The Orichalcum Crown

The Orichalcum Crown, Volume 1

J. J. N. Whitley

Published by J. J. N. Whitley, 2025.

THE ORICHALCUM CROWN

First edition. November 12, 2025.

Copyright © 2025 J. J. N. Whitley.

ISBN: 979-8993670218

Written by J. J. N. Whitley.

Table of Contents

To Clay,

Thanks for letting me ramble about Makoto and Athena for the past six years.

Prologue

Makoto sat alone by the water's edge. The pretty sparkling sea distracted from the problem that had been bugging her all morning. It was a simple problem, but one she couldn't solve.

No matter how hard she tried, Makoto couldn't remember why she'd been crying.

She'd spent the morning trying to find her missing memory. It felt like walking in the dark. She knew *something* was there but just couldn't find it. The missing memory ached her head the way hunger ached her tummy.

She felt empty. Hurt. And oh so tired. Makoto couldn't tell if the smell of salted water came from the sea or her tears.

Her mind gave up wandering the darkness to focus on the distractions. Gulls cried overhead. Grains of warm sand clung to her soles and toes. Chilling wind bristled her scarlet hair, and she clung tightly to her blankie.

It was covered in star pictures—her favorite was the big dragon. It was beautiful but looked strong. Something about that felt familiar too, which made her head hurt more.

Makoto reached forward. Twitching fingers called the tide to her side. Warm water filled the small holes in the sand where her feet rested. Another twitch of her fingers raised the water to her face.

It was clear enough to show her reflection. Hot tears left her freckled cheeks shiny like the sea. Her usually platinum eyes nearly redder than her hair.

She knew the face staring back as her own, but even it felt unfamiliar.

"Makoto?"

The voice was like the wind. Gentle, so quiet she almost missed it. Yet her body trembled at its presence. The water sprang and crashed, covering her in a bubble. Shaking hands hugged wobbling knees.

"Makoto..."

Tired eyes drifted toward a new distraction. A glittering black and silver mountain stood in the sand. Deep blue eyes met her own. Grey streaks colored otherwise golden hair, just as red stains colored axe and armor. His size scared her, but his eyes were kind. Familiar...

Sharp pain, like pricking her fingers on a thorn or shell, throbbed in Makoto's skull. She yelped, grasping her aching head. "No..." was all she said.

"Makoto!" He stepped toward her.

She thrust her arm toward him. The water surrounding her lashed out. It whipped against the ground, splashing salt and sand. But it never struck the mountain man, stopping just short every time.

He didn't flinch or move from his spot. No fear showed in his eyes. Only a kind sadness.

"You don't recognize me, do you?"

No. She hadn't a clue who he was. "I'm sorry... Should I?"

"Yes, but tis alright. I'm..." He looked away, pointing toward a stone cottage with a straw-thatched roof standing at the edge of the sand and forest. "I was a friend of your mother's. She let me stay there with you and her when I visited."

Makoto closed her eyes. She couldn't picture her mother's face, but a gentle whisper filled her ears.

"*Ole turvassa, rakkaani.*"

Sudden warmth rushed through her. Makoto didn't understand the words, but they were pleasant all the same. "I don't remember my mama."

The man sighed. "Then of course you wouldn't remember Uncle Rudolph." He dropped his axe into the sand. "May I sit with you?"

Makoto hesitated. He still scared her a little, but she wanted to trust him. At least, she wanted another distraction from her problem. She waved her hand; the gathered water returned to the sea. Uncle Rudolph approached. He was much larger up close. She almost ran, but his sweet eyes made her stay.

"You're my Uncle Rudolph?"

"Aye. *We* are Emperor of the Kauneus Empire."

"We?" Makoto unsuccessfully tried to find the second person.

"Aye. Tis tradition for emperor to use the royal we."

"Improar?"

His deep throated chuckle soothed her. "Emperor, Makoto."

"What does that mean?"

His brow furrowed. "It means tis our responsibility to protect those who can't protect themselves. We oft meet with friends across land and sea to know the needs of the people."

"Friends like my mother?"

"Aye, Makoto, and friends like you."

She smiled a little. "Why is it your responsibility?"

Uncle Rudolph shook his head. "A story too long and dreary for this day. Tis enough to say we earned it." He pointed to the gold object on his head. "And this is our proof."

"Could I earn it?"

"Buh, we should think not."

Indignation reddened her puffy cheeks. "Why not?"

"You're better suited as princess."

She liked how the word sounded. "Is princess fun?"

"It can be. We have a saying in Kauneus: Beauty in Strength. A princess is expected to exhibit both in her character."

"Oh!" Makoto gasped. She pointed to her favorite star picture on the blankie. "Like this?"

"Of course. If we learned anything from your mother, there is nothing as beautiful or strong as a dragon."

"Then I am to be the best princess," she said with a smile.

Uncle Rudolph laughed heartily. "Athena will not take such a challenge lightly."

"Who is she?"

"One of two princesses. They'll be another shortly and a prince with her." He stood and offered his hand. "I'll tell you about them on the way."

Makoto didn't take his hand. "And where would we be going, Uncle Rudolph?"

"Home, of course."

Once more, she felt cold despite his kind voice. Her hands retreated into the warm sand. "You said this was my home."

"It was. The night took many of our friends, Makoto." Uncle Rudolph paused to quell his quivering lip. "Your mother was one we couldn't save."

As the tears resumed streaming down her cheeks, Makoto realized the answer to her problem. A face she'd never see again was one she'd already forgotten. Yet her heart ached just the same as her head. This left her with a new problem.

"Why can't I remember my mother?"

"I... cannot pretend to know but do know this," he said. "Your mother loved you very much. She valued your happiness and safety over everything else."

Makoto looked at the cottage. If it was once her home, it would be so lonely now. "And... my Papa?" She couldn't remember him either, but the word was so familiar it slipped out.

"Your *Papa*," Uncle Rudolph spat the word like a curse. "doesn't deserve to be called as such." His large arms wrapped around her shoulders. "Rest assured, Makoto, we—*I* will *not* leave you here alone. You will have a place in my family. A princess, beautiful and strong."

His hug wasn't as comfortable as her blankie. She preferred fuzzy warmth over the armor's smooth but cold touch. Flowing tide tickled her wrists and ankles; its forceful ebb seemed to call Makoto to the sea. Or at least away from Uncle Rudolph. Brisk wind blowing in the same direction echoed the tide's intent.

"You'll keep me safe?" she asked.

"On my life," he said without hesitation.

Tears splashed against Makoto's forehead. His beard caught most of them, but a few leaked through.

His was another face known by her heart, not her mind. Her mind saw the worried creases of his rugged face. The largeness of his frame. How easily he could break her. Her heart was a little scared but somehow knew there was nothing to fear. *He's strong... but beautiful.*

She lifted her hands from the sand to take his. "Thank you... Father."

"Uncle Rudolph is fine, child."

He gently squeezed her hand and led her down the beach.

Minutes bled into hours. The wind and tide begged her reconsider, but Makoto would not change her mind. She was to be a dragon—beautiful but strong. Changing her mind was neither.

Uncle Rudolph led her to the monster perched on the far side of the beach. Iron scales covered its body. Smoke billowed from its mouth. Three white wings emerged from its back, but taut chains weighed it down.

"Dragon," she whispered, half afraid half in awe.

"Galleon," Uncle Rudolph said. "'Tis the ship that will see us home."

A crowd tended to the galleon by loading supplies or manning the chains. Someone shouted, and several scrambled to gather before him. Several others stayed put.

Their eyes resembled those of a viper or raptor tracking a mouse. A woman, whose teeth were either yellow or missing, spat without turning away from Makoto. A bald man with a crooked nose snarled before drinking from a flask.

She gingerly stepped back under Uncle Rudolph's legs. "Are these people your friends?" Makoto whispered.

"Some, others are mere hirelings." He gently patted her head. "Fret not, Makoto. They are loyal to our coin if not our crown. A princess has nothing to fear from them."

Makoto wasn't so sure. Even a good dog could still bite. "Why do they look at me like that? Did I do something wrong?"

"No," he said quickly. "You have done nothing to deserve their scorn. They are wounded—grieving. Your mother... she wasn't the only friend lost last night."

"What happened here?"

Uncle Rudolph's eyes darkened like the sea under a cloudy sky. "Avalon's High Priestess preyed upon our trust. She—" He paused.

A man with hair like a beast's mane approached. He wore no shirt, revealing the scars chiseled into his chest and arms. He spared Makoto no more than a passing glance. His green eyes weren't like a predator's—more akin to a guardian checking an intruder.

A boy about Makoto's age stood behind him. Light green eyes looked down without focus. She imagined looking similar when she was alone on the shore.

The boy raised his eyes, meeting hers. He was the first person to smile at her. It didn't quite reach his sad eyes, but it made his smile that much sweeter.

"The stragglers have been rounded up, Your Grace," the man said. "Your orders?"

Uncle Rudolph was quiet. He looked to the forest, reaching for something in his pocket. He winced, but the darkness in his eyes cleared. "Release them all. Not one is to be harmed."

Anger flashed across the man's face. "But Charlotte was—"

"Not. One, Lang. Enough blood has been shed."

The man's anger didn't fade, but he nodded. "It will be done, Your Grace." He bowed to Uncle Rudolph and then Makoto. "Don't forget your manners, Ephraim."

"Yes, Uncle." The boy's smile widened. He bowed and followed his uncle.

She was sad to see him go and looked to Uncle Rudolph for comfort. Instead, she noticed the grin on his face. "I don't like the face you're making," she said.

He chuckled. "Pardon our mirth, Makoto. We weren't expecting the color of your cheeks to match your hair." He offered his hand. "Shall we escort you aboard?

Indignation swelled her cheeks. "Are you always this mean?" She said, taking his hand.

His chuckling evolved into laughter. "On occasion. Your mother oft accused us of the same." His other hand moved about his pocket once more.

"What's in your pocket?"

"An old keepsake."

He showed it to her. A shining platinum gem, no smaller than her palm, strung along a silver chain. The hunger in her head and heart intensified at the sight of it. Makoto's hand reached without her mind giving the order.

"Ole turvassa, rakkaani..."

Uncle Rudolph snatched her wrist. She gasped at his speed and tried to wriggle free. His grip didn't hurt but was too firm to escape.

7

"A princess does not pilfer her father's property."

The eyes looking down on her were less than kind. Not angry but intense—as if a brewing storm could quickly swell into a winter's gale.

Makoto gulped. "I'm sorry, Father, I—"

He flinched as if slapped.

"I'm sorry, *Uncle*. I meant no harm."

The brewing storm subsided, and he released her arm. "We apologize in turn for frightening you." He sighed, pocketing the necklace.

"Know this well, Makoto. Tis our solemn pleasure to welcome you into our family. But Kauneus has no need for a disloyal princess. Do you understand?"

Not entirely, but she didn't want to risk upsetting him further.

"Yes."

"Good girl," he said, patting her head. "You must be tired after walking so much. Come, we'll show you to our private quarters."

Uncle Rudolph walked ahead, but Makoto hesitated. She didn't intend to run; she had nowhere else to go. But the gentle wind kissing her hair and cheeks begged for one final glance.

Makoto looked to the forest beyond the shore. Briars and thickets protected the forest's edge with one path cleared for entrance. Uncle Rudolph's friends and hirelings worked far from that patch of beach and forest. Her last chance to run if she chose.

Shadows rustled from the path; a small child stepped onto the beach. Too far for Makoto to make out any features save for vibrant red hair.

Pain throbbed once more in Makoto's head. She gritted her teeth and tightly shut both eyes.

The wind howled. A mighty wave crashed against the ship. Makoto tumbled toward the walkway connecting the ship and shore. She tightly gripped the handrail to steady herself.

Makoto raised her head above the railing. It wasn't the red-haired child she saw but the green-eyed boy. Ephraim looked up at her, smiled once again, and waved.

Seeing him calmed her down, and she returned both gestures without thinking. Despite the protests of the wind and water, she followed her uncle.

Hazy nightmares plagued Makoto's sleep. She awoke in a bed far too big for her, not to mention a little too hard. Moonlight streaming through the room's lone window showed Uncle Rudolph sleeping at the table. He used his fist as a pillow, while the other hand tightly clutched an open book.

Makoto moved to a chair at the table's opposite end. It was more comfortable than the bed. The wood felt a little rough in the same way as sand. She liked that feeling.

The moonlight didn't quite reach the table but didn't need to. A crystal lantern shaped like a coiled serpent stood upon the center of the table. Its mouth was open wide, as if breathing flame upon the candles at the end of its claws.

Makoto's stomach grumbled. Now her tummy was the hungry one. Thankfully, there was a bowl of soup prepared. It was lumpy and mushy. Even worse, it was cold. She gagged and tried to decide between her disgust and hunger.

Then, she had an idea.

Makoto cupped her hands around one of the candles. The flame flickered across her fingertips. She winced; fire was harder to play with than water. Focusing on the flame's warmth rather than the burn made it easier to control. Alas, hunger made such focus almost impossible.

Instead, she held the bowl near the candles to warm it up. It still didn't taste good, but at least she wasn't hungry.

Even worse, she was bored.

Makoto ventured onto the deck to watch the stars. Uncle Rudolph's lantern guided her steps. The star blanket draped across her shoulders kept her warm despite the chilling night wind.

Several people stood at the front of the ship. She remembered their looks from earlier and didn't want to be around them. It took her a few minutes to find a lonely spot at the ship's back.

The dragon star-picture stared down at her from the sky. Twinkling eyes shone like the gemstone from Uncle Rudolph's pendant. She reached for the stars without thinking. Not that she expected to touch the sky, but it frustrated her that so many things remained out of reach. The stars. The gem. Her memories...

The star blanket billowed in the growing wind. Makoto huddled closer to the lantern, cupping another flame between her hands. Eyes shut, she focused on the warmth. Her hands slowly moved away from the candle, and the flame followed.

Fire danced between her fingertips. Makoto's eyes twinkled. She blew sharply, sending a stream of fire into the sky that dissipated without reaching the stars. It disappointed her a little, but at least she was having fun.

"You little brat," a voice snarled.

A bald man shambled toward her holding an empty bottle. She recognized him and his crooked nose from the morning. Rank breath wafted over Makoto, who covered her face to mask the smell.

"Can't even look a'me. After what yer people did t'us. Then ye try an' burn the 'ol ship down." He tapped the bottle against his temple. "Not on this buzzard's watch."

Makoto instinctively stepped back. She didn't take a second. *Uncle Rudolph told me not to be scared. Be a dragon, Makoto. Beautiful and strong.* "I only play with fire because it's my friend."

"Fren?" The sailor spat. "Know 'ow many fren I lost on yer island?"

No. She didn't know how many *she'd* lost. "I'm sorry you lost friends. My mother—"

"Shaddup!' he snapped.

The first swing of the bottle slammed against Makoto's wrist. Shards of glass cut into her arm and elbow. Bleeding and trembling, Makoto collapsed to her knees. The sailor sneered down and reared back for another swing.

Makoto screamed; she threw out her arms to protect herself. Flames lashed from the candles at her call. They struck the bald man's chest.

He half-gasped, half-coughed, as he stumbled backwards. Liquor dribbled from his mouth onto the fire. Roaring flame climbed from his chest to his face.

High-pitched screams pierced Makoto's ears. She wanted to shut her eyes, but the fire's glow forbade her to look away. It was almost beautiful.

Whisps of smoke carried sparks toward the stars. None reached the heavens, but Makoto wasn't sure if they simply disappeared or if the stars took them as an offering.

A crowd gathered to douse the fire. Not one of them tended to the bleeding girl. Their wide eyes avoided meeting hers. She wasn't a mouse anymore.

"Makoto!" Uncle Rudolph shouldered his way through the crowd to her side. He gingerly helped her to her feet. "What happened—"

His voice stopped when his fingers touched Makoto's fresh wound. A storm blazed within his blue eyes so intense that none could meet his gaze.

"Who?" was all he said.

Makoto found the bald man hiding amongst fellow sailors. Shaking hands and quivering lips revealed his fear. She wasn't sure she should answer Uncle Rudolph's question. No one else did.

"Who?" Uncle Rudolph repeated.

Tension mixed with the lingering silence. The other sailors exchanged glances. A couple standing near the bald man shifted away from him.

Makoto cleared her throat. "Uncle, it was—" She intended to say an accident, but sudden pain flaring up her arm interrupted her. She cried out, clutching her bleeding wrist.

The bald man's lips twitched into a smile. There was no trace of his fear. Only satisfaction at her pain. That changed her mind.

Makoto locked eyes with the bald man. "It was him."

"Little whore!" he yelled. The man lunged but nearby sailors brought him to his knees. He continued to struggle and spit insults at her.

Makoto didn't understand his words but felt their venom. If the glass shards were stings and bites, the words pierced her like swords.

Uncle Rudolph loomed over the bald man. "You understand the penalty for your actions." It wasn't a question.

The sailor stopped struggling. "Yes, Your Grace. Let my death stand as an objection to her people and what they did to us."

Makoto gasped. *He is to die?* She didn't want that. Death was too high a price for his crime. She curled her shaking hands into fists.

"Uncle, I..."

He drew his axe. "Speak your final words."

The sailor glared at Makoto. His coal-like eyes embittered with distrust and resentment. "Remember my face, Scarlet Princess."

The axe cleanly rended head from shoulders. His body remained upright, a monument to a stubborn and hateful end.

"Leave us," the emperor said. "We require a moment with the princess."

The bystanders heeded his order. Makoto didn't watch them leave but heard their footsteps growing further away. Her gaze remained on the man's head. There was no fear in his final moment.

Only hatred for her and her people. People she couldn't even remember.

She couldn't stop shaking. It wasn't fair. She didn't deserve the man's wrath, just as he hadn't deserved her father's axe. Of all the things she wanted to remember, now she had something she wished to forget.

"Why?" was all she said.

"We lack the strength for mercy tonight. We—" He stopped talking at the tug of his cloak.

A familiar pair of green eyes met Uncle Rudolph's. "I apologize for interrupting, Your Grace, but you did intend to introduce us."

Uncle Rudolph's fickle expression changed between irritation and gratitude. "Buh. So, we did." He stepped aside and ushered the boy forward.

"Your introductions shall be your own." He moved beneath the shadow of the mast, remaining in sight but leaving them alone.

Uncle must trust him to leave us alone after the incident.

The boy's frame wasn't impressive; she wasn't sure he could even win a fight against her. Yet he stared down the emperor. None of the other sailors had the guts for that.

"You're Ephraim, right?"

The boy's smile revealed the gap between his teeth. "I didn't think I was worth a pretty girl knowing my name."

Makoto's cheeks turned redder than her hair. "Thank you. I'm—" She winced at the pain in her arm.

"You're hurt." Ephraim stepped closer. "Do you mind if I treat your wounds? My father taught me how to tend to wounded livestock."

Makoto didn't fight her indignation. "So I'm an animal to you?" she snapped.

"Not at all. It's a similar process of cleaning and dressing the wound. May I?"

His eyes showed no resentment or judgment. Only genuine kindness. Something she'd seen very little of today. She gingerly held out her arm. "Thank you, again."

"My pleasure."

Ephraim hummed while cleaning her wound. His sincerity made it harder for her to pretend to be strong. Makoto lost the fight with her tears.

"Why are you being so nice to me?"

"Mom taught me to be kind to girls, especially if she's crying." He dressed her wound with fresh gauze. "That better?" he asked.

It still hurt but did feel better.

"*Yes.*" Her voice cracked. She cleared her throat and wiped her eyes. *Beauty in Strength, Makoto.* "Your work is admirable and sufficient..."

She trailed off when she noticed him trying not to laugh. "Don't laugh at me, Ephraim!"

"I meant no offense," he said quickly. "But you don't have to act around me. You can cry if you need."

Makoto couldn't see her uncle's face under the mast's shadow but felt the weight of his judgment. "Is that allowed?"

"Why shouldn't it?" Ephraim asked. "Your father wasn't the emperor around my mother. He was just Rudolph. That's my foremost duty to you, Makoto. I'm to be your friend."

She smiled without having to force it. "I'd like that. I very much need a friend."

Makoto embraced Ephraim. His arms draped around her shoulders like a blanket and were just as comfortable.

"I don't know how I shall fare as princess. Will you stay my friend, Ephraim?"

"Of course, Makoto. Until the end of the world."

Makoto

Dawn's light streamed into Makoto's room, illuminating the amaryllis sitting atop her nightstand. Ephraim gifted one every year on the eve of her anniversary. This flower was the fourteenth.

Makoto undressed and entered the washroom attached to her bedroom. The shower head was sculpted to resemble a dragon's with the handle being a claw. She tilted the claw to the left. The eyes changed from black to red, then purple, before settling on blue. She relaxed as cold water washed away the night's grime.

Makoto glanced at her arm. There were no scars from the old sailor's attack, but he marked her all the same. The Scarlet Princess appellation followed her like a shadow in the years since. She heard it whispered behind her back. Found it scrawled on her serviette at dinner.

Although the sentiment waned over the years, Makoto found it best to downplay her Avalon traits. A daily dose of powder masked her accursed freckles. The beloved star blanket languished in the dust. Fire and water were only friends on special occasions.

Her hair, unfortunately, refused to hide. No amount of dye could cleanse her scarlet brand.

Makoto returned to her bedroom and opened the armoire. Snow-white robes with a long red skirt and sash greeted her. She changed into formal wear and nearly shut the armoire, but something caught her eye behind some old clothes. A stuffed white dragon with a matching ribbon around its wings.

Makoto pulled it into the sunlight and blew off the dust. *Athena gifted me this after my first year. Do I still have the card?*

To her surprise, she did.

Little Ruby,

Since you can't remember your actual birthday, we'll use this anniversary as our day of celebration. Your dear older sisters wanted to give you a piece of home. You're fond of the dragon on that blanket, so I had one made for you. Olive asked Father about traditional Avalon accessories and sewed you this ribbon.

Don't listen to the people who whisper behind your back. Listen to us telling you we love you every day. You're a part of this family, and we're blessed to have you as our sister. Amelia is doubly blessed to grow up with you. We know the Thronsden boys feel the same. Be careful not to break underline too many of their hearts when you grow up!

Lots of love,
Athena
Enough love,
Olivia

Makoto's heart ached. Ephraim had been her first friend, but Athena wasn't far behind. She made Makoto feel welcome in a way few others could. *Thank you, Athena. I'm sorry I left this abandoned for so long. It was unbearable to think of you each time I saw it.* A mirthless smile formed on her lips. *That's one anniversary I'm thankful we don't celebrate.*

Makoto set the dragon on her nightstand and used the ribbon to tie her hair before heading out. She reached the double doors outside the dining room and found Ephraim waiting in a black suit with his bow tie slightly askew.

"Good morning, Makoto."

"It's adequate," she said.

"Tired?"

She shook her head. "No, just memories," she said and fixed his bow tie.

"I love the ribbon. It's familiar."

"Thank you. Tis an old gift from Athena and Olivia. Speaking of which, has she been introduced?"

"Not yet. I imagine we'll hear her name shortly. Though," he said teasingly, "something tells me she's not the one you're excited to see."

"Hush, you," Makoto said with a playful shove.

She pushed the door ajar to view the dining room.

Large chandeliers hung from the four corners of the ceiling. Each one crafted to resemble one of the four great constellations: Ashen Phoenix, Platinum Dragon, Obsidian Octopus, and Gilded Serpent. The chandeliers converged in the center of the room, where a statue of the Orichalcum Crown stood atop them.

A mahogany table lay beneath the chandeliers. The table began at the Gilded Serpent's tail and ended at the crest of the Ashen Phoenix.

Emperor Rudolph Friedrich von Kauneus sat at the head of the table. He wore white robes with nary a scratch or stain. Rings adorned each finger, and no two fingers shared the same color ring. Atop his head rested a simple diadem made of a silvery metal with an unnatural glint.

He held his head high, as if he and the crown looked down on all others.

Twas gold when we met on the beach. Even orichalcum's luster is vulnerable to time.

"Introducing Her Royal Highness, Princess Olivia Elizabeth vi Kauneus and her retainer, Ser Bastien Thronsden."

Olivia slinked into the dining room. Her white dress ended in a knee-high skirt that showed off her long legs. A light jacket adorned her shoulders. Its color resided between the spectrum of purple and black, matching the gloss on her lips and choker around her neck.

Braided raven hair snaked from her shoulder down to her right arm. She cradled a sketchbook and charcoal in her right hand, while the left clasped the hem of her dress and curtseyed. Her father lifted his goblet in greeting. Olivia kissed his cheek and took her seat at his left hand.

Ephraim's elder brother, Bastien, followed Olivia. Their mother, Charlotte, served Uncle Rudolph before her death on Avalon. Her three sons carried her legacy; each assigned a different princess.

Makoto's heartbeat quickened at the sight of Bastien. He filled out his attire unlike Ephraim. The toad-faced boy had grown into a tall, broad-shouldered man. His eyes found Makoto, and a smile graced his lips. She quickly looked away lest she get flustered by his charm.

"Introducing Her Royal Highness, Princess Makoto Clarissa vi Kauneus and her retainer, Ser Ephraim Thronsden."

Ephraim pushed the doors open. "After you."

Makoto exhaled. *Remember to exude beauty, Makoto.*

She sauntered forward, stopping below the Platinum Dragon chandelier to curtsey for the emperor. He lifted his goblet, and she sat in the second chair to the right, leaving an empty seat at his right hand.

Ephraim followed Bastien's lead and stood behind his charge.

The emperor leaned forward. "Happy anniversary."

"Thank you, Fa—" She paused when he winced. "Uncle Rudolph." *He's been my father in all but name these fourteen years, but it still pains him to be called as such...* Makoto dipped her head. "I hope to do you proud today."

"Buh." His lips curled. "You do us proud every day."

His words rang a touch hollow, but she smiled nonetheless.

"Thank you, and a good morning to you, Olivia."

Olivia fixated on the sketchbook; her hands moved the charcoal at a feverish pace. "Good morning," she said with her usual monotone.

"What are you drawing?"

"The perfect specimen."

The answer puzzled Makoto.

"I'm sorry, you're drawing what?"

"The perfect specimen."

"I heard what you said, sister—"

"Yet you insist on having me repeat myself." Olivia's disdainful green eyes considered Makoto. "Tell me, sister, do you enjoy wasting my time?"

Makoto frowned. "I only meant—"

"Introducing Her Royal Highness, Princess Amelia Lucille vi Kauneus and her retainer, Ser Klaus Thronsden."

A young girl in a poofy fuchsia dress scampered into the room. Her straw-like hair was immaculately combed with naught a strand out of place. She shared the emperor's naturally tanned-skin but not his blue eyes. Rather, she inherited her mother's honey-golden irides.

"Good morning, Makoto!" Amelia sang, quickly waving both hands.

Makoto returned the wave.

A sharp cough sounded from the man behind Amelia. Klaus was taller than Bastien but not quite as wide. His white suit clear of any crease or stain. Makoto often thought Klaus resembled a sculpture more than a human being.

I'd have been honored to have him as my guardian, but he lacks the heart to be the friend I've needed these fourteen years.

Amelia giggled. She clutched the hems of her dress and curtseyed. Her father acknowledged her, and she raced to the table.

Klaus's long strides allowed him to keep pace despite not matching her energy. He pulled out her chair, and she took her seat beside Olivia. Klaus bowed to his princess before standing behind her.

Amelia leaned forward and loudly whispered, "Happy anniversary, Makoto."

Makoto matched her sister's movement and cadence. "Thank you, sister. It pleases me to know *one* of you remembered."

Olivia cocked an eyebrow but didn't otherwise react. The dispassion only irritated Makoto further.

"Introducing Count Edgar Sebastian von Kauneus and his son: Lord Richter Jonathan von Kauneus."

Two sharply dressed gentlemen entered the room. Uncle Edgar's black robes bulged around his belly. He stroked his well-groomed moustache, which was the only hair on his head. Richter's form-fitting blue suit matched his eyes, and he stood taller than his father.

The two bowed to the emperor before taking their seats. Uncle Edgar sat beside Makoto, while Richter took his place next to Amelia.

Richter clapped. "Happy anniversary, cousin. I hope this past year has been a good one."

"It has, thank you." *Especially if I ignore the unflattering whispers.*

"Ahh, tis that day already?" Uncle Edgar's laugh resounded throughout the room. "Pardon, Makoto, I'd nearly forgotten. You will be winning your hunt this year, I presume."

Makoto's countenance brightened. She partook in an annual hunt with Uncle Rudolph and Ephraim on her anniversary. She had yet to best the emperor but was confident she'd succeed.

"Yes, Uncle. You and Richter are invited, of course."

Uncle Edgar shook his head. "Afraid I'll be too busy with the senate. Richter, however, has no such excuse." He waved his hand to his son. "Keep your cousin company today."

A shadow flickered across Richter's face. His eyes darted to an empty chair further down. *He probably has plans with Margaret.* Uncle Edgar coughed and tilted his head in Makoto's direction.

The shadow disappeared from Richter's face. "The invitation is appreciated, cousin. It will be my pleasure to attend. Perhaps we can invite the countess and her sister?" He winced. "Forgive me, I don't mean to impose."

Makoto dismissed his comment with a wave. "Nonsense, Richter. Reina and Margaret are more than welcome to join the hunt, though I expect the countess to decline." Her eyes wandered to the remaining empty seats. "Do we know why they're late?"

"Margaret probably fell on the way over," Olivia said.

Makoto heard Ephraim stifle a laugh behind her. She considered admonishing him, but Klaus beat her to it. Bastien, for his part, appeared embarrassed by his princess's comment.

"You're being rude, Olivia," Makoto said, furrowing her brow.

"Yet no less honest. She visited my atelier last week and spilled paint imported from Nova City upon the floor. Her attempt to clean the mess only served to stain my workplace."

Makoto imagined the mess Margaret created on Olivia's floor. A horrid mesh of colors in an otherwise artistic paradise. The thought of her sister's frustration pleased her.

"Introducing the daughters of Regent Josephine Claire vi Kauneus: Countess Reina Erika vi Kauneus and Lady Margaret Sabrina vi Kauneus."

Countess Reina was unnaturally beautiful. Porcelain skin glistened like quartz. Nigh flawless but for the rash tracing her cheek like golden cracks upon marble. Even then, the uniqueness added to, rather than besmirched, her beauty. Makoto envied her that.

Her viridian suit with gold cufflinks matched her eyes and hair respectively. A white glove adorned each hand, which Reina kept clasped behind her back. She bowed to the emperor and waited for her sister.

Lady Margaret wore a violet dress with frills around the wrists. The dress had been stretched out to fit her unusually broad shoulders and long legs. She attempted to curtsey but tripped over her feet. A pair of servants helped Margaret and assisted her with her curtsey.

The emperor attempted to mask it, but Makoto recognized his amusement. *He's incorrigible as Ephraim.*

The sisters approached the table upon the emperor's acknowledgement. Reina sat on a short stack of books to meet the rest of the family at eye level. The space beside Uncle Edgar remained vacant to symbolize their absent mother, leaving Reina beside Richter and Margaret directly across from her.

Uncle Rudolph took a deep breath. "Fourteen years to the day since we rescued our Makoto from the turmoil of Avalon. This breakfast tis not only to celebrate a glorious new morn but to pray she sees many more." He raised his goblet. "To Makoto."

The family cheered her name. She worked hard these fourteen years to exude the beauty and strength expected of a Kauneus princess. But the emperor's earlier reaction proved it was still not enough. Rather than elated, the praise left her as empty as the goblets.

"Thank you. I know there was hesitation to accept a princess from across the sea. But—" She noticed Olivia, goblet raised but eyes downcast. *Her perfect specimen warrants more attention than her own sister. Klaus may have the expression of marble, but Olivia shares its heart.*

Makoto's shoulders sank, and she cleared her throat. "But I'm happy sharing breakfast with family."

A short round of applause followed. Amelia joined in but looked a touch concerned.

Hard to hide anything from that one.

"Well said." Edgar clasped her shoulder, gently shaking it. "Rudolph, let the girl eat. She'll need her strength if she's to best you."

"Buh. We shall see if she is up to the task."

The emperor snapped his fingers.

Servants rolled in carts carrying four course meals. The courses consisted of cheese-stuffed biscuits, oatmeal glazed with sugar, blueberry pancakes and eggs prepared to each diner's preference, and concluded with a slice of yellow cake with licorice frosting.

More servants began filling goblets with wine or virgin cider depending on preference. Amelia, Richter and Margaret chose cider, while the rest of the family preferred wine.

Makoto found wine too brut to drink often but indulged on special occasions. Today's offering was unexpectedly sweet. She mulled over the taste and found it pleasant but a tad rich. She set the goblet down to focus on her breakfast.

Melted cheese oozed from her biscuit onto her plate. *That looks divine.* She twirled her fork around the cheese and stabbed it into a piece of seasoned egg. An explosion of spice and flavor went off in her mouth with every bite.

The emperor turned toward Uncle Edgar. "How are negotiations proceeding on the Alma's proposal?"

"Quite well, Rudolph. There are some differences of opinion that need to be settled, but I expect a resolution within the coming days."

"Your thoughts, Countess?"

Reina frowned. "Permission to speak freely, Your Grace?"

"Of course."

"Your brother is underestimating the significance of these differences of opinion. Most tellingly, Nova City's representatives don't trust the Alma at all."

"You would know better than I, Reina." Edgar swallowed a biscuit without chewing. "You're practically in bed with Nova City."

"Father," Richter interrupted. "Is such a phrase appropriate at table?"

"No, Richter, let him speak," Reina said. "I hear your father is quite experienced with having foreigners in his bed."

Richter's fist slammed upon his plate, crushing two biscuits. Alas, the plate did not give. "Cease your slander, cousin! My father acts a proper gentleman at all times."

"Oh? Perhaps my sources made a mistake." She cut into her cake without breaking eye contact with Ricther. "Tell me, cousin, do you spend all your time with your father?"

Richter massaged his hand with a serviette. "No."

"Really?" Reina licked the licorice from her fork. "You claimed your father 'acts a proper gentleman *at all times*.' Yet you have no evidence of his behavior outside your presence?"

"I know my father's heart. Tis all the evidence I need."

The emperor cleared his throat. "Your loyalty to our brother is admirable, Richter, yet we find ourselves off topic. Countess, what is your estimation for the negotiations?"

"No later than the end of the month but no sooner than two weeks."

"Buh. See it done by tomorrow. We'll have no looming politics infecting the ball."

Reina dipped her head. "Consider it so, Your Grace."

Amelia's eyes widened. "But you just said two weeks? How can you be so confident?"

"One must be willing to compromise for the sake of the crown. But enough politics at the table." Reina lifted her goblet and nodded at Olivia. "What is my cousin's latest masterpiece?"

"The star attraction at The Court of Temptation." Olivia set her sketchbook down in favor of a spoon. "He's become my muse."

The emperor's fingers trembled around his goblet. "Olivia, that viper's den—"

"Be at ease, Father. I am there to observe, not partake."

His fingers relaxed, and he steadied himself with a drink. "We assume you shall not partake in this year's hunt either."

Olivia nodded. "Correct, Father. I plan on becoming enslaved to the throes of estro."

Richter's brow furrowed, as he mulled over her words. "What does that mean, cousin?"

"It means I'm going to paint."

As expected. Olivia isn't one for outdoors.

"I like paint." Margaret said. She dunked a handful of egg and biscuit into her oatmeal without noticing the incredulous stares of her family.

Reina cleared her throat. "If I may be excused, Your Grace, I would like to finish my meal elsewhere. I have work to do if I am to meet your deadline."

The emperor waved his hand.

"Thank you." Reina rose from her seat. "Richter, may I impose upon you?"

Richter glowered at her. "How bold to request my assistance after insulting my father."

"Quite. I ask you watch over Margaret for the day. I hate to imagine her lonely and idle while I work."

Richter's expression softened at Margaret's name. "I suppose I can acquiesce."

"Then I leave her in your hands. Enjoy the day, sister." She stood on her toes and pecked Margaret's cheek. Reina tapped her cheek, and her sister returned the kiss.

The countess signaled to a servant, who promptly gathered her leftovers. She bowed to the emperor and Makoto in turn before approaching Amelia.

Reina whispered; Amelia giggled in return. They exchanged kisses, and Reina disappeared behind a set of double doors.

"What was so funny?" Makoto asked.

Amelia's giggles were interlaced with bites of breakfast. "Reina and her jokes. She says I should spoil your anniversary by winning the hunt."

Makoto frowned. "Does she have quarrel with me?"

Amelia quickly shook her head. "No, just a jest at my expense, I assure you. She knows I'm too dainty."

The emperor stroked his beard. "Your disposition concerns us less than your skill, Amelia."

"Father!" she huffed. "That's rude."

He ignored her indignant tone. "Klaus, appraise our daughter's skill with a mount."

"Unsatisfactory, Your Grace." Klaus's words were quick and dispassionate. "I fear she fares no better with a bow. She is liable to be trampled in flight from her quarry."

Makoto winced on her sister's behalf. She was no expert in either field but experienced enough with her weapons and a saddle. *A dismissal of that ilk from Ephraim would wound me.*

Amelia pouted at her Thronsden. "Klaus. Your honesty is admirable, but must you adhere so strictly to it?"

Klaus dipped his head. "Forgive me, Princess, but I cannot let you proceed knowingly into dangers you are not prepared to face."

Amelia made a face at him.

Edgar clapped his hands together. "If it's experience you need, Amelia, I'd be happy to oblige. I'm an excellent equestrian. I can teach you everything I know about riding."

Amelia's countenance brightened. "That sounds lovely, Uncle. Perhaps we can practice a few dances as well."

"Consider it a date."

The two shared a jovial laugh and touched glasses.

Amelia finished her drink. "May I be excused, Father?"

"Buh, is our company not sufficient?"

Amelia giggled. "Your feigned anger does not work on me, Father."

"Aye, we know." The mirth faded from his countenance. "Do as you wish, Amelia. We permit it."

"Thank you, Father." Amelia stacked her empty plates neatly on her tray. She passed them to the server and kissed Makoto once on the cheek. "Are you alright, sister?"

"Yes," Makoto said.

"Very well. Enjoy the hunt. I hope you win." She curtseyed to her father, while Klaus bowed, and scurried out of the room with her Thronsden in tow.

Olivia gathered her sketchbook. "I shall ask to be excused as well, Father. I'm lacking inspiration. I'm hopeful a visit to Morgana's will ensnare me in a fit of creation."

"M-hmm. Should you change your mind, Olivia, you will find us at the hunting grounds. Nature has a habit of awakening inspiration."

"None as perfect as my muse. Rest assured, Father, I am careful."

He waved his hand. "Take heed. Bastien, keep any unscrupulous suitors and leeches from her."

Bastien pressed his hand upon his breast. "As always, Your Grace. It is my solemn duty."

Olivia sighed. "Honestly, Father, he's the one you should worry about. He can't refuse the attention of a beautiful woman."

Uncle Edgar grinned. "A boy that handsome must be drowning in beautiful women. You cannot blame him for enjoying his youth."

"Correct, Uncle," Olivia said. "Bastien serves his purposes, so I pay his personality no mind."

Images of Bastien fraternizing with Morgana's floosies flooded Makoto's mind. *That viper wants him in her coils. I won't stand for it.*

"Careful, sister," Olivia said. "You're dripping cheese on your robes."

Melted cheese clung to the white robes, while biscuit crumbs speckled her sash. Embarrassment colored Makoto's face, as she cleaned herself with a serviette.

"Thank you, sister," she said through gritted teeth.

"But of course. Bastien, say your goodbyes."

He bowed to the emperor and followed Olivia out the doors.

The emperor refilled his goblet. "Edgar, we request a moment alone with Makoto."

Uncle Edgar waved his hands. "Say no more, Rudolph. Richter and I won't intrude on your private time."

Richter helped his father from the seat. Margaret lumbered toward them, steadied by Richter's arm hooking around hers. Makoto noted Margaret's wistful smile at his touch.

They bowed, or curtseyed, and took their leave.

Makoto heard Ephraim stir behind her. "Is my presence an intrusion, Your Grace?"

"Buh." Uncle Rudolph set down his goblet after a drink. "Shall we separate a princess from her shadow?"

Makoto studied his countenance. His amused tone didn't match the solemn resignation in his eyes. "Something troubles you, Uncle?"

"We're Emperor, Makoto. Of course something troubles us." He refilled his goblet. "Foreign dignitaries will infest our home in the coming days. They will attempt to win our favor or snuff us out like a flickering candle."

"Yet they will find Your Grace's flame burning strong," Ephraim said.

Uncle Rudolph responded by drinking his wine. "In sooth, Makoto, what troubles us above all else..." He produced a red lacquer box from his pocket. "is if our gift befits fourteen years."

Makoto was taken aback. Uncle Rudolph forwent traditional presents in lieu of the annual hunt. Anything further was spoiling her. She appreciated the gesture, though the flush in her cheeks betrayed her embarrassment. "You didn't have to."

"Nonsense. Tis not every day a girl becomes a woman." He placed the box in her hands. "We only ask you wait until after the hunt to open it."

Makoto narrowed her eyes. *He is scheming something.* "Why the delay?"

"He means to distract you during the hunt," Ephraim whispered loud enough for him to hear. "Don't fall for his trap, Makoto."

"Watch it, boy," Uncle Rudolph growled. "Men have been executed for less slanderous words."

"Forgive me, Your Grace. A shadow should remain seen but unheard."

"Buh. Your mother oft said the same when we offended her."

Ephraim's didn't bother hiding the ensuing smile.

"We shall leave you to your shadow, Makoto." The emperor rose from his chair. Some of his muscle deteriorated to fat in his age, but his silhouette remained imposing as ever. "Expect no mercy upon the hunting grounds."

He never let her win but rarely felt the need to say so. His acknowledgment felt as if he were treating her as an equal—or at least a credible threat. She resisted the urge to grin. *Beauty, Makoto. Be graceful but show strength.* "I'd be offended if you showed me any."

He chuckled. His robes billowed behind him, as he left Makoto alone with Ephraim.

"What do you suppose it is?" Ephraim asked.

Makoto gently rattled the box. Something moved inside but only a little. "Not sure. I suppose I'll learn by tonight."

She raised her eyes to the dragon-shaped chandelier. Thoughts of the stuffed dragon and the sister who bestowed it filled her mind.

I hope you're well, Athena. Wherever you are.

29

Athena

A woman in a black cloak slithered through the bazaar. Sharp-eyed vendors hawked satin and jewelry, but she paid no mind. Rather, she followed the scent of tobacco down a claustrophobic alley.

Athena's shadow painted the walls, as she strutted to the iron door at the end of the path. She knocked once, jiggled the handle twice, and knocked thrice more. A slit in the middle of the door opened and a hand peeked through. Athena dropped two pieces of silver into it.

The door opened. Scents of coals, alcohol, and a faint hint of semen assaulted Athena's nostrils. Loud moaning and profanities echoed throughout the room.

A gaunt man with a wrinkled face led Athena to a backroom. Three people sat around a circular table. One of them slept with her head on the table, while another clutched his knees and rocked back and forth. The third's hand hovered above a glittering bowl filled with pastel ovals.

Athena shook her head at the server. He led her to another room with an identical setup but without other patrons. Athena tipped him an extra piece of silver for privacy. She sat down and let the cloak slip off her shoulders. Unkempt white hair fell over her glassy eyes.

Her ravenous golden gaze lingered on the pastel ovals. She tossed a midnight-colored one in her mouth. It dissolved into colored gas with each grape-flavored bite. Athena deeply inhaled and exhaled a mouthful of smoke. The room around her changed as the smoke dissipated.

Dingy brown walls turned stark white. A long hallway replaced the table and ovals, and the chairs surrounding the table morphed into a single throne. The emperor stood before her; irritation simmering within his blue eyes.

Athena tried to move, but her body refused her commands. She was bound by the actions of her past self until the drug's effects wore off.

Just my luck to relive the worst day of my life.

Her father wiped blood from his lip. "We are nothing if not magnanimous, Athena. We are willing to overlook this, but if you dare—"

Her punch missed; he countered with a headbutt. Her aura rippled at the impact but stayed intact. She aimed a kick at his ribs. He blocked it with one arm, while the other chopped at her thigh.

Athena's aura rippled a second time. *I didn't expect the old man to still be so strong. I'll bet he was holding back too.*

Her body lunged forward, but the emperor effortlessly stepped around her and slammed his elbow against her back.

Athena's aura shattered, as breath and blood expelled from her mouth. She collapsed to her hands and knees. The stinging pain in her back kept her grounded. *Yeah, he was holding back. He could've hit my spine or lungs if he was serious.*

He yanked her up by her collar. His eyes were more of an ember now. There was just enough rage to muddle down the condescension and disappointment.

"Your pride and inability to listen shall be the death of you, Athena."

"Better a death of self than of my family," Athena rasped.

His grip loosened significantly. "You haven't the slightest idea what I've done for our family."

Her body lunged away from his loosened grip. He stumbled, and she took the chance to dash out of the White Hall. Her back screamed at her; her heartbeat reverberated in her skull. Yet she didn't stop. She couldn't.

"Sebastien!" She roared. Hot breath burned at her throat. "Sebastien!" She turned the corner and found him. Tall, pale, a nose like the end of a meat hook.

"Yes, Princess, I heard you the first time. What can I do for you?"

Athena grabbed his shoulders. "Where is she?"

His eyes widened. "I—I'm sorry. Whom do you mean?"

She slammed his body against the wall. "You know *damn* well who I mean. Where. Is. She?"

A bead of sweat dripped from his brow. "The southern tower. At the top of the stairs."

Athena shoved him to the ground. She raced toward the southern end of Zenith Palace. It took several minutes to reach the tower's pinnacle. A door engraved with a black octopus stood before her. She rammed her shoulder into the door thrice until it opened.

Rank air raked against Athena like a crag wolf's claws. It was dark and cold inside. Only a sliver of light streamed through a lonely window with the curtain drawn. A girl, no older than five, sat in the middle of the room. The sight and smell of her sent a chill slithering through Athena's body.

The girl held a grody spider doll in front of her face. "Hello," she said in a high-pitched voice. "I'm Willard. I'm Suilla's best friend."

Athena paused to catch her breath. She considered grabbing Suilla and running but compassion quelled her adrenaline. Her past self felt a need to comfort Suilla, while her present self scorned her hesitation. *Stupid Athena, you should have just taken her. Damn it.*

"Hello, Willard. I'm Athena. It's a pleasure to meet you." She cocked her head toward the ground beside Suilla. "May I?"

Suilla made Willard nod his head.

Athena carefully stepped around the dead bugs and dirty plates littering the floor. She sat beside the window and snatched a few papers off the ground. Each had a crude drawing in red ink. The first depicted a man on his back with red scribbles covering his face. The second showed a tall woman with tentacles wearing a crown.

She patted Suilla's shoulder. "You're a talented artist, Suilla. You'd get along well with Olive."

"Heh?" Suilla shirked from Athena's touch. "What's Olive?"

"She's my—*our* sister."

"What's a sister?"

Athena considered her words before answering. "It's... someone who cares about you. Someone who wants to see you happy."

"Like a mother?"

"Yeah, like a mother." *But not at all like mine.*

"Heh. I like my mother. Do you know where she is?"

Athena winced. "Your mother is... She sent me to come get you. She's waiting for you outside."

"Outside?" Suilla shuddered. "I'm not supposed to go there."

"Maybe not, but you've got me with you. I'm great at doing things I'm not supposed to."

Suilla grimaced. "I don't know. I like it in here."

Athena scowled at the dirty room. "That's only because you've never seen anything better." She grabbed the curtain. "How about we get some more light in here?" She yanked hard enough to tear the cloth.

Sunlight illuminated the room, giving Athena a clear look at Suilla.

The girl wore a faded yellow dress that failed to cover her arms and legs. A glistening veneer of slime coated her exposed limbs. Puss oozed from picked scabs and sores, while blood seeped from open cuts.

Suilla wailed and covered her face with purple fingers. Her inky black eyes shut tightly to avoid the light.

Athena quickly embraced her sister. "Shhh." She gently stroked Suilla's greasy hair. "'Tis only the light, Suilla. You'll love it in time. It will keep you warm and safe."

Suilla wiggled Willard in front of her face. "She doesn't need light to keep her safe. Suilla already has me."

"Of course she does. Do you have any other friends besides Willard?"

Suilla lowered the doll. "Sebastien. He feeds me sometimes, but only when I've been good."

"What does he do if you're bad?"

Suilla pulled on her cheek, revealing a pair of missing canines.

"I can explain, Princess."

Athena turned around to face Sebastien. He cleaned the sweat from his brow and wasn't as pale. His apparent confidence angered her.

"Try."

"The incessant biting made it difficult to feed her, so I had her teeth removed. Your father instructed me to keep her alive. No more, no less. I have followed his instructions to the letter. Rest assured, Princess, his bastard shall remain out of sight as Empress Isabella ordered. Now—"

The first punch shattered his nose. He screamed, so Athena grabbed his throat, crushed his windpipe, and punched him again. And again. And again. Sebastien's face turned to pulp with every punch. Bones crunched; blood covered her hands.

Athena hadn't heard Suilla's screams in the moment but couldn't focus on anything else now. The girl cried—begging Athena to stop. But Athena couldn't stop. This man was responsible for Suilla's squalor. For her sister's abuse. He would pay, and the price would be his blood.

Sebastien's lifeless body stood limp in her grip, but the assault continued. *I wasted so much time. I could have gotten her out of there. Stupid Athena*

"Athena?" Klaus stood in the doorway. His usually reserved expression displaying concern.

She diverted her attention but didn't drop Sebastien's body. "I'm glad you're here, Klaus. Take Suilla."

"I... don't follow, Athena."

"Take her." Athena tightened her grip on the corpse's neck. "I have business with Sebastien."

"That's Sebastien?" His concern turned to horror. "You need to stop."

Athena glared at him. "You would have me stop protecting my sister?"

"I would have you stop..." He hesitated.

Only now could Athena see the conflict in his eyes. The horror and his conviction to stop it. *You're better than I deserved, Klaus. You'd make your mother proud.*

"My apologies, Princess. Do what must be done."

"Thank you, Klaus."

Athena's hand reared back for another punch, but something struck the back of her neck. She blinked and awoke within the White Hall, kneeling before her father's throne. His countenance was colder than a winter squall. Klaus stood behind her. His arms, which once held her so tenderly, restrained her.

Athena met her father's eyes with enough venom to fell a viper. "You had the gall to talk about family when your own daughter lives like that."

His cold façade shattered, leaving a broken, and tired, old man. "We didn't know her condition."

"How could *you* not know. You never once visited her?"

"We have not. We *cannot*. If your mother knew—had an *inkling* we set foot in that room..." His face lost its color. "Her wrath would not end at me. Mount Kauneus would be a pebble upon a mound of ash."

"It's Mother's will that Suilla suffer?"

"Her will is the girl remain isolated from our family. She may live, but she is to be alone."

Athena punched the ground. "It's cruel!"

"We agree. The All-Mother is a cruel goddess, but her will cannot be disobeyed." He wiped a hand across his forlorn countenance.

"Your recklessness may have brought disaster upon us all. We have overlooked your vices too often. You have mistaken our forgiveness for weakness far too many times. But this..."

He motioned to the amorphous head resting upon a pike. "Sebastien's execution was inevitable after what we learned today, but his life was not yours to take."

"I—"

"Silence!" The emperor's voice thundered throughout the White Hall. He rose from the throne and gripped his axe. "Our judgment is satisfied, but we know your mother demands sacrifice."

Athena tensed. "Am I to die for meeting my sister?"

The emperor silently descended the steps before the throne. Hämärä's blade dragged against the flooring. The screech of metal upon marble was oddly wet, akin to licking one's lips.

Klaus's arms shook. "Your Grace, my fate tis tied to Athena's. Tis my duty to keep her safe—even from herself. I deserve to be punished for failing my duty."

Athena met his eyes. His beautiful, regretful, eyes. He betrayed her, but even in the past she didn't hold it against him. Her brutality needed to be stopped—even if her victim deserved it.

"You attacked me while my back was turned. Cowardice and betrayal are not traits befitting of a Thronsden." She tore her gaze away from his so he wouldn't see her own regret. Klaus shouldn't share her fate. He deserved better than her. So much better.

"I dismiss you from your post. A coward has no place at my side."

I'm sorry, Klaus. So sorry...

"Athena..."

"That's *Princess* to you, Ser Thronsden."

"Klaus, we thank you for subduing our wild daughter. We disagree with her assessment of you. A Thronsden's greatest duty is loyalty. You rival your mother in that regard. We pray your brothers show the same quality of character. Rest assured, your next charge shall deserve your character."

"Next charge?" Klaus sounded numb. "I'm afraid I don't understand."

"Klaus, we entrust Amelia in your care." The emperor loomed over Athena. "We trust Athena has no objection."

"None." *I trust you've taken care of her these past few years, Klaus.*

The emperor lifted Hämärä above his head. "Do you wish to speak?"

She considered shaking off Klaus and fighting back, but her father's eyes quelled any desire to struggle. Regret and resignation replaced his usual determination or disappointment.

He truly feared the All-Mother's wrath and believed only this would pacify her. Athena cursed her father's cowardice but knew he alone was not to blame. Her mother deserved blame for this day.

"I hope Mother lives to see the end of days. When the last grains of Mount Kauneus crumble betwixt her fingertips, I hope she learns the meaning of loneliness."

Hämärä swung, cleaving the air around it. It severed a single white hair from Athena's head, which landed upon her father's feet.

"We have severed the ties between us. You are no princess—no daughter of ours. The lands beyond the mountain shall be your home. The sow and serpent your neighbors. Begone from our sight and know our axe shall sever more than our bond should our eyes fall upon you again."

Athena blinked and returned to the dingy room. She spat the residue of her oval into an ashtray. "I was hoping for a good memory. Riding through the hunting grounds with my sisters. One of my long nights with Sen."

She laughed at her misery. "At this rate I *should* return home. If Father's a man of his word he'll get rid of this headache and dry throat."

She rubbed her neck and weighed the pros and cons of buying a drink. Finding no cons, she donned her cloak and slinked into the main room.

Loud music drowned out most of the moaning and profanity. A woman stood on a makeshift stage and sang in an accent too thick to understand. Athena searched for a server to take her order. Finding none, she snatched a half-empty bottle from a nearby table and sauntered toward the exit.

Athena took a swig. Bitter-tasting swill washed down her throat. *I've tasted mud better than this.* She tossed the bottle onto the ground where it shattered into a puddle of shrapnel and terrible liquor.

"Oy! 'At's mine." A burly man with a bushy mustache towered over her. "Ya owe me fer 'at," he said, cracking his knuckles.

"Owe you?" Athena scoffed. "I did you a favor. You should be paying me for drinking that for ya."

The man replied by ripping a dagger from his waist.

Rusty blade, chipped handle. Blade shorter than my finger. It's not getting through my aura. "You've got muscles bigger than my head, and *that's* what you plan on using? I was expecting something more impressive. But I doubt I'm the first woman to tell you that."

His face turned multiple shades of red. "'Ou're makin' me real mad, girlie." He waved the dagger in Athena's face. "Pay. Me."

She coughed into her hand. "Stop breathing on me, and I'll make you an offer."

The man growled but stepped back.

Athena spread her arms and legs. "I'll give you one free shot to make me bleed. If you win, I'll pay double what the bottle was worth. And when you don't, you thank me for throwing out your terrible drink."

His beady green eyes gleamed. "Imma enjoy wipin' 'at grin off yer face." He lunged.

Athena didn't bother looking at the blade. She watched his mouth go agape when the rusty blade bent on impact with her forehead. "Aw, that's too bad." Her condescending grin stretched up to her ear. "Deal's a deal, so I guess I'll be seeing ya."

"Ya cheated, girlie." The man reached out to grab her wrist. Instead, his fingers scraped against something smooth, cold, and unseen. His eyes widened. "'At're ye?"

She winked. "The biggest disappointment you've ever met." She turned her back and sauntered outside.

Harsh sunlight greeted her. Athena scowled and lowered her eyes to find a surprisingly deep puddle of water on the ground. Her parched throat begged for relief, so she cupped her hands together and scooped. Cold water slipped through her aura. It splashed onto her palms, causing a slight shudder.

It wasn't always second-nature to let things pass through. Her power didn't manifest until she was about seven. One day she dashed through the halls playing tag with the guards. The next day an invisible force kept her from touching anything. She couldn't eat or drink. Changing clothes and bathing were impossible. It took several frustrating days to learn proper control.

Her father rarely left her side those days. *"Your divinity has taken form. An indiscriminate shield to protect against attack."*

"How do I turn it off?"

"Train it. Focus on our hand, Athena. You know its warmth and touch. Tis not a threat."

His hand was the first thing she touched in days. She remembered the warmth of his hug that night. *Shame his words rang hollow in the end.*

Athena drank until she washed the aftertastes of drugs and booze from her mouth. Her hands instinctively rubbed her arms, as if scrubbing away the filth. Fingernails broke skin, and fingers smeared trace amounts of blood from her shoulders to her elbows.

"My, what an unfortunate sight. A princess reduced to bathing like a sow. Oh, if *only* there was something I could do." The offkey notes of a lute followed the words.

A man with glittering platinum skin dressed in vermillion stood by the door. A four-fingered hand cradled the lute, and his smile revealed a missing front tooth.

"Uncle Bahamut?" Athena exhaled but there was no smoke. "Am I still high on hippodala smoke?"

He scoffed, posing with the lute above his head and his back arched. "No mere substance can recreate my beauty so flawlessly."

Suspicion darkened Athena's countenance. "Not that I'm unhappy to see you, but what are you doing all the way out here?"

Uncle Bahamut stood upright. "Why, scouring the land for you of course. My poor sister worried herself pale over you. 'Tut tut,' said I, 'and fret not. For I shall find our lost lamb.'"

The answer surprised her. "Auntie Morgana sent you?"

"No, dear child, aren't you listening? She only *worried* for you. I *sent* for you—sent myself. I'm the only one I trust with such a prestigious task." He set down his lute. "Come give your uncle a hug."

Athena embraced him tightly. "Why are you really here, Uncle?"

"You don't believe me?" He gasped. "Your doubt wounds me, Athena. Almost as deeply as your departure wounded your sisters."

She winced at the pang of guilt. "Bit harsh, don't you think."

"Too tame, I'd say." He spread his arms out wide. "This is your kingdom. Streets for bedding, rats for pillows." He mockingly clicked his tongue. "What would your father think?"

Athena rubbed her neck. "He'd think my head would make a fine trophy. If he thinks of me at all."

"Your father thinks of you as oft as Morgana thinks of coin." He chuckled and whispered. "Though maybe with not quite so much affection."

Athena sputtered a laugh. "You still haven't told me why you're really here."

He winked at her. "I hope to convince that capricious mother of yours into restoring my former glory."

"And you think she'll do that if you bring me home?" Athena scoffed. "Sorry, Uncle, but I—"

Bahamut interrupted her by playing a sharp note of his lute. "To think I had higher expectations of your intellect. I don't intend to leverage you for a bribe. I need an escort for this year's ball, and I *refuse* a companion who isn't at least half as pretty as I."

"I appreciate the sentiment, Uncle, but it might be in bad taste if I show up uninvited."

"Your family's shame hasn't stopped your behavior before."

A second pang pierced her heart. "My aura does nothing against your attacks, Uncle. I do miss my sisters. I've been trying to see them again with hippodala smoke but don't get memories I want."

"That's why you make new ones." He rested his back against an alley wall. "I wouldn't want to see your father either, Athena, believe me. There's no love lost between us after what happened on Avalon."

He plucked a string too hard, and it snapped. "But don't punish your sisters. They'll need you sooner than you think."

She didn't like the implication. "What do you know?"

"I know your father has a lot of enemies. Ones who hold tight to their grudges. They won't wait on their malice forever. I don't know about you, but I can think of no better place for malice than a ball. When the eyes of the world are watching, give everyone something to remember."

"You think my father is in danger?"

The humor left Bahamut's eyes. "I think it's better you return home sooner than regret missing your chance to say goodbye." He resumed his grin and extended his four-fingered hand. "What better way to make your grand return than as the guest of honor in this year's ball."

Uncle has a perverted sense of humor, but he might be serious. If someone is going to target my family... She pictured her sisters. *They'd have grown so much since I saw them last. I wonder how big they've gotten. What are they like now? Do they even remember me?*

The last question pierced her heart deeper than any of Uncle Bahamut's remarks. She considered her own fading memories of them. *Mother wins if they forget me.* She clenched her fists. *I won't let her win, nor will I let Father die.*

She grasped her uncle's hand. "So, when do we depart?"

Harley

Silken sheets drowned Harley in a sea of white comfort. Alas, he'd have to swim away soon. The madame would be furious if he were late.

He sat up, sheets clinging to his body like a petite dress. An assortment of items waited for him on the nightstand. A pearl necklace, topaz ring, and a note lay folded atop a red dress.

He snatched the ring and dropped to one knee.

"Harley, my sweet," he said in a mockingly deep voice. "Will you make me the happiest man alive?"

"Oh, darlin," he sighed in a honey-sweet voice. "This is all so sudden." He slipped the ring around his finger. "But with a fit that perfect how can I say no?"

Harley snickered and slipped into the dress. Form-fitting, with a skirt that showed off his legs, and a pair of large pink frills covering his chest. "Never had breasts before," he said, squeezing the frills. "No client could resist this. Even I can't!"

He tried on the necklace next. "Eh, a bit gaudy, but I jus' don' have it in me to say no. Not that the madame would let me keep it."

He finally reached for the note.

"*Dearest Harley,*

"*This dress, ring and necklace are all fit for a princess. My gifts to you in exchange for a wonderful night. I count the seconds until I see you again.*

"*Tender regards, E*"

Harley rolled his eyes. The madame would keep the gifts, of course. All Harley got to keep were the tender regards. "Coulda been worse. Least he knows to pamper prime property."

He stuffed the note between the chest frills and stepped into an empty hallway. Edgar refused to allow Harley into his villa in case of prying eyes. Rather, they laid together in the palace's seldom used southern tower. It had been too dark for Harley to notice the path they took last night, and he didn't recognize the area now.

Not that he needed to. All he needed was a little luck. Harley closed his eyes. A glowing golden band appeared in his mind.

"Shouldn' take more than a tug." The band tugged with little resistance. "Phew, still got plenty to spare." He shuddered to remember the last time one broke.

Harley shuffled across vermillion carpets with saffron fringes down a hall of tapestries. Each depicted an emperor's great feat. Marble busts stood below each tapestry with a plaque naming the emperor and their accomplishment.

The lone tapestry of the sitting emperor displayed him amongst ruins holding a bloodstained axe. *Sanguine-Hands Rudolph, Slayer of Cursed Bloods.*

A woman with golden eyes and thread-like hair had the most tapestries. In the first, she knelt before a glowing white woman. Her plaque read: *The Centennial Emperor's Coronation.*

The second showed her in a seaside jungle. She stood before a looming eight-limbed shadow. Thread encircled her fingers with large needles resting in her palms. *The Centennial Emperor, Light-Bringer to Avalon.* In her third tapestry, she leapt toward a viscous black form with rainbow splotches. *The Centennial Emperor, Scourge of the Echo.*

A rank scent distracted Harley from the other tapestries. Scuttling footsteps alongside strained breathing grew steadily louder.

Ah, they should know a way out. Jus' turn on the charm.

Harley peeked around the corner.

A girl in a yellow sweater slightly too big for her waddled down the corridor. Her hands pressed a grimy spider doll atop her head. Greasy black hair veiled her eyes, leaving Harley to wonder how she could see.

"Heh!" The girl tripped over her feet and landed on her back.

Guess she couldn'. Harley approached and offered his hand. "Need help there, friend?"

The girl's hair parted to reveal a shining inky eye. Purple fingertips slipped out from one of her sleeves to take his hand. "Heh, you're a pretty friend."

Goosepimples rippled down his arm at her slimy touch. He ignored his displeasure and helped her stand. "Ya quite the looker yaself."

"Does that mean I'm pretty too?"

"Means ya gorgeous."

She smiled—her teeth were more yellow than her sweater. "Hehhhhh. You're nice to me. I like you."

He feigned appreciation by winking. "Mos' people do. What's ya name?"

"I'm Suilla." She patted her doll. "This is Willard."

Harley's nose winkled. *That's where the smells comin' from.* "He a good friend?"

"The best in the world. He and all the other spiders in my room." She giggled. "Sometimes they nibble."

Some o' my friends nibble on me too. "I'm Harley—charmed, I'm sure. So, any idea where the exit is?"

She tilted her head. "What's an exit?"

"Uh, the place ya go when ya wanna leave."

"Leave?" She shook her head. "I'm not allowed to leave."

"Not allowed to leave? What are ya, a slave or somethin'?"

"Sebastien used to say I was a mistake. Is that the same?"

45

"What, no. Slave is when ya work for someone else, barely scrape by until they let ya go, or ya get lucky an' die."

She frowned. "That doesn't sound fun."

Harley shrugged. "Yeah, ain' exactly rainbows and sunshine." He kissed the topaz ring. "Got perks, though."

"Suilla?" A sweet voice called from down the hall. "Where are you?"

Suilla clapped her sleeves together. "My sister! I have to hide."

"Ya scared o' her or somethin'?"

"No, it's a game. She has to find me." Suilla pressed her back against the wall and hid behind her sleeves. "I don't think she'll find me here."

And I think this girl's a couple cards short o' a full deck. Hopefully her sister can help me. "I think it's a perfect spot."

Suilla smiled from behind her sleeves. "I'll win for sure this time."

"Suilla?" The sister's voice was closer and a touch panicked. "Whom are you with?"

"I'm with Harley," Suilla answered.

He scoffed. "Ya know she'll find ya by following ya voice, right?"

"Heh..." Suilla groaned.

Harley smelled Suilla's sister before seeing her; the perfume reminded him of the fruity desserts wealthier patrons ordered to charm him. She appeared around the bend with quick but delicate steps. She possessed the same golden hair and eyes as he, though she lacked his natural curls.

Pretty but not prettier than me.

Her green-eyed companion followed like a loyal dog. His posture and bulk reminded Harley of Olivia's guard. The comparison reminded Harley of Olivia's drawings—particularly those of her younger sister.

Wait a second... Incredulous eyes flicked between Suilla and the other girl. "Suilla, ya wouldn' happen to be a princess, would ya?"

"I don't know, but my sisters are."

Panic flared within but didn't show on his face. He could charm a maid in his sleep but doubted his success with a refined princess.

Especially not with her guard dog close by. Rather not have 'em askin' questions about my client either. Madame Morgana assured strict confidentiality with her clientele. Violations were addressed swiftly and severely.

Harley adopted his best debonair smile and tugged on his bangle for luck. "Good mornin'. I'm—"

"He's my friend." Suilla said.

The princess appeared confused, while the guard remained stern.

"Good morning," she said. "I am Princess Amelia. This is my friend Klaus. I'm glad to see Suilla has a friend. May I ask how you know my sister?"

Don' think I can refuse an answer. "Only known this one about two minutes. The other sis I've known for years."

Amelia tilted her head. "Other sister? Do you mean Makoto?"

"No, the other, other one. Olivia."

The man leaned down. "Her muse, Princess," he said.

"Ohhh." Amelia's concern gave way to recognition. "I recognize you now from her work. You're quite handsome."

"Thank ya, princess. I live to please. If ya ever needin' my services—" He stopped talking at her guardian's piercing gaze. He cleared his throat. "Where is ya lovely sister?"

Suilla clapped her sleeves together. "I'm right here."

"I, uh, meant Olivia—not that ya ain't lovely, Suilla. We were supposed to meet her in, uh, what's the word for her fancy room?"

"Atelier," the man said.

"Bless ya."

Amelia giggled. "She left for Auntie Morgana's earlier. It's a shame you missed her."

"Yeah, uh, real bad luck. Be a real help if I could get some directions outta here. I'm a bit turned around."

"I have a better idea." Amelia took Harley's hands. "We can be your escorts to the palace gate."

Well, bein' escorted instead of the escort sounds like a nice change o' pace. "Ya kindness is appreciated. I'd be a fool to pass up a princess's company."

"Then we best be off. My sister won't forgive me if I delay her muse. Suilla, dear." Amelia released Harley's hands to hug her sister. "Harley and I have business elsewhere, *but* I'll be back soon to continue our game."

Suilla groaned. "He's leaving?"

"'Fraid so," Harley said with feigned sadness.

She grabbed his hand. "Can we play again?"

Harley bit his lip to hide the discomfort at her touch. "O' course," he said through gritted teeth. "Promise to see ya next time I visit Olivia." He pecked her cheek and slipped out her grip.

"Heh!" Suilla squealed. "He'll keep his promise." She rubbed her cheek and waved.

Harley waved back, trying not to gag at the taste of her greasy skin, and walked beside Amelia down the corridor.

"I'm impressed you managed to get so lost, Harley," Amelia said. "Olivia's atelier is in an entirely different part of the palace."

Harley shrugged. "What can I say? The madame keeps me for my looks, not my sense o' direction."

She raised an eyebrow. "I presume your madame to be my Auntie Morgana. I'll have to make a request of her. Suilla would enjoy the company."

"Jus' know her prized property doesn' come cheap."

Amelia's eyes twinkled. "You'd be surprised what my family can afford."

Harley remained silent but couldn't suppress his grin. *Believe me, I might know better than ya think.*

True to her word, Amelia escorted Harley safely to the palace gates. Not that he needed her help for long. He knew his way about once they reached the atrium. Still, he didn't want to leave her company just yet.

It wasn't every day he got to strut around the palace as an honored guest. Olivia was a friend, but she never invited him. Edgar preferred clandestine entrances. The prospect of walking out the front door made him giddy.

Amelia led Harley through the door into the courtyard. It was warmer than expected, but he preferred it over cold weather. Groundskeepers flitted about tending to the garden. Any that met Amelia's eye stopped to bow. She greeted them each in turn with a smile, wave, or kind word.

Harley noted the servants' increased energy after she acknowledged them. "Someone's popular."

"I should hope," Amelia said. "I'm amongst friends."

"Friends? Look like servants to me."

"By occupation, yes, but I *know* them. They share their feelings—their secrets with me." She studied Harley's face. "I wonder what you'll share."

"Nothin' ya friend back there would approve o'," he said pointing at Klaus.

"Oh..." she said with downcast eyes.

Harley frowned. "Did I say somethin' rude?"

"No, I'm reminded of my sister is all. She didn't let me know her the way I know others. Said I'd pick up bad habits."

Guessin' that was Athena. Olivia talks 'bout her sometimes. "Sorry for bringin' up a bad memory."

"It's quite alright. How about a more fun topic?" She pointed at the main gate—large sheets of silver standing betwixt a wall of obsidian. "Auntie Morgana chose the obsidian stones herself. Twas Uncle Bahamut's flames that forged it. Did you know your boss used to rule Mount Kauneus?" She asked.

"Please," Harley scoffed. "She never shuts up about it." A chill shimmied up his back. "Eh, don' tell her I phrased it like that."

Amelia pressed a finger to her lips. "My lips are sealed. I'm quite good at keeping secrets." She stood on her toes to whisper, "Like your lie about visiting Olivia."

The chill spread throughout Harley's body. He tugged once more on his luck—thankful it didn't snap. "Lie? To a pretty girl like you? How could I ever live with myself?"

Amelia giggled. "There's no reason to fret about it, Harley. I just told you I'm good at keeping secrets."

"Uh, not that I'm complainin', but ya sure about that? A strange, but incredibly beautiful, boy sneaking around the palace? Shouldn' ya friend here beat me up?"

She balked at the idea. "Mother forbid. I don't know your intentions, Harley, but I don't sense hostility. You mean no harm to my family. As such, I will let none come to you."

Amelia stopped walking and pointed to the pale-skinned woman standing on the other side of the gate. "Is she a friend of yours?"

The woman wore a lacy red dress with black gloves and tights. A parasol shielded her face from view, but long white hair snuck through like a snake beneath a rock. She tilted her head, revealing the excitement glimmering in her faded, pale eyes.

"Salutations, chum!" she said with a wave.

He didn't recognize her but knew the gold medallion adorning her neck. The Gilded Serpent decorating the medallion's face served as Madame Morgana's personal emblem.

The madame sent her to collect me? Am I that late? He gulped. *How mad is she?*

"What's wrong?" Amelia asked.

Harley tapped at his neck. "Lump in my throat. Common side effect o' leavin' behind a pretty girl."

Amelia didn't giggle this time. "What're you afraid of, Harley?"

Ya freaky intuition, for starters. "Nothin' major. The madame sent an escort of her own. I'll probably get an earful when I get back for takin' my precious time."

It wasn't a lie, but disbelief showed in Amelia's eyes.

"If you're sure." She released his hand. "Don't be afraid to ask if you need anything. I'm not well versed in politics, but I could call in a family favor."

Cute she thinks she could leverage somethin' against the madame. "Thanks."

"My pleasure." She curtseyed. "I do hope to see you at this year's ball."

He returned the gesture. "I'll save ya a dance if I can schedule it."

Amelia waved to the guards, and Harley slinked past the gate without trouble.

He got a better look at the woman in red. Her eyes reminded Harley of the hungry cats prowling outside the Court of Temptation. She smelled of wildflowers, rustic but alluring.

"I am ecstatic to see you," she said. "I feared I'd catch my death in this heat if I waited a moment more."

"It's a great disservice to keep a lady waitin'." He tapped her medallion. "Friend of the madame's I take it?"

"Haven't had the pleasure of her acquaintance just yet." She caressed the medallion. "This is a gift from my mother. I'm quite fond of jewelry—especially gold. She saw fit to spoil me, and I hadn't the heart to decline."

She sighed fondly. "I'm on my way to meet with the illustrious Madame Morgana. I thought it only right to be escorted by her most valuable property."

"I like a girl with expensive taste." He extended his arm. "What's ya name, sweetheart?'

"Dorothy."

"Dorothy?" Harley kissed the back of her hand. The hot fabric of her glove wasn't pleasant, but it tasted better than Suilla. "I like it. Sounds exotic."

"Thank you," she said with a slight dip of her head. "Care to walk under my parasol?"

"Only if I can hold ya hand the whole way down."

"Oh, I can see why she values you so much. I'll be smitten if I let my guard down."

Harley gently squeezed her hand and walked beneath the parasol's shade. "Don' worry, Dorothy. I'll be sure to catch ya if ya fall for me."

She wagged a finger. "In sooth, I shan't fall alone. I'm quite charming myself."

Harley could see it. *Exotic looks, sense o' humor. She's practically competition.* "So, what brings ya to my madame's court?"

Dorothy chuckled. "My deepest apologies, but my business with the madame stays between us. Though, I suppose there's no harm saying I'm here on Mother's behest. They share a long history."

"What? Gonna fight the madame for ya mom's honor or somethin'?"

"Not in the slightest. She and Mother have been amicable for centuries."

"Centuries?" Harley scoffed. "Sweetheart, ya don' look a day over thirty."

A light flush covered Dorothy's cheeks. "You flatter me."

"My pleasure," he said with a wink.

It took them a few hours to reach the middle section of Mount Kauneus. They found a crowd gathered before an ornately lit building. Its sign displayed a beautiful woman with sharp red eyes wearing a provocative black dress. A vivaciously colored apple rested between her hand and open mouth.

The sign read: "*The Court of Temptation. The first taste is on the house.*"

Harley lightly squeezed Dorothy's hand and deftly weaved through the crowd. She followed without missing a step, whistling all the way.

A haze of red and purple lights greeted them inside; loud bass echoed in Harley's ears. The lights and music emanated from the stage in the center of the room. The naked woman on stage sensually rubbed her body against a pallet, coating herself in red, blue and yellow.

Her hands mixed the colors across her body. Equipped with purple, green and orange, her dancing painted the large canvas behind. The lights changed color to match the ones on her body, and the music's speed synched with her movement.

Dorothy clapped her hands together. "A captivating performance."

Harley chuckled. "She's a real showstopper. Brings in lots o' wallets."

He pointed his thumbs at each end of the room. The left was comprised of a long bar with several well-dressed bartenders servicing clients. The right side's tables and lounge chairs were seated near a fireplace with servers presenting the guests with bowls of powder or pipes.

"They come for a show an' indulge in a few other vices while here."

"No one offered salutations at the door. The entry is free, but each service has its price?"

"Sharper than most clients. Poor saps don' realize they're bein' played until their wallet is half-empty. By then it's too late to quit. Only the first taste is on the house, after all."

Dorothy pointed out the attendants. "I'm surprised to find how dapper the staff is dressed. I expected risqué attire be mandatory."

"Hun, no," Harley scoffed. "We're the madame's property. She wants us to always dress our best to impress clients." He leaned close to whisper, "Besides, this way the customers will pay extra to see the *real* merchandise."

"Ah, an excellent business practice." Dorothy's eyes swept over the room. "Where is the madame?"

"Wherever she wants to be. I'll bet she already knows ya here."

"Of course, we know," an all too familiar voice hissed.

Madame Morgana slithered from the shadows into view of the multicolored lights. Four golden wings wrapped around her body like a gown. The tips of her wings created an elongated collar that covered the back of her neck. The back of her wings formed a pattern of two large eyes that Harley swore she could see through.

Lavender scales made up her angular face and base of her tail. Both her sanguine eyes had slits in the middle. Half the right eye fixated on Harley, while the other half stared at Dorothy. Both halves of the left eye kept watch on the rest of her court.

"You're late," she hissed.

Harley curtseyed. "I'm so sorry, Ya Highness. I got—"

"We were not addressing our property." Her voice was soft but powerful. Half of her left eye focused on Dorothy. "Dorothy, correct?"

Dorothy's face lit up. "I am indeed. I'm so pleased you remember my name." She curtseyed. "I hoped to be here yesterday but there was trouble with my pets. Rest assured, the trouble has been resolved. I'm terribly sorry for the delay, Your Grace."

Madame Morgana smirked at the last two words. "Do you have the..." She hesitated.

"Indubitably." Dorothy touched Harley's shoulder. "Her Highness and I have matters to discuss. Do you mind if we discuss them in private?"

"Only if Her Highness has no need for my services."

Morgana dismissed him with a wave of her hand. "We will collect our property when needed." She wrapped a gilded wing around Dorothy's shoulders and led her toward the bar.

Dorothy waved at Harley before sharing whispers with Morgana.

Harley paid no mind to their whispers. He scanned the room for a patron to pass the afternoon with. His eyes fixated on a muscular man surrounded by young women. One of the women wore a court uniform, while the other hyenas showed off more skin. He met the man's eyes for a brief moment and received a curt nod.

"If the bodyguard is here then..." Harley found his raven-haired target sitting alone by the fireplace. He slinked toward her seat and slipped his hands over her eyes.

"Ya get three guesses."

"You're late."

Harley giggled. "Not my name, sweetheart. Two left."

"Does Madame Morgana know you're disturbing a paying customer?"

"Alright, alright." Harley dropped his hands and sat beside her. "How's the show?"

Olivia frowned at the woman on stage. "Mediocre. Her use of red needs work." She glanced at him. "You're out of uniform."

"Off duty." He shimmied the frilly chest. "Whaddaya think of the dress?"

"The color is overpowering. A subtle hue would bring out your features more."

"Which of my features is ya favorite?"

She considered for a moment. "It's difficult to parse what makes you perfect."

Harley fluttered his eyes. "Keep talkin' like that, and ya'll make me blush." He picked an apple off a nearby table and rubbed it against his chest frills to clean it. "Ever consider rentin' me for a night?" He bit into the apple. It tasted foul, so he put it back in the bowl.

Olivia shook her head. "Your body is a work of art. I refuse to sully it with my hands."

"What about ya hunk?" He asked, leering at the bodyguard.

"Bastien knows better than to court a child."

"Then he's one o' few. So, when do I meet the rest o' ya family?"

"Never, most likely. Makoto wouldn't be caught dead in here, and Amelia would only be here over Klaus's dead body."

"An' what's stoppin' ya from bringin' me over?"

She cocked an eyebrow. "I have no intention of bringing you inside the palace walls."

Harley clutched his chest and sank into the chair. "No intention, Olivia? That wounds me. Real deep. Lucky for me I have other contacts inside the palace."

"Can I make three guesses about this one?"

Harley pressed a finger to his lips. "Sorry to disappoint. My lips are sealed. Confidentiality an' all."

"Must be someone of high rank to insist upon confidentiality."

Harley shrugged. "Who knows? I certainly don'. I jus' know they have great taste in jewelry." He showed off the ring. "I bet this thing is nearly worth more than me."

Olivia took Harley's hand and inspected the ring.

Harley giggled. "Ooh. Gettin' a bit fresh, ain't we? I usually charge a fee for hand holdin', but since ya such a loyal customer I guess I'll—"

"This is Uncle Edgar's ring."

Harley shut up.

Olivia showed Harley a drawing of her uncle wearing it.

"Ya can think whatever ya want. We both know I ain't sayin' nothin'."

"True. I have no intention of letting this information be known. I wouldn't want my muse in trouble with his owner." Olivia pocketed the sketchbook. "I'm going to wrangle Bastien away from the wild hens. I'll see you later."

Harley blew her a kiss that she ignored. He waited till she was gone to sigh in relief. *Can't be too careful 'round that one.* He closed his eyes to let his body relax.

When he opened them, he found surrounded by darkness. One of Madame Morgana's private rooms. Despite numerous attempts, he could never find one on his own. It was only possible to enter or exit by the madame's will.

He heard the sharp sound of a match being struck. Flame flickered to life across the room, illuminating his master's red eyes.

Harley ignored his unease and curtseyed. "Greetings, Ya Highness."

"Eyes up."

Harley quickly raised his eyes. Madame Morgana used the match to light a taper. It floated toward him, stopping to hover in front of his eyes.

"We are blessed by the vast amount of property in our thrall. Despite unsavory rumors and opinions, we are magnanimous with most of it. We have no qualms loaning even our most prized possessions for a reasonable price."

She produced a fan made of ashen phoenix plumage from her wings. "But it is within our expectation for property to be punctual." Her sanguine eyes burned hotter than the taper.

"I got lost in the palace—"

Madame Morgana's fan snapped open. The white feathers covered her mouth, but her eyes stayed fixed on Harley. "Nothing a bit of luck can't fix. What else caused the delay?"

I'd tell ya if ya let me finish. Harley gulped down his retort. "Ran into a couple o' princesses. This pretty one, Amelia, and this grody greasy thing—real weirdo."

"Rudolph's bastard roams the halls? We're surprised. Either he's more brazen than we credited or our sister more forgiving." She hissed. "Did Dorothy offer our property food or drink?"

"No, Madame."

"Did she bleed in our property's presence?"

"No, Madame. Didn' bite neither."

"Good." The taper moved to his hand. "Whom did the jewelry belong to?"

"Gifts from this morning's client." He showed off the ring and necklace. "What do ya think of the ensemble, Madame?"

A ravenous glint consumed Madame Morgana's eyes. The taper moved of its own accord, following the curves of Harley's body. It lingered upon his legs before returning to his face. She slithered behind his back and gently touched his shoulder.

"We have ensnared a lucrative client. Be sure to keep him happy."

"Sure thing. He's a weirdo, but—"

Harley shut his mouth. The room around him twisted until his chair was upside down on the ceiling. Blood rushed to his head, as he held on tightly to the chair's arms. Although Madame Morgana stared at the ground, Harley saw her eyes through a gap in the ceiling.

"The Court of Temptation provides an important service to the degenerates crawling about our mountain. Pleasure. Indulgence. Quality. Property exists to provide these services. It does not exist to insult our clients."

Harley shuddered but didn't break eye contact. "It won't happen again, Ya Highness."

She said nothing further. The room shifted to its original position. Harley clutched his chest, gasping for breath. He flinched as the fan snapped shut behind him.

"The dress is lovely."

Harley faked a smile. "Thank ya, Madame Morgana. It brings out my legs."

"The face is more valuable than the legs." She brushed her hand against his cheek. "This is the most precious piece of property we own. We will trust it to Edgar and Dorothy."

"Am I spendin' a night with her too?"

"Dorothy will be attending the ball in two night's time and is in need of an escort."

"Of course, Ya Highness. It will be my pleasure."

"So it shall." Morgana slithered through the wall and disappeared.

The room itself faded away. The chair morphed into a stool, as Harley found himself at the bar. His dress and jewelry replaced with the uniform of a female attendant. A group of young men leered at him from across the way.

Harley crossed his legs and winked at them. *Better get back to work.*

Makoto

Makoto and her companions rode their horses through the hunting grounds. Fireheart, Makoto's ginger steed, cantered in lockstep with Ephraim and Sandstorm. Her cousins trailed a few horse lengths behind, while the emperor rode ahead of them all.

"Lady Margaret, today we're hunting sulfur scrofa," Ephraim said. "A great boar with mighty tusks of roaring flame." He stretched his hands wide to indicate the size of the flames.

Makoto knew Ephraim's words were no jest.

Ash and char dappled the usually lush meadow. The familiar scent of wildflowers and morning dew melded with the acrid scent of sulfur. The boar was a genuine danger to all present—even Uncle Rudolph.

The emperor donned his black and silver plate armor for the hunt. Makoto didn't doubt his desire for safety but also knew he reveled in any excuse to wear his armor nowadays.

She wore her own gambeson for the occasion. The front was vermilion, with the insides and arms a stark white. She appreciated the heat-resistant fabric but found the color a bit gaudy for hunting.

"It's all about practicality and pageantry," Athena told her during her first hunt. *"You need just enough protection to be safe, while still looking your best."*

When she questioned Athena's attire of a loose shirt and shorts her sister said, *"I'm already invincible, little ruby, and I look good in anything!"*

Practicality and pageantry. Another duality to balance alongside beauty and strength. Makoto's choice of weapons exemplified both: a parrying dagger and war hammer. The pairing was Athena's idea. She specialized in turning defense into overwhelming offense and encouraged Makoto do the same.

I've been thinking of her a lot today. She closed her eyes and placed a hand upon her breast. *I hope to make you proud today, sister. I'll win.* She noted the wriggling pouch at her waist. *I only pray I won't have to rely upon dishonorable methods.*

"You might think the best way to track one is by the ash left in its wake," Ephraim said, gesturing to the scorch marks in the meadow. "But following an old trail can leave you lost for hours. The best method is to follow the scent of the sulfur. The fresher the smell, the closer one is. Be sure to keep your nose alert."

Margaret lifted her head and inhaled sharply.

"'Tis much too early to smell one, cousin." Richter frowned at an untouched patch of meadow. "The scrofa has the night to roam. We probably won't find a trace for a few hours."

"What if it comes back here?" Margaret asked.

"It will, eventually," Ephraim said. "Their scent is comforting, so they usually come back to it after roaming. The best strategy when hunting for survival is to set up camp here, cover ourselves in its ash to hide our scents, and wait."

"Uncle believes there's no sport in hiding and waiting," Makoto said. "What of the countess or regent, Margaret? I doubt they care much for sport."

Margaret shook her head. "Mother and sister often compete. They love sport."

Richter's grip tightened on the reins. "Countess Reina." He said her name like a curse. "A harpy with a double-edged sword for a tongue."

The venom in his words surprised Makoto. "I didn't realize how much you loved our dear cousin, Richter."

"My interactions with her are usually pleasant enough—barring this morning's, of course. Father, however, tells me unflattering stories. Tis if we're kin to a fair-faced daemon. I scarcely imagine what she must say about Father behind closed doors."

"'A living stick of butter with a rabbit's libido,'" Margaret said suddenly.

Makoto covered her mouth and bit her lip to restrain her laughter.

Ephraim coughed into his elbow to mask his own mirth. "Do you suspect we'll see a dance between Count and Countess during the ball?"

"As a formality," Richter said. "Not unlike His Grace's annual dance with the All-Mother."

Makoto frowned at her cousin's words. Empress Isabella abandoned Mount Kauneus fourteen years ago. She appeared at the annual ball and shared a formal but cold dance with her husband. Other than that, she was naught but a ghost.

Rumors abounded as to why. The most common stemmed from the emperor's infidelity or a self-imposed exile following her son's stillbirth. Yet others whispered the empress found the Scarlet Princess's presence too repugnant.

I see such shame whenever she's around me. What must I have done to offend her?

"Makoto?" concern laced Ephraim's voice. "Are you alright?"

"Yes, I think a bit of ash got in my eye." She rubbed her face and pretended to flick a fleck off.

Ephraim reached into his saddlebag and produced a pair of goggles. "Try these on."

I suppose it won't hurt. Makoto slipped them on, adjusting the straps until they felt comfortable. "Thank you, Ephraim. Reliable as always."

"'Tis my duty and pleasure."

Makoto heard Richter chuckling. She nearly glowered at him but calmed herself with a deep breath. "Pray tell, cousin, what is so amusing?"

"Apologies, cousin. I mean no offense. I envy the bonds shared between princess and Thronsden. Yours especially is admirable."

"I should hope so." Makoto clasped Ephraim's hand. "He's been my dearest companion since I arrived in Kauneus. I'd not have lasted without him."

"She gives me too much credit," Ephraim said. "I treated her the way any person deserves—princess or no."

"Then I compare your relationship with Olivia and Bastien," Richter said. "They seem more like enemies than dear companions."

"Not every Thronsden can be lucky as I." Ephraim smiled at Makoto. "I'm honored our friendship resembles that of my mother and the emperor."

Makoto attempted to emulate Uncle Rudolph's posture but found the strain on her neck unbearable.

He gripped Nightstar's reigns with one hand. The other stayed close to his axe, Hämärä. She remembered it decapitating the bald sailor fourteen years ago. Even now, seeing it filled her with unease.

"I'm going to ride with him for a spell. Keep my cousins entertained, Ephraim."

"It shall be done."

"Thank you." She steered her ginger steed toward her uncle's side.

"We did not call for you, Makoto." His tone was gentle despite the dismissive words.

"Even in jest, I don't appreciate your coldness, Uncle."

"Then we apologize." He gently patted her shoulder. "To what pleasure do we owe your company?"

Makoto beamed at his touch. "What girl wouldn't spend her anniversary with her father?"

He almost smiled but for that one word. "Buh." His chuckle rumbled in his throat. "Your sister for a start. Olivia locks herself in her atelier regardless of the occasion. We suspected she may not have shown at breakfast."

"Olivia may not, but Amelia is always happy to see you."

Disagreement rumbled in his throat. "Amelia is too enamored with Countess Reina to spend time with us. Tis good she has a friend her own age, but we are jealous for her company."

"Rest assured, Uncle, you are beloved by all your daughters."

His eyes stared ahead at nothing. "We suppose..."

Makoto recognized the melancholy in his voice. She felt it herself when her mind drifted to her eldest sister. "I miss her too."

He cleared his throat. "Speaking of princesses and their friends, Makoto, do you fancy Ephraim?"

Changing the subject so quickly? Tis alright. We don't have to discuss Athena now. She humored him by feigning indignation. "I fancy him no more than you did his mother."

He laughed. "Charlotte and I oft discussed a union between our families. We hoped our siblings would marry, but Josephine rejected Ser Langdarossa's proposal. Olivia has no interest in Bastien, and Amelia is far too young for Klaus. You and Ephraim are our only hope."

She groaned. "I am honored to have Ephraim as my Thronsden, but you will do well to not expect a union between us."

"Do you prefer his brother?" he asked.

She knew exactly which brother he meant. It didn't take keen eyes to notice the glances she oft exchanged with Bastien. He was handsome, strong. Polite enough. Upon his rare caress, she felt secure.

Yet, she didn't feel loved by him. His actions, be they word, expression or touch, had charm but lacked warmth. Makoto didn't know if he were incapable of loving her or simply refused to.

Perhaps Bastien sees the Scarlet Princess rather than Makoto. He wouldn't be the first. The old sailor saw a monster, not a child. Even my fathers struggle to love me. The mere thought of me as a daughter causes Uncle Rudolph pain. Papa...

She refused to linger on him. Uncle Rudolph was too pained to speak of Makoto's mother, but the palpable disgust at the mention of her Papa told her everything she needed to know about him.

Perhaps I'm undeserving of love...

She imagined Ephraim scoffing at the concept. He never made her feel undeserving.

Never shared Bastien's coldness. Ephraim's love, though rooted in friendship, was unmistakable. Only he could soothe her aching heart, and Makoto relished his warmth.

"Bastien has grown into a fine man. He embodies the strength and courage of the Thronsdens. But Ephraim's friendship is worth more than all the riches of Mount Kauneus."

"Is that so?" her father asked. "Perhaps a courtship with Ephraim is further along than even you suspect."

"Was there something you valued more than Lady Charlotte's friendship?"

"Aye," he said.

Makoto waited for him to elaborate, but he did not. She followed his example and changed the subject. "I haven't opened your gift yet."

But she did bring it along. She hoped the order to abstain from opening it would end the moment the hunt did. Her fingers traced the lacquer, craving to see what waited within.

"Good. We'd be displeased if you disobeyed us."

"I know. 'Kauneus has no need for a disloyal princess.'"

His countenance soured. "You have never been disloyal to us, Makoto. You have been a wonderful princess." He shook his head.

"We misspeak. You have been a wonderful *daughter*. You may not desire the riches of Mount Kauneus, but you are worth all of them to us. Tell us, what do you desire?"

In sooth, she just received it. To be acknowledged as his daughter was one of the deepest desires of her heart. Alas, it conflicted with the other. Makoto longed for the memories shrouded in darkness. She treasured her replacement memories but still cursed the gaps in her mind.

But I cannot voice this to him. Doing so after receiving such high praise is a betrayal I shan't inflict. Athena betrayed him once. I dare not do the same. I am his daughter, not Avalon's. The island must be as distant from me as Athena from him.

"I'm afraid some desires are beyond your power, Father."

He didn't flinch this time. Instead, understanding flashed across his eyes. "Perhaps so. Our strength and resolve have waned considerably these past fourteen years."

"Father?" Makoto stared warily at him. "Are you feeling alright?"

He brought Nightstar to halt. He silently stared at the open field for a long moment. "If our power proves insufficient, perhaps we should prepare to pass it on."

He locked eyes with Makoto. "You shall have our crown for one full day if you are victorious."

Makoto's eyes widened. "Su—surely you jest."

"Buh. You are our princess, Makoto and a future imperial candidate. The crown may belong to you sooner than you expect. Alas, it may bestow the power to grant your desires."

His words weighed almost as heavy as the crown itself. Kauneus tradition held that imperial succession did not always pass to a firstborn child. Final say over the new emperor's selection remained with the All-Mother. All members of an emperor's immediate family were considered an imperial candidate regardless of blood relation.

I'm accustomed to Father of his age but rarely his mortality. I have no desire for imperial candidacy. I'd rather enjoy his company. "Kauneus still needs your wisdom and guidance, Father."

"Of course, it does. We are not yet wilting, but there is no harm in preparing for a future we shall not see. You must keep us abreast from beyond the grave."

"I shall," she agreed half-heartedly. "About your wager, what if you emerge victorious?"

He smirked. "*When* we are so, Ephraim shall be your sole partner during the ball."

"'Tis hardly punishment. My sisters and I dance with our Thronsdens every year."

"Buh. 'Tis your anniversary. We cannot be harsh with our wagers." He appeared pensive for a moment. "Though we wonder how young Bastien will feel seeing you dance with his brother rather than he."

Makoto flushed. *More of a punishment than it appears. He's right about not yet wilting. He's still a sly old fox.* "You have a deal, Father."

He pulled on Nightstar's reins to face the other riders. "Makoto has settled on a wager. Victory rests with whichever party slays the beast first. Ephraim will accompany her; a victory by his hand shall reside with her."

He nodded to Richter and Margaret. "You are not to assist either party. A win by you shall be considered a draw."

"Are you sure, Your Grace?" Richter asked. "Is it truly fair for you to be on a team alone?"

The emperor drew Hämärä. "We are never alone, Richter." He firmly kicked Nightstar's sides, and his horse galloped off.

Richter frowned. "It seems Margaret and I will no longer enjoy your company, Ephraim."

Ephraim patted his shoulder. "The loss is mine, Lord Richter." He had Sandstorm canter toward Makoto and Fireheart. "What are the terms of the wager?"

"*Father* will let me wear his crown for the day if we win."

Ephraim smiled and whistled through the gap between his teeth. "That's an anniversary gift to top them all. His Majesty must be especially confident or have a particularly harsh condition for our loss."

"The former. He demands you and I share each other's exclusive company during the ball should we lose."

"Is that all?" Ephraim balked. "Hardly a punishment."

"That's what I said. He finds amusement at the thought of us as a couple."

Ephraim covered his mouth to hide his mirth.

"Don't encourage his humor," Makoto snapped, though she struggled to contain her own laughter.

"I—I." Ephraim turned his head to laugh. "I'm sorry, but it's hard to imagine us in courtship." He raised his head, closed his eyes, and breathed in the fresh air. "I much prefer spending time with you like this."

"Agreed. Athena often told me of the dates she attended with young nobles. The atmosphere almost as stuffy as her dresses." Makoto shuddered. "It sounded horrible."

"Then perhaps his punishment is worse than we initially thought," Ephraim said.

It certainly will be if it further isolates Bastien from me. Makoto faced her cousins. "Apologies for cutting our time so short. I hope to speak more on our ride home."

Richter waved his hand. "Think none of it. I dare not say this around my uncle but good luck."

"I hope you win," Margaret said.

Makoto nodded her thanks and gazed upon the blackened meadow. "Which way, Ephraim?"

He procured a pair of binoculars from his saddlebag. He glanced in several directions before passing the binoculars. "Check the southwest."

Makoto obliged and found several large trees in the distance. "I didn't think scrofas climbed trees, Ephraim."

"I don't expect them to. I *do* expect them to feel threatened in an open field and take shelter under the trees."

"I trust your judgment." Makoto returned the binoculars. "'Twas your father who taught you about scrofas, right?"

"Yes. He hailed from the northern villages. Scrofas are good meals in Zenith Palace but are better served as a hearth or stove up north."

"As a hearth?" Makoto imagined curling beside a boar with flaming tusks. *The smell of its residue is bad enough. I doubt I could stand being close to one for long.*

She'd rather spend a cold night huddled beneath her star blanket with Ephraim and Bastien as company. *That would be lovely.*

"Thinking of my brother again?" Ephraim asked.

"How—"

"The drool."

Makoto wiped her mouth, cursing the telltale fluid. "Sometimes I hate how well you know me."

"A common side-effect of friendship."

He truly is more incorrigible than Father. "If you must know, I would very much like to spend a romantic evening in his company."

Determination blazed in Ephraim's eyes. "Then as your Thronsden and his brother I shall make it so. Make haste, Makoto. The emperor won't best us this day." He kicked Sandstorm's sides, and the mare galloped toward the trees.

Makoto quelled a sudden flush of embarrassment. Instead, she focused on her appreciation for Ephraim's support. His infectious energy bade her forward. She kicked, and Fireheart galloped to keep pace with Sandstorm.

Her bag lurched, and the lacquer box flew forward. She reached—snatching it before it hit the ground. Makoto slowed Fireheart and caught her breath. Excitement was for naught if she broke her gift.

They nearly reached the trees, but their trunks were too thick for Makoto to see beneath the canopy. *Asuka and I used to play amongst them after dark. We would hide from each other and...*

She didn't know anyone named Asuka. Yet the name felt familiar—important. Just as those memories that remained out of reach. Except now she could almost grasp one.

She clutched her throbbing temple and closed her eyes.

"Makoto?"

She ignored Ephraim's concerned tone. She had to focus. Tall trees pierced a darkened sky. Serrated leaves formed makeshift stars. A little girl with hair like the sunset tugged on Makoto's fingers. The girl cried, and Makoto held her. She whispered something, but the words were lost. Something pulled Makoto, and the girl was ripped from her arms.

"Makoto!"

She opened her eyes to blurred vision. The lacquer box slipped from her hand into her bag. She clutched Ephraim's shoulder to steady herself, cursing her throbbing head. "Please don't shout, Ephraim. I'm feeling a bit faint."

"This is more than feeling faint, Makoto." He lifted the goggles from her eyes. His hand brushed against her cheek and showed the salt smeared across his palm. "You're crying."

Makoto wiped saline smears from her face. She blinked and more droplets fell on her palms. "I..."

"You need to sit down."

"Very well." Makoto dismounted Fireheart with Ephraim's assistance.

He eased her onto a patch of grass unblemished by ash. "I'll be right back."

He tended the horses and returned with her canteen, insisting she drink. The cool rush of water down her throat eased her headache.

"What happened?" he asked.

"I'm not entirely sure..." She remembered seeing a little girl with similar red hair on the shoreline the day she left Avalon. *Asuka?* "Does the name Asuka mean anything to you?"

He shook his head. "Should it?"

"I don't know. I'm not sure what it means to *me*." She dug her fingers into the dew-stained earth. "I think I remembered something, Ephraim. A little red-haired girl and a name. I think it's hers."

"What all did you see?"

"We were standing beneath the trees before someone pulled me away." She rubbed her head. "It's so little. I'm not sure if this a memory or a waking dream."

Ephraim was quiet for a moment. "I think you should talk to the emperor about this."

"I can't. He has enough to worry about with the upcoming ball."

"Then afterwards. Your Aunt Josephine is Avalon's regent. She could host a visit."

"I shouldn't. I'm no longer Avalon's daughter. I'm a loyal princess, Ephraim." She stood without feeling faint.

"Are you well enough to continue? We can rest a few minutes longer."

"No, Ephraim, I have a bet to win." She extended her hand. "*We* have a bet to win."

He stared at her hand without offering his own. "So long as you promise to let me know if you're not feeling well."

"Ephraim, it's nothing—"

"Promise me, Makoto."

She flinched at the firmness in his voice. "You have my word, Ephraim."

"Then in that case—" He took her hand. "Let's win you that crown."

Makoto plucked a flower with petals matching her hair and returned to the horses.

"Forgive me," she whispered.

She pinched her fingers together and pulled. An unseen force ripped the water from the flower, leaving it to shrivel in her hand. She sprinkled cold water onto her hammer.

Makoto's breath chilled the water, coating the weapon in layers of ice. The hammer rested at one side of her belt, while the parrying dagger was sheathed on the other.

Admiration glimmered in Ephraim's eyes before they fell upon the shriveled flower. "Such a shame. This would have suited your hair."

"Thank you, Ephraim, but I'd prefer an orichalcum crown to a scarlet flower."

He drew his jitte and tonfa. "I think it's best we leave the horses for now. They're swift, but their agility will be limited with the trees so close together. We want as much maneuverability as possible when we confront the scrofa."

Makoto followed his advice and started for the trees. Ephraim stayed behind to always keep his eyes on her but close enough to step in front if she were accosted.

A trail of charred grass led her through the trees. Brimstone tainted the air. Makoto tried to muffle the scent with her sleeve to no avail. The rustling of a nearby bush caught her attention. She stilled her breath but not her heart. It pounded against her chest, as she waited for her prey to—

A rodent slithered from the brambles and bounded away. Makoto released her stilled breath and continued following the trail. The brimstone scent grew stronger—they had to be close now. Makoto avoided a low branch, and her eyes fell upon a clearing.

An ash-speckled boar paced in a circle. Flames blazed around its curved tusks with smoke emanating from the tips.

Sweat dripped from Makoto's hands—unsure if it was from nerves or heat. "Should we make our move?" she whispered.

"Not yet," Ephraim said. "Wait for it to drop its guard or leave an opening."

Beady coal-like eyes fixated on her.

"Don't look it in the eye, Makoto," Ephraim whispered. "And no sudden movements."

Makoto didn't nod—lest the movement be too sudden for the boar's liking. She stood still aside from her trembling fingers and dropped her gaze from its eyes to the tusks.

Smoke billowed from the beast's mouth. It shrieked and scraped its hooves against the earth. Sparks of flame shot from the blazing tusks.

Ephraim pulled Makoto from the line of fire, though she still felt the heat's kiss upon her.

I don't know if I'll be able to get close to it. I need to hit it from a distance.

Makoto slammed her hammer upon the ground. Icicles sprang toward the scrofa. Several bounced off the beast's hide, but one managed to pierce its eye.

Pained squealing reverberated through the trees; a flurry of flames flew from the tusks. The scrofa ran half-blind in the opposite direction, dragging the melting icicle along the charred earth.

Makoto started after it but felt a searing pain in her right hand. Flames crackled up her forearm. The gambeson shielded her arm from the fire, but her hand wasn't so lucky. She pressed the cold hammer against her hand.

"Makoto!" Ephraim snatched her wrist. "Never apply ice on a burn."

"We're wasting time, Ephraim." She tried to move, but he held firm.

"You promised me."

"I promised to let you know if I wasn't okay," she said. "I still have one arm, two legs and no damage to the rest of my body. That's okay by my standards."

"Not by mine." His eyes hardened. "My solemn duty is to protect you from any threat. That includes yourself."

"How am I a threat to myself?"

Ephraim pointedly lowered his eyes at her hand. "Proper estimation of one's ability is a skill, Makoto. As is restraint. Two things you often lack."

She hated that he was right. Her performance in previous hunts or sparring was adequate but not enough to merit her hope of victory. Continuing while injured was reckless, especially after her earlier fatigue. *But I can't win if I stand still. I must be strong to win.*

"You're not wrong, Ephraim, but standing here won't change my mistake. If we win, at least the mistake will have been worth making."

His countenance changed from condemnation to concern. "I can't leave that burn untreated."

"Unless you have a burn poultice on your belt, we'll have to reach the horses anyway."

Ephraim remained silent for a moment. "You can ride with me on Sandstorm. If we can catch the scrofa, we kill it. If it eludes us, I stop and treat your arm."

I may be the princess, but he's the one with the power here. "I accept your terms."

He nodded, and they raced toward the horses. They found Fireheart and Sandstorm nibbling on berries. Ephraim hopped on Sandstorm and pulled Makoto onto the mare's back. She neighed loudly at his kick, and her hooves thundered against the ground.

Makoto slipped her right arm around Ephraim's waist. Her left pointed at the scrofa stumbling through the open field. The icicle through the eyeball melted, but the damage had been done. *There's no sign of Father or Nightstar. This might be our last chance.*

"Ephraim, we need to go faster."

Ephraim touched the hand around his waist. "Left hand only, okay?"

Makoto didn't answer. She didn't want to make a promise she didn't intend to keep.

Ephraim gave Sandstorm an affectionate pat and kicked her sides again. Wind rippled against her coat, as she made up ground.

Panic filled the scrofa's non-mangled eye. It tried to speed up but tangled its stubby legs and fell. Ash streaked along the grass, as the fire wreathing around its tusks exploded in various directions.

Ephraim tugged on the reigns. Sandstorm halted to avoid the fire, but the sudden stop bucked Makoto off. The ground hurt, but she rolled onto her feet with only a scrape across her palm.

Her eyes found the scrofa; her hands found her weapons. *Sorry, Ephraim, but I need both hands for this.* Makoto charged—bobbing and weaving through oncoming fire.

The scrofa wriggled onto its feet. It closed the distance ready to gore her.

The dagger caught one tusk between its wing-like cross guard. One swing of the hammer cracked the tusk, leaking steam and smoke. Scalding air snapped at her hands. Makoto gritted her teeth to silence her scream. The scrofa wrested its tusk free of the parrying dagger, and Makoto retreated to safety.

The boar lunged once more. Makoto nearly did the same but was yanked aside. The tusk grazed her, but the gambeson absorbed most of the impact. Ephraim stood behind her. His eyes lingered on her right hand and the parrying dagger.

Makoto flinched at his judging gaze. "I—"

Ephraim snatched the dagger from her hand. He tossed a pouch from his waist into the air and cut the strings. The pouch flopped to the ground. Ephraim slowly backed away, and Makoto followed his lead.

An icy-white creature wriggled free from the torn cloth. It resembled a mushroom sucked dry of any heat and color with tendrils emitting from its cap.

Makoto hated everything about this creature. Its lifeless color, the sounds it made, the way it wriggled. Even its name, lämpötön, sent a shiver down her spine. They lurked in the coldest depths of the ocean, seeking out the strongest source of heat to ensnare and drain.

The lämpötön emitted a wet gurgling sound, as its tendrils swished around like dozens of little tongues. The scrofa, as if enraged it was being ignored, squealed and stomped. Steam leaked from the cracked tusk, while the other burst into flame. The lämpötön swiveled toward the boar. Pulsating tendrils stood erect, and the gurgling transformed into an eerie growl.

The scrofa charged; the lämpötön lunged. It ensnared the blazing tusk, slurping the flames. The scrofa squealed. It violently jerked its head to wrest itself free, but the lämpötön held on tight. Makoto swore she heard it laugh.

Color faded from the scrofa's body. Lethargy consumed it until its body gave way. The beast cried out once more; the initial shock giving way to mortal terror. The lämpötön unlatched from the tusk with a sharp *pop*. It was bloated, satisfied. Vulnerable.

"I'll finish off the scrofa," Ephraim said. "You—"

Makoto didn't wait for him to finish. She swung her hammer upon the fat lämpötön. It squished, spattering the area in its guts.

Ephraim hooked the cracked tusk with his jitte and splintered it with his tonfa. He traded his tonfa for the broken end of the tusk, ramming it into the scrofa's eye. It seized and lay still.

He took a few moments to compose himself. Then he retrieved his tonfa, wiped the blood on his gambeson and returned to Makoto's side. "Congratulations on your victory."

Makoto stared at the lämpötön's remnants. "There was no honor in using this. No beauty or strength."

"There's far less of those in death. Not that you showed much to begin with today. You displayed recklessness and stupidity above all else."

Makoto scowled. "I didn't promise to only use the left hand."

"Correct," he said. "I can think of no tactic more beautiful than deceiving your friend." He retrieved her parrying dagger and returned it to her. "Shall I treat your arm?"

Makoto presented her hand. "Please?" she whispered.

Ephraim whistled for Sandstorm. She cantered to his side, and he removed a poultice from his bag. He applied it to Makoto's burn, and she winced at its sting. "Good. Stupidity should hurt."

His words were harsh, but she understood their intent. She *was* reckless. Stupid. He didn't want her to repeat her mistake. Yet the mistake was worth it. She achieved victory and, with Ephraim's assistance, suffered minimal injury.

I'm not proud of how we won, but we did win. I managed to beat him, Athena. I wonder if you'd be proud of me.

Athena

Uncle Bahamut's old wooden wagon cobbled along the roads, jerking at every bump. One such jostle roused Athena from her nap. Stars kissed the blackened sky with the Ashen Phoenix constellation roosting above her head.

"The bird means we're close."

"You need the bird to tell you that?" Bahamut scoffed. "Isabella gave you eyes, didn't she? It might behoove you to use them."

The wagon stopped at the edge of a ridge. Athena shuffled toward the wagon's front to take in the view.

Mount Kauneus stood at the edge of the stars. The serfs dwelling at the base provided a strong foundation. They tended the mountain's fertile soil and raised the livestock. Their homes weren't as decadent as the higher tiers, but Athena knew from experience how well they held up against the elements.

The heart of the mountain housed gemstones and precious metals. The Centennial Emperor built a city there during her decades of mining expeditions. She established a school, hospitals, and the entertainment district where Auntie Morgana held her Court of Temptation.

Zenith Palace resided at the summit, built atop the highest point in the land. Auntie Morgana did so during her stint as emperor to keep her entire domain in view. The palace's towers and villas were built as a shrine to her glory. Her rule ended, but the shrines remained.

Athena nudged her uncle. "Your sister has a good eye for location."

He scoffed. "Don't give her all the credit. After the moon and heavens, Mount Kauneus is *my* greatest work." He sighed. "Alas, the credit is not all mine to claim. Morgana's vanity created a strong foundation, but twas Lucy who truly made Kauneus what it is today."

Athena whistled. "It's weird thinking of her as my sister. She died hundreds of years ago, but Mother will live forever." She paused. "Have any of the Enkeli died?"

"Depends on your definition of death. Hard to call Michael alive these days. But in the traditional sense, none aside from the half-breed. Although, Morgana and Almyra have come close. As for me, I am still alive." He flexed his disfigured hand. "Don't let the missing pieces fool you into thinking otherwise."

"Do you miss your finger?"

"Why should I? I don't need it, and it's found better use." He licked the missing space between his gums. "No, it's the tooth I miss. Food gets stuck in that spot a lot more often than it did four hundred years ago."

"I could imagine. I'm lucky to still have all of mine. Perks of being a half-breed." Thoughts of her father's axe soured her mood. "You ever think about death, Uncle?"

"At least once every decade. I find the idea appealing. Otherwise I'll have forever to ruminate on mistakes and miss those I loved."

He tuned his lute and flinched at an offkey string. "It might take me a while to get this right. Do you mind welcoming our new friends while I'm busy?"

"What're you—"

Something plinked off Athena's aura. A crossbow bolt tipped with a dingy green ooze landed at her feet. *No threats or demands. Just a poisoned bolt to the back of the head. This probably kills anyone else.* She thought of her sisters with a bolt through their eyes.

"It'll be my pleasure, Uncle. You sit tight for a bit."

Athena hopped off the wagon and walked around to the back. Three guests rode in a large hand car, likely pilfered from the mines or quarry. A burly woman, who appeared capable of lifting six Athenas simultaneously, sat in a cramped cockpit.

A pair of snipers armed with crossbows flanked her. A stout man in the seat above the cockpit loaded another bolt, while a lanky teenager stood on the handcar's main platform twirling a loaded weapon.

"Evening, friends." Athena cracked her knuckles. "Before I do something I might regret, that wasn't a warning shot, was it?"

The stout man aimed his crossbow at Athena. "No." He fired a second bolt that just missed Athena's ear.

"Great, thanks for clearing that up. Now I don't have to feel bad when I kill ya."

"Hear that, boys?" the woman yelled. "We got a lively one tonight. First one to shoot the bitch gets second pick of the loot."

"You got it, Ma!"

"On it, Ma!"

The snipers fired several bolts. One of them bounced off her forehead. *They've got repeaters. If a bolt hits the same place twice, they might break through. Guess it's time to pull out Aegis.*

A spark of energy surged through her. It flared up from her blood and coalesced at her palm. A white shield shaped like a phoenix feather materialized in her grip. Athena sank to her knees and hunkered behind her shield. It wasn't large enough to provide perfect coverage, but it covered the necessities.

The teenager scratched his head. "I'm sure I hit her, Ma." He tapped the space just above his nose and between his eyes. "I got her right here."

"Then how's she still standin', ya idiot?" the stout one asked.

Ma scoffed. "Ya didn't shoot her—neither of ya have. Guess I hafta use brute force."

Ma pumped a lever at a feverish pace, as steam burst from the cart. The cart's wheels slashed through the dirt, as it barreled toward Athena. "That little shield ain't savin' ya from this, bitch."

Athena didn't try to dodge or brace for impact. She whistled to herself until hearing the *thunk* of metal ramming metal. Aegis absorbed the damage without so much as a dent.

The handcar and its occupants weren't so lucky. The cart bifurcated on impact, sending the snipers flying in opposite directions. The stout man landed backwards, breaking his neck on the platform. The teenager flew forward and skidded face first across the road.

Athena used her foot to roll him onto his back. His face had been reduced to a pulp of flesh, blood, and dirt. *Almost like Sebastien's...* He slowly raised his hand toward her. Athena slammed her foot onto his hand and rammed Aegis into his chest. He lurched before going limp.

She considered feeling guilty but decided otherwise. *Nah. I love a good thief or smuggler, but these are brigands. If they're prepared to kill, they should be prepared to die.*

Athena hopped onto the cart's platform. Glass shards cut into Ma's face and chest. There was a lot of blood but no movement. Athena slapped Aegis against Ma's cheek, knocking out several teeth. No response. *Two dead?*

Athena searched Ma for any supplies. She found a butterfly knife and a packet of jerky in a jacket pocket. The jerky tasted like old dirt but was better than the slop she fought a pig for last week.

She hopped off the cart to search the stout man. There was no doubt in Athena's mind that he was dead. *I think even I'd die if my neck bent that way. Mom would probably survive, though.*

Finding nothing valuable in his coat and pants, she checked his shoes. The musty scent gave her pause, but Athena held her breath and pressed on. Her valiance was for naught as both were empty.

Athena frisked the base of his socks for any telltale lumps. There was something along the arch of his left foot. She cut a hole into the fabric with Ma's butterfly knife, and five platinum coins fell into her lap. Athena walked back toward the wagon, tossing and catching coins.

"Wait," Ma croaked from the cockpit.

"You're not dead?" *Probably not for much longer.*

"I will be if you don't help. There's no lenity up there for people like me. They'll let me die or off me themselves."

Athena shrugged. "Then you die. Can't tell you what happens after but let me know if it's nice."

"Just like that? You'd deny mercy to an old woman?"

"Mercy?" Athena failed to stifle a laugh. "You had your boys shoot me multiple times *and* tried to run me over. Leaving you intact *is* mercy." *Well, mostly intact.*

"You self-righteous, bitch!" Ma snarled. "I bet you've got a nice family. Be a shame if something happened to them."

Athena paid the taunt no mind. It wasn't a real threat. Just a dying woman's last effort to goad Athena into kill her quickly. *I don't think she deserves such kindness.*

She found Uncle Bahamut still tuning his lute when she returned to the wagon. "All clear, Uncle. Sadly, our guests didn't want to stay for supper."

"Hard to accept an invitation offered through gritted teeth."

"Hey, they shot at me. I thought I was being nice giving them a chance to leave at all."

"I don't recall you offering Sebastien the same kindness. Seems exile softened you."

"Maybe it did." Athena laid back and closed her eyes. "Do me a favor, Uncle? Wake me up when we get to Auntie's Court."

A neon halo roused her before Bahamut did. Athena donned her shawl and read Morgana's sign. "'The first taste is on the house.' She's generous as ever."

"Anything you plan to sample?" Uncle Bahamut asked.

"Nah. Doubt there's anything here I haven't tasted before."

Her uncle parked the wagon and escorted Athena to the entrance. "Age before beauty, as they say."

"You do know you're older than me, right?"

"Quite. Hence, the youth ushers the way for an aged but still handsome bard."

Athena conceded and pushed the door open. She whistled softly upon entering. "It's bigger than I remember."

"We could say the same about you."

Athena shuddered at the voice hissing in her ear. "I hate it when you do that, Auntie." She turned and stared into Morgana's slit sanguine eyes. "But it is nice to see you again."

Two eye halves focused on Athena. "The pleasure is ours." Morgana pecked each of Athena's cheeks. The other two halves regarded Bahamut. "Though our reunion *is* unexpected."

Bahamut grinned. "I needed a worthy escort to this year's ball—not that my darling sister is unsatisfactory. But you're so busy, you hardly have time for me."

"Alas, time is a force beyond even our control. Were it so, brother, we'd spend eternity with you." One of Morgana's eye halves checked another area of the room. "Does your family know you're here, Athena?"

"Not yet. I'm hoping you know a way into the palace without getting caught. I'll talk to Father after making the rounds with the kids."

"We might know a way." Morgana reached betwixt her wings and produced a violet pipe with an iron butterfly fashioned at the end. "Bahamut, if you don't mind."

His nose wrinkled. "A—a—achoo!" He tapped a finger against his nostril and released a stream of platinum fire at the pipe.

The butterfly glowed gold as smoke rose from its wings. Morgana inhaled the smoke before releasing it in a slow breath. "Do you still smoke, Athena?" She offered the pipe; every part of her eyes watched Athena.

The smoke's aroma reminded Athena of her last hippodala trip. "Trying to quit, actually."

"Pity." Morgana took another drag. "There is a patron tonight who may prove useful in infiltrating Zenith Palace. Private business with our brother calls us away, but rest assured, you'll know her when you see her." Half her right eye moved toward the stage. "Your drinks are on the house, by the way."

Athena followed Morgana's eye toward a raven-haired woman furiously scribbling into a sketchbook. She recognized her sister, not by appearance, but her passion and intensity. *Olive was always a fidgety little thing—a real terror when Father took her in. Glad I convinced her to channel all that energy into art.*

"Thanks, Auntie. You're a lifesaver."

They kissed each other's cheeks, and Athena hugged her uncle before they disappeared into the haze of lights. Nostalgia ached her heart, as she slinked through the crowd toward her sister.

Little tyke grew up fast. She barely needed her big sister once she picked up a brush the first time. Wonder how long before she even noticed I was gone. You did notice, right, Olive?

A broad-shouldered man blocked her path. Athena tried maneuvering around him, but he didn't let her. "Excuse me, ma'am, but you must remove the hood to approach the princess."

The voice was gruff but not yet hostile. *Must be Bastien.* She leaned back just enough to glimpse his face. *Still toad-like.* "I'm flattered you want to see me. But I must warn you, sir, I'm quite beautiful. Might just take your breath away."

"All the more reason to show me. If you prefer to stay discreet, then I urge you stay away from the princess."

"The guard dog has a decent bark." She adjusted her hood to let him peek at her face. "You'd make your mother and brothers proud."

Bastien gasped, and his eyes flittered between Athena and Olivia.

She chuckled. "Warned you I'd take your breath away. Don't be too hard on yourself. I tend to have that effect. I think it's my eyes." She fluttered them thrice before obscuring her face beneath the hood.

Bastien's countenance showed confusion and distrust rather than mirth. "You cannot be here, Pri—Athena. Your father will not take kindly to your presence."

"He doesn't take kindly to most things."

"We both know Olivia won't report your presence. If he finds out she spoke to you..."

Athena frowned. *Getting my sisters in trouble is the last thing I want. Would he exile them too? I can't put it past him.* "I hate that you have a point. You boys must have gotten smarter while I was gone."

She pointed at Olive with her thumb. "She looks well."

He nodded. "She is."

"Still holed up in her atelier?"

"Most days, but she regularly attends meals. Her art has improved, and she's learning violin with Lord Richter."

"Richter? Edgar's boy, right?" She lowered her hand to her waist. "He was yae high when I saw him last. He as big as you now?"

Bastien scoffed. "Not even Klaus is big as I," he said, flexing his arms.

Athena winced at Klaus's name. *The man whose heart I broke.* "He married yet?"

"To his duties. He tends to Amelia's whims as if they were matters of life and death."

"Oh?" Athena rubbed her hands together. "What kind of whims does my Lucielle have?"

"Lucielle?"

"Amelia," Athena said. "We used to call each other by our middle names."

Athena remembered holding her baby sister for the first time. She remembered the lullabies, fairy tales, and the endless giggling. It wasn't her first time being an older sister, but the first time she was there from the start. *Not that I was able to stay for long.*

"Ah. She oft meddles in affairs of the heart, but her motives are pure. I hear naught but a kind word from or of her."

Athena snickered. "Glad to hear a bit of my mischief rubbed off on her but even better to hear she stayed a good kid." *Hope she treats Klaus better than I did.* "And Makoto?"

"Makoto is well. Her strength encapsulates that of a true princess."

"And her beauty?" Athena asked with a grin.

"Unmatched."

Their first meeting came to mind. Of their father returning from Avalon with whom Athena assumed to be his bastard.

That little ruby stood up to me. She tried to be tough but was so scared. I made her promise to relax around me. No strength and beauty. Just be Makoto.

"And she's happy?"

"Yes, they're all happy."

As expected of such strong kids. None of them ever needed their big sister. She hesitated before asking. "Even Suilla?"

"I... wouldn't know. There are limitations in place, but her sisters visit. She's allowed to roam the Southern Wing rather than stay confined to one room. If I may be so bold, I suspect this came to pass because of your sacrifice."

She thought of the little girl huddled beside the window. A girl repulsed by the sun's light, because it was so foreign. There was a sense of satisfaction—of peace in knowing Athena did *something* to make that girl's life just a little bit better.

"Thank you. That means a lot."

"It's my pleasure, Princess." Bastien paused. "I won't tell anyone I saw you here. For what it's worth, I hope your father is convinced to let you return."

Athena clicked her tongue and made her way to a lonely corner of the bar. *I want something strong but still need to be presentable later.*

She flipped through a drink menu, pausing at the Madame's Special: a cocktail of watermelon juice, cucumber slices, orange juice, pineapple juice, and Nova City vodka. *Not very strong but it doesn't sound bad.* A second drink caught her eye. The Secret Keeper consisted of two shots of whiskey, grapefruit slices and blended ginger.

She rapped the table with her knuckles. "Barkeep, get me a Madame's Special and a Secret Keeper—make it a double."

The bartender mixed the drinks with aplomb. One a multi-colored feast for Athena's eyes, the other drab and smelled bitter.

"The madame informed me your drinks are on the house tonight. It remains my duty to warn you the Madame's Special's alcohol content is deceptively high. The Secret Keeper is less potent, but most patrons find a double stronger than anticipated."

His eyes fell upon a bearded gentleman passed out several stools down.

"Do you tell this to all the girls or just the cute ones?" Athena asked, fluttering her eyelashes.

He didn't smile. "I am my madame's property. My duty is to service her patrons and take great care of her guests."

"Duly noted and appreciated."

The bartender nodded. "Let me know when my services are next required." He walked down the bar and addressed a rowdy group.

Athena sampled her Madame's Special first. The sweet juices melded together to compliment the vodka. "That is dangerous. I could see myself drinking three or four of these back in my prime."

She took a whiff of her second drink. The smell alone could've intoxicated someone with weaker constitution. Athena downed half her glass—the ginger's sharp taste and the whiskey's heat singed her throat.

"Smooth as I remember." She let the flavors linger in her throat before taking another drink.

A petite figure slinked into the stool beside her. Athena kept her head low to avoid eye contact but glimpsed the modest, but pretty, black dress.

"Ya know, it mus' be difficult admirin' the madame's merchandise with a hood on."

"You'd be surprised." Her throat felt parched, so she finished off her drink. "To what do I owe the pleasure of your company?"

"It mos' certainly is ya pleasure." Their legs pointed at the stage. "They might be the star attraction tonight, but I'm the real crown jewel of Her Highness's Court. Keepin' my company is a pleasure some folks only get in dreams."

"And did the madame ask you to keep me company?"

They scoffed. "Nah, but I saw ya two speakin'. Then I hear she's givin' ya free drinks. The madame is many things but generous ain't usually one o' 'em. I decided to mosey on over here an' find out what made ya so special."

Athena chuckled. "I don't think you'll believe me if I say I'm no one."

They clicked their tongue. "Glad to see her generosity ain't wasted on a moron."

Athena slid her glass down. "Give me a refill, and I'll give you a straight answer."

Her companion hopped over the bar. Athena glimpsed their face but didn't catch their eyes. *Pretty, androgynous, almost familiar. Above all, way too young to be working here.*

"What am I refillin'?"

"Secret Keeper."

"Single o' double?"

"Single is plenty."

It took them longer to mix the drink than the bartender, but Athena didn't mind waiting.

"You got a name, Crown Jewel?"

They set the drink on the counter. "Ya first."

Athena stared at her drink and considered which fake name to use. "Katherine."

"Harley. Pleasure meetin' ya, Miss Katherine." Harley kissed the back of her hand. "Welcome to Madame Morgana's Court o' Temptation. How may I be of service?"

Athena faked a laugh. "I bet you drive a lot of patrons crazy."

"Ya know it. Girls love it, but the men are my favorite. I got one who spoils me like a princess. Speakin' o' royalty, ya ain't tell me how ya know the madame."

Athena swirled her glass around. "She and my mother have a lot of history."

Harley chuckled. "Not the first time I heard that today."

"I bet. Auntie has business everywhere. How'd her business with you start?"

"Business? Our relationship goes beyond mere business, sweetheart. She's my owner. I'm her prized possession."

Athena tilted her head toward the bartender. "He mentioned something about being her property. I thought it was a term to show loyalty or respect."

"Some go along with it, but most o' us are bought an' paid for. I'm property jus' the same as her pipe or this bar."

"How much do you think she'd sell you for?"

"Me?" Harley cackled. "Haven't ya been listenin'? I'm the most valuable thing here. Her Highness wouldn' sell me for anythin' less than the Orichalcum Crown itself. Ha, maybe even that's not enough."

Now her laugh was genuine. "I'm almost jealous. Must be nice being valued." She took another whiff of her bitter drink. "Are you happy here?"

"I'm beautiful," Harley scoffed. "That's all I need."

"I'll drink to that." Athena gulped down her shot and savored the smooth singe. "How'd she ensnare you in her coils?"

Harley shrugged. "Way the madame tells it, I was a gift from my own mama. An' let me tell ya, I'm offended she'd give me away for free."

Athena lifted her empty glass. "To terrible mothers."

Harley clinked an empty glass against Athena's. He took a fake drink and set the glass down. "Mind givin' me a peek under the hood, Miss Katherine?"

She hesitated. "Her Highness enforces strict confidentiality with clients and guests?"

"Course. Any girl who can't keep a secret ain't lastin' here. My lips might be puckered, sweetheart, but they're sealed tight."

"Then I suppose there's not much harm." She lifted her hood and saw Harley's eyes. They weren't as glassy as Athena's but shared their golden color.

Mother's eyes, but she hasn't shared Father's bed in years. Where did you come from, Harley? "You have beautiful eyes."

"I do, don' I?" He fluttered his eyelashes. "They're exotic. Madame says they're part o' my charm. Well, that an' the rest of me."

"How old are you, Harley?"

"Dunno. Madame don' keep track. I jus' know I'm old enough to work." He drummed his fingers against his cheek. "Ya look familiar too. I know I've seen ya before—oh!" Harley snapped his fingers. "I got it!"

Athena quickly pulled her hood up. "Not so loud."

Harley daintily covered his lips. "Sorry, sweetheart, but I jus' realized where I know ya from. Embarassin' it took so long. I see ya face all the time."

"All the time? How?"

"I got this friend—charmin' girl. Not much of a knockout but cute smile. Only really see it when she's got somethin' in her hands—hey, don't grin at that. Get ya mind outta the gutta—that's where mine belongs.

"I mean when she's holdin' her book and somethin' to write with. Real artist that one. Says she started sculptin', but I ain't lucky enough to see 'em yet—"

Athena tilted her empty glass. "If you're going to take this long to get to the point, you might as well get me another drink."

"No patience. My worst clients are ones without patience." Harley scoffed and took her glass. "Anyway, *the point*, is she has a lotta drawings o' ya. She draws ya almost as much as she draws me."

"Really?" Athena glanced in Olivia's direction but saw no sign of her sister. *Good. This way I won't be tempted to say hello.*

Harley finished mixing another Secret Keeper. "It's almost enough to make a girl jealous." He offered her the drink. "But jealousy is for rookies an' old bats. I'm in prime, so it's beneath me."

"Do you like her?"

"I love all o' my clients. Even the impatient ones," he added with a wink.

Athena held back a reply. She heard someone approach and kept her head down.

A familiar voice whispered, "Did you honestly expect Bastien to keep me from you?"

You're more perceptive than I gave you credit for. She gulped down her Secret Keeper and lifted her hood just enough to meet her sister's disappointed eyes. "Hey, Olive."

Olive's hand slapped against Athena's barrier. She frowned and gingerly rubbed her palm. "I need you to allow me through your barrier so I can hit you."

"Olive—"

Olive silenced her with another failed slap. "How dare you skulk in here without saying hello."

Athena tilted an empty glass against another. "I needed the proper motivation first."

Olive's expression remained unchanged. "You needed to be drunk before visiting me?"

Harley whistled. "Need a shovel for that hole ya diggin'?"

"Thanks, but I think I can do enough digging without one." Athena stared at the bottom of her glass. "Olive, I—"

"Look me in the eye when you talk to me, Athena."

Athena winced but obliged. "I came with Uncle Bahamut to visit you. And Makoto and Lucielle. Suilla too, if I can swing it. But Bastien is right. Father will be furious if he finds out you knew I was here. I planned on sneaking into the castle to see you all and Father after."

She tapped the empty glass beside her. "Wanted to enjoy a few drinks in case he doesn't take too kindly to my grand return." Athena stood. Her legs wobbled slightly, but she used the counter to catch herself. "I'll admit to enjoying a little more than I intended."

"I couldn't leave you in this state even if I wanted to." Olive silenced Athena's expected reply with a sharp glare. "I fear not our father's fury and care not for your attempt to evade me. I shall not let you out of my sight until we reach Zenith Palace."

Olive's finger beckoned Bastien join them. His expression was stern—almost Kalus-like.

"Princess, I advised Athena—"

"Your unsolicited advice has been considered and rejected." Her gaze flicked onto Harley. "I assume the client we discussed earlier told you a way to enter the palace undetected?"

"You discussed a client?" Athena mockingly clicked her tongue. "So much for puckered but not loose."

"Okay, *first*, not what I said. 'Puckered, sweetheart but they're sealed tight,' is what I said. Second, I didn' name anyone or confirm anythin'. She jus' made an assumption. That all bein' said, I may know a route or two to get inside."

Fair enough. "So, Harley, how should I sneak into Zenith Palace?"

"An excellent question. Perhaps I can be of service," a scratchy voice hissed.

A young blonde girl flanked by a tall brunette woman approached the bar. The woman wore a black uniform with a pin shaped like a pair of wings. She carried a bow in her left hand and a quiver on her back. *I didn't know Auntie allowed weapons in here. She must be accompanying a VIP.*

Despite her small stature, the girl was unquestionably in charge. Her posture, expression and regalia conveyed that she was here on business.

I remember that unreadable face. That's Auntie Jo's kid. Reina was just a brat last time I saw her. Barely aged a day in seven years.

"Good evening, Countess," Olive said.

Countess? Right, I'd forgotten Auntie Jo passed down her title. Makes sense she'd give it to Reina over Margaret. Gentle soul but a clumsy oaf. Reina was always the sharper of the two. She was only about nine when she told me about Suilla.

The countess dipped her head. "Princess." She snapped and held up two fingers. "Two drinks before you're dismissed. An ice water for myself and something sweet for my subordinate. Light on alcohol, of course—she's still on duty. Would you like a drink, Princess?"

Olive shook her head. "Your offer is appreciated, but—"

"With all due respect, I wasn't asking you." The countess sat on the stool beside Athena.

"I'll pass but appreciate the offer, Reina."

Reina smirked. "I'm flattered you remember me."

The smirk is new. She barely emoted last time we spoke. Either she's mellowed out these past few years, or she's gotten better at this. "Flattery can get you pretty far. I'm sure Harley would know all about that."

"I would." Harley slid a drink down the bar toward the woman. "Flattery is secrecy's biggest weakness." He dropped a couple ice cubes into a tall glass of water and presented it to Reina. "Am I still dismissed?"

"Unless you prefer an interrogation. I am quite curious to know about these routes into Zenith Palace."

Harkey winced. "Dismissed it is. Ain't no worse feelin' in the world."

Athena grabbed the coins she took from Ma's son and placed them on the bar. "Maybe these can keep you company."

Harley's golden eyes gleamed, and he snatched the coins. "Why ain't ya this generous?" he asked Olive.

She rolled her eyes. "Will you feel better if I hire you tomorrow as a model?"

"Really?" He pressed his hands against his cheeks. "Kauneus's coldest flower opens her room an' her heart. How could I say no to such an invitation?"

"I can still change my mind."

Harley snickered but made his exit after winking at Athena.

Athena winked back and returned her attention to Reina. "Come here often, Countess?"

"When business demands. I was in the area when I heard the most fascinating rumor. An exiled princess drinking her troubles in Madame Morgana's Court."

"Already?" Athena whistled. "Word travels fast."

"Like a plague, especially with such an interesting topic. An exiled princess not only returns but is conspiring to break into Zenith Palace. A failure to inform His Majesty of such information is a breach of trust. So, Princess, what am I to tell my uncle?" Reina drank her water, whilst staring at Athena.

I can't resist if Reina arrests me. Fighting makes me look like a criminal, which I technically am, and I might get Olive in deep trouble. Instead, she's offering the chance to spin the narrative. "I think the real question is what you plan on telling my sisters."

"Oh?" Reina raised an eyebrow. "What makes you say that?"

"I doubt Father would mind my arrest, but my sisters are a different story. You're smart enough to know selling me out won't win you any points with them. Not to mention if Father *does* allow me to stay then you'd have me as an enemy."

She scratched the back of her head. "Not that I'm much of a threat, but your life might be a little easier if I don't hate you."

Reina smiled like a cat facing off against a wounded dog: confident but still wary. "You're sharper than I expected, Princess.

Correct, I wish to fulfill my duties to the emperor without upsetting my dear cousins."

She set down her glass and folded her hands upon the bar. "Loathe as I am to disappoint them, I cannot abide blatant disrespect for the law. I need to know why you returned before I agree to help you."

"Fair enough. I didn't intend on keeping it secret. Uncle Bahamut invited me to be his escort at this year's ball."

Reina frowned. "Is that all?"

"An Enkeli's invitation isn't enough for you? Then how about his warning? Uncle tells me Father's life is in danger."

Reina nodded. "We can weave a better narrative with a warning. Am I to assume you're here to thwart any attempt on His Majesty's life?"

"It might come as a shock, but yes. I'd rather not see my sisters turn orphan."

"It wouldn't be my first time," Olive said coolly.

Athena expected a change in Olive's countenance. Shock or fear eyes from an Enkeli's warning. Olive didn't appear fazed at all. *Unflappable as ever.*

Reina raised her head. "Here's my proposal, Princess. We inform His Majesty that I investigated rumors of your return. Olivia found you before I did and delivered you unto me. You shared with us a divine warning of His Majesty's safety and requested an audience with him. I trust this version of events is to your liking."

"That about covers it. I appreciate you helping me out, Countess. But between you and me, just how many favors am I going to owe you?"

"Favors?" Reina scoffed. "I'd rather our relationship not start with subterfuge and indentured favors." She extended her gloved hand.

Athena regarded Reina's hand. *The girl's sharp and well-informed. That's a valuable ally so long as I don't get on her bad side. Best not to be too comfortable around her.* "Are we going straight to my father, or will I be waiting somewhere while you speak to him?"

"Linnette will escort you to my villa. My subordinates will attend to your needs, while I report to the emperor. Olivia and Bastien will accompany me and support my story. You will be collected once the emperor is ready for an audience."

"Works for me." *I'm guessing this cute brunette is Linnette. As armed escorts go, the company could be worse.* She firmly shook Reina's hand. "Let's go see the emperor."

Makoto

Torchlight and moonbeams illuminated the stable. Makoto ferried Fireheart into an empty stall. She offered a handful of oats and thanked him for his service. Fireheart whinnied and laid down to rest.

Makoto's joy faltered once she glanced at the next stall over. A sleek black mechanical bike stood under the moonlight. *It's been ages since I've ridden it.* She approached the bike; her hands lightly squeezing the handbrakes. *Athena used to let me steer during our rides. These seemed so much bigger back then...*

Athena's hearty laughter echoed in her ears. *"Wanna burn rubber with me, little ruby?"*

She remembered the rippling wind tickling her face. The hum of the wheels grinding against the earth. The burning rubber smell bothering her nose. *It's nice to have a memory without a headache. Seems the anniversary has me in a nostalgic mood.*

"Take your time reminiscing, Makoto. We shall see you at dinner." The emperor flourished his cloak, nearly hiding the drop of his shoulders, as he left.

Father rarely drops his posture. He misses her more than he lets on. I think most of us do. She touched the bike one final time and met Ephraim outside the stable.

"How fares your hand?"

Makoto examined the bandage. "Sore but otherwise okay. Should we change the bandage?"

"It's fine tonight, but be sure to change it tomorrow morning," he said.

"Very well. Then let us egress, Ephraim. Our business here is concluded."

"Yes, Makoto. Or," he said with a twinkle in his eye. "Should I start saying 'Your Grace?'"

"Not yet," she chuckled. "I imagine Father will transfer the crown after tonight's dinner or tomorrow's breakfast. It's still 'Makoto' until then, Ephraim."

He smiled as he walked beside her. "Don't think I didn't notice you calling him 'father' during our hunt. May I ask?"

"Of course. He said I have been a wonderful daughter. Worth nothing less than all the riches Mount Kauneus has to offer."

"He's right on both fronts. Though, all the riches of Mount Kauneus are too low a value for you."

"Too low?" she scoffed. "Flattery is useless when it's transparent, Ser Thronsden."

"Yet I meant every word." There wasn't a hint of jest in his words or countenance. "Not even all Bahamut's tears would be enough."

She looked up, hoping he wouldn't notice her flushed cheeks. Bahamut's tears formed the stars according to the Alma's preaching. To her knowledge, neither the Platinum Dragon nor All-Mother denied the story.

Makoto admired the heavens. The Gilded Serpent loomed overheard—its stars coiling around invisible prey. The Ashen Phoenix perched nearby with unfurled wings. *The Platinum Dragon only graces the southern skies with his presence. Though, he may appear at this year's ball with his sisters.*

Makoto grimaced. Last year's ball had been a disaster. She forewent her annual attire upon Olivia's insistence. Instead, she borrowed one of her sister's black dresses. It had been a bit tight, especially around her chest. *Twas hard walking in that—let alone dancing. No beauty or strength that night.*

"Why don't you dress up more often, Ephraim?" The ball was the only night he did, and he never deviated from the same red suit. *In sooth, tis a shame. He's quite dashing when he tries.*

"I don't own anything fancy. The suit is borrowed from Amelia. She has several to dress Klaus in. He's her favorite doll."

The visage of Klaus wearing Amelia's ornate dresses filled Makoto's mind. "I'm sure he—" She covered her mouth to stifle her laughter. "I'm sure he's very pretty."

"Not half as pretty as you."

"That should go without saying." Makoto curtseyed and extended one hand toward the stars. "I have been raised to exemplify the beauty of a Kauneus princess. It wouldn't do to be shown up by your brother."

"Your beauty is matched only by—"

"My reckless behavior?"

"I was going to say your poor dancing."

"Poor dancing?" She was indignant. "I struggled only because my dress was too tight."

"An excuse for one of thirteen struggles. What will you blame for your fourteenth?"

"You *dare* insinuate that a Kauneus princess struggles on the dancefloor?"

"I do." He extended his hand with a crescent moon-like smile. "Care to prove me wrong?"

Makoto's indignation faltered, as she regarded his hand. "Surely you're not serious?"

"Surely you're not scared of dancing."

She scoffed. "Very well. I'll fall for your taunts this time." She took his hand and set the other at her waist. "Your lead, Ser Thronsden."

Ephraim led them in a semi-circle into the palace garden. Moonlight-dappled ivy clung to the garden wall as firmly as the dancers gripped hands. He twirled her in place before dipping her low to the ground.

"Oh?" Makoto gasped. "You don't do this very often."

"Must be the moonlight in my veins. It's gotten me feeling quite romantic."

"Romantic?" Her heart fluttered unexpectedly. "H—how so?"

He let go of Makoto's hand and plucked a white acacia. "Now you can wear a pretty flower *and* the crown."

She tucked the flower behind her ear, letting the petals caress her hair. "And how do I look?" she asked with an exaggerated flutter of her eyes.

"Beautiful," he said.

His cavalier tone bothered her. Today was her anniversary—the day she reached adulthood. But the only man asking for a dance regarded it as a joke. The realization left her melancholic, if not bitter.

"Am I?"

Ephraim blinked. "Of course you are."

"How am I beautiful?"

"I... don't think I follow."

"My sisters each have a unique beauty. Athena's rugged charm attracted gentleman and ladies to her side. Olivia is like a waterfall, imposing but beautiful to behold. Amelia is naturally pretty like a freshly bloomed flower."

Makoto stepped away from him and sat on a wooden bench stationed between a bed of roses. "Olivia's admirers send presents, and Amelia is complimented daily. Suitors threw themselves at Father's feet for a chance at Athena's hand. Yet not one asks for my hand or so much as a dance on my anniversary."

She sighed deeply. "I don't lament my lack of suitors, Ephraim. But I wonder... what must be so wrong with me that I have none?"

Ephraim sat beside her. His former cavalier countenance laced with concern. "What of Bastien?"

"Bastien?" Makoto scoffed.

She remembered the last time she were alone with him. A sleepless night led her to the training hall. There she found Bastien, shirtless and glistening with sweat. They sparred until sunrise.

He complimented her form, in more ways than one, and didn't hesitate to show off his physique. The encounter didn't lack passion, but he remained formal and cold ever after.

"I'm an ornament he admires, not a woman he loves." She frowned at the night sky. "Seems the moonlight in my veins prefers melancholy to romance."

Ephraim was quiet a moment. He tilted his head back and gazed up at the stars. "There was fire in the sky the night we met. Do you remember?"

"Of course, I caused it." She grimaced at the memory of the drunken sailor and his bottle. "I'll never forget it."

"Neither will I. A beautiful blaze streaking across the night sky." He gently squeezed her hand. "Your beauty is that of fire, Makoto."

"I burn whatever I touch?" she scoffed.

"Fire takes many forms. It simmers when relaxed and blazes when indignant. Yet nonetheless mesmerizing. I haven't been able to take my eyes off you in fourteen years."

Makoto turned to hide her flushing cheeks. "You're embarrassing me, Ephraim."

"Good. My duty is to be your retainer until the day I die. My *pleasure* is to be your friend and make you happy. I'm not so presumptuous to think a few compliments will relieve all your troubles. But if only one person in this damn palace will praise you, then I shall do so until you tire of me."

"And if I shall never tire of you?" she asked, squeezing his hand.

"Then you will shed the appellation of 'Scarlet Princess' and be simply 'Makoto' for the rest of your days. "How does that make you feel?"

Makoto rested her head upon his shoulder. "Beautiful."

They remained in the garden until a servant fetched them for dinner.

Makoto curtseyed for the emperor, who greeted her with a half-hearted lift of his goblet. *He's still thinking about Athena, isn't he?* She sat across from an empty seat. *Another absent daughter can't help his mood.*

"Introducing Her Royal Highness Princess Amelia Lucille vi Kauneus and her retainer, Ser Klaus Thronsden."

Her father's spirits, or at least his posture, lifted at the sight of Amelia. She frowned at Olivia's empty seat but greeted Makoto with an emphatic smile. "Congratulations on winning. I've heard it's not easy to beat Father."

"Buh," he growled. "She is lucky we started off in the wrong direction."

Luckier still the lämpötön didn't turn on Ephraim or I. Makoto regarded him with exaggerated disappointment. "It's bad form to blame your loss on luck, Father."

He matched Makoto's expression. "You should be more gracious in victory, Makoto, lest you fall victim to divine humbling."

"I shall take my chances." She sensed Ephraim's disapproval at her boasting.

"Introducing Count Edgar Sebastian von Kauneus and his son: Lord Richter Jonathan von Kauneus."

Uncle Edgar waddled to the chair beside Makoto. He clasped her shoulder just hard enough to make her wince. "Congratulations," he whispered.

Makoto nodded her thanks. "How has your day been, Uncle?"

"Quite productive. I had lunch with the heads of several noteworthy families. We may reach that compromise discussed at breakfast sooner than expected."

"Have you met with Countess Reina, Father?" Richter asked after taking his seat.

Uncle Edgar's sigh caused his moustache to flutter. "Unfortunately, not. She's been indisposed since the afternoon. Some business with Madame Morgana. I hope to speak with her at dinner."

"Introducing Lady Margaret Sabrina vi Kauneus."

Only Margaret? Reina must be hard at work.

Margaret managed to reach the table without tripping. "My sister apologizes for her absence."

"Then we shall enjoy the feast in her and Olivia's stead," the emperor said and snapped his fingers.

Servants rolled in carts carrying four course meals. The first course consisted of peppers stuffed with lardons. The second course a bowl of egg drop soup. The scrofa had been curried for the main course. Finally, a slice of yellow cake with licorice frosting for dessert.

Twice in one day? Father is spoiling me.

The emperor raised his goblet. "As the sun sets on this joyous day, tis our pleasure to end it in good company."

He regarded Makoto with pride. "Our princess celebrates fourteen years by besting us. She is rewarded not with the pride of victory but the weight of responsibility. Makoto will wear the Orichalcum Crown after dinner. Though she shall return it by the morrow's end, her word shall be as binding as our own."

Amelia gasped. She snatched up her goblet, sloshing cider onto Klaus's arm. "Three cheers for Her Grace. May her reign be glorious!"

The others followed Amelia's lead.

Makoto basked in her family's cheers. None rang hollow this time. "Thank you. I—or perhaps *we*—shall do our best."

She drank from her goblet, cursed the wine's sweetness, and cut into the first course. Each bite of pepper and lardon tasted better than the last.

Uncle Edgar slurped down his soup in one gulp. "Margaret, do you know when the countess will be available?"

Margaret shook her head. "The villa staff told me she's out this evening on business. She'll return when she's finished."

"Tis diligent as always. Like a rat scurrying within a labyrinth," Uncle Edgar said.

"Buh," the emperor grunted. "Better a diligent rat than a slothful walrus."

"Slothful?" Uncle Edgar chortled. He licked remnants of curry off his fingers. "Tis the least of my vices, brother."

The emperor grimaced. "Vices run in our blood. Our daughter and niece spend their evening in a debaucherous den."

"I doubt she's there for pleasure, Rudolph," Uncle Edgar said.

"Athena often was. We wonder how she learned of Suilla. Few knew of our bastard and fewer still were foolish enough to talk. We suspect the snake still has her ways about Zenith Palace."

Palpable discomfort enveloped the room. Uncle Edgar's jovial spirit dissipated. Amelia winced but relaxed when Klaus touched her shoulder.

Margaret remained ignorant of the intensity. "The food is good."

"Yes!" Makoto sprang at the opportunity to lift the mood. "What's your favorite?"

Margaret answered by dunking a frosting coated pepper into her curry. Curry and licorice dripped into the last dollop of Margaret's soup. Makoto's stomach churned, but Margaret ate her culinary abomination with gusto.

Richter glanced between Margaret's expression and his own plate before trying her concoction.

"How is it?" Makoto asked.

"Not... awful." He swallowed a second mouthful. "You should try it."

Makoto failed to mask her disgust. "My palate tis not refined enough to enjoy Margaret's creativity. Perhaps Uncle Edgar would be so willing?"

"Unfortunately, I'm too full to eat another bite." His hands drummed against his belly. "Since I will not be able to meet with the countess tonight, I shall retire for the evening. Makoto, I once more wish you congratulations and happy anniversary."

"Thank you, Uncle. I shall meet with you tomorrow."

"It will be my pleasure to meet with the sitting emperor." He bowed to his brother and waddled toward the door. "Oh, Richter, may I impose upon you before bed?"

Richter finished the scraps off his plate before answering. "Name your request, Father."

"I ask you watch over Margaret for the evening. I hate to imagine her lonely and idle."

"Is this agreeable, cousin?" Richter asked.

"Yes. May we walk in the garden? Reina takes me there when I've been good."

"Of course, whatever you prefer. Please excuse us, Your Grace."

The emperor waved his hand. "Enjoy your night."

"Thank you, Your Grace. Happy anniversary, Princess. Best wishes on the morrow." Richter waited for Margaret to finish her last pepper before escorting her out the dining room.

Makoto noticed how tightly Margaret clung to him. *She fancies him. Does he return the feeling?* The thought soured her mood. *Even Margaret has a suitor before me.*

"Speaking of the garden." Amelia pointed at Makoto with her soup ladle. "I caught your dance with Ephraim, Makoto. I must say you two make a lovely couple."

Makoto rubbed her brow. "Many have misinterpreted our friendship, sister. Yet I never expected *you* to be amongst them."

A mischievous giggle bubbled from Amelia. "Oh, I'm not misinterpreting *anything*."

Makoto regarded her sister with a restrained glare. *Is enduring Olivia's teasing not enough? Must I suffer the sapling's taunts as well?*

Amelia frowned. "I apologize for offending you. I jest only because I love you. Something I learned from Sophia." She placed her hands upon her bosom. "In sooth, I hope for your happiness from the depths of my heart."

"Thank you, sister. Though I'm amazed your heart still has room for me, amongst the other occupants."

"There's plenty of space, I'll have you know," Amelia said, feigning indignation. She giggled once more and set her ladle into her empty bowl. "Father, may I be excused? It's almost time for Suilla's lessons."

"Aye."

Amelia hurriedly jumped from her chair. She hugged her father and kissed his cheeks. Then she hugged her sister tightly. "Tis no jest when I say you two make a handsome couple," she whispered.

In sooth, the idea had crossed Makoto's mind. She admired many things about Ephraim, several of which she hoped to find in a partner.

I'm thankful for his policy of candor over appeasement. His loyalty is second to none. Our companionship goes beyond the requirements of his position—Bastien and Olivia are testament to that. And he is quite easy on the eyes...

The more she appreciated Ephraim's warmth, the more she feared losing it. *A heart is a fragile thing. I'd not recover if he broke mine.* "I don't doubt your words but am content to not let romance spoil our friendship."

"Your mistake." Amelia clutched the hems of her dress, curtseyed, and left the dining room with Klaus in tow.

Dinner ended just as breakfast had with only Makoto and the emperor at the table. Her eyes lingered on the seat at his left hand. It felt more empty than usual. "Why do you allow Amelia to visit Suilla?"

"Amelia is no prisoner and may wander the palace as she pleases. Bastard she may be, but Suilla still carries our blood. We can afford her the luxury of Amelia's occasional company."

Ephraim cleared his throat. "Forgive me, Your Grace, but I believe the princess is asking why *Amelia's* actions are excused."

"Tis as we said, boy. We can afford to give Suilla occasional company. A mere visit can be excused by happenstance. Sporadic meetings are light mischief."

A shadow crossed over his face. "Murder is not happenstance or mischief. Athena was brazen and violent. Wresting Suilla from her prison and staining it with blood is a disrespect Isabella would *not* condone without consequence."

He stared upon the empty seat at his left hand. "A father's love kowtowed to an emperor's fear. Twas not the first time our children paid for our mistake." He beckoned Makoto. "Sit with us. You have the same right to this seat as Olivia."

"I do?"

"Yes, unless you would deny an old man's wish for his daughter's company?"

"No, I..." It would take time before she was used to being known as his daughter. "Are you sure you'd feel comfortable with *me* in your firstborn's seat."

"We do not mind, Makoto. You are as much our child as she." His hand masked his eyes, but tears flowed through the gaps between his shaking fingers. "Damn these eyes of ours! They betray our weakness."

Father... Makoto took Athena's seat. She gently touched her father's shoulder, finding it weaker than expected. Age marred his face with wrinkles. Silver hairs outnumbered the golden in his beard.

These fourteen years have taken their toll upon him. He spoke of his mortality during the hunt. Please, let it be no more than an old man's musings.

"You're dismissed, Ephraim," she said.

"Of course. I'll keep vigil by the door."

"Thank you."

She waited until he left to embrace her father. Now that they were alone, he could be as weak as he needed.

Emperor Rudolph wept upon his daughter's shoulder. "We miss her, Makoto. We would give our empire to see her one more time."

"When was the last you heard from her?"

"We cannot recall. She slipped from our eyes years ago. Her pride will not allow her to be spied upon."

"I wonder from where she gets her pride," Makoto said.

He regained his composure. "Aye, she inherited our stubbornness." His downcast eyes stared at his still shaking hands. "Will you listen to an old man's tale, Makoto?"

"Of course." *Hopefully one of his war stories will renew his vigor.*

He used to regale her with tales of the daemons he slew in Nova City. Cursed bloods, he called them. Monsters almost equal part man and beast that feasted upon human flesh, and the telltale whistle of their unseen master. Her father described it as the song of a predator relishing its prey's terror.

I could barely sleep after such stories, but I can stomach them now. "It will be my pleasure."

"We suggest you get comfortable lest we ramble." He sank into the chair.

"Emperor Roland Charlamagne von Kauneus was our father. We won't bore you with his troubled history with women. The important one was Beatrice, his concubine. She was a sickly, unassuming, woman, but he loved her dearly. They never married, but she bore him two children. Can you name them?"

"You and Aunt Josephine."

"Correct. Mother barely survived our birth. Josephine's killed her." His fingers curled, venom consuming his eyes. "We were orphans of royal blood. Perfect prey for the jackals prowling our father's court."

"Orphans? What about your father?"

"Buh," he scoffed. "He treated us with indifference for weakening Beatrice. Josephine suffered outward contempt for dealing the death knell. Father," he spat the word like a curse. "encouraged our half-brothers to torment her.

"Edgar taunted her on occasion to save face but showed her kindness in the dark. Laurence, however, reveled in our sister's misery. He preyed upon her like a vulture—too cowardly to scorn her in our presence yet emboldened when alone."

His bones cracked from flexing his fingers. "Laurence did something *unforgivable* to our sister. We nearly killed him for it—we *should* have. Father tied us to a hitching post on the hottest day of the year with no food and a bowl of water out of reach as punishment."

Beads of sweat dripped down his furrowed brow. "We still feel the heat. The desperation for water so tantalizingly close." He licked his lips and paused for a long drink.

"We remember the third day vividly. Our mind, wild with delirium, conjured the visage of the All-Mother. She shielded us from the sun and asked our crime.

"We told her the truth; our sister demanded vengeance. When she untied us, we descended upon the water as a hungry dog to fresh meat. We lapped at it like an animal. Even when it spilled into the dirt."

Makoto gagged at the thought of licking wet dirt. "Quite an impression to make on your future wife."

He chuckled dryly. "She took a liking to us and protected Josephine from further torment."

"And you were anointed emperor after killing Uncle Laurence."

There was a twinkle in his eye. "Aye. Laurence tried buying the crown after Father's death. He bribed the other imperial candidates to relinquish their claim. He demanded we do the same and for Josephine to be his empress."

Disgust simmered in Makoto's heart. "He wanted to marry his own sister?"

Her father's face mirrored the sentiment. "Laurence excused his lust through a desire to unite our father's household." He stood and beckoned Makoto follow him to the opposite end of the table. He motioned to the large dent dappled with sanguine spots.

"This is where we smashed his head upon the table. We insisted it not be replaced or fixed as a warning to any who dare trifle with us. With no other candidates vying for the crown, the All-Mother anointed us emperor."

He traced his hand over the red splatter. "Our fingers dripped with the blood our brother was so proud of. Sanguine Hands Rudolph, they called us. A fitting name."

More macabre details. Makoto followed him to their seats. "Your succession is no secret. Why tell me this?"

"To illustrate a point. We made three solemn vows to Isabella, Makoto. First, to never bend the knee. Second, to succeed our father as emperor. Third, to take her as empress. We kept all three, but the first remained paramount. We surrendered to none. Not Father, Laurence or the daemons lurking within Nova City's mists."

He sighed deeply, as if exorcising an invisible specter. "Avalon is only one battle we take no pride in winning."

Makoto tensed. She knew the basics of the Avalon incident. The High Priestess attempted to assassinate the emperor but was killed. The island remained under Kauneus control with Josephine named its regent.

Father avoided the specifics of that night. Fourteen years later, Makoto still didn't know her mother's name.

It's the High Priestess's fault. She may not have stolen my memory, but she's why I lost my mother. Had she not already been killed I...

"Josephine informed us of the assassination plot mere days before we visited Avalon." His fingers tightly gripped his goblet. "To be killed in our sleep like a wounded dog. The *gall!*"

The glass shattered in his hand. Blood and wine stained his robes crimson.

"Father!" Makoto tied several napkins together as a makeshift bandage. She wrapped his hand, and the bandage quickly turned red. *Sanguine Hands...*

The ghosts of Avalon haunted his countenance. "Avalon's betrayal wounded us deeper than any blade. The High Priestess died by our hand just as the dawn broke. We're haunted by the vermillion rays on her bloodied face. Fourteen years..."

He met Makoto's eyes and relaxed. "Fourteen years with our beloved daughter. Did you bring the box?"

"Yes." She offered the lacquer box. "You teased me this morning. Not only with its delay but its riddle. A gift befitting fourteen years?"

"Judge for yourself if it is worthy of such a title."

He opened the box, revealing a pendant. Makoto gasped—she recognized the platinum gem. It had a power over her then. Even now its allure was undeniable.

She reached for it but hesitated. Her father's harsh words from the ship returned to her. "I thought I was not to pilfer your property."

"Twas never our property, Makoto. Tis your mother's necklace—an heirloom of her family. Our grief was raw that morning, and we could not relinquish it. If we may." He retrieved the pendant from the box and slipped it around her neck.

Makoto's hands encased the gem. Its touch was warm and comfortable, like her star-blanket.

"You look like Tamamo Akemi—your mother. She'd be proud of the woman you've become."

Her mother's name. It sounded so familiar despite being the first time hearing it. Yet another memory obscured by darkness and just out of her reach. She hadn't missed the feeling, but it was tantalizing nonetheless. *If only I remembered her face...*

She closed her eyes, and the darkness cleared.

A woman stood before her. Makoto recognized her own scarlet hair. This woman shared her freckles but didn't hide them. They shared the same eye color, but the woman's were far kinder.

She reached out and caressed Makoto's cheek. "Olen ikävöinyt sinua, rakkaani."

Makoto trembled, but it wasn't fear or anger that consumed her. "What does that mean?" Her voice was much softer than normal—like a child's.

"It means, 'I have missed you, my love.' You and your sister."

Makoto clutched the gem even tighter. She needed to focus on something lest she break into tears. "Asuka?"

The woman nodded. "She waits for your return, rakkaani."

"I can't go to her. Kauneus is my home."

Her mother's eyes retained their kindness, but there was no denying the sadness in them too. "I understand. You will go to her when you are ready, rakkaani." The woman kissed the top of Makoto's head, and the darkness consumed her.

Makoto opened her eyes; she tightly gripped a nearby chair to stay upright.

"Makoto?" The emperor stood and steadied her. "Are you alright?"

"Tell me about my mother." She closed her eyes in a vain attempt to fight her tears. "Please."

It was her father's turn to hold her as she cried.

"Tamamo possessed a soul like fire. She burned brightly for those she loved but scorched her enemies. She saved our life once. We told you before she was our dear friend." He kissed the top of Makoto's head. "Raising you are our own is the least we could do for her. We are prouder of being your father than any act as emperor."

Makoto smiled despite her tears. "Thank you for raising me all these years."

"Buh, thank us not for our duty. We should thank you."

"What have I done to be worthy of the emperor's gratitude?"

"You have been our friend through our losses. Charlotte and Tamamo on Avalon. Josephine and Edgar treat us as business partners, not a brother. Our firstborn a pariah. Our only son lost to his birth. We betrayed our wife in our loneliness and raised Suilla as a prisoner not a daughter. We have lost many to our mistakes and are grateful for your companionship."

They stood in silence a moment, before he stepped away. "Enough of the past, Makoto. Tonight should be spent reveling in the present and anticipating the future."

He lifted the Orichalcum Crown and placed it upon her head. "This will be yours for the next twenty-four hours."

The weight of orichalcum burdened her. She attempted to adopt her father's posture, but the strain on her neck forced her to slouch.

He grumbled a laugh. "You grow accustomed to the weight."

Makoto grimaced and adjusted the crown's position. "Why use orichalcum at all? Surely a crown of sapphire would have sufficed?"

"The Centennial Emperor deemed it so. Isabella recited her words when she anointed us." He closed his eyes and recited:

"'The crown is neither prize nor burden. 'Tis a symbol of the trust our people have put in me, and that I in turn put in my successors. We are no better than our subjects. Thus, we have no need for ornate or lavish regalia. The design must be modest lest we forget ourselves. The material heavy, for the duty of leadership weighs upon us. Humility and responsibility will lead us to prosperity. Pride and cowardice shall be our undoing.'"

Beauty and strength for a princess. Humility and responsibility for an emperor. Makoto fiddled with the crown until it almost felt comfortable. "Do you think I'm ready for this?"

"For one day?" He chuckled. "I trust you to not burn down the mountain, deplete the treasury or start a war in that time."

"No, I mean..." Her father's age and musing on his mortality weighed almost as heavily as the orichalcum. "If I were to become an imperial candidate. Do you think I could serve as emperor?"

"Do you doubt yourself or your origins?"

She lowered her gaze. "Both."

"Then I shall address both. You are my daughter, Makoto, the same as any other. Any fool who cannot see past your place of birth is not worthy of your consideration. *All* my daughters have qualities befitting a great emperor.

"You have the pride needed to not take slights against your empire. Olivia's keen eyes are difficult to deceive, and Amelia's compassionate soul will care for her people. But unchecked virtues become weaknesses. Compassionate souls can be manipulated. Keen eyes may lead to jaded vision. And pride can fuel a stubborn heart to reckless action."

'Tis true I take pride in being a Kauneus princess. Pride insists I must be strong and beautiful. That I repay my debts. I must repay Father for raising me by being a loyal princess.

But if her father spoke in sooth, there was no debt to repay. At least, not to him. *Do I owe a debt to the girl in the canopy—Asuka? No, not a debt but perhaps a responsibility. Ephraim advised that I speak to Father about her. That I seek permission to return home...*

Pride binds me to Kauneus. Responsibility will give me the courage to reach Avalon. But which is stronger?

"Introducing Princess Olivia Elizibith vi Kauneus and Countess Reina Erika vi Kauneus."

Impeccable timing as always, Olivia. Makoto made no effort to hide her displeasure upon her sister and cousin's entrance.

Reina didn't waste a glance at Makoto. "Your Grace, I—"

Rudolph waved his hand. "Do you see a crown upon *my* head, Countess?"

Reina's eyes darted onto Makoto before returning to the head of the table. "How long will this be in effect?"

"One full day as per the wager. I will advise and honor the decisions she makes."

Pride swelled within Makoto at her father's words. "So, Countess, you desire to speak with *us*?"

The intensity in Reina's eyes nearly made Makoto flinch. "I met with your eldest sister this evening, Your Grace."

Makoto waved an indifferent hand at Olivia. "With all due respect, Countess, we meet with Olivia nearly every day."

Indignation mixed with Reina's intensity. "With all due respect, Your Grace, Olivia is not your *eldest* sister."

Makoto's eyes moved between her sister and cousin. She discerned for hint of an elaborate jest but knew neither of them were foolish enough to risk such a prank. Her eyes settled upon her father. He nearly portrayed an uncaring façade but for the slight quiver of his lip.

"Tell me—" Makoto cleared her throat. "Tell *us* everything."

Olivia stepped forward. "Athena traveled with Lord Bahamut for a few days. They stopped in Madame Morgana's Court on his behest. I spoke to Athena, and we agreed she needs to see you, Father. Due to your absence, I sought Countess Reina. She suggested we let you rest and eat after your hunt before informing you."

He hid his shaking hands below the table. "Where is my daughter now?"

Makoto heard the strain in her father's voice and noticed Olivia's eyes soften.

"She is in my villa," Reina answered. "She is awaiting an audience with—" She faced Makoto. "With *you*, Your Grace."

"We shan't keep her waiting. Bring our sister to the White Hall."

Reina bowed. "Shall I tell her with whom she will be speaking?"

Makoto briefly considered this. "No. Keep it a surprise."

"As you wish, Your Grace." Reina left the dining room with Olivia in tow.

Makoto lifted her goblet. Her reflection stared back with barely restrained excitement. *She's home. Athena is home! I have the power to grant amnesty. I can...* Her reflection's countenance darkened till it was bitter as licorice.

Tis a deceptively simple choice. Of course I want my sister back, but I must remember the tenets: humility and responsibility. The humility to set aside personal desires and responsibility to the crown.

"Athena's crimes are high. Attempting to kidnap a princess *and* murder. Granting amnesty for such acts sets a dangerous precedent." *Not to mention how the empress might react.* "What would you do, Father?"

"We—*I* recommend listening to her. You must consider if her reason for return is altruistic enough to warrant lifting her sentence or too selfish for mercy. Trust your judgment and know I will honor any decision you make."

"Then we shall see you after we meet our sister." Makoto dipped her head and headed toward the throne room. The Orichalcum Crown felt heavier with each passing step.

Athena

An unkindness of thirteen ravens perched atop the villa's black gates. Two of them fought over a piece of meat, while the others stared at Athena. She held out her arm as an invitation, but each bird either ignored her or cawed in disgust.

"Friendly buzzards, aren't they?" she laughed.

Linnette said nothing. Athena tried getting her to talk the entire time. Linnette occasionally smiled but not a word escaped her lips. She attempted to nudge Athena forward, but her hand bounced off the aura.

"Hey, I'll only let you get handsy if you say please." Athena noticed the slight flush in Linette's cheeks. *Not a word, but I'll take it.*

She was led onto a dirt path set betwixt a modest garden. White flowers with petals like dewdrops lay on each side of the path. *So the countess has an affection for moondrops? Surely she won't miss just one.*

Athena reached for the nearest flower.

"The mistress requests her guests refrain from touching the flowers."

Athena turned to see a chalk-white woman wearing a black suit and gloves standing before her. Jagged black lines covered her face, akin to the surface of eroded rock. The left glove held a water pale, while the right brandished a knife. What at first appeared to be a belt was actually a tail wrapped around her waist.

Don't see too many Elämää with blood this pure outside Nova City. How much did Reina pay to hire her?

Athena stepped away from the flower. "Sorry, but they're just so pretty. Is this your handywork?"

"Tending the garden is one of my duties. Thank you for appreciating the moondrops." The woman whistled for a raven to perch on her shoulder, and it dropped a rolled-up scroll.

Athena admired the knife's unnatural glint. "Do gardeners normally carry orichalcum daggers?"

"The mistress prefers not to take chances with her security."

"Gardening *and* security?" Athena whistled. "She must keep you busy."

"Of course. My duty is to serve." The gardener returned the note to the raven's beak and politely shooed it away. "You are dismissed, Linnette. The guest is in my care."

Linnette nodded and headed toward a smaller dwelling nearby.

She recognizes Reina's gardener as her superior. Linnette must belong to Reina directly rather than Father. Just how many more does she have? Another reason to stay on her good side.

"Reina has you lot well trained. I bet my father is jealous."

"I wouldn't know. I spend little time within Zenith Palace." The gardener slipped the knife into her boot. "Pardon me for neglecting my manners, Princess. My name is Anna," she said with a bow.

"The mistress informed me of your situation. I will grant you a tour of Linna Varjoissa whilst you await an audience with the emperor."

"Why thank you, Miss Anna." Athena strutted down the path. A home blacker than the ocean's abyss loomed ahead. "The Castle in the Shadows, right?"

"You're familiar with Linna Varjoissa?"

"I do enjoy a bit of history. I'm pretty sure big sis Lucy built this place."

"Correct. I'll show you the dedication."

Anna pointed to a stone standing amongst the sea of moondrops. Several words were engraved into the stone's face. Despite their age, none of the letters had been lost to time.

"*My dearest Elena. Your light shines through my darkest shadows. May your radiance shine for all generations.*"

"The Centennial Emperor retired here with Lady Elena after her one hundred and eighth year as emperor. They lived together thirty years until Lady Elena passed away, and Empress Lucy abandoned the mountain," Anna said.

"Tragedy still haunts Linna Varjoissa's halls. Most recently, your grandfather's barren empress took her own life after her assassins failed to murder Prince Laurence. Assassinations, diseases, and unfortunate accidents are all too common here."

"I assume preventing such tragedies to your mistress is another duty?" Athena asked.

Anna hesitated outside the front door. She scrutinized Athena, seemingly determining if her words implied a threat. "Correct," came her terse reply, and she ushered Athena inside.

The foyer stretched from the front door to a pair of marble staircases spiraling toward the upper floor. Trinkets and treasures littered the foyer—vases, paintings, and jewelry lined the walls or stood upon stands.

Athena swiped her finger against a nearby pearl necklace. "Spotless."

"Of course. Mistress Reina expects nothing less than perfection." Anna stopped beside a painting of a decrepit green ship sinking into the dark water. "She purchased this from Princess Olivia three years ago. One of her finer pieces, in my opinion."

"No kidding?" Athena leaned forward to admire the painting. She recognized the small black circle in the upper right corner as her sister's mark. *Olive's improved; her brushstrokes are less messy.* "How much did this sell for?"

"Mistress Reina prefers to keep her contracts confidential. The eastern stairs lead to the common areas: the kitchen, library, and observatory. The western stairs to private chambers and the mistress's study. I trust you understand—"

"Yeah, yeah, I get it. Western side is off limits, right?"

Anna cracked an ephemeral smile. "You may wait in the observatory. Can I interest you in a vintage wine?"

"Only if you share a glass with me." Athena grinned. "Never been a fan of drinking alone."

"If those are my orders." Anna dipped her head. "I shall bring it upstairs. Excuse me." She headed down the hall and disappeared behind a door.

Athena's eyes wandered between the east and west stairs. *If only I wasn't trying to make a good impression today.* Swallowing her curiosity, she climbed the eastern stairs.

Reina's observatory was divided into an upper and lower half. The walls, ceiling and floor each had a mural depicting a great constellation. The Ashen Phoenix soared overhead with Olive's mark in its eye. *I wonder how much Reina paid for this.*

Athena climbed a small ladder to access the upper half. Shelves lined with books and maps formed a half-circle around a door with a crescent moon painted on it. She pushed it open and stepped onto the balcony. A desk, pair of stools, and a telescope awaited her. Detailed star charts with notes and coordinates scribbled in the margins lay beneath the telescope.

"Your wine, Princess."

Anna offered a tray with two wine glasses brimming with deep purple liquid. A small plate with a pair of ribs lay in the middle.

"That's the second time you've snuck up on me," Athena said, picking up a glass. "You trying to spook me?"

"I make no effort to hide my presence, Princess. Perhaps you should be more perceptive."

Athena sniffed the wine before drinking. It smelled like a rich slice of cake with a hint of peppers in the frosting. She lapped at it and smacked her lips.

"Sweet—*very* sweet. There's a layer of heat that doesn't overpower it. Fantastic flavor." She gulped it down with a hearty swig.

Anna regarded her with a bemused expression. "Isn't it customary to toast before sharing a drink?"

"Yeah, yeah, we'll toast before the second round." Athena grabbed the bottle and read the label. "Nova Flame Sugarplum. This an Elämää blend?"

"Correct. A friend of the mistress gifted her the bottle. He has an eye for expensive sweets."

"Sounds like my kind of guy." Athena lifted her refilled glass. "To your friend and his expensive tastes."

She touched her glass against Anna's and drained it. Her eyes drifted between her glass and the bottle. "This might be the last drink of my life..." She set it upon the tray. "Thanks for making it a good one." She paused and added, "And thanks for keeping me company."

Anna took a long sip, leaving her glass half full. "Does being alone frighten you, Princess?"

"Nah, frighten is too strong a word. I just find it unpleasant."

"Is that why you returned?"

"Not exactly but kinda." Athena bit into one of the ribs. "Oh, that is *tough*. Does my cousin really like them undercooked?"

Anna pulled a cleanly picked bone from her mouth. "Correct. She prefers her meat on the rare side."

"To each their own. You can have the other one if you want." She stopped talking when another raven perched onto Anna's shoulder. "What's the word from Mistress Reina?"

Anna stroked the bird's back and let it drink a dollop of wine. "Your presence is requested at the White Hall. Mistress Reina and Princess Olivia will meet you there."

"Really? I expected them to escort me there. I'm assuming that's another one of your jobs."

Anna shook her head. "I am to keep watch over your stay in Linna Varjoissa. I have no such orders to extend that watch to Zenith Palace."

"Reina didn't mention an escort taking me to the White Hall?"

"No."

"Father trusts me more than I expected. That's encouraging."

Athena hopped off the stool and stretched her back. "You gonna—" She heard a loud *pop* from her back and stopped to whistle. "That felt *good*! Anyway, you gonna wish me luck?"

Anna tipped her wine glass toward Athena. "Good luck, Princess. For what it's worth, I hope you're granted amnesty. The ball will be far more interesting with you attending."

Athena needed no assistance navigating Zenith Palace. No one explored this place like she used to—not even Olive in her hyper years. The architecture stayed the same; it was the faces that changed. None of the passing faces dared speak a word to her.

It must be like seeing a ghost. She rubbed her neck. *That might not be too far off, actually.*

Athena reached the White Hall within a half hour. Her sister and cousin waited outside.

Reina's eyes fixated on a pocket watch. "Right on schedule." She met Athena's gaze. "I trust your stay was pleasant."

"It was. Linnette and Anna made for fine company—we shared a great wine."

"Ah, I trust it was one of Noah's. He'll be pleased to know it satisfied a princess's palate."

"Noah? Doesn't ring any bells. Anna said he's a friend of yours."

"My father, actually. He's a Nova City Peacekeeper."

One of Auntie Jo's paramours is an NC officer? I wonder how that union came about. "You're on a first name basis with your father?"

"Correct. Our relationship has always leaned more formal than paternal. But with all due respect, we're not here to discuss *my* father."

Athena nodded her head several times. "True, true. How is Father's mood on this fine night? You girls think I have a chance of keeping my head?"

Reina shared a glance with Olive. "His Grace's mood is unexpected."

Athena's eyes darted between them. "What are you two not telling me?"

"My apologies, but the emperor ordered us to hold our tongues on the matter. Rest assured, Princess, this surprise is to your benefit."

Athena attempted to read their expressions for a further hint, but her sister and cousin gave nothing away. "Does it have anything to do with Bastien's absence?"

"None," Olive answered. "I dismissed him for the evening. I suspect he's flirting with the first maid to ogle his muscles." Her eyes hardened as she added, "Just as I suspect you're stalling."

"Nothing gets past you, sis." Athena's hand twitched as it reached for the door. *Last chance to back out, Athena. Last chance to keep your head.*

She slapped her cheeks to exorcise her cowardice. "Count of three." She exhaled deeply. "Three."

"Introducing Her Former Highness, Athena Sophia vi Kauneus," Reina declared.

Former Highness? That's brutal.

Athena kicked the door open and swaggered into the White Hall.

Nostalgic scents of metal and her father's peppermint cologne welcomed her home. Yet the surrounding walls were suffocating. The white paint glowed brighter than freshly fallen snow.

Athena winced; her eyes searched for color. She found no solace on any wall or the columns lining the edges of the hall.

Running out of options, she finally focused on the center of the room. An empty throne stood before her, elevated by a short set of steps. Its silvery-black hue gave Athena color, but the orichalcum's sheen still bothered her eyes.

"Too bright, sister?" Olive asked.

"Yeah, but I'll adjust." Athena blinked several times. She knelt at the foot of the steps, flanked by her sister and cousin. Her eyes wandered toward the eastern wall. *Father should be—*

A door opened from the center of the wall. A woman clothed in white and scarlet robes glided across the floor. Her movements, both delicate and deliberate, seemed intent on keeping the crown balanced upon her head.

Makoto? Has Father already—no, someone would've told me. It's a trick or temporary measure. Either way, this is what Reina meant by a surprising benefit.

Athena watched Makoto take the throne with a greater sense of admiration than shock. *My little ruby is all grown up. She looks the part of a proper emperor.*

"Before we begin, tis imperative you understand this is no jest." Makoto tapped the diadem upon her head. "We are to rule Kauneus with all authority of the emperor until the morrow's twilight. We are not your sister this evening but your judge. Just as you stand before us a criminal in breach of exile. We will hear your case and pass judgment." She motioned for Athena to stand and speak.

She even moves her hand like him. I need to take her as seriously as I would Father. I'll offend her otherwise, and Makoto was always testy.

Athena rose, studying her sister's eyes. Makoto did her best to appear impartial but couldn't fully mask her excitement and confusion.

"Your Grace, I—" The door creaked open behind her. "I believe this conversation is no longer private."

Makoto bolted upright. The sudden motion knocked the crown askew, but she caught it just in time. "Who *dares* eavesdrop on us tonight?" Her words echoed throughout the hall.

A younger girl crept inside. "A thousand apologies, Mako—Your Grace. I sensed the turmoil here and came to investigate. When I heard Sophia's voice, I..."

Her voice caught in her throat. She closed her eyes and exhaled. "I really wanted to see my sister again."

Athena recognized Lucielle immediately. The golden locks from their paternal grandmother. Their mother's telltale golden eyes.

That's why Harley is so familiar. He's Lucielle's paler reflection. About the same age too. Mother's affair must have been just after Father returned from Avalon... Ugh, that woman is the last thing I want to think about now. Don't let her ruin this, Athena.

Athena tilted her head toward her little sister. "May I, Your Grace?"

Makoto waved her bandaged hand.

Athena crossed the White Hall. Lucielle bounced with excitement but didn't move toward her. Athena knelt until she was just shorter than Lucille. "You've gotten so big. You're taller than me when I kneel down."

Lucielle giggled. "In a few years I'll be taller than you when you stand."

"I bet you will. You'll catch up to me in no time." She gently patted her sister's head. "Rumor around this place is you're a real troublemaker. That true?"

Lucielle scoffed. "Not at all. I'm a good girl."

"Really now? Prove it. What's the most good thing you did today?"

"I visited Suilla. I give her lessons on being a princess. She's a... slow learner but doing her best."

Thank goodness she's allowed to have company. Even if it's just once a week. No doubt Lucielle is leaving a better impression than I did.

"Princess lessons? What kind of things are you teaching her?"

"Only the most important. How to curtsey. All the best blends of tea to drink. The proper way to use her utensils."

"*And—*" Athena cleared her throat to mask the crack in her voice. "And she's doing okay?"

"Better—a lot better. She's less picky with her meals. She used to only eat bread and drink water. Father gave her the freedom to roam the southern wing. Her world is still confined, but it has expanded."

"That's good to hear. And how's Klaus? Taking good care of him?"

"Yes," she nodded before giggling. "My apologies, I thought you were going to ask if he takes good care of me. I don't do much for Klaus, unfortunately. His service is excellent. I couldn't ask for a better companion."

Athena scoffed. "How's he taking care of you if he lets you wander the palace alone at night?" She punched her fists together. "Do I need to knock some sense into him? He knows I'm not afraid to punch him."

"No, Sophia, Klaus wouldn't dream of letting wander alone. He's waiting outside the door. Do you wish to see him?"

Yes. He's owed an apology for starters. Though I don't think I could ever apologize enough for everything I put him through. Let alone what I said to him that last night.

"Nah, I have another meeting to take care of. Klaus can wait a little longer for me."

Athena returned her focus to Makoto. "Do you protest to Lucielle's continued presence, Your Grace?"

Makoto shook her head. "We do not. Amelia, feel free to stay as long as you please."

"Thank you." She curtseyed and grabbed Athena's hand.

They joined Olive and Reina before the throne. Lucielle knelt but kept hold of Athena's hand.

"The reason for my return is simple, Your Grace," Athena said. "Uncle Bahamut invited me to return as his date for the ball. He said, and I am quoting here. 'I *refuse* a companion who isn't at least half as pretty as I.'"

Makoto's eyes widened. "I—*we!*" She slumped against the throne. Her eyes lost their impartial edge and glimmered with exasperation. "Please, tell us you jest."

Athena chuckled. "I reacted the same way, Your Grace. Such an excuse, though true—I am *very* pretty—wouldn't be enough to justify my return. Then Uncle shared a warning. He's convinced Father's enemies will move against him. If the eyes of the world are watching, there's no better stage."

She scratched the back of her head. "I hate to admit I'm a bit concerned for the old man. But I'm more worried for the rest of my family, because I doubt his enemies will stop with him. I know coming back here is a risk, but I'd rather lose my head than any of you lose yours."

Makoto was silent for a few minutes. "We find our sister's concerns admirable, albeit misplaced. Security is heightened during the ball to protect the dignitaries. The princesses have Thronsdens for extra security—not to mention Empress Isabella's presence as a deterrent. Tis hard to take any threat seriously with her in the wings."

"Unless she *is* the threat."

Makoto's countenance darkened. She reached for the pendant around her neck. Its touch eased her tension, though she remained dour. "You dare utter such nonchalant blasphemy with naught but the rumors and whims of a fangless dragon."

Athena raised her arms. "Not saying I suspect her, but Mother's whims are more frightening than Uncle's. We both know our security means nothing to her. If she's the enemy, we may as well start preparing our funerals. Assuming we stand a chance against our unknown threat, it still pays to be wary."

Makoto snapped her fingers in Reina's direction. "Countess, we request your counsel. How do you respond to rumors?"

Reina stood with her hands folded behind her back. "Rumors abound behind every corner, Your Grace, but potential assassination should always be taken seriously. Once I've determined the threat credible, I scour for more details to develop a counter strategy."

"Do you find this warning credible?

Reina's brow furrowed. "In sooth, Your Grace, I do. Though he oft speaks in quips and riddles, Lord Bahamut *is* an Enkeli. His warning should be taken as gravely serious."

"Do you advise we cancel the ball, then?" Makoto asked.

"No, Your Grace. Doing so will be a logistical nightmare," Reina said. "We risk offending our allies by recalling their invitations at such short notice. If we reveal our reason, they will see us as weak. If the great Mount Kauneus shudders at a mere whisper, it won't take much to see it crumble."

Athena grinned. "Which is exactly why we let the ball continue as planned. Let Father's enemies think we don't see them coming. And when they make their move, we spring our trap."

"What kind of trap do you propose?" Makoto asked.

Athena punched her hands together. "These have a pretty good track record."

Makoto's eyes wandered from Athena to the open door in the eastern wall, as her fingers drummed along the throne's armrests.

"As your sister, we want nothing more than your return. We are grateful for the years spent together. Yet we do not confuse gratitude with responsibility. Tis our duty to uphold the sanctity of the Orichalcum Crown."

She sat up straight. Her face strained, as she pushed against the crown's weight. "You were exiled for a reason. Father described your acts as brazen and violent. Even now that doesn't seem to have changed. Your return may have angered the empress, and you accuse her of conspiracy. You're an idiot," she seethed.

She's got me there. "I—"

"*I* wasn't finished." Makoto stood from the throne. "Your haste to be the family's savior expelled you from Mount Kauneus but may yet save your fate. Providing knowledge of an assassination is worthy of commendation. I know not if Empress Isabella can be placated, but I will be *damned* if I lose my sister a second time without advocating for her."

Makoto descended the steps, stopping on the final one. "I propose a stay of exile—subject, of course, to the empress's approval. What say you, Countess?"

"I second the proposal," Reina said. "Athena's intentions appear pure—even her distrust of the All-Mother is rooted in desire to protect her kin. It's unorthodox, but I recall Athena never being one for convention. She may stay at Linna Varjoissa as my guest until properly reinstated as a princess at Empress Isabella's discretion."

"Then we leave our sister in your care, Countess. We trust you to keep her out of trouble." Makoto's fiery gaze fell upon Athena. "We trust this accord is to your liking?"

Athena rubbed her neck. *Honestly just keeping my neck is to my liking. Anything beyond that is me being greedy.* "Yeah, I can manage good behavior for a couple days. So long as I can cut loose when we find our assassin."

Makoto waved her hand. "Countess, you are dismissed. Inform our father of this night's events. He will adhere to our decision."

Reina dipped her head. "Of course, Your Grace." She extended her hand toward Athena. "It'll be my pleasure working with you, Princess."

That's twice she's helped me out today. I'll be in her debt forever.

"Likewise, Countess." She firmly shook Reina's hand. "Get me a good bed, yeah? I could use a good night's sleep."

"Only the best for my cousins." Reina kissed Lucielle's cheek and left the White Hall.

Athena saluted Makoto. "Hey, little ruby. The crown looks good on you."

Makoto's hand bounced off Athena's barrier. "Ow!" She rubbed her bandaged hand and glowered. "I need you to lower that, so I can slap you properly."

"When did you lot get so violent?" Athena spread out her arms and legs. "Give me your best shot, sis."

Makoto tackled Athena to the floor. She cried, holding her big sister tightly. "Don't you dare leave us again. I'll never forgive you if you do."

"*We'll* never forgive you," Lucielle said, joining the pile.

"Yeah, yeah. You little tykes are stuck with me." Athena closed her eyes and embraced them. "You getting in on all this love, Olive?"

"If I must." Olive wrapped her arms around Athena's shoulders. "We'll handle Uncle Bahamut's warning together."

"Together, huh? Sounds like a nice change of pace for me." *I just hope we're enough.*

Makoto

An emperor, not a princess, stared at Makoto from the mirror's surface. Her father insisted upon regalia befitting her temporary status. Tailors worked through the night to complete her ensemble on time.

Makoto's new robes matched both her eyes and pendant. A pair of scarlet dragons were embroidered onto the sleeves. One wreathed in fire, the other coated in ice. The Platinum Dragon constellation displayed upon her back.

"Tell us, Ephraim, are we the Scarlet or Dragon Emperor?"

"Dragon," he said without hesitation. "It fits your family's motto. The strength of a winter storm alongside the beauty of roaring flame." He raised his eyes. "The crown suits you, *Your Grace.*"

Makoto frowned. "It would suit me better if it weren't so damned heavy."

"No, Makoto, your response should befit an emperor," Ephraim said. "How would your father respond?"

He'd grunt and either accept Ephraim's words or chastise his tone.

She cleared her throat and adopted her father's posture, despite the great discomfort to her neck. "Buh," she grunted. She noticed Ephraim trying not to laugh.

"We—" She coughed to hide her own chuckle. "We care not for your tone, Ser Thronsden, but your words flatter us."

Ephraim cleared his throat. "It is our pleasure, Your Grace."

"Buh. Cease your groveling, boy—" She didn't try hiding her laugh a second time. "I'll need more than a day to grow accustomed to this. At least I look the part."

She regarded Ephraim. "You're quite dashing this morning too."

The tailors hadn't stopped at Makoto. Ephraim donned a white jacket with crimson trimmings around his wrists and collar. Matching jitte-shaped cufflinks chiseled from the scrofa's tusks adorned each wrist. Its hide sewn into the belt adorning Ephraim's new pants.

"You think so?" He fiddled with the cufflinks. "This part is a bit tight, but I like the design. I must say I'm fond of your new pendant. May I?" he asked.

"Of course."

Ephraim plucked the pendant's thread. "It should hold nicely. As for this..." His fingers scraped against the gem. "Not quite a diamond. I'm not sure what it is. I'm guessing this was your father's gift?"

Makoto nodded, careful to keep the crown from slipping off her head. "My mother's. Father called it 'an heirloom of her family.' I'm happy to inherit something other than her hair color."

She clutched the gem; its warmth traveled from her fingers through the rest of her being. "I saw her face, Ephraim."

"Really?" he gasped. "What did she look like?"

"Like my future reflection, only so much kinder. She..." Makoto lingered on her mother's call to return home. To Asuka. "She was beautiful."

"Ah, so she does look like you."

"Stop it," she said with a roll of her eyes. "Save those lines for Athena."

Ephraim flushed. "I don't still fancy her," he muttered.

Makoto lifted her head and waved. "Good morning, Athena."

Ephraim stood at attention. "G—good morning, Princess. I—" He stared at the closed marble door, while Makoto smirked at him. "You will make a cruel emperor indeed."

Makoto playfully nudged him. "I can put in a good word for you. Just imagine, Ephraim. If you do end up marrying Athena, you'll be my brother."

"That's bound to happen when Bastien finally proposes."

Makoto choked on her teasing words. *Is Bastien cold because he's shy? I hadn't considered that. I'd prefer a proper courtship first, but I could be swayed by a strong proposal.*

She fiddled with the gem, as Ephraim's words sank in. "Is he contemplating proposal?"

His brow creased. "Unfortunately, I jest. I've never known Bastien to commit to any relationship besides his brothers and duty to Olivia. But with enough encouragement, he might be persuaded."

She scoffed. "I don't want my proposal influenced the same way as a drunken dare." *A proposal should require conviction not encouragement. Does it ask too much for love to be doubtless?*

A knock at the door roused her from thought. "Buh, who intrudes upon our privacy?"

"Countess Reina Erika vi Kauneus, Your Grace."

Really? I expected Father. Perhaps he's busy. She waved for Ephraim to open the door.

The fair-faced countess entered the room. She traded yesterday's uniform for a cream and lilac dress Makoto had seen in Amelia's closet.

"We mean no offense, Countess, but we hoped to meet with our father this morning."

"None is taken, Your Grace. Uncle and I spoke last night. Today is his first day off in decades, and he intends to spend it as such. He entrusted me to look after you today and keep you on schedule."

"If you're here, then we trust your guest is mischief free this morning."

"Correct. I had Anna procure garments for your sister. She was asleep when I left."

"Good. It would reflect poorly on us both if she caused trouble so quickly." Makoto's stomach growled. "We don't suppose breakfast is on our schedule?"

"It was an hour ago. I presume you missed it to be fitted." Reina tossed Makoto a bread roll and boiled egg. "This should keep you satiated for the morning."

"We thank you, Countess," Makoto said as she caught the bread. The egg slipped from her bandaged grasp, but she caught it on the second attempt. *Father maintains dignity and grace at table. I must show nothing less before another member of court.* "We request you turn your back to us."

Reina's eyes hardened. "I make a habit of not showing my back when alone with another party, Your Grace."

"You are not alone, Countess," Ephraim said.

"A Thronsden's presence intensifies the isolation rather than alleviates it. I may leave the room if Your Grace requires privacy."

Makoto was taken back by Reina's intensity. "You may stay but avert your gaze."

"Of course." Reina stood against the door and fixated on the window. For a moment she stood so still that her skin blended with the marble.

She reached for the silver flask at her waist. An adder was engraved onto the flask with its head acting as the cap. Reina flicked the head backward, revealing the fangs.

Makoto turned her back. She swallowed the egg whole but took her time chewing the roll to savor the buttery texture. "What is our schedule today?"

Reina holstered her flask and stood with her hands folded behind her.

"You will oversee a representative meeting within the hour. I took the liberty of scheduling afternoon tea with your sisters on Amelia's behest. Finally, you will debrief with your father before dinner."

"Thank you, Countess. What should we expect at today's meeting?"

"I expect to begin with general housekeeping regarding the ball," Reina said. "Count Edgar is in charge of the decor and refreshments, while my duties are the logistics of travel, amenities and security. As for unique matters, the Alma is requesting a stipend to aid the hungry and oversee training of new paladins."

She and Uncle Edgar mentioned the Alma yesterday morning. The All-Mother's devout paladins have served the Kauneus family dutifully for generations. I have no reason to doubt their intent.

"Their request sounds reasonable," Makoto said.

Reina's smile was condescending—as if she found Makoto adorable. "Permission to speak freely with you today, Your Grace?"

"Tis given, Countess."

Reina dipped her head. "The cathedral walls are impenetrable as your sister's shield. Only the bishops know where the funds truly go."

"You're suspicious of the church?"

"I am suspicious of all but myself. I trust little besides corroborated facts and paper trails." Reina scoffed. "Alas, even those aren't infallible."

"What do you suspect them of?"

"I can't be sure," Reina said. "Bishops filling their pockets rather than hungry mouths and stomachs. The training of paladins more loyal to the Alma than the crown."

Makoto frowned at the last sentence. "Do you think the Alma may be plotting the assassination?"

Reina chuckled. "In sooth, no. Your father is lax with the Alma, and I suspect they prefer him over a suspicious emperor. Off the record, shall I name the parties I suspect?"

Makoto nodded curtly. "None of my sisters, I trust?"

"Correct, I don't suspect Uncle's family—including his empress. Her family is another story, as Enkeli motivations oft elude me. I recommend keeping an eye on them, but they're not my prime suspects."

She held up two fingers. "I propose two. First, Nova City to the west. They fashion themselves a phoenix that will rise from the ashes of your father's ruination. Perhaps they grow impatient with his longevity.

"Likewise, the Orabelle Queendom in the southern waters. Their propaganda is best compared to a virus. It spreads, evolves, and is harder to kill each passing day. Their bias toward Kauneus is passionate as it is irrational."

"What of Prince Elias?" Makoto asked. "He graces our home every year for the ball and shows none of the viral hate you claim is endemic to his kingdom."

"I acknowledge Prince Elias may be an exception, Your Grace, and hope him to be the much-needed cure. Yet his claims of friendship are without action," Reina said.

"Attending the ball may be no more than lulling us into false security or for espionage. Until I see definitive friendship from Prince Elias or his siter, I consider any alliance or treaty with the Orabelle not worth the paper used to draft it."

"Your words are as venomous as his supposed intent," Ephraim said.

Reina smirked. "A side-effect of political discussions, Ser Thronsden. Pray your charge isn't easily infected." She frowned at the black bird lightly pecking at the windowpane. "Regent Josephine brings a message. May I?"

"You may."

Reina opened the window. The bird swooped inside and landed on her shoulder. It cawed into her ear and dropped a scroll. Reina quickly read and pocketed the scroll. She dismissed the bird and closed the window. "Many thanks, Your Grace."

"Of course. Any news the emperor should know?"

Reina shook her head. "Nothing more than her usual requests."

"Which are?" Makoto asked.

Reina raised two fingers. "First, that I write bi-weekly, which I neglect due to my lack of spare time and for my own sanity. Second, an influx of Alma paladins. The regent is never satisfied with those at her disposal."

"What does the regent need paladins for?"

Reina smiled. "You're asking the right questions, Your Grace. She alternates between three reasons. She needs workers in the mines, soldiers to provide security from local fauna, and hunters to find the conspirators from the previous assassination attempt."

"They haven't all been found?" Ephraim asked. "It's been fourteen years."

"Correct. The regent is convinced the island itself hides them from her."

"Can it do that?" Ephraim asked.

Reina shrugged. "I wouldn't know, Ser Thronsden. What I do know is I live amongst Enkeli and demi-Enkeli with abilities beyond my own understanding. I doubt any of us will ever have a grasp of Avalon's true power."

Makoto glanced at her pendant. *Avalon is an island of secrets. My past. My sister. Its abilities are just another in a collection.* "If the regent can show genuine need for paladins, then she will have them. I'll leave it to the representatives' discretion if her needs are genuine."

Reina nodded. "Wise choice, Your Grace. A final piece of advice, if I may?"

"Of course, you do have permission to speak freely."

Reina's eyes turned steely. "Seasoned politicians hunt for any angle to undermine their rivals. Your 'origin' and 'Scarlet Princess' moniker will no doubt be used as weapons against you today. Don't let them nettle you lest they pounce on perceived vulnerability."

My pride will not allow slights against me for my origins, but I cannot let it blind me either. Remember, Makoto. Humility and responsibility. "We thank you for your advice, Countess. You have given us much to consider. Please, take us to the meeting chamber."

"Right this way, Your Grace"

Makoto and Ephraim followed Reina to a chamber within the heart of Mount Kauneus. There was no artificial ceiling, allowing the attendees to gaze at the gem encrusted crags far above their heads.

A crystalline serpent spiraled from the base of the chamber to the ceiling. Its coiled tail formed a large roundtable, and the scales on the serpent's back acted as a staircase. Moth-like wings stretched into the walls with seats situated on each one. The head looked down on all of them, intense but unimpressed.

Representatives from the lower mountain and surrounding villages gather at the tail. Ambassadors and nobility sit at the wings, and the Kauneus family are on top. Makoto felt dizzy looking up. *Why did it have to be so tall?*

"After you, Your Grace," Reina said.

Makoto grimaced. "Is there no faster way to ascend?"

"Not unless you can fly," Reina said. "Not that you should. There are one hundred and eight steps in total—one for each year of the Centennial Emperor's reign. I find I appreciate the journey when I rise to the top."

She glanced at the serfs standing at the base of the tail. "It gives a better appreciation for those at the bottom."

"That's surprisingly empathetic," Ephraim said.

"One learns empathy quickly in politics, Ser Thronsden. Tis a better motivator than fear."

Makoto ascended the serpent. She felt the attendees' intense stares—several of them openly balked at the sight of the Orichalcum Crown upon her head. One in particular caught Makoto's eye. He sat on the edge of the right wing with a lute across his lap. His wry grin showed off a missing tooth.

He's far less impressive in flesh than stars. "Does Lord Bahamut oft appear at these meetings?"

"The Enkeli are welcome but seldom appear. Even Madame Morgana rarely graces the chamber with her presence." Reina said. "Though I suppose in some ways she always does."

Makoto regarded him once more. Sunken eyes, missing finger. *The Platinum Dragon is mortal as Father.* "How old is he?"

Reina smirked. "Fancy elder gentleman, Your Grace?"

Makoto narrowed her eyes. "We *can* order your execution, Countess."

Reina chuckled. "I imagine the order would find little resistance here. Lord Bahamut has seen the end of several centuries, though I do not pretend to know how many."

Makoto searched for any attendees with ties to Avalon. Red hair, similar robes, or the Platinum Dragon motif. Aside from Lord Bahamut, she found none. "Are there no representatives from Avalon, Countess?"

"Regent Josephine acts as the island's voice with input by Bishop Lateo. I speak on my mother's behalf when she sends letters."

An island with no voice and a declawed defender.

Makoto reached the serpent's head. Two thrones stood at the edge with nine more behind. *One for each member of the family minus Suilla.* An orichalcum throne stood at the center. No question whom it belonged to. She assumed the diamond throne beside it was for the empress.

Makoto considered the remaining thrones: amethyst, platinum, garnet, lapis-lazuli, peridot, emerald, jade, and opal. "Is this one mine?" she asked, pointing at the garnet throne.

"Goodness no, dear girl. My brother insisted your throne match your eyes."

Makoto jumped at Count Edgar's voice. "You scared me, Uncle."

"My sincerest apologies." He twirled his moustache. "Emperor for a day. My brother knows how to play a high rolling bet. I should join in the next hunt." He chortled. "I remember negotiations with the Orabelle for the platinum. Rudolph nearly started a war to build you that throne."

Guilt pierced Makoto's heart like an arrow. "We should use it more."

Reina shook her head. "You are confusing gratitude with responsibility, Your Grace. Your time is precious—no need to waste it here."

"Our meetings are a waste of time, Countess?" Edgar inquired.

"For those without the stomach for politics or the necessary influence."

Makoto noted the change in the stares. Collective surprise was giving way to impatience.

"Tis customary for the highest-ranking person to begin the meeting," Reina said. "Today, Your Grace, tis you."

"Contrary to the countess's claims, there is no rush, Your Grace. We can start whenever—"

Makoto interrupted her uncle with a flurry of her robes. She approached the edge of the serpent's head and adopted her father's posture.

"Good morning. We are Makoto Clarissa vi Kauneus. In our capacity as acting Emperor, we call this meeting to order." She sat upon the orichalcum throne.

Edgar clasped Ephraim's shoulder. "She is quite the treat. Go, dear boy, stand by her side." He ushered Ephraim toward the center throne, whispered in his ear and strutted toward his own throne.

"What did he say?" Makoto whispered.

Ephraim leaned down. "He warned me about letting you get too close to Reina."

Reina sat upon the garnet throne and took another drink from her flask.

Should I be wary of her or is Uncle trying to play me? She frowned at the thought. *Being distrustful of family is nauseating. I nearly passed out during my meeting with Athena last night.*

"We shall start by discussing the status of tomorrow's ball," she said. "Count Edgar, how go the preparations?"

"Swimmingly, Your Grace." He stroked his thick moustache. "The ballroom has been cleaned spotless and the décor prepared. Most of the desserts are already resting. There are a few minor adjustments to make. Rest assured, they will all be made by tomorrow."

"Excellent." Makoto waved her hand at Reina. "Countess, how goes your side?

"Well, Your Grace. Our dignitaries from Nova City have arrived. They send their regards and apologies for missing today's meeting, but they do require rest. I'm told the Orabelle prince and princess will arrive tonight."

"If they are resting, then we assume accommodations have been provided?"

"Of course. The guest housing has been fully furnished and cleaned, though one of our Nova City guests is staying with Madame Morgana. The Alma's paladins will provide security, as always. I have met with the good bishops and have been personally assured of each paladin's strength and dedication."

"Very good. Whilst on the Alma, we understand there are negotiations at work. Who wishes to address us first on the matter?"

A man stood wearing gold and white robes and a matching hat. Both hat and robes bore the insignia of an ethereal egg hatching. "Bishop Lateo, First Order. If it pleases Your Grace, the Alma requests a stipend to better serve the people of Kauneus and its allies."

Makoto flipped her hair. "A well-intentioned but ultimately vague proposal, Bishop. Tell us, what are the specifics?"

Uncle Edgar raised his hand. "Your Grace." His tone carried reverence with a slight hint of exasperation. "The Alma is not under audit. Tis established tradition to leave the church in charge of its own accounts."

"Yet they ask for us to provide funds, Uncle. If they wish to oversee their own accounts, they can raise their own funds. If they request our funding, then we *will* know where it goes."

"Your Grace is wise to advocate transparency." Reina said.

Makoto waved an open hand toward the bishop. "Specifics, if you please."

Bishop Lateo pressed each hand into the opposite sleeve. "The Alma will build homes and shelters for the homeless throughout the empire. We will teach them various crafts; such as carpentry or masonry. Some will be trained by medical personnel to take up the rod. Others will take the sword and undergo paladin training."

He nodded to Reina. "We understand Regent Josephine has a great need for paladins in Avalon."

Makoto noted the intensity in his eyes at the end. *He means to taunt me, just as Reina warned. He may not oft be challenged, but I will not balk before you, Bishop.*

"We are of the same understanding when it comes to the regent's request. The merit of which shall be discussed in time. We thank you for the specifics of your plan, Bishop. Next we require an estimate of the proposed funds."

A second man in similar robes stood. "Bishop Bayard Finnian, Your Grace, First Order. We estimate two hundred thousand gold pieces."

Makoto barely restrained her shock. *Two hundred thousand to teach carpentry and swordplay?* "Your aims are as amicable as they are expensive. How do you propose we raise the funding?"

"Taxation, Your Grace," Bishop Lateo answered quickly. "The people help us to help them in a cycle of charity."

Cycle of charity. I wonder what those most affected think. Makoto watched those at the serpent's tail make shadows on the wall or eat. *They're unconcerned with the state of the meeting. How often is their input requested or heeded?*

Makoto cleared her throat. "We ask our friends at the serpent's tail to consider your offer of charity."

The serfs ceased their shadow puppetry. Their eyes were upon her now.

"Those in favor?" she asked with a raised hand.

A handful raised their hands.

"Those opposed?" She asked.

The majority of the serfs raised their hands.

"Your proposal has been defeated, Bishop. We may revisit later if there are edits."

Bishop Lateo's eyes narrowed. "May I be heard, Your Grace?"

"No." Makoto turned away. She successfully fought her ensuing smile and appeared composed. "Does anyone else have a proposal for us?"

"If I may, Your Grace?" a wispy voice asked.

"You may. Speak your name and your piece."

A large woman wearing black robes stood. Her pale skin glittered like the gems encrusted in the walls. She adjusted a hairpin made of quills and pushed it to the back of her scalp.

"Ambassador Delmar of the Orabelle Queendom. My brethren cannot step above the surface at Gravesend Bay without being flayed, murdered, or trafficked. You will oversee a swift and thorough investigation, and the perpetrators will be delivered unto the Orabelle Queendom for retribution."

Gravesend is that old port Father's sailors retired to. They are our people, but they forfeit our protection by murdering innocents. "And if no such perpetrators are found?"

"Should your investigation prove *insufficient*, my queen will take matters into her own hands."

Makoto's eyes hardened. *So they demand blood even if the allegations aren't supported. We will not give up innocents to satiate their bloodlust.*

"You will have your investigation, Ambassador. Should it bear fruit, they will be delivered unto you. If your queen deems it insufficient, we require her determination as to why before we let her act freely upon our soil."

Ambassador Delmar's skin turned prickly. "*Your* soil? Gravesend's waters belong to the Queendom."

"And its *soil* belongs to Kauneus. Are we incorrect to say so?"

Ambassador Delmar plucked a long quill from her eyebrow and set it in her hairpin. "No, Your Grace. We thank you for your understanding." She bowed and took her seat.

I've angered the Alma and the Queendom. Thankfully Nova City's representatives aren't here to add to my list.

Reina cleared her throat. "I wish to make a proposal, Your Grace."

Makoto nodded. "Yes, Countess?"

"I propose the Orabelle Queendom assist in paying for the Alma's proposal—specifically, for the training of paladins. This will provide extra eyes to conduct the investigation. Regent Josephine will do her part to secure funding as needed. Let's say fifty thousand each. It's less than the Alma's goal but eases the taxation burden upon our masses."

Ambassador Delmar removed another quill, this one from her lower lip. "You would hold my people hostage to appease the church and your mother?"

"You misunderstand me, Ambassador. I only incentivize working together. Your funding helps the church, which provides the paladins needed for your investigation. Cycle of charity, no?"

Ambassador Delmar nodded. "If the motion passes, then consider the Queen's aid granted."

Bishop Lateo raised his hand. "The Alma accepts this modified proposal. Should we put it to a vote, Your Grace?"

"All in favor of the Alma's modified proposal?"

A sizable majority of the villagers raised their hands.

"The Alma's motion is granted, and the Orabelle will have their investigation. Are there any—" A sharp note from Bahamut's lute interrupted Makoto. "Do you have something you wish to add, Lord Bahamut?"

He raised his head. "An emperor who wishes to hear my counsel? You are a rare sight indeed, Your Grace." He winked at her. "Between the Alma and the Orabelle, it seems you're in the giving spirit. So, I humbly ask Your Grace to grant Avalon its independence."

His lack of tact caught her off guard, but she kept her outward composure. *I almost appreciate him dispensing with subterfuge. But he's mistaken if he believes my connection to Avalon a weakness.*

"We will afford you the same opportunity as the other attendees. Give your proposal, and we shall consider it."

"Proposal?" He clicked his tongue and wagged his finger. "This is not a quid pro quo, Your Grace. Tis a matter of humility and responsibility."

Makoto tensed at his choice of words. She grasped the gem around her neck and felt its soothing warmth. "And what responsibility do we owe Avalon?"

"I'd have thought it obvious. Tis the duty of any who sees fit to adorn their head with Lucy's trinket." He set down his lute. The mirth left his eyes, and a cold smolder filled his platinum gaze.

"The All-Mother's home should be revered, not subjugated. Avalon twas not meant to be ruled by Kauneus or any nation."

"Subjugation seems a fair price for attempted assassination. A quid pro quo, no?" Makoto said. "We wish to hear other opinions on the matter."

Reina raised her hand. "My mother tis Regent of Avalon. Thus, my opinions are poisoned with bias. I shall recuse myself from discussion."

Bishop Lateo stood. "The Alma always supports the liberation of the All-Mother's homeland."

"Count Edgar, your thoughts?" Makoto asked.

Edgar stroked his moustache. "Avalon tis a tricky issue. Its orichalcum deposits are greater than those in the Kauneus homeland, but Lord Bahamut speaks true of its reverence."

Ambassador Delmar and the serfs offered no input.

Makoto folded her hands and met Bahamut's eyes. "We don't disagree with your sentiment, Lord Bahamut, but my uncle speaks in sooth regarding the orichalcum. Even Mount Kauneus finds it rare. We will abstain from deciding the motion now but will confer with our father."

The intensity didn't leave Bahamut's eyes. "You shirk your responsibility to your people, Makoto. You are the most powerful voice they have. Restore their freedom and be their savior."

And there it is. The appeal to my origin rather than refute my argument. Father was right. Those who cannot see past my birth are unworthy of my consideration... No, Father and Reina both warned me of this. Remember, Makoto. Humility, not pride. He may yet have something to offer.

Makoto exhaled. "We are burdened and shackled by our ties to Avalon. They blind those wishing to see a Scarlet Princess instead of Emperor before them. The notion of *our people* extends beyond Avalon's shores. Our people include the family who reared and loved us, and the people who rely upon our protection. We will not be goaded by you, Lord Bahamut."

She extended her arm towards him. "But we are not deaf to your plea nor so heartless to shun an entire people. Rest assured, we *will* speak to our father on the matter."

Makoto studied Bahamut's eyes. The intensity faded, but it was difficult to tell what replaced it. He was disappointed to be sure, but part of him appeared relieved. *Reina was right. Enkeli are nigh impossible to make sense of.*

"You carry more than your mother's eyes and hair, Makoto. You embody her very spirit."

Makoto reached for the gem around her neck. "You knew my mother?"

"We were practically family."

The words bit like an adder. *Why? I have a family. A father and sisters I love very much. Why does talk of my mother hurt me so?*

She closed her eyes. *You are representing the throne of Kauneus, Makoto. You must be beautiful. You must be strong. Tears are ugly and weak.* She gripped the gem tightly. *I need to be beautiful and strong. I must be beautiful and strong. I will dazzle and show no weakness.*

Makoto opened her eyes. "This is hardly the appropriate venue to reminisce, but we thank you all the same. We will steal your company during the ball, Lord Bahamut."

"It will be your pleasure." He picked up his lute and strummed a few notes.

Makoto's eyes swept over the chamber. "Is there other business to discuss with us?" She waited a moment, but no one spoke up. "Then we declare this meeting adjourned. We thank you for your time and understanding."

She stood but a sudden tightness gripped her chest. She descended the snake's tail, careful to keep both posture and balance on the way down.

Ephraim followed close behind. "What's wrong?" He whispered.

"Nothing serious," she said. "Just a bit tight in my chest. A heavy heart, I suppose." She grimaced. *It itches terribly.* She resisted the urge to scratch. "How was I?"

"Excellent," he said. His countenance betrayed his worry. "Are you sure you're alright?"

"Yes, but I may change my answer once I've spoken with Father."

"Are you going to meet with him now?"

She shook her head. "We have lunch with our sisters. After, a bit of fresh air."

Athena

Athena awoke to a feeling of bliss. Her usual aches and pains nowhere to be found. *I haven't slept this well in years. Do I have to get up?*

A knock on the door told her yes. Athena groaned but slinked out of bed. She opened the door and found Anna cradling a set of silk purple robes. "Morning."

"Afternoon," Anna said.

Then I missed breakfast. She wasn't sure if the extra rest was worth the growing hunger pangs. *At least I'll get to shower. I've been craving a good cleaning but didn't want to change into my grody clothes after.*

"I'm about to shower. Care to join me?" Athena asked.

"*After* your shower."

"I'll try not to keep you waiting." Athena closed the door. She shed her unclean garments like an insect's shell. Scalding water cascaded down her back. It stung, but her cleaning needed to be thorough.

Athena stepped out of the shower with steam emanating from her back. The robes, likely Margaret's, didn't quite fit but weren't uncomfortable. She stepped outside and modeled the robes for Anna.

"How much do you think I'd fetch at Auntie's Court?"

"A higher price than her crown jewel."

Athena laughed. "That's a compliment of the highest order." She remembered Harley's golden eyes. *I need to ask Mother about him next time I see her. And she's not the only parent I have business with.* "I think I'm ready to see the old man now. Any idea where he's at?"

"Follow me."

Athena walked with the gardener from the villa to the White Hall. "I thought Makoto would have been in here."

"My mistress is escorting Emperor Makoto to the meeting chamber down the mountain. It seems your father is drawn here even on his off day." Anna stepped away from the door. "I shall wait out here until I am needed."

Athena scratched the back of her head. *Just like yesterday, Athena. You're ready for this. Just kick down the door. And if he gives you problems, punch him.*

She kicked the door open. A familiar face in unfamiliar attire sat upon the throne. Her father traded his noble regalia for pajamas. He was slovenly and fat. *But I bet he still has a mean right hand.*

She strutted toward him. "Sorry, old man, but you can't take a nap there. That's the emperor's chair."

"Buh," he growled. "Impudent as I remember."

"We both know you wouldn't recognize me if I showed proper etiquette." She stopped at the steps before the throne. Struggling to find words worthy of the moment, she opted for the first thing that came to mind. "Were you always this fat?"

His lip curled. "Tough words from one so scrawny. A stiff wind could snap you in two."

"At least it would take a stiff wind. You look weak in your old age."

"Weak?" He stood; his looming shadow eclipsed the steps. Muscles flexed; the buttons on his pajamas burst. Her father remained strong, albeit pudgy. "I have *never* been weak. Perhaps you need a reminder, Athena."

She cracked her knuckles. "I'd love to for all time's sake. Between you and me, I still have some issues to work out." Her shoulders slumped. "But, alas, I don't think the reigning emperor would take kindly to us exchanging punches."

"Tis no crime to indulge an old man." He draped the busted shirt over the throne. "I'll be sure to speak with her on your behalf."

"Ugh, it would be rude to turn down an offer like that." She summoned Aegis. "First move is yours, old man."

"With pleasure." Rudolph slowly descended the steps before the throne. Each movement echoed throughout the White Hall like a beating drum.

The sound reminded Athena of her first ball. She heard the string quartet and percussion. Visages of dancers flooded the White Hall. A noble boy she fancied danced with her until clumsy footwork caused him to seek a different partner. She wandered the White Hall, envying the capable dancers. Her father, clad in opulent purple and gold, bowed to her from across the room.

Athena ran toward her father's waiting arms—

—and thrust her shield into his face. Her father blocked Aegis with one hand. He spun around and swept her leg. Athena lost her balance and swung a wild punch at her father—

—who caught her before she fell. They spun toward the center of the room. Other dancers parted for the emperor and princess. Athena spun away until her arm was fully extended. Her father's eyes shone with affection, hers with adoration. He pulled her toward him—

—and punched her face. Athena grinned and jabbed her father's jaw. The impact stunned him enough for her to ram Aegis into his chest. She smirked; her father did too. He wrapped his arms around her—

—and lifted Athena into the air. She laughed and surveyed the crowd. Her eyes fell upon the boy she fancied. She pulled down her eyelid and stuck her tongue out. Her father smiled rather than scold her. Athena leaned her head down—

—and smashed her forehead against his. Her head spun, and the memory of the ball faded. Her father stumbled up the steps and plopped onto the throne. He rubbed a fresh cut on his head and stared at the blood on his hand.

"Your head is harder than I remember."

"I'm surprised you can remember anything after that hit." She clutched her forehead and steadied herself. "I could use a drink after that."

"So early in the day?" He tore a piece of cloth from his shirt and pressed it to his cut. "Have some respect for yourself, Athena. What would Isabella think if she saw you?"

Athena thought back to the last meeting with her mother. To the disappointed golden eyes. "Wouldn't matter much. She's never been much of a mother."

"Athena." Her father's tone conveyed a thinly veiled warning. "Do not speak ill of her."

She mimicked her father under her breath. "When did you last see her?"

He responded with a long sigh. "The last ball. Your mother rarely forgets a grudge. I imagine immortality makes time insignificant." He rubbed his tired eyes and added, "I am happy to see you once again. I—"

"Don't," she spat. "I didn't return for you, old man." She turned her back on him. "Best save that nostalgia for someone who missed you."

His dry laugh filled the White Hall. "Your words wound more than your fists. But tis as you say, Athena. Your sisters will want to see you at tea this afternoon. Spend your company with those deserving of it."

Athena heard his voice waver. He slumped against the chair, struggling for breath. She'd never seen him look so old. *There won't be many moments like this one.*

She almost approached him, but another memory reared its head. His face several years younger denying her sister's freedom. *You're right, Father. Immortals are experts at holding grudges.*

Athena kicked her feet onto the table and exhaled peppermint-flavored smoke. "Being your guest has better perks than being a princess."

Reina set a fifth chair at the table. "You are too kind, Athena. Margaret and I have no desire to indulge in Regent Josephine's gifts, so I am more than happy to share." She poured two cups of tea and paused. "Tea or something stronger?"

"Tea with a few spoonsful of sugar."

Reina grimaced. "More than one ruins the flavor. You may as well be drinking candy."

"Would if I could." Athena sucked at her cigar and exhaled. *So much for quitting. Maybe I should've taken a toke from Auntie's pipe.* "But I am your guest, so I'll accept your terms."

Reina poured a cup and added one spoonful of sugar. "Amelia is on her way. Olivia insisted upon an invitation, though I doubt she'll be punctual. Makoto will join us shortly. She requested a bit of fresh air after the meeting and sent me ahead."

"How was she on her first day?"

"Aside from nearly starting an international incident, she did quite well."

Athena sucked too hard on the cigar. She coughed out the smoke and drank tea to ease her throat. "What did she do?"

Reina shook her head as she filled the final cup. "Not over tea. I avoid discussing work and politics when with Amelia—save for emergencies, of course."

Near international incidents don't qualify as emergencies? Athena ashed the cigar. "Was I an emergency?"

"I was already attending business when I heard of your arrival. Had I not, you certainly would have qualified. An unscheduled visit from an Enkeli with the exiled princess in tow. Only a fool wouldn't mount an immediate investigation."

Reina sipped her tea and relaxed into her chair. Her eyes glimmered affectionately at the cup. "Orabelle tea is a blessing from the gods."

"Is that what you have in that flask?" Athena asked, pointing with the cigar.

Reina's brow furrowed. She studied Athena's expression before answering. "The flask holds something more precious."

"Like what? Water?"

"In a sense."

Athena waited for her to elaborate, but Reina held her tongue. *Alright, Reina, keep your secrets.* She closed her eyes and squirmed until she felt comfortable. "Wake me up when—"

"You're taking a nap, Sophia? But I just got here!"

Athena opened one eye. A pair of silhouettes loomed over her. The light obscured their features, but she knew the short one bouncing on its heels to be Lucielle from the voice. That meant the giant next to her was Klaus.

"Sorry, kiddo, old habit. I used to take naps out here all the time. I'd have to sneak away from him first though. Right, Klaus?"

Klaus's near invisible smile sent a nostalgic shiver up her back. "'Tis refreshing to not blink and lose my charge."

"M-hmm!" Lucielle wrapped her arms around Klaus's hand. "Klaus is always around to take care of me. He's like a big, sweet, dog." She clicked her heels together and took the empty chair between Reina and Athena. "Now I have the best seat at the table."

Athena noticed her sister wearing a uniform not unlike the one Reina wore yesterday. "Do you two exchange clothes?"

"M-hmm," Lucille nodded. "Once a week. Your new clothes are lovely, by the way."

"Oh, these?" Athena stretched to show how the robes didn't fit her. "A bit big but still comfortable. Though not as comfortable as Father's pajamas."

Lucille gasped. "You saw Father today? Did it go well?"

Athena shrugged. "He missed me more than I expected. His aim is failing in his old age."

Reina raised an eyebrow but didn't laugh. Klaus's countenance aged at least three years. Lucielle stared at her sister with a befuddled expression.

"I think I'm missing a joke, but I'm glad he missed you."

"Me too, kiddo," Athena said and patted her sister's head.

Her sister giggled, as she swatted Athena's hands. "I'm not a 'kiddo' anymore, Sophia. I turn fourteen soon."

"Fourteen, huh?" Athena whistled. "But you've still got a lot of growing to do." She tapped her solar plexus. "You stop being 'kiddo' when you come up to here."

Lucielle pouted. "But that will take so long. I need at least another year."

"Sorry, squirt, but I don't make the rules."

"Nooo!" Lucielle cried. "'Squirt' is so much worse. Oh, do you remember this?" She reached into her collar and produced a silver locket.

"*From Sophia to Lucille,*" Athena read. "That was for your birthday the year I left."

"M-hmm. I hid it from Father and wear it when I visit Suilla." She opened the locket, showing a picture of Athena dropping a slug on Makoto's shoulder. "Suilla loves this picture."

"I'll bet. I remember how mad Makoto and Olive were at me for ruining the sibling portrait. I swiped some liquor from the kitchen a few nights later, and the three of us had a secret party. Olive might still have the sketches of drunk Makoto dancing."

"Let me know the next time you have a secret party, Sophia."

Athena winked and relit the cigar.

"You are incorrigible, Athena." Reina refilled her cup and added cream to Lucielle's. "I can't imagine how you stayed sane with her, Klaus."

"Who says I did?" came the terse reply.

Athena leaned back in the chair. "Come on, Klaus, you know you love me."

Klaus lowered his eyes and said nothing.

Athena regretted her choice of words. "Klaus, I—"

"Apologies, sisters and Countess. I was waylaid after a pleasant encounter."

Olive slinked toward the table clutching a sketchbook against her chest. She was paler than yesterday. Her burgundy lip gloss matched her snug sweater and pants.

"Encounter with someone I know?"

"Who knows?" Olive said with a frown. "I hoped to be the last to arrive."

"Wanted to make a memorable entrance?" Athena asked.

"Hardly. I wanted to avoid the sun. Tis terrible for my skin."

"Don't fret, sister," Lucielle said. "I sense Makoto just around the bend."

True to kiddo's prediction, Makoto scampered into view with her hand adjusting the crown.

Athena noted her sister's relaxed expression. *She's rather calm for nearly causing an international incident. Reina was either joking or little ruby is blissfully unaware.* She checked Reina's expression and found a wry smile. *Ah, joking it is.*

"How'd the meeting go, *Your Grace*?" Athena asked.

Makoto's brow furrowed. "It went well, I—*we* suppose. That may change after speaking with Father. At the very least, we're confident we have not disgraced the Kauneus family name."

Athena snickered. "Good, that's my thing. I'd be incensed if you stole my thunder, sis." She offered Makoto the cigar. "Any of you girls smoke?"

Her sisters shook their heads. Athena then offered the cigar to Klaus's brothers as they filed in behind their charges.

"I ran into Bastien yesterday, so this handsome stallion must be Ephraim," she said.

"Y—yes. Tha—that." He stopped talking to compose himself. "Yes, that's me."

Athena pointed the cigar at him. "He always this jittery?" she asked Makoto.

"No. He fancied you growing up, and you just called him handsome."

Ephraim rubbed his furrowed brow. "Remind me to not share secrets with you, Makoto."

"Hey, don't be embarrassed. You're not the first poor soul I've beguiled." *It's flattering but no. He and Bastien are practically my little brothers. Not to mention Makoto would probably kill me.* "Are you two a thing?" She asked him and Makoto.

Makoto flushed, but Athena couldn't tell it stemmed from embarrassment or indignation.

Ephraim, on the other hand, was rather pleased with himself. "Shame to disappoint you, but we intend to remain bosom friends."

"Oh really? Careful, Makoto, someone might snatch him up if you don't."

Athena's elbow nudged her sister, but Makoto didn't so much as chuckle. Her glare conveyed a simple message. Back. Off.

That confirms it. Makoto would definitely kill me. Athena cleared her throat and took another hit off the cigar. "So, what's on the agenda, girls? Do we talk about feelings? Suitors?" She blew a smoke ring in the shape of a spider. "Can we bring Suilla?"

"Suilla is still forbidden from leaving the southern wing. She's still *technically* not supposed to have visitors, but Father is lenient. If you'd like, the two of us can visit her afterwards," Lucielle said.

Athena stared into her empty cup.. *Would she even want to see me?* "I think I'd like that."

"Just the two of you?" Reina asked. "I feel left out."

"Don't!" Lucielle whined. "You get to spend all day with Makoto. I'm jealous."

"I'm not," Olive said. "Speaking of sisters, Countess, where's yours?"

"Helping Anna tend to the flowers. I can pass on a message at your request, Princess."

"No need." Olive opened her book to a blank page. "I speak for us all when I say we wish to know of *your* adventures, Athena. What have you been up to? Are you married? Have you seen the All-Mother since exile?"

Athena refilled her cup. "Once in passing. I was skulking through Nova City a few years ago—you'd love it, Olive. It's a city high in art and culture."

Olive straightened up. "I've sent several works to Nova City University for their consideration. But you were saying."

"Right, right. Mother made a scheduled appearance. A parade was thrown in her honor, though most of the locals were grumbling about how it ruined their schedules. I figured I'd drop by to see it. She, uh, looked at me—right at me. Her eyes followed me everywhere I went."

"Was Mother pleased to see you?" Lucielle asked.

Athena hesitated. The All-Mother's countenance was famously unflappable, but her emotions that day were palpable.

"She was disappointed—like any plans for me were forlorn and beyond saving. Like I wasn't her first mistake, and she was wondering where she went wrong."

Makoto's eyes softened. "Who said you were a mistake, Athena?"

"Me about three seconds ago." She blew three smoke rings that quickly dissipated. "It's hard not to be after being disowned *and* exiled. All I'm missing is an execution."

"It can still be arranged," Reina offered.

"Reina!" Lucielle gasped. "Enough of that. Klaus, tell Athena she's not a mistake."

"No, really, it's fine. I just—"

"You are not a mistake, Athena," Klaus said.

Athena scratched the back of her neck. "Ooh. That felt weird for both of us, eh, big guy?"

His expression remained unchanged. "Not at all. I meant every word."

Dutiful as ever. I still need to apologize to him. "You asked if I was married, Olive? That's a no—no kids either. Nothing to report at all. I just traveled anywhere but here."

"Did you ever see Avalon?" Makoto asked.

Athena shook her head. "Unfortunately, no. Spent a few years with the Orabelle, though."

Olive scoffed. "'Nothing to report,' she says." She readied her charcoal. "Describe."

"Very wet but not uncomfortably so. Okay." Athena clapped her hands and made a half-circle. "The Orabelle have an artificial light source, and this thing is *bright*. Like a second moon. It's always day there."

"How do they sleep?" Ephraim asked.

Klaus nudged his brother's ribs. "Speak when spoken to, brother."

"No, Klaus, it's cool. He can speak as much as he wants." Athena winked at Ephraim, who flushed.

"Anyway, they got cursed back when Lucy wore the crown, which is why the second moon is in the depths of the ocean. Don't know why—could never find a book on it. Now, Ephraim asked a great question."

She held out her hand and stretched out her fingers. "Orabelle homes are shaped like this. There's a big space, like my palm, which reaches out to a bunch of other rooms. When it's time to sleep—"

She curled her fingers into a fist. "The house folds over. It's like a flower that blooms and unblooms every day."

"Is it comfortable folding like that?" Bastien asked.

"Hey, what did your brother just say? Speak when spoken to, Bastien. You're not as cute as Ephraim, so you don't get the exception."

Bastien hung his head, but a quick head shake from Makoto restored his ego.

Athena laughed. "I'm kidding, Bastien. To answer your question, I got used to it pretty quick. The houses in the upper seas have it a bit rough, but the transition gets smoother the deeper you go."

Olivia finished a rough sketch of an Orabelle home. "I suspect you spent the majority of your stay in the upper seas?"

Athena clicked her tongue. "Correct. The High Nobility have it out for us surface dwellers, and the Lesser Nobility are only slightly more friendly. The average folk don't care that much. I spent a few months working in a mill before the owner chased me out for catching me with her husband and sister and—"

Klaus coughed, as Lucielle sat on the edge of her seat.

Oh, right. Kids. Athena cleared her throat. "And then I met *her.*"

"The owner?" Lucielle asked.

"No, someone else. A few nights after losing that job, I go to a bar putting on a show. I got something fruity with an edible coral straw and watched an amateur production. Cheap props, inconsistent makeup. I was more interested in my drink for two-thirds of it."

She still smelled that night no matter how hard she tried forgetting. The must from the bar and fruity tang of her drink. And a dash of sea anemone perfume.

"But the last act introduced a new character and actress. She took my breath away when I—don't scoff, Olive. I swear, I forgot to breathe. The light hit her just right, and a kaleidoscope filled the stage."

Luminescent flowers hung from the rafters. Their dim glow converged as a makeshift spotlight. An Orabelle woman with skin like a sunrise graced the stage. The light illuminated her pale face and the white streaks on her arms. Her flowing pink hair glowed and crackled.

"Every movement was elegant. Her words held my attention, *and her eyes!*" Athena swooned at the thought of those blue pearls. "I'm getting overwhelmed just thinking about her."

"You haven't said her name yet," Reina said.

Athena paused for dramatic effect. "Defluo Sententia." She waited a moment to gauge the reactions.

Reina raised an eyebrow, and Olive nodded. No one else appeared to recognize the name.

Athena groaned. "You guys don't know Sen? She's the biggest star under the sea."

Olive offered a reassuring shoulder pat. "I apologize for our uncultured sisters. They rarely show interest in the cinema."

"Oh, she's in movies?" Lucielle clapped twice. "I like the ones with a lot of blood."

"Yeah she—what?" Athena narrowed her eyes at Olive and Makoto and hugged Lucielle like a protective parent. "What are you letting this precious creature watch?" She switched her gaze onto Klaus. "You're not off the hook either, buddy."

Klaus grunted but said nothing.

"Ask this one," Makoto tilted her cup toward Olive. "I don't much care for movies."

Ephraim leaned forward and whispered, "That's because she falls asleep every time."

"Tis true. The chairs are better than the pictures."

"The cinema is too loud for me," Reina said. "I prefer stage shows. Though I have heard Sententia's name in talks with Orabelle and Nova City diplomats. She's quite popular."

Olive finished drawing and sipped her tea. "I must admit to being a fan. Her performance as both a murderer and inspector with a split personality in *Depths Shadows Won't Reach* impressed me. I believe that film elevated her to Lesser Noble."

Athena clicked her tongue. "It did, but I met her before she got her big break. She was swarmed by the audience after the show. People wanted to shake her hand, get her signature, and all that. Orabelle alcohol hits different than ours, so I shambled out back to clear my guts."

"Ugh," Makoto set her drink down. "I didn't need to hear that at table."

Lucielle, on the other hand, clapped eagerly. "I bet it was gross!"

"The grossest, kiddo, but I don't want Her Majesty exiling me for making her sick." Athena winked at Makoto.

"Most of the crowd cleared out when I made it back inside. Sen was still at her table, though. She ushered me over and offered me a virgin cocktail. She noticed me duck out and didn't want to leave without meeting me first."

"Aww," Lucielle giggled. "You're smiling, Sophia. You must like her a lot."

"Yeah, I do. I spent a lot of nights with Sen after that. We talked about our homes and families. She made me an expert on Orabelle cinema—the silent films are the best, by the way. The cinematography is unmatched, and the stars of the era really shine.

"We dated for a few months before her first movie. The director was an anti-Kauneus psycho. Whole thing was mendacious propaganda, but the effects were fantastic.

"Sen stole the show, as always, playing the Centennial Emperor. She only had a few scenes, but she made every one count. She got several roles after and could afford a home in the deeper sea. I moved in and worked as her housekeeper."

Olive and Makoto exchanged doubtful glances; even Klaus was bemused.

"Doubt all you want, but I became a cleanliness connoisseurrrr," she rolled her tongue. *Sen talked like that when she was flirty or drunk*

"But, like I've said, the lower depths have something against Kauneus. There were photos of us together and more than few articles about our affair. Sen was denied jobs she was more than qualified for, and one of the sponsors dropped her. It came down to me or her career. The right choice was made." She took a final hit of the cigar and set it down.

She received several sad looks and a pat on the shoulder from Reina. "My condolences. Still, tis hard to blame her decision given the circumstances."

Athena grimaced. *If it were that simple I wouldn't feel guilty.* "Impossible to blame her. I made the choice to leave. I wrote her a goodbye letter and took off one night."

Bold of you to call it a letter, Athena. It was barely a paragraph. "*You'll shine brighter without me blocking your light. Thanks for everything.*" *I couldn't even say I love you without losing my nerve. Cowardly Athena. Stupid Athena.*

"I didn't want to ruin her life. A disappointment like me—"

"If you say 'isn't worth it,' we shall slap you," Makoto snapped.

"I second Her Grace's sentiment," Olive said.

Athena laughed. "Seriously? Can you girls only communicate through threats of violence?"

"Sophia." Lucielle reached for her sister's hand. "There are people who love you even though you don't love yourself. Losing you hurts more than you can possibly know. At least we three had each other and the Thronsdens. You abandoned Sen."

"I—" Her reply died in her throat.

"I refuse to give up on you, Athena. My star will shine so bright they won't be able to ignore my light. We'll get through this together. I promise."

"I made a mistake, and I wallowed in my misery by heading out east. There's not much out there past Morgana's Bounty. It's a wasteland—full of highwaymen and gangs. I figured no one would bother me out there, but that old lizard Bahamut proved me wrong. But I'm glad he did. It's, uh, real good to see you all again. I didn't think I ever would."

Olive closed her sketchbook. "Inspiration has struck. I'll be indisposed until dinner..." She paused to ponder something. "Possibly a dash later than dinner. I'll see you all when it's ready." She kissed Athena on each cheek. "Come, Bastien. I have work to do."

Reina checked her pocket watch. "I believe it's time we left as well, Your Grace. Your father is expecting you."

"Then we shan't keep him." Makoto hugged Athena. "Love you."

"You too," Athena replied with a pat on her sister's back. She saluted Ephraim, as he ushered Makoto and Reina through the garden.

Lucielle hopped out of her chair. "Yes, I too have something vague I need to complete in the garden. Klaus, it's private, so I need you to remain here with Sophia until I finish."

"Princess, I must insist—"

Lucielle scurried off without listening. She admired the flowers in a nearby bush and steadily made her way further from them until disappearing behind a wall.

"She's a good kid. You've done a great job with her, Klaus."

"Thank you. It warms my heart to know I've impressed you."

She pointed her thumb at the empty seat beside her. "What do you say to keeping me company?"

"I prefer to keep watch of my charge." He took a step, but Athena caught his arm.

"Wait, hold on. I..." *Come on, Athena. Say you're sorry. It's just a couple words.*

Klaus's languid face wasn't unlike the All-Mother's. Frustration. Exasperation. The disappointment in her. *Why bother? It won't fix anything.* "I think someone spiked the tea. It was *strong.*" She flashed a grin. "Swear it wasn't me."

Klaus didn't so much as smile. "May I go?"

"Yeah. Tell Lucielle I'll be waiting for her in the southern tower when she's ready."

"Of course." He dipped his head and walked away.

Athena lightly kicked one of the empty chairs beside her. "The more things change, right?" She grinded the cigar's remnants into the large pile of ash. *Stupid Athena.*

Harley

Harley sauntered toward Zenith Palace's gates holding a letter from Madame Morgana.

"Princess Olivia paid a handsome sum for our property today. This letter shall be delivered to her. Its seal shall remain intact."

Two sentinels awaited Harley at the gate. Both wore white and gold armor. Their breastplates and shields bore an insignia of a silver egg blooming. Their visors were turned upward, granting Harley a view of their faces.

The right sentinel had a rugged face with grizzled hair. His ungroomed moustache carried leftovers from a previous meal. His burly partner averted her grey eyes. Harley recognized her as an occasional client. He winked but approached the right side of the gate.

The grizzled sentinel stepped forward with his spear readied. "State your business."

Harley spun the letter on his finger. "Delivery."

"Dressed like that?"

Although he wasn't showing much skin, Harley's attire could hardly be called modest. He wore a form-fitting crimson shirt. Its frilled collar drew attention to the plunging neckline, but a tight black undershirt covered his chest and neck. The white bowtie was optional, but he wouldn't be caught dead without it

"O' course," Harley scoffed. "I'm part o' the delivery."

The grizzled sentinel grunted. "I must inspect you first."

Harley shrugged and handed over the letter. "Jus' be careful. The madame has a strict break it ya buy it policy. An' between us, she has *real* expensive taste."

The grizzled sentinel rattled the letter but heard nothing other than the slight shifting of paper. "Appears clear." He returned it to Harley. "Stretch out your arms."

Harley did as he was told. "Should I stick out my tush too?"

"That won't be necessary."

Harley snickered. "Don' get too handsy, else I'll charge ya."

The guard sighed and conducted a pat down. "Whom is the delivery for?"

Harley playfully squirmed as a hand brushed against his leg. "Princess Olivia."

The grizzled sentinel's brow furrowed. "She oft ignores summons from the gate." He nodded to his partner. "All clear." He retreated to the guard station and scribbled a note. A raven snatched the note and flew towards the palace. "An escort will take you to the princess's atelier."

"An escort?" Harley pouted. "Ya don' trust me, handsome?"

"Less with each passing second."

Harley giggled. "Then I'll wait here like a good girl."

It took approximately half an hour for his escort to arrive. Harley recognized Bastien's large frame and toadlike face.

"The princess is expecting you," he said. "Best not to keep her waiting."

Harley bowed. "Course not. Punctuality is almost as important as confidentiality."

Bastien offered his arm; Harley eagerly hooked his own around it.

"Smart not to take my hand. Costs extra."

Bastien massaged his furrowed brow. "Are you always like this?"

Harley clicked his tongue but said nothing.

Bastien led him through the front gates and into the courtyard. The southern tower loomed above. Harley remembered the clumsy princess and his promise to see her.

Breakin' a promise is bad luck. I'll sneak away when I get a chance. His nose wrinkled at the thought of her grody presence. *I'll keep it short.*

Harley relished the staff's questioning stares and whispers. "Darlin'," he whispered in a breathless gasp. "They're starin'."

"I bet they are. Not often a whore is so brazen to use the front entrance."

Harley gasped. "I prefer the term 'valuable property,' thank ya very much. How'd ya like bein' called Olivia's dog?"

"Don't call me that," Bastien growled.

"See, ain't fun is it? But I know ya'll forgive me." He pressed his finger against Bastien's torso and traced an outline around his heart. "All good dogs play nice with their master's friends."

Bastien's eyes blazed. "I said—"

"Oh, don' be like that," Harley scoffed. "Jus' havin' a bit o' fun. Don' tell me ya don' like fun." He clung a smidge tighter to Bastien. "I'm sure the two o' us could have lots o' it."

Bastien ripped his arm away. "Watch that mouth of yours. It'll get you into trouble you won't squirm your way out of."

"Not the first time I've been told I got a dangerous mouth." He pressed his forefinger against his lips. "But I'll keep it shut if it suits ya fancy."

He followed Bastien through the atrium. They walked through a scarlet hallway decorated with portraits of previous princesses. Harley admired the portraits, although he decided he was prettier than most of them.

They stopped before a door marked by a large portrait of Olivia. It depicted her below a crepuscular sky amidst a field of white flowers. The wispy pink clouds above her formed hands reaching for her, though she remained oblivious.

Bastien pressed one hand against the door to ease it open. Harley rubbed his hands together and took his first look inside the revered atelier.

Black pillars held up a dark grey ceiling. Blue raindrops slashed down the pillars. A pair of sculpted arms protruded from the rafters, extending toward an empty chair. A violin and bow rested upon the left arm, while the right held a collection of lip gloss.

Olivia sat upon a gurney in the room's center amidst a cone of canvases. She worked on several at once, deftly wielding a brush in each hand and foot.

"She paints with her feet?" Harley whispered to Bastien.

"Her focus is ironclad. It's not uncommon for her to work without ceasing for hours at a time. I've reminded her to sleep on several occasions."

"No kiddin'? I almost feel bad intrudin.'"

"Don't," Olivia said without looking at him. "Your presence helps." She laid back on the gurney. Her left foot reached for a canvas dangling from a pillar, while her hands fought for positioning on a blank canvas. "I hear you have a letter for me."

"Right here." Harley held it out. "Compliments o' Madame Morgana."

Olivia's left hand smeared a navy line across a burgeoning sunset. She lifted her head to scrutinize the picture. "Put it on the chair. I'll get to it when I have time."

Harley slipped inside the room. He glided across a large splotch of painted floor, pausing briefly to appraise the floor mural. The colors failed to blend neatly and formed no coherent shape. It felt haphazard rather than avant-garde.

He circled the abomination with a sheepish grin. "Whadda ya call this one?"

"An Oaf's Magnum Opus."

Harley snickered and dropped the letter on the empty chair. He tilted his head to get a better view of Olivia's new paintings. One foot blocked his view when it reached up to massage her scalp.

"Didn' know ya were that flexible. Should I rub it instead"

Olivia's foot grabbed a fresh brush. "Please."

"It'll be ya pleasure. Anythin' I can use as oil?"

"Nothing besides paint."

"Naked fingers it is."

Harley's fingertips slipped behind Olivia's ears, tracing the skin up towards the scalp. He gently rocked back and forth to massage her without applying too much pressure.

Harley split his fingers into a V-shape and slid them down the sides of her head. The V's center caught Olivia's ears, letting him massage both sides at once. She squirmed when his pinky touched her earlobe.

"Ooh, ticklish?" Harley whispered into her ear.

"More than I care to admit. You're quite good at this."

"I should hope. Madame Morgana made me master massages before learnin' how to kiss."

His hands rested upon her scalp. His fingers curled into a comb around Olivia's raven hair. He leaned back, lightly tugging her hair. "Anythin' else ya need rubbed, Princess?"

Bastien cleared his throat and narrowed his eyes.

"No, thank you. This is sufficient. Though I must apologize. I hoped to have you pose for me."

"Don' worry, I believe in pleasure before business." His hands slipped to the bridge of her nose. He traced her nose to her forehead and spread his fingers out to her temples. "'Sides, we got time."

"Less than you think. I have afternoon tea with my sisters shortly, and I assume you have other business based on your attire."

"This old thing?" he giggled. "I insist on dressin' my best for my favorite customer."

She smiled for once. "It seems even I'm not immune to flattery. If you don't mind waiting, I'd like to work on posing after tea."

That'll be my chance to see Suilla. "Course I don' mind. Anythin' for ya." He glanced at a formerly blank canvas. Now it had been sprayed with crimson and gold near the top. "What're ya paintin'?"

"I'm unsure but will know when it's done."

"Be sure to show me, alright?"

"It will be your pleasure."

"Such modesty." Harley remembered the white-haired patron he met the previous night. "Tell that big sis of yours I say hi, by the by."

"You fancy her?" Olivia shook her head. "Here I thought I was your favorite princess."

"Trust me, it'll take somethin' special to dethrone ya." Harley stepped back and bowed. "Satisfied with my services?"

"Very." Olivia stood and observed the canvas cone. "Bastien, tis almost time for tea. Stand outside and be ready to escort me to the garden."

"Yes, Princess." Bastien shot Harley another warning look before stepping outside.

"So mean. Maybe I need to try harder." Harley took Olivia's spot on the gurney. He draped one leg over the other and practiced a smoldering gaze. "Think he could resist this?"

Olivia was unimpressed. "I've seen you do better." She said and left the atelier.

Harley scoffed. "'I've seen you do better.'" He glimpsed his reflection. "Eh, she's right. Hopefully Suilla is less picky..."

He used a skosh of luck to find the staircase and avoid any praying eyes. *Ugh, it's gettin' tight. Only a few pulls left before I run out.* Still, he reached the musty stairs without incident.

He crept his way up, careful to avoid getting too dirty. He stopped at the door marked with a black octopus and knocked twice.

"Suilla, my grody pearl, are ya in?"

"Heh!" An excited clapping sounded from beyond the door. "He came, Willard. I told you he would."

Harley pushed the door open and peered inside. Black curtains blocked all but a sliver of light, which shone upon the young girl and doll upon her lap. She patted it with one hand and waved with the other.

"I hope you don't mind, Harley. I like the dark."

"I do prefer actually *seein'* the pretty girl I'm with."

Suilla giggled. "He called me pretty, Willard. I think he's in love with me."

She held the doll up to her face. "No way, Suilla," came the high-pitched reply. "I don't trust him."

"Eh. Bad, Willard." She slapped her doll and set it down. Suilla crawled to the window and pulled back the curtain.

Illumination showed the barren room. Harley counted three pieces of furniture. First, a small bed with yellow sheets in the corner furthest from the window. Second, a desk in the center with a painter's pallet slung across its edge. Papers cluttered its surface and the adjacent floor.

Third, a hope chest beneath the window that Suilla currently sat on. A host of spiders scuttled toward her from the floor and ceiling, settling on her lap or nestling in her hair.

"They're nibblers," Suilla giggled. "You want a nibble, Harley?"

Harley didn't bother hiding his disgust. "I'll pass."

He approached the desk, glancing at the papers. Comparing them to Olivia's work, they were hardly drawings. But Harley recognized one of himself standing beside this same desk. "Interestin' drawin'."

"Heh." She smiled, seeming proud of herself. "I knew you'd come see me. I saw it."

"Ya saw it? Like in a dream?"

"I have lots of dreams, especially when I touch people." She extended her arms. "We should hug."

A spider scuttled across her teeth and disappeared behind her neck. Harley gulped. "One hug, sweetheart, but then I gotta go."

She squirmed in place, and her neck submerged into the sweater. "You don't want to play with me?"

"Not that I don' wanna. I'm jus' busy. An' even with how busy I am I *still* made time to see my favorite girl." He approached her, dread welling up with every step. "Who wants her hug?"

"Me!" Suilla rested her slimy head against his chest.

Eugh, she's naturally greasy. He watched in horror as the spiders crawled over him. They didn't bite, but goosebumps rippled down his arms and legs. Harley stayed in Suilla's arms for a few moments before squirming out of her grasp. "Ya, uh, got a towel?"

Suilla called the spiders back to her and opened the hope chest. She scurried toward Harley carrying a yellow towel but tripped. He grabbed her hand before she hit the ground.

"We gotta stop meetin' like this."

She frowned. "Do we have to? I like meeting with you."

"Not quite what I meant, Suilla." He wiped the grease off. "I jus' mean ya gotta stop literally fallin' for me."

"I'll try. Can I see you tomorrow?"

Harley shrugged. "Hard to say. Tomorrow is the ball, an' I'll be *real* busy." He kissed the tip of his finger and touched it to her nose. "But I'll see what I can do." He rubbed the grease off his finger and tossed her the towel.

"Heh!" She fell over catching the towel and wrapped it around her face. "See, Willard? He does love me."

Harley considered correcting her, but Suilla's bliss warmed his heart just enough for him to bite his tongue. He blew a kiss, as he slinked outside.

Using a little bit more luck, he returned to the atelier without incident. He sighed in relief when he realized Olivia hadn't beaten him back.

Harley approached the window and stared at the horizon. His gaze passed over the fields in the shadow of Mount Kauneus, settling on the visible sliver of coast and ocean. He whistled loudly. "A girl could get used to a view like this."

He wondered if his parents were down the mountain. The madame never told him much beyond his mother abandoning him.

"To think my own flesh an' blood gave me up." Harley snickered "Who does that for *free*? Her Highness robbed that woman blind. Serves the crone right. Hope she's rottin' wherever she is."

The atelier door flew open. Olivia scrambled inside with Bastien behind. She laid a pair of blank canvases onto the gurney and painted at a fever pitch.

Harley crept behind her to peek at her work. "Save some of that passion for me, eh?"

Olivia ignored him.

"Guess we're doin' this again." He winked at Bastien. "How was teatime?"

Bastien pressed a finger to his lips and tilted his head toward the door. Harley rolled his eyes but took the hint. He followed Bastien outside, who quietly shut the door.

"Inspiration struck during tea. I'm afraid the princess will be unavailable for the time being. My job is to keep away any annoyances."

"An annoyance? Me?" Harley fluttered his eyes. "It's a step up from 'whore' or 'homewrecker.' So, ya gonna escort me out?"

Bastien's brow furrowed. "I escorted you in as your business involved my charge. My business with you concludes with hers." He winced as though tasting something unexpectedly bitter. "Apologies, that sounded less harsh in my mind. What I meant is—"

"Eh, it's fine. I know the way out from here. We'll get together another time."

Harley retraced the steps between atelier and courtyard. The gardens welcomed him with a fragrant aroma, and he paused to bask in its scents and warmth. *Olivia should request me more often. I could get used to usin' the front door.*

Alas, Madame Morgana would be furious if he wasted time. Time spent idle was time not making coin. And Harley was expected to make his master a lot of coin. But he got distracted by the sight of Princess Amelia peeking around a wall. *What's she doin'?*

"Planting seeds."

Harley blinked. "Ya read minds?"

"No, your curiosity is just loud." She scurried toward him. "I sensed Suilla's joy from down here. Thank you for making her happy."

"My pleasure." He bowed. *An' whadda ya know? I ain't idle no more. Now I'm investin' in another princess.* "I'd be insulted if she wasn'. Who wouldn' enjoy a kiss from me?"

Amelia gasped. "You kissed her?"

"Course. Ain't a proper greetin' without at least a peck." He licked his lips. "Interested in a sample?"

"Not now when I know where your lips have been," she giggled. "I refuse to compete with my sisters."

"Ya loss." Harley looked around, realizing they were alone. "Where's ya friend?"

Amelia's smile was gentle but a tad condescending. "I have lots of friends, Harley. You'll need to be more specific."

"Uh, the big one with the brothers. Follows ya like a dog."

"Oh, you mean Klaus." Her eyes glimmered mischievously. "He's busy with the planting."

"What kinda seed do ya plant hidin' behind a wall?"

"A special kind of seed. I'll tell you about it tomorrow."

He feigned indignation. "Holdin' out on me? Thought we were friends."

She pouted. "Friends don't pull those kinds of tricks, Harley."

"Alright, keep ya secrets." *Not like I don' got my own.* "Ya excited for tomorrow?"

"Ecstatic!" She clapped her hands. "The Orabelle prince and princess are making their appearances, and I do enjoy their company. And what of *your* date?"

Harley gasped. "That's gossip, sweetheart, and these lips are sealed."

"Oh, pish. What's gossip between friends?" Amelia giggled. "If our companions find themselves busy tomorrow, we simply must get together."

"Agreed. Maybe ya can show me some fancy desserts."

Amelia curtseyed. "It would be my *sweetest* pleasure."

"Then I better not disappoint." Harley kissed her hand. "Not every day I can pleasure a princess."

Amelia flushed. "I know *not* what you mean. But I *do* recommend getting scarce lest my Thronsden or sisters hear you."

Harley winked and took the hint. He slipped through the courtyard and passed the gate. He blew a kiss, and Amelia waved back. *Whadda ya know? I might have actually made a friend.*

Makoto

Reina and Ephraim flanked the temporary emperor as she stood before the White Hall.

"We thank you for your time and guidance today, Countess," Makoto said, "but we wish to speak with our father alone."

Reina nodded. "As you wish. I assume Ser Thronsden will remain at your side?"

"Ephraim is our shadow. We would not be at ease without him."

"For what it's worth, I hope he errs on the side of Avalon's freedom."

I'm not sure if I should thank her or not. I'm still not sure which side I'm advocating for.

Ephraim pushed the doors open, and Makoto sauntered inside. She held her head high despite the crown's strain upon her neck. The tightness in her chest remained, and the itching grew worse with each step. Makoto pressed her hands at her sides to avoid being unsightly.

"Father!" she called to the man standing by the large window. The word reverberated through the shining white walls. "I have a request of you."

Her father was garbed in modest dress: pajamas with an orange stain and several burst buttons. *He appears comfortable. I suppose I'd be the same after decades of stressful work.*

He drank sparkling liquid from a tall glass. "You neglected use of the royal we, Your Grace. Perhaps you should try again."

"No, Father." Makoto removed the Orichalcum Crown but kept it in her hands. "I stand before you not as an acting emperor but as your daughter."

"Retiring so soon?" A chuckle rumbled but quickly died in his throat. "Is everything alright? How was your meeting?"

Makoto frowned. "That's what I want to discuss. Don't fret, Father. There is no imminent emergency. First, I must ask how went your reunion with Athena?" She studied her father's face. "The cut above your head wasn't there yesterday."

"Nothing to concern yourself with. Our fool-hearted daughter has not the strength to besmirch our face." He massaged his jaw. "Though her punches remain hard as iron."

Makoto sighed. "It took less than one afternoon for you two to fight."

"Buh, twas light sparring. Nothing more than recreation."

Makoto rubbed her frustrated head. "Sometimes I wonder where she inherited her incorrigible fool's heart."

"Tis a mystery for the gods alone. No need to worry, Makoto. All is well enough between your sister and I."

"Good to hear. She said the same at our lunch." She turned the crown over in her hands. "During the meeting, Lord Bahamut requested I grant Avalon independence. I deferred the decision with the promise I would discuss it with you."

Her fingernails scraped against the crown. "You told me the Orichalcum Crown represents humility and responsibility. I'm conflicted if my responsibility is as your daughter or the voice of a people I don't even know."

She thought again of Asuka. "Ephraim suggests I return to Avalon for a spell. He may be correct..." *I truly am shackled by Avalon's spectre.*

The shadows from her father's eyes darkened his countenance. "I have oft considered returning Avalon her freedom. Yet the scars of that night remain fresh despite the years."

He reached for the crown and placed it atop his head. His back straightened as he resumed his usual posture.

"We respond to your request not as your father but Emperor of Kauneus. We shall send you to Avalon as our emissary. Evaluate and observe the island's status, alongside the actions of its regent and people. We will heed both your report and recommendation. If you wish for the island's freedom, it shall be granted."

"Fa—father." She was shocked. "When am I to depart?"

"We will discuss the matter with Countess Reina and Regent Josephine. They will prepare your travel and lodging. Does this please you?"

"Yes, it—" Makoto stopped talking.

Golden lights shined from the wall—a pair of eyes regarding her. Athena and Amelia oft expressed their compassion, mirth, and mischievous natures with their eyes. But these were cold. Indifferent. She knew instantly whom they belonged to.

A woman clad in a translucent shawl stepped away from the wall. Sunlight streaming through the window struck her. She glowed like a lantern, but Makoto knew it would burn brighter without the shawl's restraint.

"Empress Isabella." Makoto dipped her head. "Tis an honor to—"

"Raise thine head, child. Tis unbecoming of a dragon to prostrate itself."

Makoto obliged and found the All-Mother standing before her. Ephraim started toward them, but Makoto stopped him with a wave of her hand.

"I acquiesce to thine decision, child."

Makoto blinked. "Of returning to Avalon."

"Tis not within mine domain to restrict thy access to the Pyhä Äiti."

"Then I'm afraid I'm not sure of which decision you speak."

"Thou granted amnesty to thine sister, child. I shalt not object."

Isabella's words were so casual Makoto thought she misheard them. *Not that her words are ever easy to understand.* She studied the All-Mother's expression. The golden eyes remained indifferent. Her expression didn't betray a hint of a joy. *That's not the countenance of a mother.*

"You mean that?"

"Foolish child." There was no inflection in Isabella's voice despite her chiding words. "Tis not the nature of light to deceive."

A rush of joy swept over Makoto. She lunged forward and embraced the empress. "Thank you! Thank you so much."

She clung to the hems of the All-Mother's shawl. *I can't wait to tell her. Athena and the others will be so pleased. I wonder if she and Amelia are with Suilla right now.* The thought gave her pause.

"If Athena can return to the family, can Suilla do the same?" Makoto asked.

The light emanating through Isabella's shawl morphed from flickering candle to blazing inferno. "Thine father's abomination taints his crown's legacy." Isabella's cadence and countenance remained even, but Makoto felt the disgust shine through.

She quicky stepped away and dipped her head. "Y—yes, of course. My apologies for being so bold." *What emboldened me to ask that of her? She may renege her amnesty if I've angered her.*

"Thou hast no need for apologies, child. The abomination twas not thine mistake."

Makoto saw her father flinch. *She hasn't even looked at him.*

Isabella reached forward; Makoto instinctively shrunk back. The All-Mother paid no mind and touched the pendant. "Thou shalt heed thy father's command. Observe his mistakes and judge thusly."

The gem glowed brightly, and Makoto smothered the light betwixt her hands. "Why does it do that? Why does touching it bring me such peace?"

"Thou shalt understand mine brother's heart in time." Isabella released the gem, but the glow remained. "Such magnanimous luster infects me so. Tell us, child. Will mercy purify a tainted crown?"

Makoto glanced at Ephraim for a hint. At his nod, she did the same. "Yes," she said with feigned confidence.

"Then mercy shall be observed upon the abomination." Isabella glided across the floor. She pressed her hand to the wall, opening a hidden chamber, and disappeared without another word.

Makoto's father maintained his composure. There were no tears in his eyes or quiver of his lips. To most he would appear stern, but Makoto knew him well enough to recognize his solemn joy.

The emperor strutted toward his throne and sank into it. "Clemency for our daughters. We miss only our sister now." He rubbed his cheeks with his large hand. "Makoto, you have given us the greatest gift. We are forever in your debt."

She curtseyed to him. "The gift is mine to enjoy as well, Father. I'm... beyond words. Why do you think she changed her mind?"

"We cannot say. Isabella's nature has always been foreign to us. Perhaps we caught her in a good mood."

He scoffed and slapped his belly. "'Tis unbecoming to conduct business in our current attire. Makoto, inform Countess Reina we shall receive her in our chambers once we are presentable. We shall see you at dinner."

"Consider it done, Your Grace." Makoto bowed to her father and exited the White Hall.

Reina waited outside with a curious expression. "Am I to resume referring to you as 'Princess'?"

"Correct, cousin. Father will receive you in his chambers once he is decent."

"Then I shall await his summons at Linna Varjoissa." Reina dipped her head and left.

Ephraim exhaled once Reina left his eyesight. "I hope to never see that much of her in one day again."

"Come now, Ephraim, no need to be so rude. She's been helpful today."

"To what end? The way she looks at people, Makoto, as if judging a cut of meat." He wrinkled his nose and shuddered. "I felt naked before her eyes."

"Oh? This dashes my plans. I hoped to match you two."

Ephraim's countenance betrayed his shock. "Why?" He gasped.

She chuckled at his reaction. "Noblesse oblige, Ephraim. I want to see you happy and thought her your type. Independent. A savvy head on her shoulders. Athena in a smaller frame."

"Nothing like Athena," Ephraim scoffed. "Reina is an adder hiding 'neath a rock. Your sister an untamable bruin." He smiled wistfully. "Athena oft gave me presents after Mother passed. Her kindness touched me most of all. Something I doubt Reina capable of."

"I make no promises, but I'll put in a good word for you with Athena when I can."

"Thank you, Makoto. I will strive to... are you ill?"

"Ill? No, why do you ask?"

"You haven't stopped scratching your chest since you stepped outside the White Hall."

Makoto glanced at the nails digging against her robes. "'Tis nothing serious, Ephraim. Possibly a light reaction to the Orabelle tea."

"Do you want me to check?" He asked, reaching his hand forward.

"My chest?" Makoto crossed her arms and turned from him.

"Not that I wouldn't enjoy a peek, but that's far from my intention. I've treated several of my brothers' rashes. Its shape and shade will give clues to its nature."

Makoto narrowed her eyes. "I trust you, but must you mention enjoying a peek?"

"Just being honest. Not sure why it's a big deal. You and I have seen each other naked."

Yet Ephraim keeps his eyes on mine if I'm disrobed. I've never once mistrusted his eyes or hand. "Very well. I shall show you in my chambers."

Makoto led Ephraim to her room and locked the door behind them. "Close your eyes, Ephraim." She untied the sash once he obeyed. Her robes slipped, but she pressed them against her skin before they touched the ground.

A gasp escaped her trembling lips. A series of platinum rhombuses melded with the skin around her heart, compacting together like a honeycomb. Their luster almost dazzled her.

It's beautiful—no! It's some sort of rash. This is what has been bothering me.

She traced her finger across a line of them. Cold and metallic to the touch—lacking the texture of her flesh. Sharp edges resembled the scales from her father's armor. *Dragon scales? Is it an Avalon ailment or allergy?*

"Makoto?" Ephraim stepped forward. "What's wrong?"

"N—nothing. I—"

"I'll open my eyes now if you insist on lying."

Embarrassment and frustration colored Makoto's cheeks. "That's no way to speak to a princess, Ephraim Thronsden," she snapped.

"But it's how I speak to my best friend. I'm opening my eyes, Makoto."

"Wait!" Makoto adjusted her robes to cover the rest of her chest. "You may open your eyes. Just... promise to keep this between us."

"I promise." Ephraim opened his eyes. He didn't gasp but tilted his head. "I..." He closed his mouth and tilted his head to the other side. "I've never seen a gleaming rash before. May I?"

He stepped forward once Makoto nodded. His fingertips scraped the edge of the platinum. "This doesn't feel like skin—more akin to scales. Lord Bahamut didn't touch you, did he?"

Makoto shook her head. "Not at all. Unless he can curse me from across the senate chamber, he's innocent." *Can he curse me from such a distance? Perhaps its within his repertoire of tricks.*

"We can ask a doctor," Ephraim said. "Perhaps he's seen this condition before."

"No," she snapped. "I made you promise to keep this between us."

"But, Makoto—"

"Ephraim!" Her voice mimicked the tone her father used when ordering servants. "Knowledge of this shall not leave this room."

I've been branded the Scarlet Princess for my hair. What epithets will I receive from this? Her mind returned to the ship's deck and the bald sailor's hateful, disgusted eyes. *A platinum brand tis no better than scarlet.*

Ephraim's eyes challenged her but relented. "You'll let me know if it gets worse."

"Of course." She touched his arm. "There's no one else I'd rather have at my side."

He beamed at that. Ephraim knelt, placing her hand upon his heart. "I'll follow you to the end of the world."

Makoto's hoarse laugh felt dry in her throat. "Don't let Athena hear you say that. I don't think she'll be willing to share."

"Then that's her loss. My future wife must understand your needs come before hers."

"Ephraim!" Makoto gasped. "You can't marry someone and tell them they're second place."

"Why not? Father understood Mother loved him, but her duty to the emperor remained paramount." Ephraim placed his hand upon her scaly heart. "To the end of the world, Makoto. Scales and all."

"Thank you, Ephraim," she said, squeezing his hand tighter than expected.

Athena

Athena stood outside the black octopus door. She paced in a tight circle, tapping her forefingers against her elbows. *I shouldn't be here. Mother will kill something if she finds out—most likely me. Ugh, hurry up Lucielle. I need you or Klaus to talk me out of this.*

"Nervous, Sophia?"

Athena pressed her back against the wall, as Lucielle and Klaus climbed the staircase. "Thought that power of yours didn't work on me."

"I don't need my power to see your nerves." Her little sister offered her hand. "It's going to be okay."

Athena pressed her forehead against the door. "What are you feeling from her?"

Lucielle closed her eyes. "Hmm... I'm a tree standing on a moonlit night. I bear no fruit, and there are no critters or birds making nests in me. It's lonely, but there's a gentle breeze blowing against my bough. I think she's lonely but happy."

She approached the door with her hand at the ready. "Shall I do the honors?"

"I think it's better if she sees you first," Athena said. "I don't want to scare her."

Lucielle rapped her knuckles against the door. "Suilla, are you decent?"

"Heh?" came the startled grunt.

"No, Suilla, we've been over this. Not 'heh'. Use your words, dear."

"Heh... I'm decent."

Luicelle clapped. "Very good. I'm coming in. I have a guest with me today."

"Is it Harley?" Suilla asked excitedly.

Harley? What's Auntie Morgana's boy doing here?

"No, dear, not Harley. Maybe I can bring him tomorrow if you're good."

Suilla grumbled something unintelligible.

"Suilla, your words."

"Oh, sorry. Um, come in."

Lucielle pushed the door ajar. "Good afternoon, Suilla. You look positively radiant."

"Heh, good afternoon, Amelia. You look, uh, pretty."

"Thank you." She pushed the door open enough to slip inside. "Come in on my signal," she whispered to Athena.

"Sure."

Athena waited for Lucielle to get further into the room before peering inside. The room was cleaner than last time. It didn't smell *great*, but the air was breathable without inviting sickness. *Could probably do something about all these spiders, though.*

The little girl Athena remembered had grown up a bit. Suilla's clothes appeared to fit and there were no obvious cuts or bruises. A bit greasy, and her hair could be trimmed, but she seemed healthy. Suilla caressed a towel and nestled her head against a ratty spider doll.

Lonely but happy.

"Suilla, dear." Lucielle sat on the bed and took her sister's hands. "You trust me, right?"

"M-hmm. We're gonna play dress up."

"A favorite for sure. And you know I wouldn't bring a guest that would hurt you, right?"

"Heh—er, yes."

"Perfect. Then allow me to introduce my guest. Athena?"

That's my cue. Athena pushed the door open all the way and gave her best grin. "Hey, sis. Remember me?"

Suilla tensed. Joy drained from her face. A silent scream contorted her countenance, as she tightly gripped Lucielle's wrists.

So she does remember me.

"Suilla, dear. Remember what I said?"

Suilla's inky eyes fixated on Athena. "But she's the scary lady..."

"She won't hurt you, Suilla. Will you, Athena?"

Athena quickly shook her head. "Never."

"See? You can trust her because you trust me."

Suilla shifted to huddle behind Lucielle. "Heh..."

Lucielle stroked her little sister's hair and beckoned for the eldest to enter.

Athena sat on the edge of the desk to keep her distance. She sifted through the papers—half-decent drawings of Suilla and sometimes other familiar faces. *One with Harley. So they do know each other.* "You like drawing, Suilla?"

Suilla didn't say anything. Long hair veiled her face, leaving a single black eye to glare at Athena.

"Suilla, remember your words," Lucielle said.

"No, it's fine." Athena set down the papers and hopped off the desk.

Suilla jolted backward and hit her head against the wall. "Owwww," she said furiously rubbing her head.

Lucielle kissed the top of her sister's head. "Is that better?"

Suilla lifted her head. "It would be if she wasn't here."

"Suilla, that's rude."

"No, Lucielle, it's fine." *I knew this was a mistake. Nothing good ever happens when I come up here. At least it's not worse.* Athena scratched the back of her head. "She used her words just like you asked. I'm happy just knowing she's okay."

"Not okay," Suilla grumbled. "Head still hurts."

"Mostly okay," Athena said. "I'll see you at dinner." She faced the door but froze at the white glow filling the staircase. *Oh, no...*

The telltale sound of footsteps echoed from the bottom of the stairwell. Slow, nonchalant. Each step tolled the All-Mother's arrival.

Athena tensed. Though the light grew brighter, her skin felt colder. Her heartbeat accelerated—three beats for each footstep. She released a long, dry breath. Then another. Slow, deliberate.

"Mother!" Lucielle grabbed the hems of her dress and scurried past Athena. She stood beside Klaus, and they curtseyed and bowed respectively. "I'm so thrilled to see you."

Isabella passed them without a word. The coldness in her eyes didn't match the white-hot light of her person. "Hello, child," she said to Athena.

Athena steadied her shaking hands by clenching them into fists. She positioned herself between her mother and Suilla.

Isabella's countenance remained unflappable. "Thou stand as a tree, strong and proud before a winter's gale. Tell us, was thine Father's mistake worth thine freedom?"

"Always," Athena said without hesitation.

Slow, nonchalant footsteps carried the All-Mother across the floor. Her hand pierced Athena's barrier and touched her daughter's cheek. Athena winced, though her mother's touch was gentle. Almost loving.

No. That creature doesn't have a loving bone in her body. "Here to execute me yourself?"

"Thy will burns like flame upon the shore. Though the waves may crash and break against thee, thou remains ever-burning."

Isabella stepped back. "I have pardoned thine insolence, child. Thy sister requested I forgive mine husband's. We shall acquiesce for now."

Athena blinked. "You... you what?"

Isabella didn't answer. She returned to the doorway, pausing to gently pat Lucielle's head. "'Tis a joy to see thee as well, child. Be unto thy sister a calming wind lest her flames blaze even Avalon's waters."

Her youngest daughter beamed at her. "I shall do my best, Mother."

Isabella started down the staircase. Each step slow and nonchalant until they could no longer be heard.

Athena unclenched her fists, her palms red from pressure. Not the first time her hands had been red in this room. She sank back onto the edge of Suilla's desk.

"Sophia!" Lucielle threw her arms around Athena's neck. "Did you hear what Mother said?"

"Yeah... I'm just not sure I believe it."

"Well, you should, because it happened," Lucielle sang. "And we haven't a moment to spare. Suilla, dear?"

"Heh?" Suilla lifted the hair from her eyes. "Is the scary lady gone—" She squeaked when she noticed Athena.

Lucielle hopped onto the bed. "We are going to pamper and gussy you up. You're going to be the prettiest princess at the dinner table when we're through."

"Really? Even prettier than you?"

"Most definitely." Lucielle helped Suilla to her feet. "Klaus will escort us to my chambers where we can work. Will you be joining us, Athena?"

Suilla won't be able to enjoy herself if I'm there. "Nah, never been one for gussying up. You two have fun without me."

Lucielle frowned. "Very well. We'll see you at dinner."

She practically dragged Suilla out the door. Suilla struggled to match her sister's pace and energy but managed to keep upright, as they disappeared down the stairs.

Athena stared at the spiders scuttling along the ceiling. "Girl lives in the dark with spiders, and I'm still the scariest thing she knows. Not that I blame her." She groaned and splayed her body over the desk.

I didn't even have the decency to apologize to Klaus. Suilla is terrified of me. Mother did something I actually liked—She remembered the golden-eyed boy at Morgana's Court. *I forgot to ask Mother about Harley! Another mistake...*

She draped an arm across her eyes. "I could use a drink. A smoke wouldn't be too bad either. Or a massage." She imagined Sententia's hands rubbing her shoulder blades. "I miss her magic hands."

"*You abandoned Sen.*"

"Yeah, yeah, no need to remind me." She slammed the back of her head against the desk. *I'm sorry, Sen. Klaus. Suilla. I'll try to be better.*

"Introducing Her Royal Highness Athena Sophia vi Kauneus."

Athena shook the jitters from her hands and sauntered into the dining room. Familiar scenery overwhelmed her with nostalgia, especially the dent from Uncle Laurence's head. *Glad to see that hasn't changed.*

Her father lifted a goblet in her direction. A simple yet familiar gesture. One she hadn't realized she missed.

She saluted him. "Where do I sit, old man?"

He rattled her old chair with a grunt. "Your seat shall always be at our left hand."

Athena took her old seat and rocked back and forth. "The back legs have been fixed."

"Of course. Olivia kept your seat occupied. She insisted it be fixed."

"Typical Olive. I remember the creaking used to drive her nuts." Athena kicked at the empty seat across from her. "Looks like your beloved empress won't be joining us tonight."

His eyes told her to watch the tone; her eyes told him she wouldn't. She peeked into her goblet and frowned upon seeing it empty. "Do you miss her, Father?"

He nodded without hesitation. "Aye. The chasm between us was borne of our own mistakes. It grows longer and our heart colder each day without her light." He regarded his daughter accusingly. "Though we suspect you missed her little."

Athena balanced her goblet upon the bridge of her nose. "Mother is an enigma. Personally, I always preferred Charlotte Thronsden." She leaned back in her chair. The goblet wobbled but didn't fall. "She taught me how to do this when I was five."

"Costing us several goblets in the process." His expression softened. "Charlotte oft told us you were the daughter she never had. Just as stubborn and indignant. You share her penchant for vices."

"And here I thought you liked her."

His hearty laughter echoed throughout the room. "She was our bosom friend. We would not have changed a thing about her."

"Would you have changed a thing about me?"

"There are *several* things we'd change about you."

Athena's laugh was just as hearty. "And here I thought we'd never agree on anything." She clinked her empty goblet against his.

"Introducing Her Royal Highness Princess Makoto Clarissa vi Kauneus and her retainer, Ser Ephraim Thronsden."

"Makoto?" Athena frowned at the chairs. "Shouldn't Olive be next?"

"Olivia informed us she will be late tonight. We presume a new project has its talons in her."

"Right, she said something about inspiration when she left the tea party." Athena's stomach growled. "Hope it doesn't take her too long."

Makoto started for her seat but hesitated when she saw Athena. "Oh, right. I'm on the other side now." She walked around the table and sat beside her sister. "Not that I'm complaining about your return, Athena, but this will take some getting used to."

"Sorry for throwing you off," Athena chuckled. "Actually, why *are* you sitting here?" She stood up and patted Makoto's head. "Where's your crown?"

Makoto shooed Athena's hand away. "Don't you have eyes?" she asked, tilting her head towards their father.

"Yeah, but why don't *you* have it? Don't you still have a few hours left?"

"I discussed matters with Father after our tea party. It seemed like a well enough time to return his crown." She rubbed the back of her neck. "I don't miss its weight."

"Thy sister requested I forgive mine husband's. We shall acquiesce for now."

"But you bore it well." Athena patted her sister's head once more.

Makoto frowned but didn't swat at Athena's hands a second time. "Please, sister, refrain from treating me like a child."

"Can't help it. You'll always be my little ruby." She kissed Makoto's forehead. "Thank you for helping Suilla."

"Of course. It was my—" Makoto stopped and appeared puzzled. "How do you know about that?"

"Introducing Her Royal Highness Princess Amelia Lucille vi Kauneus, her retainer Klaus Thronsden, and Her Royal Highness Princess Suilla vi Kauneus."

Guess Father never bothered giving her a middle name. "Heard it from the All-Mother herself. How's it make you feel, old man?"

194

His stern eyes showed no signs of gratitude or remorse. "The All-Mother's clemency is received with grace," he said.

Ever the emperor, even when he should be a father.

His youngest daughters entered the dining room. Lucielle's dress consisted of various shades of pink Athena didn't know the names of. She styled her hair in a ponytail and wore a pair of earrings with stones that matched her dress.

To Athena's surprise, Suilla's dress wasn't yellow. Instead, it was cerulean with lighter shades of blue for her shoulders and gloves. Her long hair twisted into a pair of braids that stretched down to her torso. Suilla tugged at the hems of her dress and grumbled something about its color.

"Suilla, dear. Eyes up when greeting Father."

"Heh?" She raised her head, eyes falling on Athena. She shrank back behind Lucielle. "It's the scary lady."

"Did the scary lady hurt you earlier?" Lucielle asked.

Suilla shook her head but didn't look convinced.

"Then you have nothing to fear from her. Do you remember how to curtsey?"

Suilla shook her head again.

"Like this." Lucielle grabbed the hems of her dress. She dipped her head and bent her knees. "Now you try."

"Heh..."

Suilla bent her knees but lost her balance. She stumbled forward, and Athena jumped from her seat, catching her sister in a hug.

"Whoa there, kiddo. You—"

Athena didn't mistake the terror on her sister's face. She immediately let go, and Lucielle steadied Suilla.

"See, Suilla, she didn't hurt you. She helped you."

Suilla hugged her shoulders and tightly shut her eyes. "I want to go to my room."

"But, Suilla dear, we—"

"*I want my room*!" Suilla screamed loud enough to rattle the cutlery. Even the chandelier moved precariously.

"Klaus, please escort Suilla to her room," the emperor said.

Lucielle hugged Suilla and kissed the top of her head. "You were the prettiest princess tonight."

Suilla silently took Klaus's hand and followed him out the double doors.

Lucielle took her new seat on the left side of the table. "I'm sorry about that, Sophia. It will take her some time to adapt."

"What did you feel from her?" Athena asked.

"I don't think you want to know."

"That bad, huh? I'd try apologizing, but being around me only makes her worse." She groaned. "Was being a sister always this hard?"

"You should try being Olivia's," Makoto muttered.

"You know she'd never admit this," Athena said. "But she used to ask me for advice on how to be your big sister."

"I find it hard to believe Olivia would ask anyone for advice on anything," Makoto said.

"Introducing Count Edgar Sebastian von Kauneus and his son: Lord Richter Jonathan von Kauneus."

Athena perked up. *Uncle Edgar's jollity is what this table needs after the Suilla debacle.*

Uncle Edgar and Richter entered the dining room wearing matching light blue and white suits. Edgar twirled the end of his moustache.

"Ho, ho! It seems the rumors are true. How are you, my girl?"

Athena gave him a sheepish shrug. "Can't complain, Uncle. Turns out a warm bed beats a literal pigsty. The years have been kind to you too. You lose weight?"

Uncle Edgar chortled. "I should hope not." He slapped and rubbed his belly. "This is a symbol of my status. It'd be a shame to lose it. Though my son doesn't share my sentiment."

"Sorry to disappoint, Father."

"Hey, I can drink to that." Athena lifted her empty goblet. "To disappointing our fathers."

Only Uncle Edgar laughed. Athena frowned and set the goblet upside down upon the table.

"I see the seating has changed," Richter said. "Am I to sit beside Amelia?"

Lucielle shook her head. "There's been a complication tonight. But rest assured, cousin, the seat beside Makoto is occupied."

Edgar's countenance lost its jollity. "Rudolph, surely you don't—"

The emperor raised his hand. "Calm, brother. Our empress approves. We have gained two daughters this day."

"Ho, ho. Then this is a day for jubilation." Edgar patted Amelia's shoulders and sat beside her. "I can only imagine how excited you must be, my dear."

"Delighted, Uncle. You're quite happy yourself."

"Of course. Happiness is contagious."

Richter walked around the table and sat in the second empty seat from Makoto. "I suppose I'll be sitting beside Princess Suilla now."

"That a problem, cousin?" Athena asked.

"I don't see why it should be. It will take some getting used to is all."

"Introducing Countess Reina Erika vi Kauneus and Lady Margaret Sabrina vi Kauneus."

Reina wore the same dress from the tea party, while Margaret wore a stretched-out viridian dress.

Reina took her seat beside Richter. "Pleasure to see you again, Athena."

"Tis all mine." Athena raised her empty goblet. "Same to you, Margaret. I appreciate you letting me borrow your old robes."

Margaret flashed an ugly smile. "Ha—happy they fit," she said and sat beside the empty space next to Uncle Edgar.

"They fit well enough," Athena said. *So Auntie Jo still has a seat at the table even though she's half a world away. She and Father used to be close. Is that still the case, or is she part of the assassination plan?*

Her eyes shifted between Reina and Margaret. "My memory is a bit hazy on Auntie Jo, but I do remember playing cards with her. She never let me win."

Reina chuckled. "I don't doubt it. Mother balks at losing."

"Buh," Emperor Rudolph grunted. "Our sister's thirst for competition is a vice the same as any other."

Then hopefully she doesn't see that damn crown as a competition. "Speaking of thirst." Athena turned her goblet over once more. "I was ready to eat and drink an hour ago. What are we waiting for?"

"We told you that Olivia will be late but not absent. We have decided to wait for her arrival," her father said.

The double doors opened. Athena perked up only to frown when Klaus, not Olive, entered. Athena slumped against her chair. "Whatever you're working on better be worth it, Olive," she grumbled. "Any suggestions on how to pass the time?"

"You could always share a story," Reina said.

"Hoh? I do love a good story," Edgar said. "Please, Athena."

"Story, huh?" She grinned at the red-haired girl beside her. "Alright, this one's a favorite of mine. Let's go back fourteen years. Olive and I are at the lake house with our Thronsdens."

She tilted her thumb at Lucielle. "Mother is by the lake with this little scamp in her belly. And the old man is galivanting across the sea with Auntie Charlotte."

Klaus remained taciturn at the mention of his mother, and a forlorn twinkle graced Ephraim's eye.

Sorry, boys. Can't even tell a story without hurting someone.

Athena rapped her knuckles against the table in a rhythm. "Then I hear hoofbeats, and I figure the old man is back. Olive stays inside, and I ask Klaus to make her some tea while I investigate. And what do I find?"

"Oh!" Lucielle raised her hand. "You found Father?"

"Yes." Athena wrapped her arm around Makoto's shoulder and pulled her into a hug. "And he had this little ruby with him. I thought for sure he was having an affair, and you were his illegitimate child. He and I almost came to blows. Do you remember what happened next, Makoto?"

Makoto

Uncle Rudolph escorted Makoto and Ephraim on horseback to his family's vacation home—a handsome stone cottage perched on a hilltop overlooking a lake. A young woman greeted them at the bottom of the hill. Between her golden eyes and white hair, Makoto thought her an alien. She started yelling at Uncle Rudolph and accusing him of dishonorable acts.

"*Pardon me!*" Makoto shouted.

That caught the woman's attention. Her powerful golden eyes fixated on Makoto.

Beauty in strength, Makoto. Be strong. She stood before the white-haired woman with outstretched arms. "My name is Makoto. I am a strong and beautiful Kauneus princess, and I will *not* allow you to speak to my Uncle Rudolph like that."

The woman squatted to meet Makoto at eye level. "Oh? And do you know what I do to strong and beautiful princesses?"

Makoto's arms shook, but she held eye contact. *Be strong, Makoto.* "What do you do?"

The woman grinned; her distrust and frustration gave way to mischief. "I kidnap them!" She slung Makoto over her shoulders and started running.

Makoto screamed. Her fists pounded against the woman's back, and she kicked furiously. Alas, her struggle proved ineffective. She reached for her Uncle Rudolph and new friend. Neither of them moved to help or even showed concern.

"Why won't they help me?"

"Because they're waiting for you to relax and enjoy the ride." The woman stopped running and set Makoto on the ground. "You're wound up tight, little ruby."

"Little ruby?" Makoto patted her red hair. "I told you my name is Makoto."

"And I'm Athena." The woman pointed at herself. "And as your big sister, I reserve the right to call you 'little ruby.'"

"Athena?" Makoto remembered her father mentioning one of the princesses having that name. "So, you're not kidnapping me?"

Athena howled. "No way. Just taking you for some fun." She plopped onto her back and rolled around in the grass. "Are you having fun?"

Makoto absorbed her surroundings. The scents of wildflowers disarmed her. A gentle breeze rustled the petals and kissed her fingertips. She found herself reaching toward the lakeshore. It was so far away but seemed within her reach.

"Yes..." She cleared her throat. "I mean, it's pleasant and acceptable."

Athena condescendingly shook her head. "Alright, first rule. Don't bother with all that 'Beauty in Strength' pageantry around me. Just be you. Can you do that for me, little ruby?"

"Only if you agree to call me 'Makoto.'"

"I make no promises, but I'll keep it in mind." Athena hopped onto her knees and patted her sister's head. "So, *Makoto*, want to run through the flowers?"

Makoto nodded emphatically.

"Then it shall be done, my liege." Athena scooped Makoto onto her shoulders and started running.

The flowers released multicolored pollen as Athena dashed past them. The pollen glowed like pastel stars and floated out toward the lake.

"Having fun yet?"

"Yes!"

"You made me feel like your little sister." *A real sister, not just one from Avalon.* She lightly pushed away from Athena. "I also remember you promising not to call me 'little ruby.'"

Athena wagged her finger. "Never said I promised. Just that I'd keep it in mind. You were so cute back then. Now look at you—you're prettier than me. Trust me, I don't say that very often."

Makoto's posture improved at her sister's compliment. "I'm beautiful like fire," she said.

"Introducing Her Royal Highness Princess Olivia Elizabeth vi Kauneus and her retainer Ser Bastien Thronsden."

Olivia strutted into the dining room with Bastien in tow. Violet gloss replaced the earlier burgundy, though the rest of her attire remained the same. Bastien pushed a large cart, with its contents obscured by a grey tarp, into the dining room.

"I apologize for being late," she said. "Yet I am confident you will agree my time was well spent." She snapped her fingers at Bastien.

He removed the tarp, revealing two portraits. The first stood in a frame of platinum, while the second in a frame of gold.

The platinum frame contained a mostly monochrome portrait of Makoto in traditional Avalon clothing. The only color staining the portrait was the vermillion used for Makoto's hair, making it blaze like burning flame.

She held a pair of wooden weapons ending in curved blades approximately the size of her forearm. Makoto held one above her head and the other at her side.

The portrait in the golden frame depicted Athena standing before Zenith Palace. She raised a closed fist to the sky with the rising sun at her back. She held Aegis on her other arm and her father's crown upon her head. A flowing robe of crimson and purple covered the golden armor on her body, shining in the sunlight.

"Inspiration struck when I saw my sisters at tea this afternoon. I've been working nonstop since." Olivia took her seat at the table. "I'm exhausted, truth be told, but am satisfied with the results."

She gauged her family's reactions. "Are the results to my sisters' satisfaction?"

"To my satisfaction?" Athena said. "Olive, your work gets better every time I see it. This is incredible."

"I'm grateful for your praise." Olivia's eyes moved toward Makoto. "Your thoughts?"

Once more I am reduced to being their Scarlet Princess. Avalon's clothing. Avalon's hair. I only assume those to be Avalon's weapons. I bore the Orichalcum Crown upon my head, but tis only present in Athena's portrait. Unfit for a head such as mine.

Makoto's fingernails scraped against the scales. "What are those?"

"Kamas. Traditional weapons used on Avalon. They suit you."

Makoto's nostrils flared. "You think so?"

"Yes. The blades have an elegance I feel matches your personality."

"My parrying dagger tis equally elegant."

"Yes, but that hammer isn't. I don't think it suits you at all."

Amelia coughed. "Now that Olivia is here, when will dinner be arriving?"

The emperor snapped his fingers. Staff poured into the dining room with trays of food and drink. Makoto and Olivia held eye contact as their glasses were filled.

"You didn't color my portrait."

"I colored your hair."

"You colored *all* of Athena."

"Yes. I had a specific visage of Athena to convey."

Makoto glowered. "What were you trying to convey with mine?"

"I wanted to accentuate your strongest feature, so I left the rest monochrome."

"Strongest feature?" Makoto huffed. "The feature that points to Avalon, you mean."

"Precisely. Your heritage is unique."

"Unique?" Makoto hissed. "As a brand upon my body."

"Makoto..." Amelia reached out toward her sister. "I know Olivia meant no offense."

"Of course not," Olivia added. "I intended only to capture your natural beauty."

"You cannot intend offense when empathy escapes you," Makoto said. "You are selfish, entitled and oblivious to the feelings of others."

"Cousin," Richter snapped. "Your words—"

"Correct, sister," Olivia interrupted. "I am oft oblivious to the feelings of others, but I know yours well, Makoto. Your belief in the nobility of suffering aids nothing but your desire to play victim. By silence or accusing me of false slight, you gain comfort in others' pity."

Olivia snatched her goblet and raised it. "A toast to Her Former Grace—too fragile for orichalcum's weight. Revel in your fragility, sister. May it bring you peace."

She emptied her drink in one gulp and set the empty goblet upon the cart. "I do apologize to my fellow diners. The dinner table tis no place for savagery."

"*I am no savage!*"

Makoto's hand slammed against her dinner plate. Cracked porcelain cut into her bandaged hand and wrist. Attendants rushed to her side, but she waved them away. She pointed a trembling finger at Olivia.

"I am not your scarlet pet from across the water. I am not your little ruby either." She spared a passing glare at Athena before returning her focus to Olivia.

"I am more than an Avalon orphan *Father* took pity on. I am part of the Kauneus family—the same as you. The same as any of you." Her eyes swept over the other diners before returning to Olivia, her breaths shallow. "You will see me as such."

Olivia met Makoto's eyes without flinching. "Our grievances aside, I have seen you as nothing more or less than my sister since the day we met."

She snapped her fingers at Bastien, who delivered the portrait beside Makoto's chair. "Tis a gift. Burn it should that please you." She stood. "Excuse me, Father. I have lost my appetite. May I be excused?"

"Aye."

Olivia kissed her father's right cheek and exited the dining hall with Bastien.

Makoto clutched her bleeding hand. *Why did I react like that? It frustrated me, yes, but to that degree? I've had many a quarrel with Olivia, but she did not deserve such ire this day. What is wrong with me?*

She remembered the question she asked Ephraim the previous night. *What must be so wrong with me?* Her injured hand trembled, and her chest itched furiously. "I wish to retire for the evening as well, Father. May I?"

"Aye, you are no prisoner at our table, Makoto. Countess, how are the preparations?"

"Well, Your Grace. I will send a raven to the regent with my recommendations after the ball."

"Excellent." He stood with his goblet raised. "To Princess Makoto Clarissa vi Kauneus—born to Avalon's shores but raised in

Kauneus's cradle. A princess with a scarlet exterior and a heart of pure orichalcum. To *our daughter*. May her travels be safe."

"Aye!" Athena raised her own goblet. "To my sister. May she be happy."

Amelia closed her eyes and pressed her hands together. "To my sister. May our love for her be never in doubt."

Makoto folded her hands into her lap. "Such kindness is wasted on me," she said avoiding eye contact.

"Buh. You cannot demand respect but shirk when tis given." Her father downed his wine. "You may recuse yourself."

"Thank you." She stood, but her eyes remained downcast. "Athena, I'm sorry for—"

"No worries." Athena leaned back in her chair and pointed her thumb at the door. "We both know who you *should* be apologizing to."

Makoto nodded glumly and left the dining room. Incessant scratching failed to quell her discomfort but kept her focus off the outburst.

"Makoto?" Amelia called after her.

She flinched at the concern in her sister's voice. "No need to worry about me, sister. I'm—"

"Not fine. My skin prickles when I look at you. A deep ache claws at my heart. Do you really believe we see you as our pet?"

"No, Amelia. I..." Makoto took a moment to compose herself.

"I am viewed as the Scarlet Princess first and Makoto second. I am tolerated by many but doubt I am loved by more than few. It hurts, Amelia—as you say it aches. I should have learned years ago that silence abets the aches. Perhaps Olivia understands me better than I do."

Amelia's arms wrapped around Makoto's waist. "I'm sorry I failed to feel the depths of your pain, Makoto. But I'm sorrier I hurt you in the first place."

Makoto tensed but quickly relaxed in her sister's embrace. The warmth soothed her, and the itching subsided. "Thank you." She kissed the top of Amelia's head. "I needed that."

Amelia giggled. "My pleasure. I'll go tend to Suilla. I'd invite you to attend, but I suspect you have business elsewhere?"

"Yes. Olivia deserves my apologies. Give my regards to Suilla?"

"Of course." Amelia pulled away but squeezed her sister's hands. "You are loved, Makoto. More than you know."

Makoto's smile wasn't forced, but it wasn't happy either. "Thank you, again. I love you too."

Amelia returned to the dining room, but Makoto wasn't alone in the hallway.

"Ephraim," she started. "I doubt you'll want to accommodate my request, but I do wish to be alone."

"You can still be alone with your shadow. I thought its presence put you at ease."

"Precisely why I am dismissing you for now. I don't wish to be at ease when I meet with my sister. I think it will be more sincere if I'm alone. *Truly* alone."

"You're right. I *don't* want to allow this." He was silent for a few moments "Promise me we'll talk tonight."

"You have my word."

"Very well. I wish you luck."

It took her several minutes to reach the atelier. *No need for beauty or strength tonight. Be humble and accept your responsibility to her.* She exhaled, knocked twice upon the door, and waited for Bastien to swing it open. Yet it remained shut. She knocked again—louder this time. "Olivia? Are you in?"

"Depends on what you want."

Makoto flinched at her sister's tone, harsh and strained. "I want to see my sister so I can apologize properly."

The door cracked open with Bastien on the other side. She'd grown accustomed to him as a stern protector who dropped his guard to leer at her. So rarely had he shown outright disdain.

"My lady is many things, Princess, but she is not so heartless as you accuse."

"I know. Tis why I'm here."

Bastien held her gaze for several moments. Finally, he stepped aside for her to enter.

Makoto found her raven-haired sister standing by a wall of paintings. A half-empty bottle of wine dangled from Olivia's right hand.

"Well?" Olivia said.

Makoto said nothing. Measured steps carried her to Olivia's side. Black lines streaked from Olivia's eyes to her cheeks. Her breaths stayed short and staggered. Yet her complexion was less pale.

"Get on with it so you can ease your conscience." Olivia drank directly from her wine bottle.

Makoto clasped Olivia's shoulder. A wall of landscapes stood before her. The center frames formed a cityscape shrouded in mist. Silhouettes of man and beast prowled the city. The glow of their eyes piercing the veil.

"Is this Nova City?"

"Yes. One of the nights before Father cleansed the streets. This was one of the louder nights. The screaming and growling accompanied by that accursed whistle."

"You still remember Nova City?"

Olivia scoffed. "I never forget."

"I wish I could relate." Makoto approached the portraits in the corner.

An island floating above a sparkling blue ocean with mighty waves crashing against rocky shores.

The heart of a lush jungle. Trees with leaves like stars reached to place them into the heavens, and white flowers blooming in the sunlight streaming through the canopy.

"They're beautiful."

"Of course, they are, I made them." Olivia's arm wiped her puffy eyes. "Though I'm surprised to see *you* find beauty in Avalon."

Makoto didn't flinch at the venom in her sister's tone. "The quality of your work is never in question, Olivia. Its intent picked at a wound I let fester far too long. The 'nobility of suffering' I believe you called it. Tis not an incorrect assessment of me. We have our differences—we always will. But I will love you until my dying breath, and I am sorry for my savagery."

Olivia finished her bottle and dropped it on the floor. "Bastien," she barked.

Bastien grimaced but produced a new bottle. "I must insist, Princess—"

Olivia snatched it from him. She removed the cork with her teeth and spat it toward the window. "My acceptance of your apology is conditional."

"Name it."

"I hear Father will send you to Avalon as an ambassador. I wish to accompany you."

Makoto smiled, feeling genuine happiness this time. "Done. It would be my pleasure."

Olivia said nothing but offered the bottle. Makoto took a drink in solidarity.

"Eugh," she gagged. She expected a sweet or bitter wine. Instead, it tasted metallic and salty. "Tis vile."

"More for me, I suppose. So, when do we leave?"

Makoto swished her tongue in a vain attempt to rid herself of the taste. "I'm unsure. After the ball, of course. Countess Reina will work with her mother to prepare for our arrival."

She returned her focus to the paintings. "Though I don't suppose you need to see it in person. You've captured it perfectly."

"You're not the only member of this family to see Avalon, Makoto. I listen to Father's stories—I've painted several of them. I exchange letters with Aunt Josephine on occasion as well." She licked her lips. "Tomorrow's lip gloss is a present from her."

Makoto's hand brushed against the painting of trees and flowers. "I've seen this canopy before. I wonder if..." She closed her eyes and reached for the gem around her neck.

Makoto found herself inside the grove. Darkness leered and hummed around her. A ginger-haired toddler gripped her hand. A grown woman lay slain by her feet. A stream of crescent moonlight illuminated the woman's face. She knew it from photographs. *Charlotte Thronsden?*

Another woman loomed over Charlotte. Moonlight shimmered against her rugged face and silver hair. The blood-stained weapons in her hands matched the kama from Olivia's portrait.

"Kagura..."

"Who is Kagura?" Olivia asked.

Makoto opened her eyes. "I... I'm unsure." She fiddled with her pendant. "Someone I may have known from Avalon."

Olivia cocked an eyebrow. "Your memory has returned?"

"Not exactly. Names without knowledge of the person, but faces are becoming clearer."

"Try focusing on the name or the face then."

Makoto clutched the gem, but it wasn't Kagura she tried to focus on. *I wish to see my mother again.*

She closed her eyes and found herself running through a misty forest. Tangled feet made her trip. Ignoring the fresh scrapes through gritted teeth, Makoto scampered until she reached a grove with a great stone bird.

A pair of silhouettes circled each other without saying a word. Each of them passed under the silver light breaking through the canopy. The moon revealed a scarlet-haired woman wielding a pair of kama. *Mama!*

Unlike Kagura's metal weapons, Tamamo's blades were of bestial nature. The other silhouette remained dark. Their outline retained the haze of Makoto's other memories. She could not discern a form or a gender. All she recognized was an axe glowing under the moon.

The unseen partner allowed Tamamo to lead their dance but matched her step for step. They exchanged blows rather than words. A cacophony of clashing weapons filled Makoto's ears.

Tamamo ducked under the axe's swing, but a swift kick struck her face. She lost her footing, giving her opponent the opening to cut off her left hand. Makoto called out to her mother, but her voice died in her throat.

Tamamo gripped the kama in her mouth. She lunged, twirled, and slashed with abandon. Sparks flashed amidst a vermillion vortex. Losing her arm didn't slow Tamamo; it only stoked her inner fire. Makoto glimpsed her mother's face; the glint in Tamamo's eyes nearly sharper than her opponent's axe.

Alas, the axe *was* sharper. It plunged into Tamamo's chest, cleaving her open.

Makoto's hands shook. Her parched throat strained. She bounded to her mother's side and held Tamamo's bloody body in her arms.

"Ma... Makoto?" Her mother gasped. "Kagura, she—" A bloody cough interrupted her.

"No, Mama. Don't talk. Just rest. We'll get you fixed right up." She ripped a piece off her mother's robes to dress the wound. The azure cloth was instantly stained crimson. "I... I'll fix you."

"My darling." Tamamo's feeble hand cradled her daughter's cheek "Take care of—" Tamamo coughed again, spraying blood upon Makoto's face. "I'm sorry, my darling."

"No, Mama." Makoto clutched her mother's hand, flinching at its coldness. "It's not your fault."

Tamamo's smile ached her daughter's heart. A weak hand reached for the glistening gem around her neck. "Makoto, my darling, may I sing for you once more?"

"Of course, Mama." Makoto's tears splashed against her mother's face.

"Kuivaa kyyneleesi ja kohtaa pelkosi. Rakasta kuin tuli, kaikella mitä sinulla on. Anna tähtien ohjata sinut kotiin, kun olet eksyksissä. Olet kaunis. Olet vahva. Olen kanssasi aina. Rakastan sinua. Ole turvassa, rakkaani."

Tamamo's singing grew labored. She reached for her daughter's face, but her hand fell short.

"Mama?" Makoto cradled the limp body. "Mama, why did you stop?"

The silhouette's heavy breathing filled the grove. They spoke, but their garbled words remained as muddled as their figure.

"No, I don't want to remember you. I don't want to remember any of this!"

The dawn's light illuminating her mother's face blurred, ushering in the dark haze.

Makoto blinked and stared into Ephraim's familiar green eyes.

"Good evening, Makoto."

"Ephraim?" Makoto stirred and recognized the interior of her bedroom. *I was just in Olivia's atelier. When did I end up here?* "What happened?"

"I was going to ask you that question. Olivia says you passed out. Bastien carried you here. I've been at your side since."

Makoto flushed at the thought of being in those strong arms. "Not that I don't appreciate the assistance of either Ser Thronsden, but I am—"

"I swear to the All-Mother if you say fine I will scream." His eyes hardened. "The tightness in your chest, the scales, and now fainting. Not to mention your outburst at dinner. There's something wrong."

He regarded the pendant the same way he did the sulfur scrofa. "Where did your father say he found that gem?"

Her hands instinctively covered the gem. "From my mother. Why do you ask?"

"You've been ill since taking a liking to it."

"It's not cursed."

"And you know this how?"

"I... well, I don't believe in curses, for one."

"I find it better to believe in everything. That way I can be prepared."

Makoto glared at him. "I shan't let you take it from me, Ephraim."

He met her glare with a level expression. "And I won't. I wouldn't forgive anyone if they took my mother's legacy from me. I only ask you be cautious of its influence and consequences."

She relaxed but didn't let go of her pendant. "I had another vision."

"What did you see?"

"I was running through dark mists. I found my mother. She was with someone—I couldn't see whom. They dueled under the moonlight. Mother, she..." Makoto swallowed the lump in her throat.

Ephraim lightly squeezed her shoulder. "I'm sorry," he whispered.

She tapped his hand. "My past-self recognized the killer, but *I* could not see their form or hear a voice."

"You're sure it's a memory?"

Makoto recalled the vivid feeling of her mother dying in her arms. "Yes."

"Then we'll discern your mother's killer when we reach Avalon. But for now, I urge rest. You'll need your strength tomorrow."

"My beauty too," she said, halfheartedly.

"You always have that."

He stood, and Makoto grabbed his arm

"Ephraim, will you stay with me tonight?"

"Of course. I was grabbing a chair. I'm not going anywhere."

"Good." She released his arm. "Promise to get your rest too. I don't want you making a fool of me when we dance."

"Wouldn't dream of it."

Athena

Athena drove her bike down an old trail. Stars zoomed overhead. Her aura acted as a makeshift windshield, but she chose to let the air through. She relished the cool night breeze rippling against her body. *I missed this feeling!*

"Eyes front!" Reina shouted above the engine's hum.

Athena rolled the throttle for more speed and glanced back at Reina. "Say something, Countess?" she asked with a grin.

Reina's arms coiled around Athena's waist. "I need a drink," she muttered.

That's the intent. Athena craved a strong drink all evening. Her father returned the bike's key upon the condition Reina act as chaperone, and it be kept at Linna Varjoissa afterwards. *Reasonable terms. It would reflect poorly if I were found passed out in the street or missing a couple teeth.*

Athena howled and rolled back the clutch, slowing them to a comfortable cruise. "Guessing you've never given her a ride before. Not your speed or other reasons?"

"My unending schedule for one. It's also easier to communicate in a carriage's seats."

"You could always ride by yourself."

Reina scoffed. "Perhaps if my feet could reach the pedals."

Athena admired her own long legs. "Yeah, never had that problem."

The cousins reached Morgana's Court of Temptation within a half hour. Its looming sign dappled their clothes with neon. A second sign Athena had never seen hung outside her auntie's door.

"She's closed," Reina said.

Athena scoffed. "Auntie never closes." She knocked, and the door swung open. "See?"

She strutted inside. Gone were the dancers, well-dressed servants and loud music. Instead, three familiar souls occupied the bar. Uncle Bahamut held a drink in his disfigured hand, while her mother didn't touch the tall glass before her.

Auntie Morgana stood behind the bar fiddling with an abacus. All her eyes trained upon her siblings. "Don't you know how to read?" Morgana asked.

"Don't *you* know how to lock your doors?"

Morgana chuckled but didn't spare so much as half an eye on Athena. "Both your drinks are on the house tonight."

"Thank you, Madame." Reina dipped her head and sat at the bar. "I'll have the usual."

"Usual?" Athena echoed. "You come here that often?"

"For business, not pleasure."

Morgana beckoned a bottle shaped like a roaring dragon. It poured a deep red liquid into the countess's glass. Reina inhaled the scent of her drink and relaxed. She took a long sip and set a half empty glass onto the table.

Athena sat beside Reina. "I'll have what you're having."

"A drink at this hour?" Bahamut wagged his finger. "Like father like daughter."

"Really? Never knew him to be much of a drinker."

"He is quite blood thirsty," Bahamut said. "We do hope you appreciate his company while you're able."

"Is that a threat, Lord Bahamut?" Reina asked.

"No," he laughed. "Not at all. Merely a humble suggestion. Athena's been away from her family so long. She should *cling* tight to them and make up for time lost." He hugged himself and spun around the stool.

Morgana set a tall glass of crimson liquid before Athena. "We warn you, Athena, tis quite strong."

Athena took a whiff of her drink. Strong but not pleasant. *Smells like brimstone. Reina finds this relaxing?*

She took a curious sip and nearly spat her drink on Morgana's countertop. It was hot and gravelly, like how she expected molten earth to taste. It didn't feel any better on the way down. Her stomach felt uncomfortably warm and twisted in knots.

This has more kick to it than I do. She banged on her chest and burped out wisps of smoke.

"Enjoy your drink?" Reina asked.

"Eh, I've had worse." *Seriously, though, what is this kid made of?* She pushed the drink aside and leaned against the countertop. "So, Auntie, I notice your property isn't out and about."

"We were supposed to be closed."

"Even still, you don't keep the good stuff available for family?"

That got Morgana's attention. One full eye fixated on Athena, while the remaining halves remained on the other Enkeli. "We prefer to not wear it out before its next use."

"Fair enough." Athena swirled her finger around her glass. Even her aura didn't fully protect from the liquid's burn. "I can't help but wonder where he came from. I mean, golden eyes are *quite* rare. Ain't that your thing, Mother?"

Isabella remained silent.

Athena counted on her fingers. "Me. Big sis Lucy. Lucielle. Only people I've ever known that's got 'em. What do you think, Uncle? Seen any other golden-eyed scamps running about?"

"None besides Lucy's siblings."

Which means he is Mother's kid. "And how old do you suppose that prized property is, Countess?"

"I'd wager no older than fifteen."

"So not much older than Lucielle? Well, isn't that strange, Mother? Here I thought you and Father haven't shared a bed since she was born. Which would mean, the only way another kid would be born so quick is if you had an affair."

Athena shook her head. "No, that can't be right. After all, you threw a divine fit when you learned about Suilla. Damning her to that tower for having the *audacity* to be born when you had your own secret kid?"

She glared at Isabella. "That'd make you a hypocrite, right, Mother?"

"Foolish, child," Isabella said. "Claiming truth whilst grasping darkness."

Athena took another sip. *Never mind what I was thinkin' earlier. That burn feels good.* "Then enlighten your foolish child. Where did my little brother come from? Why did my little sister have to suffer all that time in her tower?"

"If clemency cannot satisfy thine gluttony, perhaps thou art unworthy of it."

"I'm unsatisfied, because I don't trust what I don't understand."

Bahamut clicked his tongue at her. "Then I suspect you don't trust much."

Athena tipped her glass toward him and finished its remnants. *It tastes a bit better every time. Maybe it's just an acquired taste.*

"Nostalgia for mine eldest," Isabella said.

Athena turned her head. "You what?"

Isabella's light flickered like a dying candle, and Athena felt a touch colder. Auntie Morgana regarded Isabella with surprise, and Uncle Bahamut appeared concerned.

"Thine temperament and potential mirror mine eldest. Nostalgia begot amnesty for thee and the sister thou struggled for."

I remind her of big sis Lucy? Maybe I'm not a disappointment after all. "And about my brother?"

"Our property is *not* your brother," Morgana said. "You will do well to remember that, Athena."

Athena's fists clenched on instinct.

Reina cleared her throat. "I think it wise not to anger the madame in her court."

Athena wanted to argue but thought back to tea with her sisters. *I've hurt a lot of people by acting without thinking. Reina's right. There's a time and place for this but not now. I'd rather not have Auntie after my head when someone else is after Father's.*

She let out a deep breath and relaxed her hands. "Of course, Auntie. My mistake."

"Fret not. We will forgive your mistake as our sister has."

Bahamut laughed. "It seems even a ravenous hunter can learn restraint. And as for you, sister." His crooked smile showed off the missing tooth. "Such magnanimity. Where did you learn temperance?"

Malice seeped into Morgana's eyes. "Centuries of coexistence with our sister."

"Oh, my beloved family. How I've missed you," Bahamut sang. "We should palaver more often." He feigned a yawn. "Alas, the night grows short, and the morrow grows closer."

"I agree," Reina said. "There will be time for merriment tomorrow. Athena?"

"No way you're tired already." Athena arched her back until it popped. "Maybe you're just excited for the ride back."

Reina frowned. "Do you take pleasure in spoiling other's moods, Athena?"

She snickered. "Just a bit." *I'm going to get a real kick from spoiling someone's mood tomorrow. First, I save Father. Then, I save my brother.*

Makoto

Each of the great constellations was engraved upon the atrium door. The Ashen Phoenix perched upon the Platinum Dragon's head. The twins—Gilded Serpent and Obsidian Octopus—entwined themselves in a waltz below. Betwixt the dragon's talons and the serpent's head was the Orichalcum Crown.

Vermilion and saffron carpets laid upon the marble floors. Candelabras with aromatic scents lined the walls. Savory and sweet hors d'oeuvre and sparkling drinks decorated the porcelain tables set about the room.

Quartets of paladins were stationed at each door, stairwell, and corner of the room. Their ornate armor and still figures gave the impression of a statute rather than sentry.

Makoto and her sisters stood at the atrium's second floor, near the balcony entrance, alongside the emperor. The Thronsdens, dressed in suits matching their princess's hair, stood behind. Athena and Olivia stood by their father's right shoulder, while Makoto and Amelia stood at the left. Suilla, who even Amelia couldn't coax from her room after last night's episode, remained absent.

Emperor Rudolph stood tall—a touch weary but proud as ever. He didn't wear his armor lest it interfere with his formal dance with his empress. Instead, he donned pristine purple robes with silver trimmings.

He was clean shaven this evening per his wife's preference, and his rustic cologne evoked the wilderness she was so fond of. He didn't wear the rings he often wore at breakfast, but the Orichalcum Crown remained upon his head.

Makoto's annual ball regalia consisted of two silk robes and a decorative sash. Vermillion flames colored the sleeves of her inner white robe with a dragon decorating the back. She occasionally wore it separate from the ensemble as a night garment. Twas comfortable but the fabric a touch too thin to wear around company without feeling exposed.

Olivia didn't share Makoto's concern. She lamented for years how the outer robe covered the watercolors. *"I'll not have you hiding my work another year,"* she'd said last year, demanding Makoto let her wear it.

Oliva wore the robe confidently. No surprise since her ballgowns oft used thin fabric or showed skin. This year's black dress matched her lip gloss and exposed her back with slits revealing her legs.

Makoto felt more confident tonight than in balls past but not brazen enough to emulate her sister. She skipped the powder this morning, choosing to flaunt her freckles, and her mother's pendant was proudly displayed.

She treasured her outer robe's deep blue color. Not only was she rarely gifted clothing without a shred of scarlet, but it matched the emperor's eyes. A small detail that made her feel connected with Uncle Rudolph through the years. *Perhaps this was a hint he always saw me as his daughter.*

Though Makoto's usual robes required a sash to tie them, her ball robes were each tied with a thin rope circling her back. Tonight's sash was purely decorative. Bright gold, speckled with white flowers. Chrysanthemums, she'd been told, symbolized nobility and longevity.

Amelia's pink dress lacked flowers but was no less ornate. White lace and ruffles trimmed its sleeves and multiple skirts. Little pink bows adorned the dress with one white bow at her collar.

Hardly surprising to see my sister wearing a cake. I wonder if she's dressed Klaus or Reina in this one.

Makoto cracked a smile.

"Glad one of us had reason to smile," Athena grumbled. Her white dress was pretty, albeit plain, but she couldn't stop fiddling with the sleeves or her choker.

"Not used to dressing up?" Makoto asked.

"It's tight but not in the fun way."

"What's the fun way?" Amelia asked.

Both Emperor Rudolph and Klaus shot Athena warning looks.

Athena winked. "I'll tell you when you're older. What I'll tell you now is I feel better in a suit."

"I think you look lovely, Sophia," Amelia said. Her eyes glimmered as she added, "I suspect Klaus feels the same."

Makoto chuckled. "Funny, I was about to say the same about Ephraim."

Athena snickered. "Only the two of 'em? I'm not good enough for Bastien?"

Olivia turned toward her Thronsden. "My sister asked you a question. You have my permission to answer."

Bastien grunted. "She's better for me than most."

"Better than Makoto?" Amelia asked.

"Amelia!" Makoto gasped. "Keep your silly questions to—"

"None could be better for me than Princess Makoto."

Makoto flushed. "Tha—that's quite the..." She cleared her throat. "Quite the compliment, Ser Bastien. Your praise flatters me." She caught the collective mirth in her sisters' eyes. "But if my sisters insist on teasing me, I may request mine own Thronsden act in my defense."

She turned to see Ephraim trying not to laugh at her expense. "On second thought, I may have him executed for treason."

"An execution you say? Here I hoped tonight be a bloodless evening."

Reina approached wearing a blended suit and dress. A black dress shirt with gold buttons and a red pauldron that ended in a long white skirt that covered her legs.

She exemplifies beauty and strength better than we do. Even her weapons were beautiful but strong. Rather than a saber, Reina kept a pair of ivory pistols holstered at her sides.

Powder-based weaponry was heralded as the future of marksmanship. In sooth, these weapons were rare and, in Makoto's limited experience, woefully inaccurate. Her father received one of the first, which he subsequently gifted to Olivia. Reina's were the only others Makoto had seen.

Unreliable but preferable to being unarmed. I pray there's no need to use them tonight.

Reina touched a hand to her chin. "Count Edgar and I may be busy with the dignitaries, but I can always arrange for Ser Ephraim's execution if necessary."

"Of course not," Makoto said quickly. "I was only joking, cousin."

Reina frowned. "Pity. I could have used the distraction."

Amelia giggled. "You're so funny, Reina."

Reina shrugged, amusing Amelia further.

Makoto bristled at them finding such mirth in her friend's death. Before she could retort, her father cleared his throat. Amelia regained her composure and stood at attention.

"Have you any business with us, Countess?"

"Yes, Your Grace, concerning your eldest."

He furrowed his brow. "What did she do?"

"Yeah, what *did* I do?" Athena asked.

"Nothing concerning, I assure you. I only think it wise for her to keep my company tonight. Several of the dignitaries and ambassadors haven't had the pleasure of her company in many years—if ever. Introductions, or reintroductions, are in order with Athena's return."

The emperor nodded. "There is merit to your words, Countess, but our daughter shall remain in our company for the early part of the night. We will leave her to her own devices afterwards, but she *will* keep decorum when speaking with our guests."

"Is this acceptable, Princess?" Reina asked.

"Perfectly," Athena said, cracking her knuckles. "I look forward to meeting each of tonight's guests in turn."

Makoto noted the edge in Athena's voice. *I doubt she'll feel satisfied unless she checks every guest herself.*

"Then I shall take my leave, Your Grace." Reina bowed and kissed Amelia's cheek before joining her sister, Uncle Edgar, and Richter at the atrium door.

Flowers embroidered Margaret's large yellow dress. An ornamental white flower adorned her long hair, which dappled the white flowers on her shoulders.

Uncle Edgar and Richter wore smart dark blue suits and black ties. The curls of Edgar's moustache were glossier than usual, and its tips extended to his cheeks. Whereas Richter's hair was tied in a bunch with twin pins resembling short swords.

Emperor Rudolph snapped his fingers, and the sentries opened the door.

Makoto expected Empress Isabella to enter first. Instead, Madame Morgana slithered inside. Golden wings clung tightly to her body, creating the illusion of an hourglass figure.

A retinue of attendants followed behind. Six pairs walked behind her in two straight lines. Men in black suits marched on her left with ladies in conservative dresses and heavy makeup on her right.

Morgana stopped to greet Uncle Edgar and Reina, but every half of her eyes focused on the rear window. Makoto suppressed a shiver. She saw the Gilded Serpent every year but never felt comfortable around her. History painted her as a greedy and vengeful creature. Even without Athena's warning, Makoto had little reason to trust Morgana.

Morgana drew a fan from her wings and snapped it open. Her attendants dispersed into six pairs, and another trio of guests entered behind them.

A young girl in a vibrant red dress arrived on the arm of a pale-skinned woman holding a parasol. The girl's golden hair and eyes resembled Amelia, though Makoto couldn't imagine her little sister wearing something so brazen.

The pale-skinned woman wore a white dress with a tulle collar and dangerously low neckline. A pair of painted red hearts adorned her cheeks with a larger one embroidered on her dress.

A wiry man strutted behind them, lute in hand. He donned an overcoat lined with fur that matched his hair and eyes. He winked at Makoto.

We'll have much to discuss, Lord Bahamut. Not only Avalon but that warning of yours.

She once more considered Morgana's involvement in the supposed plot. Her attendants carried no obvious weapons aside from their natural charms. *Unless that woman's parasol conceals a blade.* Makoto dismissed the thought as paranoia.

The next pair of guests drew an excited gasp from Amelia. A girl approximately her age entered with a much larger man on her arm. Makoto knew them as the Orabelle Queendom's crown princess and her illegitimate brother.

White patches mottled Princess Amira's right eye, throat and the backs of her arms. The dress's chocolate and cream swirls resembled dessert rather than ballroom attire. A crown of white-striped, brown spines lay atop her head.

Black spots speckled Prince Elias's grey skin and hair. He wore a white shirt beneath a dark blue vest with patterns resembling a swelling ocean wave. A cape draped from his left shoulder and tied around his waist.

A group of attendees from Nova City followed the Orabelle siblings. Makoto recognized them from the black feathers incorporated into their attire. Maxwell Thurston, a young artist and one of the city's council members, stood at the front.

He's the only councilman present. I've still yet to meet Representatives Pythagoras and Fairchild.

Other guests arrived in equally lavish or garish ensembles. Even the bishops Makoto spoke with yesterday wore larger hats and more opulent cloaks. *Perhaps Reina wasn't wrong to suspect them of lining their pockets.*

"The guests spared no expense. They wish to make an impression on you, Father."

"Buh. Like peacocks posturing for favor."

"Nah, I'd say they're like butterflies," Athena said. "Their opulence and feigned loyalty serve to distract from their true intentions."

Makoto clutched her pendant and prayed her sister, and Bahamut by extension, were overly paranoid.

"Sophia," Amelia scoffed. "You shouldn't assume the worst in people."

Athena's countenance soured. "I respectfully disagree."

The congregation parted to make way for a familiar figure. Empress Isabella silently approached the staircase. The white dress beneath her shawl was the same she wore every year. Its color matched her skin, making it almost impossible to discern flesh from cloth.

Amelia bubbled with excitement, the ruffles on her dress rustling incessantly. Olivia almost smiled—likely imagining a mural of this moment. Athena clenched her fists; frustration and doubt burned in her golden eyes.

If the guests are distracting butterflies, how does she see Isabella?

The emperor snapped his fingers. Every eye in the atrium—aside from two halves from Madame Morgana—fell upon him. His daughters took their places upon the staircase in order of their birth. Athena stood upon the first step, Olivia exactly one quarter of the way down, Makoto at the halfway point, and Amelia at the final quarter. His empress awaited him at the bottom.

Their father descended upon the first step, and Athena kissed his cheek. He repeated this with the other three until he reached his wife. He offered his hand. Isabella took it without a word. He led her to the center of the room. His free hand once more snapped its fingers.

Olivia's bow kissed the violin's strings. Her song's lullaby-like rhythm was chosen to elicit the intimacy of a dance between husband and wife.

Yet there was little intimacy to be found here. Emperor Rudolph feigned a smile, but Makoto knew her father well enough to see through it. Isabella made no effort to hide her disinterest in her husband.

Makoto thought of her own mother and unknown Papa. Had they danced upon Avalon's moonlit shores? Was such a dance cold or passionate?

A hand upon her shoulder startled her. She expected to find Ephraim. Instead, a larger man stood beside her.

"Shall we?" Bastien asked, extending an open hand.

Makoto's heart raced. "Did Ephraim put you up to this?"

Ephraim shrugged. "I *may* have suggested Bastien request your first dance and acquiesced when he did. Though," he paused to chuckle. "I should have reneged after seeing your freckles."

She considered scowling at his attempt to fluster her. Yet she couldn't deny her gratitude. "Very well." Makoto entwined her fingers with Bastien's. His hand was much larger than hers. It was firm, rough, and oddly warm. "It shall be my honor, Ser Bastien."

Makoto felt several pairs of eyes scrutinize her. *Beauty, Makoto.* Her gait was deliberately delicate and graceful, as Bastien led her to the dance floor.

"Do you know how to waltz, Princess?"

"I know the count but struggle with the steps."

"That's half the work. Think of it as a duel. Your objective is to keep pace with your opponent. Don't give them an opening. For example, if I step forward—" Bastien took a step toward her; Makoto reflexively stepped back. "Very good. Next I try your side."

Bastien stepped to his right with Makoto mirroring his movement toward her left. She slid her feet together to keep her balance, and he nodded his approval.

"Every duel has its rhythm. Ours will be one, two, three. Are you ready?"

Makoto squeezed his hand. "Of course."

They moved in a circle around the room. She matched his movements, though her timing was slightly off. He adjusted his own speed to accommodate. She appreciated it, lest she look foolish. Still, it wouldn't do to lose face in front of the guests. *Strength, Makoto.*

She repeated the count in her mind until she reliably matched his timing. The music's tempo quickened until the rhythmic beating of her heart matched the waltz count.

"We can rest if you require it, Princess."

In sooth, she was growing tired. She had the horses' assistance during the hunt, but her own legs were less durable. Still, she persisted in spite of the perspiration on her brow. Makoto tightened the grip on his shoulder.

"You will not be rid of me so quickly, Ser Bastien. Or are you afraid I will win this duel?"

His ensuing laugh rumbled through his body. "I dare not shame my mother's memory by denying such a challenge."

"Did Madame Charlotte teach you to dance?"

"Aye. My duel analogy is not my own. Mother had a friend from Avalon who likened combat to dancing."

She studied the contours of his rugged face. *Strong and beautiful. He—* She lost her concentration and slipped.

Bastien caught her in a tight embrace.

Makoto thought naught of beauty or strength in that moment. She was not a daughter of Kauneus or Avalon. She was a maiden in the warm arms of a young man she fancied.

"None could be better for me than Princess Makoto."

"Bastien, did you answer Amelia's question honestly?"

He hesitated a moment. "Yes."

"Then why have you waited so long to hold me like this?"

"Fears and doubts weighed heavy upon me."

"Such as?"

Bastien shook his head. "They are mine to bear, but your words last night convicted me. You are no savage, Makoto, but a strong and beautiful Kauneus princess. You should be treated as such, and it shall be my honor to do so."

An unmistakable smile graced her lips. "Thank you." She shut her eyes and relished the moment.

Athena

Athena's mother remained cold as always, while her father displayed performative affection. Whatever love he once felt for Isabella gave way to fear. She'd given amnesty to him, and Suilla by extension, but it could be revoked as easily as it were granted. *And from what she said last night, she only forgave him on a whim.*

Her sisters' emotions were less farcical. Makoto's veneer of dispassionate elegance dissipated the moment she fell into Bastien's arms, and she relaxed for the first time since Athena's homecoming. Olive was focused but serene; her passion felt in every note.

Lucielle made no habit of concealing emotions. She giggled, prancing around the dance floor with Klaus. He hunched down to hold both her hands but didn't return her mirth. *Maybe he'd enjoy himself a little if he didn't have to break his back escorting his partner.* A twinge of guilt nagged at her, but she ignored it.

If Uncle Bahamut is right then one of Father's guests wants to ruin this peace. Athena cracked her knuckles. *Who should I party with first?*

"Princess?"

Ephraim Thronsden offered his hand. "It seems you're without a partner. Tis my duty as a Thronsden to remedy this." He didn't fidget. Rather, he was relaxed and confident.

Athena rubbed the back of her neck. "Not that I don't appreciate your advances, kiddo, but I'm more in the mood for breaking heads than hearts."

Ephraim scoffed. "Do you think me so fragile as to break from one dance?"

Athena couldn't help but grin. He didn't have his brothers' builds, but she wouldn't call him fragile. "Alright then. If you won't break—"

She snatched his hand and pulled him close. She brushed her hip against his hand to gauge his reaction. His composure remained despite a slight blush. "Then you can keep me company in this den of vipers."

"I thought they were butterflies," he said.

"Handsome *and* he listens? Makoto doesn't know what she's missing."

Athena hoped ribbing with Makoto's name would get a reaction from him. His posture slightly improved but nothing else. *Maybe he really isn't interested in her. Should I ask Lucielle how these two feel about each other? Nah, that's low even for me.*

"The butterflies are the distractions, Ephraim, to keep us from observing the vipers. Let me give you an example." She cocked her head toward a Nova City guest flirting with a brunette attendant.

"Linnette isn't a servant—she's one of Reina's. Hiding in plain sight, so any enemy thinks there's less security. My guess is that crumple in her dress is hiding a knife."

"I understand." Ephraim opened his jacket. His tonfa and jitte were cushioned in each of his inside pockets. "The jacket is a butterfly, my weapons the vipers."

"Exactly. Now we just pick the viper from this kaleidoscope." Athena surveyed the attendees. *Aside from Mother, who here most wants to kill Father?* She grimaced. *It's probably a shorter list if I ask who doesn't. My sisters and their Thronsdens. Me, at least most of the time. I'm choosing to trust Reina and Uncle Edgar. Who else has the most to gain or biggest grudge?*

Auntie Morgana's left eye fixated on the emperor and empress, while the right was split between Athena and Uncle Bahamut. Her aunt invited her over with a wave of her fan.

Speaking of butterflies and vipers. The original emperor reduced to ruling an empire of sin rather than one of beauty and strength. How long does a grudge like that last?

Athena tugged Ephraim's hand. "I was supposed to come here with someone else but never heard back. Want to make him jealous?"

"Of course. Anyone foolish enough to spurn you deserves to know what they're missing," he said.

Athena snickered, and the pair approached Morgana and Bahamut. Morgana didn't greet them, while Bahamut bowed too deeply to be sincere.

Athena feigned her displeasure. "You wound me, Uncle. I was waiting for your escort, and here I find you with the most beautiful woman in the empire."

"Wounded? Then is poor Ephraim nothing but a scab?" Bahamut shook his head. "If either of us should be offended, Athena, it's me. I've been replaced at your right hand as easily as your father once replaced you."

Ephraim bristled, but Athena just rolled her eyes. She turned toward her aunt and bowed, lightly tugging Ephraim's arm. He took the hint and copied her.

"Forgive me for not addressing your first, Auntie. Uncle's slight against me, however small, needed to be addressed."

"There is nothing for us to forgive. Bahamut may not act the part, but he *is* our older brother. Outside our court, tis proper decorum to address him first." The half-eye trained on Athena's flicked onto Ephraim. "Aren't you the Scarlet Princess's Thronsden?"

"Aye, Madame. I'm pleased to be known by a being of such renown."

"Don't flatter yourself, boy. Tis our job to know our sister's family and its associates." She took a drag from her pipe, blowing smoky butterflies into the air. "Tell us, boy, why does your princess spurn our invitations?"

"She means no offense, Your Grace. Makoto prefers her father's company is all."

Morgana scoffed and blew a much larger butterfly. "Then she should enjoy her time with him while it lasts."

This time Athena bristled. *Uncle Bahamut said something similar last night. From him it's a joke but a threat from her. Is Auntie still testy I brought up Harley?*

"That almost sounds like a threat, Auntie."

Morgana rasped out a chuckle. "Despite your mother's blood, you still think like a mortal, Athena. We have no fear of time. We watched this mountain grow from a pebble in the dirt and will live to see it eroded. We have held grudges longer than your father has lived."

Her entire right eye looked upon Athena. "If we want to see him die, we need only wait." She blew a viper of smoke that consumed the large butterfly.

"Forgive my little sister, Athena—she's feeling a bit playful this evening." Bahamut strummed his lute and played a gay tune. "Her words express sympathy that His Majesty's daughters will one day see him die. Mixed, however, with a slight edge that Makoto chooses his company over hers."

Morgana didn't object and silently offered Athena her pipe.

Olivia played a final sharp note, and the song ended. The atrium rumbled with applause—Bahamut's the most obnoxious. Morgana clapped slowly. It was polite but for the disdain in her countenance. Athena put the pipe in her mouth and joined in the applause.

The emperor kneeled before his empress. She touched his shoulder and exited the atrium without a word. Athena caught the loneliness in her father's gaze. *Maybe the poor bastard still loves her after all.*

Morgana's tobacco tasted like Orabelle wine. It reminded her of Sententia, and she felt a pang of the same loneliness.

Unlike her parents, her sisters remained with their partners. Lucielle dragged Klaus toward Harley. They hugged and started chatting. Athena wasn't sure how she felt about that. *I'm glad to see they're cordial, but how does she even know him? She's too young for the Court.*

Athena gauged the woman on Harley's arm. Despite her enthusiastic applause, the woman blazing eyes and ear-to-ear smile were aimed at Athena.

Not that I mind being admired, but I can't tell if she wants to eat me or sleep with me. She took a moment to admire the woman's figure. *I really hope it's the latter.*

Makoto and Bastien gracefully walked across the atrium. Athena whistled to catch her sister's attention. She pecked Ephraim's cheek and winked at Makoto. She expected an eye roll, grimace or flush from her sister. Instead, Makoto smiled.

Damn, did I really misread them both? I'm losing my touch.

Bahamut pointed at Makoto with his missing finger. "Don't look now, Ser Thronsden, but the Scarlet Princess is replacing you as easily as Athena replaced me."

"Somehow I doubt anyone could be replaced as easily as you, Lord Bahamut."

"Well done, boy." Bahamut clapped Ephraim's shoulder. "You may not believe me, but I genuinely want to see that girl happy. Promise me you won't abandon her when she needs you."

Ephraim clasped Bahamut's hand. "On my life."

"Good. That means I can kill you if you break that oath."

"Such hostility, Uncle. I didn't realize Makoto meant so much to you."

"What can I say? She has my heart." He clutched his chest and twirled in place. "Speaking of which, she promised me a conversation." He winked and scurried in Makoto's direction.

"Athena," Auntie Morgana said. "A private word?"

Athena tapped Ephraim's back. "I'll be right back. Get us something to drink?"

Concern flashed across Ephraim's countenance, but he hid it with a bow. "Of course, Princess."

Morgana slinked into a corner with Athena at her side. "You didn't hear this from us," she whispered, "but there are rumors the Orabelle Queendom is not happy with your father."

That wasn't news to Athena. That tension led to her leaving Sententia. She pushed down the creeping loneliness to stay vigilant.

Prince Elias told an animated story to her father. Elias dropped into a fighting stance, threw a couple jabs, and fell onto his back. He and the emperor shared a hearty laugh, while his sister rolled her eyes and helped him to his feet.

Is his good nature a facade, or is Auntie's tip sleight of hand?

She considered their earlier conversation. Morgana's life was eternal but not her patience. There was no love lost between her and Isabella. Was she petty enough to kill the emperor and throw Kauneus into chaos to spite her elder sister?

No. Morgana's great loves are coin and control. She'd lose it all if she crossed Mother. Auntie is powerful, but Mother could kill her without trying. And if I'm choosing to trust Auntie, then I need to have a talk with Prince Elias or his sister. And there's my excited admirer. How does she play into this?

Athena cocked her head in that direction. "She one of yours?"

"Not quite. She's a Nova City socialite. She's been begging us to extend an invitation for years."

"Finally gave in? You're growing soft, Auntie."

"Hardly. She made her fortune at Representative Fairchild's casino. She purchased his invitation and paid to stay a few nights in my Court."

Fairchild's been on Nova City's Council forever but never attends the ball. I wonder what he's planning. "Wealthy and pretty? She's just my type, Auntie."

"Allow us to introduce you two."

Morgana snapped her fan closed. The sound carried throughout the atrium; each member of her retinue flinched. Morgana's fan beckoned Harley and his partner. The woman grabbed his wrist and bounced her way toward Athena. Harley tried to keep up but was mostly dragged behind her.

I used to drag Klaus around this room like that. Poor thing.

The pair reached Athena's side. Harley tried his best to maintain dignity despite clear exhaustion. Conversely, his companion had no pretenses. Her eyes gleamed and lips trembled. *Even my own family wasn't this excited to see me.* Athena snuck a glance at the woman's ample cleavage. *The feeling's mutual.*

"Athena, this is Dorothy," Morgana hissed.

Dorothy's hands lashed out, cradling Athena's. "Truly an auspicious day to finally make your acquaintance, Princess."

"Didn't realize I was so popular." Athena tried moving her hand to no avail. *Strong for such a dainty thing. Her hands are like an iron vice.* "Sorry if I'm supposed to recognize you. I don't owe you a debt, do I?"

Dorothy's giggle was almost sickeningly cute. "No. We have yet had the pleasure of meeting. Your reputation proceeds you is all. Oh!" She stepped back and let go of Athena's hand. "I apologize if I'm too brazen."

"Don't worry about it." Athena rubbed the back of her hand. *It doesn't exactly hurt, but it's not comfortable either.* She considered Dorothy once more. The gleaming eyes and energy begging for release. *Is this excitement or barely contained malevolence?* Even the parasol at her side seemed more threatening—like a sword ready to be drawn on a whim.

"Believe me, Dorothy, the pleasure's all mine."

Dorothy touched the painted hearts on her cheeks and turned away. "You flatter me, Princess." She nudged Harley with her hip. "Another comment like that, and I may leave with a different partner tonight."

That would let me keep an eye on her. Athena winked at Harley. "You up for a little competition?"

Harley scoffed. "It would dishonor Her Grace if her prized property refused *or* lost." He embraced Dorothy from behind. "I guarantee she's leavin' with me tonight."

Dorothy sighed. "I've oft longed to be the belle of the ball. Mother often told me stories of—"

"I hope I'm not interrupting." Countess Reina approached their group. She folded her hands behind her back and bowed. "Apologies for the delay, Your Grace, but the modifications to your table have been completed."

Morgana regarded Reina with half an eye. "Good, though your timing could use some work. Dorothy, we request you escort us to our table."

Dorothy frowned. "But must I? I'm having such a wonderful—"

"We shan't ask again," Morgana hissed.

Dorothy frowned. "I suppose I must." She cast a longing glance toward Athena before skipping alongside Morgana, who slinked across the atrium.

"It's been a while since someone looked at me like a piece of meat," Athena whispered to Harley.

"Trust me, ya learn to love it."

They shared a laugh, and Athena winked at Reina. "How's the evening, Countess?"

Reina rubbed her brow. "Stressful as always. Several of our guests are complaining or requesting accommodations they didn't think to ask for beforehand. Anything to throw us off kilter or show weakness."

Anything to distract from our real enemies. "What do you think of our Orabelle friends?"

"Oh, fish gossip." Harley rubbed his hands together. "I wanna know everythin'."

"This is a private conversation," Reina said.

Harley rolled his eyes. "Hun, I do all my best work in private. 'Sides, these lips are sealed. Nothin' escapes."

"I somehow find that hard to believe."

"Rent me for a night an' I'll make ya believe anythin'," Harley winked.

Reina remained unflustered. She regarded Harley for a moment before walking away.

Athena offered Harley an apologetic shrug. "Thanks for your company yesterday. I'd love to talk more, but I do need to debrief with Reina."

Harley returned her shrug. "Hey, don' sweat it. I know better than anyone how stressful it is bein' popular. Save me a dance later, an' we'll call it even."

Athena clicked her tongue at him and followed her cousin to a refreshment table. She popped a chocolate strawberry in her mouth, relishing the sweetness.

"It's funny you mention our Orabelle friends, Athena. I discussed Prince Elias with your sister yesterday. I've been waiting for a commitment from him beyond words of friendship."

"Judging from your tone, it sounds like he made that commitment."

"I do appreciate someone who picks up on my subtleties," Reina said. "Today's rumor is he's interested in a political marriage with one of the princesses."

"Really now? That's one way to make a commitment." Athena folded her arms. "Suilla is obviously off the table, and Amelia is too young. That leaves Olive and Makoto. Not that I doubt his charms, but I don't see him having much success with Olive. That leaves the little ruby."

Reina smirked. "I suspect wooing Makoto was the initial plan, but he'll make a move on you instead."

"Me? Why? I was only just reinstated as a princess."

Reina raised an eyebrow. "You're the biological daughter of both the reigning emperor and All-Mother. Your bloodline makes you the optimal choice."

Just like big sis Lucy. Athena grunted and rubbed the back of her head. "You don't think Prince Elias is a threat. What about his sister?"

"An absolute dream."

Athena didn't miss the sarcasm in Reina's tone. "You're not a fan?"

"She's a touch too sweet for my liking. Amelia, for what it's worth, finds her delightful."

Athena remembered her sister's excited squeal when the Orabelle siblings entered the atrium. "No offense, but I think I trust her judgment over yours."

Reina shrugged. "I won't begrudge trusting your sister, but I will advise against blindly trusting her power."

"You don't think it's infallible?"

"Is yours?"

No, it wasn't. The aura protected her entire body but could be broken with enough force. Trading it for Aegis granted her indestructible defense that left most of her body exposed.

"Fair enough. Better to rely on my own instincts. What do you say, Countess? Think it's time I meet the royal Orabelle siblings?" She admired Prince Elias. He was handsome but a bit too many sharp teeth for her liking. *If I play things right Dorothy could have a night with a princess and a prince.*

Reina cleared her throat. "I'm sure I needn't remind you to keep proper decorum, Athena."

"Yeah, yeah, I'll behave—"

"Sophia!"

Lucielle scurried their way clutching the hems of her dress. Klaus was nowhere to be seen.

"Lucielle?" Athena jogged toward her sister. "What's wrong? Where's Klaus?"

"It's terrible. You need to come quick. Klaus, he—"

Panic gripped her. Had she missed something? *Father and my sisters are all okay. Who could have hurt Klaus? Who dared hurt Klaus?*

"Reina, keep up appearances. Speak with the Orabelle siblings. I'll deal with this."

Reina frowned but nodded. "Keep me informed."

"Of course. Lucielle, take me to him."

Lucielle grabbed Athena's wrist and led her up the stairs, through the rear window, and onto the balcony. Klaus stood stone-faced as ever, though a slight tilt of his head betrayed confusion.

"Klaus needs a partner, while I socialize downstairs."

What? "Lucielle..."

"Gotta go, bye!"

"You little brat!"

Athena reached for her sister, but Klaus snatched her wrist.

"Princess or no, I won't have you assault my charge, Athena."

Lucielle waved and daintily skipped down the stairs.

Damnit. I've been concerned with the guests, but she's the most dangerous person here. She rolled her wrist. "Mind letting me go?"

He released her.

"Thanks." She rubbed her wrist. Klaus's grip was strong but gentle. Just as she remembered it. *Still second nature to let his hand through.*

Athena took in the view. The palace's lush gardens reached out to a far-off ocean that looked to be less than a stone's throw away. Dappling sunlight lit the water aflame. *It's beautiful.*

"Do you remember this place?" he asked.

"Zenith Palace? Yeah, I kinda grew up here."

He grunted. "Never mind."

Athena's expression soured. She leaned against the balcony railing. "Did I offend you?"

"No." The reply was terse but honest.

Not that I can trust my reads today. I misread Makoto, Ephraim. Even Lucielle pulled a fast one on me. How am I going to find a conspiracy when I don't even know my own family anymore? Better yet, how can I save my father if I'm too scared to say a proper apology?

"I'm sorry," she said before cowardice could silence her.

"There's no need to apologize, Princess. I said you didn't offend me."

"Not for that—well, maybe for that just in case. I mean I'm sorry for how we left things. How *I* left things. I said horrible things to you that night, Klaus."

He hesitated before speaking. "They hurt, but they weren't wrong—"

"Yes, they were! I knew you'd follow me otherwise. I damned myself trying to save Suilla. I wasn't going to damn you with me. You always deserved better than me, Klaus. As far as princesses go, I think your new one is an improvement." She chuckled. "Though I guess she has her own mischievous streak."

"I won't compare my charges."

Athena jokingly winced. "Ooh, bad answer. Girls *love* being compared to each other, Klaus. Just as long as we look better than our competition. Keep that in mind and you'll keep any girl happy." She patted his shoulder and walked toward the door.

"The first time we made love."

"Hmm?" She turned around. "What about it?"

"It was here. On this very balcony."

Athena folded her arms. "No, I distinctly remember it being behind one of the rose bushes."

"No, that was *your* first time. One of the wealthier boys from up north. Ours was right here." Klaus exhaled. He slumped and rested his hand upon the balcony railing.

"Father had taken ill. We didn't think he'd survive the winter. Mother's grief was harsh. Bastien and Ephraim too young to understand. I had to be strong for them. I couldn't let them see me falter."

His fingers were white as marble. "I came here to be alone, but you followed me. Never a moments rest with you."

It wasn't an accusation, but she still prickled at his words.

"You held my hand. Told me you'd think no less of me if I needed to cry," he said.

The memory came back. Klaus's usual taciturn expression marred by grief. Moonlight dappling his face. Shining eyes wet with tears that refused to fall.

"I kissed you. And you held me so fiercely as if you feared I'd leave you too." *And I did, didn't I?* "I promised I'd be there when you needed me. Your shield when you needed rest." *But I wasn't, was I?*

Stupid Athena.

"Athena..." His voice shook, and he didn't meet her eyes. "Did you ever love me?"

"I..." What answer would hurt him less? *My words broke him once. I can't do that to him again.* "I don't know. After that night, you were the only person I slept with until my exile. I was loyal, for whatever that's worth. But I don't know if I was truly capable of love back then."

"Are you capable now?" he asked, still avoiding her gaze.

She thought of time spent with Sen. Time removed from her father's judgment and mother's disappointment. The joy she felt every morning waking up to Sen's eyes. The blissful afternoons spent in her company. The passionate evenings in her arms.

"Yes."

A long silence followed. Athena hated silence. One of the few things she had no protection from.

Klaus faced her, his expression taciturn as ever. Shades of doubt or regret invisible to Athena's eyes. He pressed a hand upon his breast and bowed.

"Forgive me, but I've kept my princess waiting long enough."

Athena faked the biggest grin she could and curtseyed. "Don't let me interfere with your duty, Ser Thronsden. She's lucky to have you. Any princess would be."

"Thank you." Klaus stood upright and left the balcony.

Athena rested her head against the railing and stared at the ocean.

Harley

"Harley, I do believe that *I* am a genius." Amelia raised her glass. The shining gold liquid reflected her satisfied face.

Harley tipped his glass against hers and sipped. A touch bitter for his liking, but he'd had worse. At least he enjoyed the fizzy bite against his throat. "How ya figure?"

"Well, I told Klaus to wait for me on the balcony while I visited the privy. Instead, I grabbed Athena and told her there was something urgent. She realized Klaus wasn't with me and rightfully assumed it involved him. I led her up to the balcony and made my escape. Now they're reunited on this romantic evening on the very balcony they first confessed their love."

She smugly sipped her drink. "Eugh!" She gagged and dumped it into a nearby plant.

Harley snickered. "That's diabolical!"

"Diabolical?" Amelia gasped. "It's wonderful. Klaus's love for her simmers like coals in a hearth yearning to blaze once more. And her love is just the spark he needs."

Harley tossed a peppermint cake into his mouth. He frowned at the strong taste and spat it into the same plant. Another sip of the bitter drink washed away the taste. "Sure she loves him back?"

Amelia's brow furrowed. "Not quite. Sophia is impossible to read." She tried a piece of peppermint cake, and her countenance brightened. "But not to worry. Klaus is too lovable for her to reject him. He's handsome. Loyal. A great listener."

"Sounds more like a dog."

Amelia stuck out her tongue. "Everyone loves dogs, Harley. You'll see."

"Ya play matchmaker often?" He asked, splitting a cookie in half.

"I dabble." Amelia sandwiched the half-cookie between her remaining peppermint cake. "My friends ask me for advice."

Harley ate the cookie plain. It was moist enough to not require milk. The cookie and filling became goo almost instantly. *Mhmm. Finally, somethin' good.* "What's ya success rate?"

Amelia licked her fingers clean. "One hundred percent..."

Her satisfaction melted away. Pride turned to shock and then horror. Amelia's head whipped toward the staircase and balcony. Klaus descended the stairs ungraced by even a ghost of a smile. And there was no princess walking on his arm.

Harley drummed his lips. "Tough break, Princess. Guess ya can kiss that hundred percent satisfaction goodbye."

"But... it was perfect. He still loves her, I can..." She reached a hand toward Klaus but flinched.

"Ya alright?" Harley asked.

Amelia's teeth chattered. "He's... so cold. His coals smothered." The shock and disappointment remained on her face, but the chattering ceased. "I don't understand, Harley. How could that happen?"

He patted her shoulder. "Relationships are complicated. It's why I don' bother. Sure ya alright?"

She pouted but nodded slightly.

He took her glass. "Need a new drink?"

A smile returned to her face. "Yes, please. Something fruity."

"Shame we ain't at the madame's Court. I could make somethin' with enough fruit to turn ya orange."

"Orange? I'd quite like to try that someday."

"Eh, maybe not any time soon. Between ya big guard dog and family, I think they'd have my head before lettin' ya take so much as a sip."

Amelia giggled. "No, I wouldn't let them take your head. You're my friend, after all."

Harley almost blushed. "Still on that? Sure I'm not playin' ya? Ya read ya friend all wrong."

She puffed out her cheeks and jabbed a finger against Harley's chest frills. "I read him perfectly, thank you very much. But reading hearts is not the same as reading minds." Her finger retreated, and she flushed. "Sorry for poking you. Very uncouth of me."

"Ya know, ya might be the only person ever sorry for pokin' me." *Or to trust me. The madame always has to make threats.* "Thanks. I'll uh..." He clinked the glasses together. "Get ya somethin' fruity."

Harley sauntered to the nearest refreshment table and sampled various drinks. *Too bitter. Too sweet. Mhmm, this one's good.* He poured the second drink into Amelia's glass and refilled his own with the third one.

"Is that for me?"

Harley jumped at Dorothy's voice. She stood beside him, rocking back and forth on her heels. "Ya nearly gave me a heart attack."

"Apologies and salutations, chum." She took Amelia's glass. "Such a gentleman pouring me a drink."

"Uh, actually, this is—"

Dorothy downed the drink in one gulp. She shuddered with a sharp giggle. "I'm having a delightful evening. Everyone has been such great company."

"Glad ya havin' a good time." He leaned forward and whispered, "Jus' between us two, I think the eldest princess likes ya."

"Harley, you dog. You're supposed to fight for me."

"I'm supposed to make ya happy. An' from the way ya was eyin' Athena, that princess would make ya real happy."

"Oh dear. You noticed me admiring her?"

"Ya weren' exactly hidin' it."

A wistful twinkle consumed Dorothy's pale eyes. "I suppose not. For what good is love hidden behind a veil? My love shall shine brighter than even the All-Mother herself."

She laughed and wrapped an arm around Harley's shoulders. "Yet there's still one guest who eludes me. When may I make acquaintance with Ms. Suilla?"

"Dunno. She's probably still in her room."

"Could you escort me?"

"Why ya wanna meet her so bad?"

Dorothy pressed a finger against her lips. "A maiden can't reveal all her secrets, Harley. But if you're unwilling then I may have to forgo the meeting. Madame Morgana said you could take me to her. I do hate for her to be wrong."

Harley bit his lip. *If the madame gets a complaint...* "H—hey, I never said I wouldn' take ya." He finished his own drink, a delightfully tart strawberry cocktail, and hooked his arm around Dorothy's.

"Follow me, my dear."

"Here we have the, eh, hall o' pretty towels." Harley said of the tapestries hanging in the southern tower.

Dorothy clapped. "They certainly are pretty." Her eyes danced between them. "Which is your favorite, Harley?"

Harley shrugged. "Eh, Olivia's the art coni...-ah, what's the fancy word for expert?"

"Connoisseur?"

"Yeah, that. She's the one to ask about art. Any o' these strike ya fancy?"

"Hmm." Dorothy let go of Harley's arm. "It's hard to choose. They're all so expertly... woven..."

She approached a tapestry Harley recognized from a previous trip—the golden-eyed woman deftly wielding thread against a monster.

"Like that one?" he asked.

"Very much so." Dorothy placed her hand upon the fabric but quickly drew back. "Such resentment in this piece. Such sorrow. Lucy must have weaved it herself."

"Lucy? That's the hundred year broad, right?"

Anger flashed within Dorothy's eyes. Harley instinctively stepped back and pulled on his luck. The golden bangle remained intact, but he was running out of slack.

"The Centennial Emperor," Dorothy said, returning her focus upon the tapestry. "Mother has regaled me with so many stories of her life."

"Ya mother a historian?" Harley asked, hoping to distract from her frustration.

"In a sense." Dorothy giggled. She flexed her right hand, while the left pressed against the tapestry. Her fingertips traced the fabric, as she skipped down the hall.

Harley took a step of his own after her.

Dorothy twirled around, slashing her right hand across the tapestry. For a moment, all was still save for Harley's breathing and heartbeat. Then the fabric depicting the Centennial Emperor peeled off the wall.

Dorothy caught the torn tapestry before it touched the carpet. "Mother will be so pleased to see you," she cooed.

"Dorothy, what're ya doin'? Ya gonna get us in trouble."

"Doing what?" She draped the cut cloth over her shoulder. "Whatever do you mean?"

"I, uh..." Harley gulped. "Ya know, I jus' remembered somethin' the madame needed from me. Tell ya what. Go see Suilla, tell her she's beautiful, and I'll—"

"Harley." Dorothy's normally airy voice was a touch harder. She flexed her right hand again, showing off her fingernails' sharp glint.

"Boys who see too much or ask too many questions are liable to suffer accidents. I'd really..."

She rubbed her thumb and middle finger together. An awful sound of iron scraping against iron grinded in Harley's ears. "rather not see you suffer an accident." Dorothy paused to admire her nails before offering her hand. "Thus, I insist you keep my company. Otherwise, I won't be responsible for what finds you."

Instinct begged him to run. To do anything but take her hand. He felt the sharp edges of her nails across his skin just by looking at them. Her smile wasn't friendly anymore. It didn't convey a maiden falling for his charms or fantasizing of being the belle of the ball. This was a predator toying with its prey. She was daring him to escape—to give her a reason to pounce.

But he'd played with predators before. His patron, his clients. They were easy to placate once they revealed their true nature. *Play along, an' I won't get cut. Easy enough to understand. Sorry, Suilla.*

Harley took Dorothy's hand. Her nails weren't as sharp as he expected. They tickled more than anything. He led her down the hall and up the stairs to Suilla's room.

Dorothy rapped her knuckles against the door. "Pardon, but is Princess Suilla in?"

"Heh?"

Harley heard an exclamation of shock followed by the shuffling of feet against wood.

"No!" A scratchy voice shrieked. "She's not here and wants to be left alone."

Pretty sure that's her spider doll voice.

Dorothy was crestfallen. "Pity. I hoped to make her acquaintance."

I doubt this door would stop her if she really tried. "Allow me, darlin'," Harley whispered. He knocked twice. "Suilla, my grody pearl, I was hopin' to see ya."

"Harley!"

The door swung open, nearly hitting Harley in the face.

Suilla stood in the doorway wearing a fuzzy yellow dress. Purple streaks colored her hair, matching the color of her fingertips. A small green bow rested upon her head like a garnish upon a fancy dish. She would have passed for a princess but for the spider crawling across her face.

"I didn't want to leave my room, but Amelia still made me pretty. Am I pretty, Harley?"

"Beautiful—gorgeous even." He didn't have to be facetious this time. "I missed ya down there, so I snuck out. Wanted to introduce my date."

"Charmed and delighted."

Suilla shrank behind the door with her murky eyes peeking around the edge. "She scares me, Harley."

"What? Her?" Harley drummed his lips. "There's nothin' to be scared o'. Dorothy here wouldn' hurt a bug."

"Indubitably." Dorothy stepped inside.

"Heh?" Suilla scampered to her bed. "You promise not to hurt me?"

Dorothy curtseyed. "On my mother's name and honor. It won't hurt even a little."

She crossed the length of the room in a blink. Dorothy gripped Suilla's shoulder and chopped the back of her neck. Suilla crumpled to the floor with nary a whimper.

"Suilla!" Harley rushed to her side. She was unconscious but breathing.

"See? I kept my promise. Not one moment of pain." There wasn't a morsel of remorse in Dorothy's face or tone. "She won't wake up for several hours, which is perfect."

"What're ya gonna do?"

Dorothy giggled. "Harley, we just talked about asking too many questions."

He shut his mouth and gulped.

"Don't be so serious. I'm teasing is all." Dorothy laughed and roughly shook his shoulder. "I'm taking her with me."

"Don' think I'm supposed to ask where."

"Good, you're learning." She laid the torn tapestry beside Suilla. "Do you think she'll fit?"

"Uh... no?"

"I suppose she doesn't need to. It would have been more convenient to carry you three together, but I suppose I'll make do somehow."

Harley didn't like that last sentence but didn't dare ask for clarification. At best she'd threaten him for asking another question. At worst...

He reconsidered his earlier appraisal. Predators were dangerous—often enjoying power over their prey. But even the most ardent predators understood the food chain. Rougher clients understood certain acts against Morgana's property were taboo.

Even the madame herself refrained from taking advantage of the royal family. Predators sometimes toed the line, with varying degrees of success, but the lines were acknowledged.

Dorothy was a monster without compunction. Being a princess's friend or the madame's precious property wouldn't save him if her whims wanted him dead. His instincts told him to run once more.

He pulled once more on his bangle. It shattered.

Dorothy rounded on him. She caught him by the throat and pinned him against the door. Sharp nails dug against his skin, each one like a sword against his throat. She didn't cut deep, but it still hurt.

"You guaranteed you'd leave with me tonight, Harley. I'm holding you to that promise."

She leaned forward and licked a dollop of blood from his neck. Her body seized. "Self-control, Dorothy. Mother always reminds you." Her lips curled into a gleeful but blood-curdling smile. "Maybe one taste before the show starts."

Her teeth sank into his exposed shoulder. Harley tried to scream, but the hand on his throat silenced him. Color returned to her face, as she drank his blood.

He squirmed in place, but she was too strong. *Far* too strong for someone her size. His own body grew weaker, his breaths shorter. Coldness set in, as the time between each heartbeat grew longer.

His heavy eyes blinked once. Twice.

Then his eyes remained closed.

Athena

"You have the right idea, Princess."

Prince Elias stood at the balcony entrance holding a pair of drinks. He smelled like a salty ocean breeze. The scent was inviting, stirring memories of carefree walks on the sandy shores.

"Fresh air, an unbeatable view." His eyes lingered for a moment on Athena's backside. "Far better than the stuffy atmosphere downstairs."

She'd have reveled in that look a few minutes ago. Instead, she regretted it didn't come from another's eyes. *Damnit, Klaus. You couldn't make me feel emotional until after the handsome prince made his move on me? I should play along. I won't get any information if I spurn him. Plus I could use the pick me up.*

"Unbeatable view? You talking about me or the ocean?"

"It's the same view from where I'm standing."

Athena cracked a smile, thankful she didn't have to force it. "The view from here isn't bad either." She patted the railing beside her. "Care to join me?"

Elias sauntered toward her. He hopped on the railing and offered a drink.

Athena considered the glass. *If Reina's right about his intentions there won't be any poison. And if there is, I'll have a violent excuse to vent my frustrations.*

She gulped the drink. The only poison she tasted was alcohol. *A bit on the strong side but nothing like what I had at Auntie's last night. Prince checks out for now.*

Elias followed her lead, though he needed an extra gulp. "Not that I'm complaining, but I'm surprised you'd accept a drink offered by a stranger. Didn't your father teach you to be more careful?"

"My father taught me a lot of things I ignored. Besides, I have a pretty good track record against poison. And this," She tapped her empty glass. "was no poison I'm not already used to."

"And what if it wasn't one you're used to?"

"Then at least one of us would be in a heap on the ground."

"I'd rather both of us be in a heap on a bed."

Oh, he's good. He flashes another smile at me, and even my defenses won't hold up. "You're as tactless as you are handsome."

"So you think I'm handsome?" He smiled and offered his hand. "Handsome enough to accompany inside?"

Athena stopped herself from swooning. "Not to say no, but let's enjoy the fresh air a little while longer. Tell me about yourself, Prince."

"One of my favorite topics," he chuckled. "I'm a fan of art in all its forms. I have a few of your sister's paintings in my gallery. Quite talented that one. I've considered inviting her to my mother's palace for a spell. Tell me, Princess, what are your talents?"

She wiggled the empty glass between her fingers. "You just saw one of 'em firsthand. I've also got a mean right hook."

"Hopefully I won't experience that one." He gazed out at the water. "We live in a beautiful world, both above and below the water. I so enjoy the moments when I can escape and see it."

"I could drink to that." Athena raised her empty glass and pretended to drink from it. "And what's your favorite part of these moments where you can get away?"

"The pleasurable company I find along the way."

That sent goosebumps up her arms. "Don't go making me jealous now," she snickered. "Whose company could be more pleasurable than mine?"

"I think you can guess. Sententia tells me you two were quite close."

Athena felt a tightness in her chest and throat. "I hear she's doing well."

"I suppose she is. She shines quite bright without anything to block her light."

How does he know about that? Her fists clenched on instinct. *No, careful, Athena. Don't let him get under your skin.* She relaxed by admiring his figure once more. *Not yet anyway.* "Really? I imagine you'd be quite the distraction."

He shrugged. "I likely would've been if she accepted my advances. I tried courting her for a time. After the third rejection I finally took the hint. She remains a dear friend all the same."

He stood and rolled his shoulders with a loud crack. "I hate to be pushy, but it is getting dark, and I am rather looking forward to dancing with you."

"That's all?" Athena asked, as she took his hand. "I was hoping you'd ask for more than a dance."

He made no effort to hide his leering eyes. "Oh, I plan on it," he whispered in her ear.

He's dangerous alright but maybe not malevolent. Else he's the butterfly to his sister's viper. "Careful, Elias. You might just get everything you're asking for."

Athena found Olive standing beside Bastien, while Makoto and Ephraim chatted with Uncle Bahamut. Her father stood alone by a refreshment table. *Still no sign of Mother. And where is that little brat?*

She found Lucielle pacing in front of Klaus with her head down. *Hopefully he gave her an earful for the trick she pulled. I might just do the same.*

"You're scowling. Does that mean the poison is finally kicking in?" Elias asked.

Athena grinned. "Nah, just light family drama. You got any of that?"

"Of course, I'm the family bastard. A mistake my mother would rather forget."

A solemnity she hadn't expected clouded his eyes. She lightly tugged his arm to drag him out of any negative thoughts. "And your sister? You two close?"

"Dewdrop is wonderful. My best friend."

"I thought her name was Amira."

"Pet name. I call her Dewdrop, and she calls me Elly."

"Elly, huh? I kinda like that."

"Careful, she gets upset if someone else calls me that. I'm not sure even your defenses would protect from her poisons." His tone was jovial, but the jest didn't reach his eyes.

So his dewdrop is the possessive type. It'll be hard entrusting one of my sisters to him if they might get a spine in their neck. "Speaking of little sisters, mind if we pay mine a visit?"

"Introducing me to the in-laws already? You move fast."

Says the guy calling them his in-laws. "Course. These long legs help set a quick pace."

Elias didn't waste a moment admiring them.

"Hey, eyes up here, buddy," she said with mock frustration.

"Funny, I almost said the same thing to you on the balcony."

They laughed and descended the stairs. Athena led him towards Lucielle and Klaus. Her sister's pacing grew more frantic—the terror clear in her eyes. *She's not faking that.*

Athena let go of Elias and ran to her sister's side. "Lucielle, what's wrong?"

"It's Harley," she whispered. "He offered to refill our drinks but hasn't returned. I can sense his fear, Sophia, as if I'm standing on a crumbling ledge overlooking the abyss."

"Can you tell where he is?" Athena asked.

"This feeling is coming from the southern tower."

From Suilla's area? She's off-putting but not scary. Who else is there? She discerned who was missing from the atrium. Aside from her mother and Harley, the only missing person was Dorothy. *Another butterfly or is this the viper?*

"Is everything alright?" Elias caught up to them looking concerned.

Athena answered honestly. "I'm not sure. It might be nothing, but I'm going to find out."

"Do you need my help?"

Athena hesitated. *If going after Suilla is a butterfly to draw me out, I'll need people down here to keep my family safe.* "Nothing I can't handle on my own. But if you *really* want to get on my good side, then keep an eye on my sisters while I'm out."

"It will be my pleasure."

"That goes double for you, big guy." She said to Klaus.

"Ill shall not befall any of them."

"Good." She nodded to them and patted Lucielle's head. "I'll see you all soon."

Athena raced out of the atrium as fast as her legs would carry her, taking several precious minutes to reach Suilla's door.

Eerie quiet awaited her. No shuffling of feet or the weird 'heh' sound her sister made. She didn't hear Harley either despite how much he liked to hear himself talk. The only thing more concerning was the metallic stench of blood seeping through the door.

She thrust Aegis into the door and splintered the wood.

Dorothy stood in front of the open window with a tattered cape draped down her back. A pair of unconscious figures were cradled under her arms. She beamed at Athena's presence.

"Salutations, Princess. Oh, it does distress me so to leave without a proper farewell but—"

Athena charged, slamming Aegis into Dorothy's kneecap. Dorothy doubled over, dropping her hostages. She tightly shut her mouth, and the ensuing sound was more of a hiss than a scream.

Dorothy drew her parasol and thrust. Athena jumped back; the sharp tip missed her neck by a hair's breadth. Dorothy lunged, swiping at Athena; her nails raked down Aegis's face. Athena winced at the metallic screech, but Dorothy swooned.

"Music to my ears. I've long craved to sink my claws into you." Her second slash was deflected again by Aegis. "To test how impenetrable you really are."

Athena scoffed. "Please, I haven't been impenetrable since I was sixteen."

She lurched forward for a headbutt, but Dorothy grabbed her head with one hand. The fingers curled, cutting into Athena's forehead and cheeks like daggers. Dorothy giggled and slammed Athena onto the ground with enough force to crack a rib.

Athena coughed up blood and spit. She lifted Aegis just in time to deflect another parasol thrust. *How is she this fast?* She slammed Aegis into Dorothy's wrist twice before her head was free. *How is she this strong?*

Dorothy rubbed her broken wrist. "So vulgar. You fight more like an animal than a princess." She snapped her wrist back in place. Pleasure seeped into her countenance. Dorothy licked her glistening teeth, as she stared hungrily into Athena's eyes. "I couldn't be happier."

"Just what are you?" Athena asked between breaths.

"Me?" Dorothy beamed. "I'm flattered you ask but am afraid I have nothing new to say. I'm Dorothy." She twirled the parasol around her forefinger, slung it across her back, and curtseyed. "Mother sent me on an errand."

Mother? "Anyone I know?"

"No, well—perhaps?" Dorothy frowned. "Oh no, Dorothy, you've done it again and said too much. Mother told you not to get distracted. But here I am doing something *other* than what she asked."

Thank goodness she's a talker. I'm starting to catch my breath. "What are you here for?"

"This." Dorothy faced the window and stuck two fingers in her mouth. Her ensuing whistle was so loud it echoed outside.

Some kind of signal? But for who or what? It wasn't long before she heard the screams. Shock, pain and terror melded into a horrific cacophony.

"Who did you call?" Athena demanded.

"My lovely hounds, of course. My darlings should be ripping and tearing their way through the ballroom as we speak. Oh, Mother will be so pleased—"

Athena's fist smashed into Dorothy's nose. She dismissed Aegis and unleashed a flurry of blows. A right hook to the jaw. A left jab to the throat. A pair of uppercuts to the chin. Each one was faster and harder than the last. *Much* harder.

But Dorothy didn't go down. She smiled through the impact of each punch. Her incessant giggling fueled Athena's desire to shut her up.

"Why?" She broke Dorothy's nose. "Are you?" She fractured an orbital bone. "Still smiling?" She knocked out one of Dorothy's canines.

But that smile remained plastered on Dorothy's face. "You're just so pretty with my blood on your hands."

The next punch stopped short of its mark. Athena watched the blood dripping from her fist. It wasn't the first time she had bloody fists in this room. That she'd been consumed by anger.

I haven't even checked that they're alright. This is exactly what my sisters were talking about. Stupid Athena. Some protector you are.

Athena's eyes darted at the unconscious bodies on the ground. *I need to get them away from Dorothy and return to the atrium. Which means I need to take care of this problem now.*

Dorothy let out another sickening giggle. "You dropped your guard," she sang.

The tip of Dorothy's parasol pierced Athena's aura and stomach. It didn't hurt. If anything, it only annoyed her. *How'd I let her get the drop on me? I thought I was better at this. Well, at least she can't use her weapon if it's stuck in me—*

Pain seared through Athena's side, as Dorothy ripped the weapon free. Athena clutched her side; it was warm and wet. *Haven't been hurt like this in a long time. Almost forgot what pain was.* She started forward, but the pain kept her at bay. *Damnit. Wound is deeper than I thought.*

Athena managed a grin. "Credit where it's due. You're as tenacious as you are pretty."

Dorothy clapped her hands together. "You really think I'm pretty?"

Athena took a moment to admire the work she'd done to Dorothy's face. A swollen right eye, her nose split open, and several cuts to her cheeks and lip. "Never seen a prettier face."

Dorothy twirled in place. "Did you hear that, Dorothy? She thinks you're pretty. Oh, I can hear our wedding bells echoing in the distance." She raised the parasol's crimson-stained tip to her lips and ran her tongue against it.

The split halves of her nose melded together as if sewn by a tailor's thread. Her eye regained its shape. Blood flowed backwards into her cuts, and any sign of injury dissipated like smoke.

Athena was suddenly reminded of her father's old war stories about the monsters he slew in Nova City. Pale creatures appearing human but more feral than wild beasts. Thirsting for blood and drinking it made them stronger, faster, and nigh impossible to kill.

He called them cursed bloods. Athena used to call them hogwash. Now she wasn't so sure.

The glint of Dorothy's nails reflected in her gleaming red eyes. There was no playfulness on her face now. She was feral. Hungry. "You are exquisitely scrumptious."

Panic bade Athena throw another punch, but Dorothy easily weaved around it. She lunged and plunged her fangs into Athena's neck.

Athena's yell was more from anger than pain. She grabbed Dorothy's chin in an attempt to wrest the monster off, but the fangs only sank deeper. Strength left her. Athena could barely ball her fists, let alone throw another punch. She only stood because Dorothy propped her up.

So this is how I die. Unable to help the people I love. Withered. Weak. "Always figured a pretty girl would be the death of me."

"Dehh o' you?" Dorothy ripped her fangs from Athena's neck.

"Don't be daft. Mother forgives many of my eccentricities, but I doubt even I'd survive her ire if I killed you. I only wanted a taste is all. An appetizer before I can really enjoy you."

Dorothy swiped a finger across Athena's neck and licked it clean. "I have a delivery in Nova City, but then I'll be back for you. If Mother permits, we can play for keeps. Doesn't that sound lovely?"

Delivery? "You're taking the kids?"

"M-hmm but don't fret. I may nibble a little, but they'll be safe." Dorothy pecked Athena's forehead and retreated toward the window.

Athena stumbled toward Suilla's desk. She clung to it in a feeble attempt to stand, as Dorothy collected her little brother and sister. *Not yet. Not while I'm still standing.* Adrenaline surged through Athena's body. She grabbed Dorothy's cape and yanked.

But Dorothy didn't budge. "I'm ecstatic to see there's still fight in you, Athena, but I really must be going. So if you don't mind—" She kicked the side of Athena's head.

Throbbing pain pulsed from her temple to the rest of her skull. She clutched her head, finding it wet from blood too. Her vision blurred, but she could make out shapes. Shapes coalesced together and disappeared.

What? Did she take them out the window?

Athena scrambled forward until she reached the wall. She lifted herself against her body's wishes.

Dorothy's nails gripped the stone and brick, as she climbed down the palace walls. Suilla dangled betwixt her feet, whilst her fangs carried Harley by his scruff. Dorothy moved deftly despite the added weight.

I can't climb in my condition, and there's no way I'd survive a fall from this height. And I can't attack her without putting the kids in danger. She slammed her fist against the windowsill. *I'm sorry Suilla, Harley. I promise to rescue you both.*

The irony of the situation brought out a grimace. *Suilla finally gets out of this damn tower, and I'm trying to bring her back.*

Her burning abdomen demanded attention. The pain sharpened her awareness, returning her senses back to zero. Athena ripped the sleeves from her dress. She pressed the first sleeve against the wound and used the second to tie it around her waist. *That should stop the bleeding enough for me to not die.*

She turned toward the door and the ongoing screams.

Alright, Athena. If you can still stand then you've still got fight in you. Don't let that monster take another of your sisters. Her first step was more of a stagger. She buckled but didn't fall. *Dorothy better start praying to the All-Mother none of her hounds get my sisters.*

Athena limped her way toward the atrium. The abdomen wound burned with every step, but she pressed on until she reached the door separating the atrium from the southern tower. The screaming quieted a few moments ago. Whatever chaos raged within those walls quieted.

Please, let my family have survived.

The door swung open at her push, and she stumbled onto the atrium staircase.

Makoto

Makoto walked across the atrium floor with Bastien on her arm. She enjoyed their dance greatly and hoped it would lead to spending more time together. However, she had business with Lord Bahamut. *Where is he?*

A sharp whistle caught her attention; Athena kissed Ephraim's cheek and winked at her. *No doubt an attempt to rile me up. At least my outburst hasn't changed the way she treats me.*

Makoto smiled at Athena, delighting in her sister's incredulous expression. *I doubt she expected a calm response. But so long as he's happy, he can spend time with whomever he pleases.*

"You're quite pleased," Bastien said.

"A friendly jest between sisters."

He grunted. "I wouldn't know the feeling. Klaus is too taciturn for jests."

"And Ephraim isn't?"

"He's more your friend than my brother."

"You two aren't close?"

He shook his head. "We have no quarrel, but our time is rarely spent together."

"I suspect that will change when we embark for Avalon."

Bastien said nothing.

"It's rare to see a dragon keep company with a toad."

Makoto bristled at Lord Bahamut's choice of words. *Does he know about the scales?* She instinctively placed a hand upon her chest.

"Dragon, you say?" She tried to gauge if his words were a compliment or insult. *Strength, Makoto. Settle on the former.* "To what do I owe the pleasure of the compliment?"

"You spat brimstone at the church folk. And with the Orabelle?" He whistled. "I know a territorial dragon when I see one, Scarlet Princess."

"I suppose that makes me the toad," Bastien said.

"Of course, dear boy. Haven't you ever looked in a mirror? The resemblance is uncanny."

Bastien grunted but said nothing further.

"Don't pout because I'm stealing your princess from you."

Bastien stood between Makoto and Bahamut. "Is that a threat, my lord?"

"Not in the slightest. That girl may have many enemies, but I will never be amongst them. No, I'm merely making good on a promise to keep her company." He snapped his fingers and extended an open hand. "May I have this dance, Scarlet Princess? One dragon to another."

Makoto touched Bastien's shoulder. "'Tis alright. I did promise him."

"Very well. I should return to my princess's side."

"Better yet, bring her here. I'm sure she'd love to bend Lord Bahamut's ear when we've finished." Makoto took the Enkeli's hand but winced at his touch. It was beyond cold—like a hearth with the last embers snuffed out.

"One thousand pardons, Princess. I oft forget how cold I can be."

"How did this come about?"

Bahamut pranced onto the dance floor. "My sister cursed me."

"Morgana?"

Bahamut laughed once more. "No, my baby sister *wishes* she had that kind of power."

"Then you mean the All-Mother."

"Ah, quite the interesting creature that one. She's as much our creator as yours but *insists* we know her as our sister. Her equals. Yet we're all under the same porcelain thumb." He wiggled the thumb of his mangled hand.

"Are your injuries part of your curse?"

He sighed as deeply as he laughed. "Your ignorance of your home never fails to astound me."

"My home is—"

"Avalon will *always* be your home, Makoto." His words lacked their usual cavalier tone. "You feel it's call even now." He pressed his thumb against her pendant. "Else you wouldn't be wearing *that* so brazenly."

Instinct urged her to pull away from him. Indignation argued for the same. But curiosity begged her to stay in place. Presently, she found its call the most compelling. "What is this gem?"

"You wouldn't believe me if I told you."

"Are you being evasive or just coy?"

"Who says they're mutually exclusive?" He grinned, and his tongue licked the spot with the missing tooth. "As for these," he said, wiggling his four-fingered hand. "Every soul on Avalon knows their story.

"The Platinum Dragon fell for a young maiden. She was weak, but he cared for and protected her. He bestowed upon her two gifts when the war started. His fang and claw to keep her safe against the Orabelle King."

King? "The Orabelle have lived under a queen for centuries."

"Of course they have. The All-Mother saw to it there'd be no king after what our brother did to Avalon."

"So why did she curse you?"

Bahamut's hollow eyes chilled Makoto more than his touch. "Because when that young maiden lay dying in my arms, I gave her my very life. What I intended to be an act of pure love was seen by the All-Mother as an insult. She cursed me to live forever as one of the humans I so desperately cleaved to. And now I stand before you fangless and heartless."

Now Makoto let go of his hand. "You're a living corpse."

"Living is a strong word, Makoto. I prefer being a revenant in limbo." He sighed again, though with more mirth than before. "Alas, our time together is cut short."

A slightly crestfallen Ephraim approached with Athena nowhere in sight.

"I take it your time with my sister wasn't so well spent?" Makoto asked.

"It was pleasant until she sent me to get drinks. Then she disappeared on me."

"Abandoned by your escort twice in one night?" Bahamut clicked his tongue. "'Tis not your night, boy."

"And yet I find myself doing better than you, my lord."

"Hoh? Do tell."

"I may have been left by Princess Athena, but she saw fit to lend me her arm. Yet she discarded you as easily as Madame Morgana had."

Bahamut shrugged. "The honest words are always the most hurtful. And now that your arm is free, I presume your princess prefers it to mine."

"She does," Makoto said, taking Ephraim's his hand and reveling in its warmth. "But your company is appreciated."

Bahamut clutched his heart. "I've been spurned and pitied. My poor soul can't take such humiliation." He stomped away.

"I'm surprised to see you fancy him over Bastien," Ephraim said.

"I do not," she whispered sharply. "I promised to speak with him is all."

"What did the old lizard have to say?"

Makoto pondered how to answer. "He told me an Avalon fable and of the All-Mother's eccentricities. She's not one to be crossed."

"None of them are. Which reminds me, the Gilded Serpent wants you in her coils."

Makoto suppressed a shudder. "Whatever for?"

"She's jealous for your company or so she claims."

"Probably for this," she said, brushing her hair from her face. "I imagine I'd fetch quite a fortune. Don't you think, Ephraim?"

"I think it'd be rude to say no but inappropriate to agree."

Makoto chuckled. "What do you think I'm worth?"

His brow furrowed. "You're priceless. Impossible to value."

"That's a good answer," she said. "Though, I imagine Athena would take offense to not receiving a number higher than our treasury."

"I wouldn't doubt it," he said.

Makoto touched his arm. "I'm sorry it didn't work out with her."

"I didn't expect it to. Just a boyhood crush finally reaching its end. Speaking of crushes, how was my brother's company?"

Makoto giggled, despite herself. "It was lovely."

"Then should we join him and Olivia?"

Makoto almost agreed but something caught her eye. Athena and Amelia spoke hurriedly. She couldn't see Athena's expression, but Amelia was worried. Athena dashed out of the atrium without another word.

Athena was more worried about Father than any of us. She wouldn't leave without an emergency.

Makoto found her father standing by one of the refreshment tables. There were no princesses, Enkeli or Thronsdens by his side. No one to catch an assassin putting something in his drink or to intercept a blade. He was vulnerable, and her sisters were worried.

The Nova City guests flocked around Madame Morgana. Lord Bahamut fraternized with Olivia and Bastien. Princess Amira chatted with Countess Reina and Margaret, with her own eyes trained on her brother.

None of them are directly threatening Father. Are they innocent or Athena's so-called butterflies hiding daggers in their wings?

"We're going to my father," she said.

The emperor greeted her by raising his goblet. "Even an Enkeli's company pales to that of Ser Ephraim's."

Ephraim bowed. "Whose company did you prefer between my mother and the All-Mother?"

"We shall not say," he said with a chuckle. "What did you discuss with Lord Bahamut, Makoto?"

"An old fairy tale of a wounded dragon. Seems it's an Avalon legend."

"Aye. Your mother told us old Avalon stories during our campaign in Nova City. Perhaps we should have shared some."

"I suppose I'll learn soon enough." She clutched the gem around her neck. "I'm more nervous than I am excited."

"Buh. Tis no way for a once reigning emperor to hold herself."

"Strength and beauty, right? Or should it be humility and responsibility?"

"Neither. You are returning to your birthplace. Strip away the tassels of royalty and you will be left with yourself." He touched her shoulder. "And you, our daughter, are enough as you are."

Makoto didn't fight her smile. "Thank you, Father. Your words—"

The echoes of a sharp whistle cut her off. It was exuberant, like a songbird singing on the first day of spring. Yet Makoto found it haunting. Its chimes a ringing bell tolling doom for the hungry bird's prey.

Suddenly her father's old stories came back to her. *The song of a predator relishing their prey's terror.*

A wave of apprehension crashed over the atrium. The guests shuffled and whispered amongst themselves, but none sprung to action.

It didn't come from the atrium. Athena must be confronting our viper. Does that mean we're safe? "Father, we should—"

His axe was already in hand. "We know that sound well. It haunts our sleepless nights. Tis a harbinger of death."

He slammed Hämärä upon the ground. The impact thundered throughout the atrium. All attendees' eyes were upon him—including Madame Morgana's. "Retreat from the door and windows and brace yourselves."

A series of thuds sounded from beyond the atrium door. One. Three. Seven. The thuds increased with each second. Incessant scratching scored by low eerie growling followed each one.

"Is this a game, Emperor Rudolph?" The Orabelle princess asked. "I'm afraid I don't understand the rules."

The balcony door shattered. A creature cloaked in mist bounded down the stairs. Ashen skin as though baked in the volcano's womb. Its spear-like fingers forged within the mountain's belly.

It had no eyes, but the indents chiseled into its cheeks resembled nostrils. The sides of its head split to open its maw. Drool oozed from its lashing tongue; a wheel of teeth grinded around its cheeks.

It was grotesque. It was monstrous.

And its growl curdled Makoto's blood.

Her father rounded upon the beast. Hämärä cleaved through its skull into its throat, slamming the monster into the ground. Its flailing tongue lashed toward Makoto but was parried by Ephraim's tonfa.

Hämärä grinded against the ground. With a final jerk of his hand, Emperor Rudolph rended the beast's head from its shoulders. "Here is your rule, Princess," he said, lifting his bloody axe. "Survive."

The atrium door gave way. A hive of beasts swarmed the ballroom. Blood and screams filled the air, as the mists seeped inside.

Maxwell Thurston's head was ground to pulp inside a beast's jaws. Four fingers impaled one of Morgana's attendants and slowly splayed her chest open. A tongue wrapped around one of the Nova City guest's arms. The grip tightened and twisted until the arm burst open at the elbow.

The monsters sat on their haunches and lapped at the crimson shower.

Like hounds bred for butchering.

A familiar scream caught her attention. Amelia writhed on the ground. One hand clutched the side of her head. The other arm dangled helplessly at her side. But there wasn't a hound within spitting distance of her. Klaus made sure of that. Every punch he threw hit its mark and broke a limb.

Dear gods, she's feeling everything. How many deaths did she just die?

"Makoto!"

Ephraim pulled her away from a jabbering maw. He thrust his tonfa, cracking a set of the hound's teeth. "I know you want to keep track of your family, but—" He ducked under a slash of the hound's tongue. "I need you to focus, okay?"

Tis no time for beauty and pageantry. Tis a time for strength. She clutched the gem around her neck for calm and focus.

"Rakkaani," Tamamo's voice echoed in her mind. *"Pyhä Äiti kuulee aina rukouksesi."*

If I am a territorial dragon, then these hounds shall see a real beast. "Pyhä äiti, anna minulle lohikäärmeen voima!"

Hot platinum light emanated from her fist. It enveloped her body, creating a visible aura resembling a dragon's wings. Makoto felt *something* coursing through her very being. It flowed between her veins and the sinews of her flesh.

Despite the chaos surrounding her, Makoto felt a sense of calm. No, more than that. The doubts and frustrations shackling her had been cleansed. She felt healthy. Free!

And these monsters had the gall to threaten her and her kin. Anger burned within her soul at their audacity. The flames lighting the torches roared with her anger.

"Liekit, tule luokseni!"

Flames bloomed and streamed toward Makoto. They coalesced above her head into a burning crown. She preferred it to a crown of orichalcum. It felt lighter, more comfortable. And she felt *far* more powerful with it adorning her head.

"Get back, daemon!"

Makoto recognized Bastien's voice. He fended off a trio of hounds with his axe. Olivia stood behind him; concern shimmered in her usually unflappable eyes. Lord Bahamut was nowhere in sight. Not that he was needed.

"Sisareni ei ole saaliisi."

Bolts of flame burst from her crown. The bolts didn't strike the hounds directly. Instead, a circle formed around them.

"Polttaa," she hissed.

Wreathing fire blazed within the circle at the snap of Makoto's fingers. It consumed the hounds, forming a cocoon around their bodies. Melting faces melded into the gnashing wheel-like teeth. Satisfaction filled Makoto, as the daemons were reduced to cinders.

Such was the fate of any who dared stand against her.

Bastien stood aghast with sweat dripping from his brow. Olivia nodded her head in Makoto's direction.

"Takanasi," Tamamo's voice hissed.

Makoto turned to see a pair of hounds lunge at her. Such insolence deserved her ire. She reached behind her, feeling the mists curl around her body.

"Vesi, ole keihääni."

The mists froze, creating a lattice of tiny spears. One soft breath sent the icicles in motion. They spiraled and danced their way to pierce the hounds' throats with enough force to sever their heads.

Their bodies toppled; one of the heads rolled toward Makoto's feet. Her crown acted upon her burning disgust. One bolt was all it took to melt the head.

"Makoto?" Awe and concern crept into Ephraim's voice. "How are you doing that?"

She ignored his question. Her eyes found ten hounds pelting into the atrium from the balcony door.

Reina stood at the base of the stairs. Her pistols each fired once. Her shots were careful but not precise. She missed once and clipped one hound's side. Her oafish sister huddled behind her crying.

Makoto reached the stairs in two strides. Ephraim rushed to catch up, while Reina led Margaret away from the staircase. Unfettered hounds descended—daring to attack Makoto's family. Perhaps she needed a greater show of force.

The burning crown compressed into a coal small enough to fit in her palm. Makoto swallowed it whole, feeling the fire sink into her body.

"Räjähtää."

The coal burst within her. Flames swelled within her belly and rose to her throat. She opened her mouth and vomited a stream of fire. Most of the oncoming hounds were consumed and blackened by the fire's kiss, but three avoided her attack.

Their punishment would be most severe.

Something cold caressed her cheek. Its sharp kiss glided down to her throat. Pain radiated from her cheek and neck. She clasped one hand against the stinging areas and found blood.

Something hurt her—no. The glint of the bloody knife on the ground caught her eye. Someone targeted her.

The energy flowing within her ran its course. The light enveloping her shimmered and dissipated. Makoto reached for her pendant. The chain had broken; her mother's gem was gone.

All at once, she suffered the consequences of her actions. Her chest burned from swallowing and breathing fire. She coughed violently, hacking up smoke. Fear rained upon her, dousing her confidence. Her panic-drenched heart shackled once more.

She felt vulnerable. And there was no Ephraim in range to save her.

I'm going to die.

She faced Ephraim. "I'm sorry," she whispered, as the beasts descended upon her.

The first stabbed two fingers into her chest. The second's mouth grinded against her shoulder. Makoto writhed to no avail. Screams sputtered into coughs. She was helpless and weak.

I die neither strong nor beautiful. Only a fool one too proud to look away. She watched the third hound leap with open maw and extended claws.

And she watched as a larger beast's jaws clenched around it.

The hound's severed tongue flailed on the ground, spraying black blood. The daemon feasting on her shoulder had its head caved in by a scaly platinum tail, while her Thronsden tackled the one ripping open her stomach.

Ephraim wrestled with its gnashing teeth and wild tongue. He shoved his tonfa into its mouth, barring it from closing. His jitte pierced the hound's throat multiple times until it no longer connected the head and body.

He wasted no time dressing Makoto's wounds with torn pieces of his suit. "Where else are you hurt?"

"I... I don't know. Be careful. There's another beast—much larger."

"'Beast', she says. That's the thanks I receive?"

275

The voice was deep, regal, but she recognized its insincere tone. "Lord Bahamut?"

"In the flesh."

Makoto tried to sit up. A fit of coughing overtook her, and Ephraim eased her back down.

But she saw him. A being made of flesh and scales rather than stars. The shape of his body reminded her of a serpent, but the head was like a wolf with a cat's whiskers. Despite the blood and viscera strewn about the atrium, the platinum scales looked pristine.

The only flaw Makoto noted was a missing claw. *I suppose I'd see a missing fang if he smiled.*

"But your curse?"

He did smile, revealing more than his missing tooth. Her mother's gem was lodged within his gums. "Avalon's blessing trumps the All-Mother's curse. Quite a powerful trinket you had."

"Had?" she coughed.

"Of course. Anything lost so easily should not be so easily returned." He snorted a cloud of glittering smoke. Disdain filled his gaze and voice as he growled, "After all, what have you done to deserve it?"

She was at a loss for how to respond. What *had* she done? She fought with a power not her own, and even that wasn't enough to overcome her weakness.

I am capable of so little on my own. Ephraim saved me from the scrofa. Bahamut saved me from the hounds. I'm no dragon. Naught but a leech clinging to others.

The atrium reeked like a hospital after a plague. The smell overwhelmed her, and she vomited. *Weak. So weak!*

Bloody tears streamed down Amelia's deathly pale face. She hugged her knees while violently shaking.

Klaus was at her side holding her hand. "Princess, look into my eyes." He waited until she raised her head to continue talking. "Repeat after me. I am safe. No one can harm me."

Makoto couldn't hear Amelia's hushed words but presumed she repeated Klaus's mantra. Olivia crossed the room with Bastien and hugged Amelia tightly without a word. Color returned to Amelia's face.

Makoto caught Bastien's eye. He didn't hold her gaze long. She knew distrust and resentment when she saw it. *Just like that sailor's face in his final moments...*

Uncle Edgar's shoulder supported a bloody Richter. Reina's handkerchief wiped blood from Margaret's crying face. Anna slinked to her mistress's side with her hands in her pockets. A coat of frost dappled her right cheek and arm.

I must have gotten her by mistake. I wonder if she resents me too.

Her family fared better than the guests. Several of the Nova City attendees were dead. Entrails decorated the ground and walls like tinsel. Morgana stood amidst the viscera of at least four of her attendants. Her eyes scanned the room, seemingly taking stock of her dead.

Chunks had been taken out of Prince Elias's left leg and torso. He rested in his sister's arms. Princess Amira patted his head and cooed softly. She was slightly battered but otherwise unharmed. The hounds at her feet lie twitching with spines from her crown lining their necks.

At the center of it all stood Emperor Rudolph. A dozen slain beasts rested at his feet. Their blood dripped off Hämärä's blade

I don't need Amelia's power to know what he's feeling. Frustration at his failure to stop this. The embarrassment of it happening in his own home. Anger at whatever daemon planned this.

But there was something else too. Something she felt guilty for but felt nonetheless. *Pride in my fight. It wasn't on my own power, but I took several down and made it through.*

"I—" She coughed smoke and sick upon the atrium floor. "I survived." She thrust her hand toward him. "Now return my mother's treasure."

The dragon's eyes gleamed, though she knew not if he took pride or offense at her answer.

Footsteps echoed throughout the atrium, and a white figure approached the staircase. Makoto felt the All-Mother's unfeeling eyes on her and the Platinum Dragon.

A mocking laugh rumbled in his belly. "A good answer, Princess. Though even a bad answer would have netted your reward." Bahamut leaned down. His tongue wrested the gem from his gums, and he spat it into Makoto's hand.

She clutched it tightly, ignoring the slimy texture. She waited for the energy to return to her but felt nothing aside from the pain in her chest and throat.

The dragon's tail wrapped around him. The tip of his nose touched the ceiling, and he sank within his coils. The platinum melted, forming a puddle of flesh and scales. Lord Bahamut stood where the Platinum Dragon once had.

"I hope you appreciate the sacrifice I just made for you, Princess. Choosing your happiness over my beauty." He leaned beside her ear. "You'd do well to not lose such a treasure again," he hissed.

"I won't."

"Good. Ah, there's my dear sister. Between you and me, I think I should make myself scarce. I'm already an endangered species. Wouldn't want to risk extinction if she doesn't approve of my little stunt." He scampered off toward Morgana.

The All-Mother reached Makoto's side. "A hatchling but nonetheless a dragon. Thou hast honored thine blood, child." She placed a hand upon Makoto's injured shoulder.

The energy moving through Makoto wasn't empowering nor did it reach her spirit. Instead, it was soothing. Isabella's gentle touch mended her wounds. The dryness in her throat eased, and she drew breath without issue.

"Thank you, All-Mother." Makoto regarded the wounded. "Will you do the same for them?"

Isabella regarded the guests. "His Grace and family require space. Morgana shalt accommodate the survivors."

Morgana blew a trio of butterflies from her pipe. "We are not so crass to refuse our dear elder sister. The Court of Temptation's halls will be open to all. Its services at a reduced price."

"How generous, Your Majesty," said Bishop Lateo nursing a wounded arm. "I'm sure debauchery is the exact service we all need."

"Finally, someone gets it," Prince Elias croaked.

His sister hushed him but helped him to his feet.

Madame Morgana waved her pipe. "It's no concern of ours if you accompany us or not, Bishop. After all, those beasts will need company if they return for an after party."

Bishop Lateo turned pale and said nothing.

Morgana blew another slew of butterflies and slithered toward the door. "Follow us, if you please."

"And I'll provide the entertainment." Bahamut strummed his lute. "Free of charge but tips are appreciated, of course."

The majority of the guests followed without further hesitation.

Prince Elias, however, limped toward Makoto with his sister's support. "My apologies on the delayed salutations, Princess. I assure you I intended for us to become *very* well acquainted over the course of the evening. Alas, there was another who enraptured me. But after that display I may have fallen for the wrong princess."

Makoto was too taken aback to answer. It wasn't surprising to be passed over in favor of Athena. It surprised her he chose this moment to bring it up.

"Elias," his sister said sweetly. "Is this *really* the right time to propose courtship?"

"I can think of none better. We're alive and still in the prime of our youth. What do you say to joining me for a holiday under the sea?"

"I'm afraid the princess's travel plans are spoken for," Ephraim said.

Elias grinned at him. "It seems other things may be spoken for as well. Not that I've ever been opposed to sharing," he winked.

Ephraim's face remained taciturn. "Is there anything else I can help you with?"

Elias shrugged "Only a favor. Pass on a message for me. Tell Athena I didn't need to keep that promise after all. The Kauneus family and their attendants are strong enough alone, but they have friends below the water's surface."

"We'll be sure it gets to her."

"My good man." Elias clasped Ephraim's shoulder. "Perhaps we can share a drink some time. I'm sure you're quite the firecracker if we loosen you up. I'll buy the first round."

"Perhaps next time."

"I'll hold you to it, Ser Thronsden. Dewdrop, are you ready?"

"Yes, brother."

The Orabelle siblings followed the rest of the attendants behind Madame Morgana, leaving the atrium empty of all but the Kauneus family, their attendants, and the All-Mother.

Isabella's hand touched her husband's shoulder. "'Tis alright, Rudolph. Thine enemy hath not forced thee to bend thine knee."

"Did you know?" he asked. His voice was hoarse. Frail.

Isabella said nothing. She released his shoulder and turned her back.

Emperor Rudolph took three steps and then collapsed.

Makoto rushed to her father's side, cradling his head. His faint breath rasped against her hand. She remembered Tamamo's body growing weaker in her arms. Growing colder. *No. I just lost my mother for the second time. I won't lose my father too.*

Makoto pressed the gem against his chest. She searched for healing words in her mother's tongue but couldn't find them.

"Save him," she said.

Nothing.

"Heal him. Restore him. Cure him!" She growled.

Nothing.

"Please," she whispered through her tears.

But the power she felt earlier refused her plea.

Athena

Athena watched her father fall. Her sisters had appropriate reactions. Makoto rushed to his side to render aid. Lucielle wailed to the heavens from the bottom of the staircase, whilst Olive held her tight. Each of the Thronsdens stood behind their charges with their heads down.

But Athena stood paralyzed at the top of the atrium stairs. She felt no desire to cry or offer comfort. Failures had no right to do so.

Instead, she took stock of the atrium. Dorothy's hounds fulfilled their master's orders of ripping and tearing. *How many people could I have saved if I stayed down here? Would Father still be standing?*

She took solace, albeit not much, that the rest of her family appeared intact.

Uncle Edgar sweated profusely. The color drained from his face until he was almost paler than Dorothy. He clung to his son's shoulder. Richter's suit was tattered, and blood caked his right arm. Still, he stood by his father.

Margaret sat underneath one of the refreshment tables hugging her knees. Her large frame rocked back and forth, whilst Anna stroked her hair and cooed.

Countess Reina stood at the other side of a different refreshment table inspecting the goblets. She glanced in Athena's direction—the only person so far to notice her presence. The countess's usual composure gave way to apprehension.

Athena sensed the questions whirling in Reina's mind. *Where were you? Why weren't you here? Could you have helped?* But the countess held her tongue. She offered a solemn nod; Athena returned the gesture.

Reina snapped her fingers at Richter. "Gather a group of servants."

"What for?"

Reina rubbed her temples. "To help our uncle, of course. It won't do to have him lying in the middle of a bloodied atrium. He'll need to be moved, guarded, and attended to."

Richter wasted no further time arguing. He whispered to his father and ran up the atrium stairs alone, pausing when he reached Athena. "I'm sorry, cousin. Do you need assistance?"

Athena feigned a grin. "What? For this?" She lifted her hand from the wound. "It'll take more than massive bloodletting to kill me."

Richter didn't say anything. His eyes judged her for making jokes in this situation, and he ran off.

It's the last defense I have, kid. Let me hide behind it a little longer.

Athena skulked down the staircase; Isabella met her about halfway down. Her mother's countenance displayed the same distant expression as always. *Even her husband falling can't get a reaction from her.*

"Quite the party, huh? What did I miss—"

Isabella wrapped an arm around Athena's back, while the other hand gently patted the crown of her daughter's head.

"'Tis not the first time mine arms embraced a daughter grieving her father."

The tenderness of her mother's voice and touch pierced the last of Athena's defenses. Her eyes sparkled from the welling tears. "Did Lucy cry?"

"She wept for all her losses that day."

Athena thought about her own losses. The younger siblings she was too weak to save. The hearts she'd so stupidly broken. The years lost with her family. The ones she'd never make up with her father.

Athena's cry echoed throughout the hollow atrium. Her sisters finally noticed her—finally saw how vulnerable she was. Athena didn't want to be the big sister right now. She needed to be her mother's daughter.

Cry now, Athena. Let it all out. What you're giving in salt will be paid back in blood. Dorothy's. Her mysterious mother's. And anyone else they allied with. Father's Sanguine-Hands will be white as snow compared to mine.

"Art thou restored, child?"

"Yeah, I..." Actually, she did feel restored. Healthy even. Her pain and lethargy were gone. She touched the wound but found no blood or damage. "You healed me?"

"Yes, child."

"Why don't you heal him?" She knew the answer already but needed to hear it. *There's naught that can be done for the dead.*

"'Tis not mine life to save."

Athena blinked. "Not yours to save? Wait, is he still alive?"

"He hath been afflicted with nukkuva kuolema. 'Tis a slothful poison that will take time to snuff his internal flame."

Athena narrowed her eyes. "How do you know it was poison?"

"Sophia," Lucielle started. "Mother is not our enemy."

Athena pressed her forehead against her mother's. "How did you know?"

"Rudolph's body made its affliction clear."

"Why didn't you heal him?"

"Rudolph lost mine protection when he violated the Pyhä äiti. His sins caught him."

"Then why did you heal *me*?"

"Thou art an imperial candidate. Thine death would be a waste lest thou claim the crown."

Athena gripped the collar of her mother's shawl. "That's all I am to you? You act like a mother for the first time in years, because I'm a piece on the board. I should've known you didn't really care."

"Yet thou stand renewed. Just as Lucy did."

Athena's fist slammed against her mother's forehead. The cracking of bones thundered within the atrium. Blood trickled down Isabella's face, but her expression remained unchanged.

"Shall I heal thee again, child?"

Athena gritted her teeth. She ripped her hand away and massaged her bleeding knuckles. "No. I'll keep this one. Reminder not to trust anything I can't break."

She watched Makoto crying over their father's body, and her sisterly instincts kicked in. "How do we save him?"

Isabella opened her hand. A sparkling white flower appeared in her palm. "Mine husband's cure lies within Avalon's jungles. The ihmelääke's petals cureth all ailments and injuries short of death." She crushed the flower, sending sparks of light onto the floor.

So he can be saved. I was afraid she wouldn't give me an answer after I punched her. If Makoto is going to Avalon, then I can trust her to save Father while I save the other two.

Athena marched past her mother to join Lucielle, Olive and their Thronsdens at the base of the stairs. "You girls alright?"

Lucielle stared at nothing. "I've felt death before, but never so many at once." She reached for Athena's hand. "I can't feel Suilla or Harley anymore. Are they—"

Athena lightly squeezed her sister's hand. "They're on their way to Nova City. I'll be heading that way tonight."

Olive frowned. "You're leaving us again?"

"Afraid so. Someone has to save Suilla."

Olive grunted but said nothing further. She didn't have to. Athena didn't mistake the bitterness in her sister's eyes. *You wouldn't have to leave if you'd protected her. You've failed us all yet again.*

"Sophia," Lucielle started. "I'm demanding a promise from you."

"Oh? Making demands, are we?" Athena crossed her arms. "What do ya got for me?"

"Promise not to lose yourself, Sophia. I trust you to save our sister, but don't be rash. Don't hurt yourself in the process."

Athena showed off her split knuckles. "I won't make promises I can't keep. But I'll keep your words in mind, kiddo."

"I suppose that's the best I can ask for. Thank you." Lucielle's tone was despondent, and she didn't meet Athena's eyes.

She's not trying to hide her disappointment. I'm sorry I can't be better, kiddo. Athena kissed the top of her sister's head.

Klaus wore his taciturn mask well, but she knew how fragile he could be underneath. Bastien, meanwhile, didn't bother hiding his emotions. The anger was clear in his countenance.

"It's not your fault. You boys did your duty."

Bastien stiffened. "I performed my duty for my princess." He balled his large hands into fists. "But in its course I failed my emperor."

Athena touched his shoulder. "His Grace would have been shamed had you neglected his daughters in favor of him. You do him proud. Both of you." She tilted her head toward Ephraim. "I'll make sure he knows that too when I see Makoto."

Klaus dipped his head. "Thank you, Princess. Your words do us more justice than we deserve."

She shook her head. "Trust me, Klaus. They could never do enough."

His façade cracked—the hurt clear on his face. Lucielle took his hand, and Klaus regained his composure. "My brothers and I will see our duties through to the end, Princess. You need not worry."

"Good, because if I find one hair out of place on any of my sisters, the All-Mother herself won't protect you from me."

Klaus pressed a hand upon his breast and bowed. "We would not request her aid. Falling upon our swords or thine shield shall be our due penance."

Bastien mimicked his brother's pose. "I don't often speak for my brother, but Ephraim and I feel the same."

"Then I'll trust them in your care." Athena continued toward Makoto and her father, meeting Ephraim along the way.

"Princess," he said with a bow. "My condolences. I only wish—"

She pulled him into a tight hug. "Thank you for everything you've done for Makoto. She couldn't ask for a better Thronsden."

He was quiet for a moment. "Thank you. I'll be sure to live up to those words for the rest of my days."

"You will. You and your brothers." She patted his shoulder and approached her sister.

"Hey, little ruby."

"Hey."

"Mind if I sit with you?"

"Of course." Makoto wiped her eyes with her sleeves. "He's your father too."

Athena sat down and rested her elbow across her knee. "I think he was more your father than mine at the end."

"Hardly. You're the one who shares his blood."

"Yet both of us have his stubbornness." Athena nudged Makoto with a light chuckle.

Makoto's smile was ephemeral. "He spoke of his mortality startlingly often the past few days, even before your warning. Great help that was."

Makoto's words cut her to the quick. Disappointment cloaked Athena wherever she roamed. She didn't enjoy its company but understood it. Her sister's words were something deeper. The accusation pierced through the cloak into the heart.

You failed to save him. He'd be standing if you provided better information. It's your fault. Athena rubbed at her chest. *That hurt more than anything Dorothy did.* "Yeah. I didn't amount to much, did I?"

Regret flashed across Makoto's face. "No, Athena. I—I don't mean to blame you. The fault lies not with us. I'm just..." Her nails dug into her wrist.

"Frustrated?"

"Yes." Makoto relaxed her hands and set them in her lap. "Very much so." Her eyes wandered toward Isabella. "This would be so simple if she helped."

"Believe me, sis, I'm *loathe* to give her any credit. But telling us about the poison and cure is a big step. You were already planning on returning to Avalon. This just bumps up your departure date."

"Alongside adding stakes and a time limit. Neither of which I wanted."

Athena pondered that for a moment. "What do you want, Makoto?"

"I want to save my father," she said.

"Anything else?"

Makoto caressed the gemstone around her neck. "I... want to know more about the family I left behind. And..." She grimaced. "No, that's all."

"Sure? I won't share your secrets. Big sisters are bound by their promises, you know?"

Now Makoto's smile endured. "Thank you, but there's nothing else to share. And what of you? What does my darling older sister want?"

Athena answered without hesitation. "I want you tykes to be happy. All of you." Her foot gently nudged her father's shoulder. "I want this stubborn bastard to hold on a bit longer." She cracked her neck to each side. "And I want to bust some heads."

"Are you sure that's all?"

"Hey, no fair turning all my questions against me." Athena's laugh sounded hollow. "I want to stop making mistakes. Mother said I remind her of big sis Lucy. I want to live up to that pedigree by saving Suilla and Harley. Then I'll join you on Avalon to finish saving this one."

"When will you leave?"

Athena patted the closed wound on her abdomen. "I don't need to spend time resting anymore, but I do need to swap information with the countess. After that, I'll pack some provisions, get changed, and head out."

She cradled her sister's head and kissed its crown. "You're right, by the way. You're no 'little ruby' anymore, Makoto. You're a blazing fire, and you'll burn brighter than all the stars in the Platinum Dragon."

She pulled away, but Makoto grabbed her hand.

"You're bound by your promises, right? Then promise me you'll return home."

"What's with you kids thinking I won't—"

"Promise me."

Athena knelt and met her sister's eyes. "I'll make it back home. I promise."

Makoto released her. "Good. I'll see you on Avalon. Oh, before I forget. A message from Prince Elias. He said to tell you he 'didn't need to keep that promise after all. The Kauneus family and their attendants are strong enough alone, but they have friends below the water's surface.'"

Then hopefully I can trust him. "Did he make a move on you?"

"Somewhat. He invited me to an Orabelle holiday." She smirked. "He insinuated that he regretted choosing you first."

"Hey, don't tell me that. I can get cranky when I'm jealous."

The two of them shared a laugh.

Never been one for goodbyes, and I've regretted it every time. She leaned to whisper in her father's ear. "Enjoy your nap while you can, old man. We've got years' worth of accounts to settle once you wake up."

She swore she saw him smile.

"Athena," Reina called from across the atrium. "I hate to interrupt your bonding, but would you mind joining me?"

Perfect timing. "I'll be right there." Athena hopped to her feet, patted her sister's head, and joined Reina at one of the refreshment tables. She recognized the emperor's goblet in her cousin's hand. "Thought you preferred to drink from a flask."

"Believe me, I do. I could use a drink now for my nerves. Alas, it's empty." Reina set the goblet down. "I was checking for traces of poison, but the goblet is clean."

"How can you tell?"

"I am the countess of a cursed villa and a member of His Grace's imperial senate. I live every day in terror of an assassin's knife. I should hope to recognize traces of poison."

Athena crossed her arms. "Has anyone else shown symptoms?"

"No. Our assassin managing to poison only the emperor without touching his drink distresses me." She regarded Athena with thinly veiled frustration. "Which is why I don't appreciate you leaving the palace tonight."

"Don't trust me?" Athena grunted.

Reina scoffed. "I don't need Amelia's magic to read you, Athena. You loved and hated your father in near equal measure, but you'd be damned before trying to kill him. You will fight for your family's safety at the risk of your own without hesitation. And as I work to uncover the assassins' identity, I'd have appreciated that tenacity and dedication keeping *me* safe."

"Don't you have soldiers and a gardener for that?"

"Yes, and yet none of them can summon invincible shields with a flick of their wrists. As for my gardener, she will be staying with my sister tonight while I work."

Reina reached into her breast pocket, retrieving both a lighter and cigar. Her attempts to light it proving futile.

"Pass it here." Athena lit the cigar in one try. "Thought you didn't indulge in your mother's gifts?"

"Thank you." Reina took a long hit and exhaled a cloud of green smoke. "I make exceptions during exigent circumstances." She frowned at the emperor's body. "My condolences, by the way."

"Appreciated but hardly necessary." Athena cracked her knuckles. "He's a tough bastard. He won't be leaving me anytime soon. We won't let him."

"If only it were that easy..."

"You doubt me and my sisters?"

"Your family's tenacity isn't in question. I'll work on preparations for travel to Avalon tonight. I expected to do it soon, so there's already a tentative plan in the works." Reina twirled the cigar between her fingers. "Still, I urge caution. Even gods aren't immune to grief. Don't let it consume you should the worst come to pass."

Athena's knuckles reminded her of one god who was. "Who'd you lose, Countess?"

Reina shook her head. "No one personally. My grandmother—father's side, not the regent's, lost her husband decades before I was born. I see the zeal in her eyes when she speaks of him. Without him she's colder than a starless winter night. She'd have traded the world for his life, but he lost it all the same."

She ashed her cigar into the emperor's goblet.

Athena chuckled. "He'll hate that when he wakes up. Trust me, I'd know."

Reina smirked. "I'll be sure not to blame it on you." She took another long hit. "I'd like to hear your thoughts on potential suspects."

"You remember Dorothy?"

"I believe so. The exuberant young woman in Madame Morgana's company." She glanced at Athena's abdomen. "Is she the one who injured you?"

"She did a lot more than that. She took Suilla and Harley to Nova City."

Reina's brow furrowed. She finished her cigar and lit another without Athena's assistance. "One emperor's bastard and another's prized property. I suppose that excludes Morgana as a suspect."

"Agreed. Auntie would never agree to a plan that cuts a hole in her pocket." Athena pulled down her collar to show the scar from where Dorothy bit her. "What do you know about cursed bloods?"

Reina frowned. "Not much I'm afraid beyond your father's tales. You think Dorothy is one?"

"No doubt about it. She's too tenacious to be human. And she healed after drinking my blood."

"Gods... And here I was hoping for a relaxing evening." Reina ashed the cigar and offered the remains to Athena. "Did Dorothy refer to any accomplices?"

Athena declined the offer. "Auntie mentioned Dorothy got her fortune at Fairchild's casino. I'll look into him when I get to Nova City. Dorothy herself mentioned a mother a few times, but I—"

Reina coughed violently.

"Alright, Countess?"

"Fine," Reina rasped. She grimaced at the cigar. "Harsher than expected at the end." She tossed it after dousing the flame.

"I agree with you regarding Fairchild, especially since another council member was killed in the attack," Reina said. "Assassinate the emperor to destabilize the realm. Remove another councilman to take greater control of the city. It's a genius power play."

Reina frowned. "Though I don't know what he stands to gain by pilfering from Morgana. There are few beings I'd less want to be my enemy than her."

"What would he gain by kidnapping Suilla?"

Reina raised an eyebrow. "Isn't it obvious? He removes you from Zenith Palace."

"How'd he know I was here?"

"Likely the same way I did two nights ago. Word travels fast through the right channels. I suspect he wants to keep you as far away from your family as possible. What better way to tempt you than by dangling your little sister in front of you?"

"And leading me into a trap in his territory."

"Precisely." Reina smirked. "Apologies, but I must admire the plan. If I were trying to conquer the realm, you'd be one of the first pieces I'd take off the board."

Suilla took me off the board seven years ago too. She considered Reina trustworthy for giving her that information and accommodating her the past few days. Now she wasn't so sure.

Athena narrowed her eyes. "You're not trying to, are you?"

Reina didn't flinch. "Afraid not. I'm overworked as it is." She laughed mirthlessly. Her eyes moved toward the platinum puddle in the center of the atrium. "What of Lord Bahamut and our Orabelle friends? What are your reads on them?"

Athena didn't quite dismiss her doubts but chose to continue the conversation. "My reads have been terrible all day, so take these with a grain of salt. But Uncle B clearly knew *something*. I'm not sure if I should trust him for tipping us off or doubt him for not sharing everything. As for our aquatic friends, I can't speak for Dewdrop but do trust Elly."

"Sure you're not thrown off guard by his charms?"

She shrugged. "Can't ever be sure someone's legit until they break your heart."

"Even if they die first?"

"Maybe they just never got the chance to hurt you."

"You're as jaded as grandmother," Reina said. "She'd love you."

"Oh yeah? You should introduce us sometime."

"Doubtful. I haven't seen her in years." Reina massaged the skin between her nose and forehead. "It'll be a long night for both of us. I imagine I'll be burning oil long after midnight. I won't keep you any longer, Athena."

"What? No 'Former Highness'?"

"I don't see the point of titles now. You and I share the same rank. Imperial candidate. Speaking of which, I believe our cousin has returned."

Richter sauntered down the stairs with several attendants in tow. He stood beside his father and once again offered his shoulder as support. "They're ready to move His Grace. Are there any objections?"

"Mine husband shan't leave this room until the void in his wake hath been filled," the All-Mother said.

Athena bristled at the implication. "You're talking about a temporary emperor."

"Precisely, child. Thou shalt anoint one to bear the weight of orichalcum."

"I thought you picked the emperor," Athena said.

"Only if mine husband's slumber consumes him. The burden of selecting the crown's permanent home is mine alone."

"Well, any volunteers?" Athena asked her family.

Margaret gingerly raised her arm. "I... I believe my sister is best suited for such a role."

"Reina?" Richter scoffed. "Hardly. I nominate my father for the position. He's had decades of experience over the countess."

"Quantity does not equate quality, cousin," Reina replied. "My record of service speaks for itself."

Richter looked about the bloodied room. "Clearly."

Reina narrowed her eyes. "I accept your rebuttal. Unfortunately, the night's security was not prepared to fight daemons. I'll have that addressed in the future. Athena, is there anyone you'd like to nominate?"

There was. *Makoto and I are already spoken for, and it sounds like Olive is going with her. I'm choosing to trust Reina, but she's overworked as is. Uncle Edgar is too much of an unknown. That just leaves one person.*

She pointed at her nominee. "I nominate Amelia Lucille vi Kauneus for temporary emperor."

Lucielle gasped. Olivia nodded, while Makoto quizzically tilted her head.

"Not that I don't trust your judgment..." Makoto started.

"But why me?" Lucielle finished.

Athena gauged the reaction of her cousins and uncle. Margaret and Richter shared her sisters' befuddlement. Reina appeared amused but not the least bit surprised. Edgar's pale face regained some of its color, and his eyes gained a steely glint. *Uncle's finally ready to play.*

"As Mother said, Father's incapacitation gives us all opportunity to seduce her into anointing us emperor. And of everyone not embarking on a journey to save my father, Lucielle is the only one I trust to be completely selfless."

"No—not true, cousin!" Margaret sputtered. "Sister works so hard for her family—" She stopped once Reina raised a hand.

"Thank you, sister, but I'm afraid Athena will not be swayed by your platitudes." Reina regarded Amelia for a moment before asking, "How do you plan to keep your sister safe from further assassinations?"

Athena grinned. "You hear that, Klaus? Reina is doubting you."

"Then let us pray it will be her only mistake."

"Yes, forgive my foolishness, Ser Thronsden. Your record of protecting charges is spotless, after all." Reina stepped back with her arms folded. "The floor is yours, Uncle."

"I thank you, Countess." Edgar stroked his chins with a shake of his head. "You speak of trust as if you were immune from suspicion, Athena."

"Never said I was, Uncle. An exiled princess returns just as the old man gets poisoned *and* leaves the night of? If I didn't know better I'd say I was the most suspicious person here."

"You certainly have a lot to gain," Richter added.

Edgar nodded solemnly. "Rudolph and I had our differences, Athena, but I never once despised him. I need you to believe that I would never hurt him."

He's either devastated by what happened to Father or cackling behind the façade. I wish I knew him well enough to tell.

"And I need you to stop wasting my time, Uncle."

Edgar balked, and his moustache fluttered. "I beg your pardon."

"And you shall have it. Ten thousand pardons for a swift decision. My father needs rescue, and your concern is to argue with me over who should keep his seat warm. All in favor of Lucille?"

Athena raised her hand. Olivia and Makoto followed suit. Lucielle made a face but did the same. To Athena's surprise, Reina raised her hand as well.

"Reina?" Lucielle asked. "You too?"

"Of course, Amelia, I trust you. I'll concede Athena's judgment. Five votes constitutes a majority with the absences of Regent Josephine and Princess Suilla."

Isabella nodded. "Amelia Lucille vi Kauneus shall bear the weight of orichalcum."

"Great." Athena clapped her hands together. "Pleasure doing business with you, Reina."

"Likewise."

They shook hands, and Athena jogged toward Lucielle and Klaus. Her sister was unusually pensive, though Athena understood given the circumstances.

"You really trust me with the empire?"

Athena knelt down and grasped her sister's shoulders. "I'd trust you with the whole world. Your ability will guide you through this mess better than the rest of us. I have my own suspicions, but I'll advise you to not trust *anyone* your power hasn't cleared."

Lucielle pouted. "It's a lot of pressure, Sophia."

"Don't I know it. But I also know that pressure makes diamonds. And you're going to shine brighter than all the gems in Mount Kauneus, *Your Grace*."

She frowned. "I think that sounds worse than 'kiddo.'"

"And I promise to stop calling you that once I get back."

Lucielle giggled. "I'll hold you to your word—" A long yawn interrupted her. She covered her mouth with a slight flush. "Pardon me, Sophia. Tis been a long day."

"That it has. I imagine tomorrow will be even longer. Get yourself some sleep."

Her sister tightly hugged her. "I'll make you proud, Sophia."

Athena hugged with one arm and patted her sister's head with the other. "You already have." *That's everyone I needed to speak with.* "Wish me luck?"

"You won't need it," Lucielle said. "Luck is for those who lack the necessary skill."

"Look at you already sounding the part of an emperor."

Athena ruffled her little sister's hair and jogged out the atrium. She didn't spare another glance for her sisters or father lest they slow her down. There was a daemon to catch, after all. Not a moment to waste.

Her feet carried her to Linna Varjoissa. Not a soul was present—not even the ravens. Only the Ashen Phoenix constellation greeted her from the heavens.

Alone again already? Usually takes longer than a couple nights.

It was quiet out. Not eerie but peaceful. Moonbeams kissed her arms and forehead. The cool night air caressed her hair. These moments of serenity used to mean so much to her. Where she could bask in the moonlight away from stress and expectation.

Silence grew deafening over the years. Serenity turned to loneliness. It ate away at her heart, leaving a pit at its core. Her sisters' laughter drowned out the silence. Their joy filled that pit. A deep ache set in now that they were nowhere in sight.

I don't remember loneliness hurting this much. It'll hurt more if I dawdle.

It hadn't taken her long to get ready. The tattered dress replaced with a form-fitting top, shorts, and a jacket. The clothes were more comfortable to move in, and her powers made up for the lack of protection. She slung a sack over her shoulder with enough food for a couple days and enough coin for a few more.

And as Athena stood beside her bike, it only now dawned on her that Reina still had the key. *Stupid Athena.*

"Having trouble with the engine?" Olive stood a few paces away holding a long black key with Bastien just behind her. "Reina said you might need this."

Athena chuckled. "Thanks, sis." She stepped forward, but Olive pocketed the key. "Something wrong?"

Olive scowled. "We've only just reunited, but here you are preparing to leave me again."

Athena winced. "I don't want to, Olive, but Suilla's been taken. Harley too. I'll need to leave by tonight to have a chance of making up time—"

"Why is she more important than me?" Olive snapped.

"She—what?" Athena was taken aback by her sister's outburst. "No. I don't have a sister ranking."

"Then why are you always leaving me for her? She doesn't appreciate what you did for her, Athena, let alone like you." Olive openly glared at her elder sister. "How can you think she's worth it?"

Pangs of nostalgia ached Athena's heart. *The kids probably only know the reserved, artistic Olive. Petulant and emotional are how I remember her best. This is my Olive. The one who taught me how to be a big sister.*

"The same reason you were worth it all those years ago. I recall you not liking me much either for taking Father's attention."

Olive averted her eyes. "That was different. I had to adjust to having a family."

"Sure it's that different from Suilla?" Athena walked forward, and Olive didn't retreat. "It doesn't matter if she likes me or not. It's my job to look after her."

Olive's hands trembled at her sides. "But I *love* you. Just as Makoto and Amelia do. Why won't you look after us when we need you too?"

Athena cracked a grin. "Because I can trust you knuckleheads to be strong while I'm gone. And I can rely on the Thronsdens to pick up the slack," she said with a wink at Bastien.

Olive's eyes glinted in the moonlight. "Consider my proposal. The three of us save Suilla and Harley together before journeying to Avalon for Father's flower. Amelia stays behind to handle the empire's affairs."

Her sister's eyes pleaded with her. *Don't abandon me again. I just lost Father; I can't lose you too.*

Athena imagined the misadventures she could get into with her sisters. *A road trip without loneliness would be a nice change of pace.*

"Tempting offer, but I have to decline. Our best option is to divide and conquer. Otherwise we may run out of time on both ends. Trust me, I can travel faster by myself."

Olive winced. "So we're a burden to you?"

"Not a burden, just extra weight. Besides, you've been Makoto's big sister seven years longer than I have. She'll need you more than ever."

Olive sighed. "I did promise her my company. I can't imagine how she'll fare without my steady temperament."

Athena cackled. "Words I never expected to describe you."

Her little sister smiled and offered the key. "You're sure you'd rather go alone?"

Athena ignored her breaking heart and took the key. "It helps that I won't be alone for long." She patted her sister's head. "This is 'see you soon,' Olive, not goodbye."

Olive brushed Athena's hand off her head. "Such an annoying habit. Amelia has my sympathies."

"More of a hugger?" Athena asked with open arms.

Olive embraced her sister without hesitation. "Make haste, Athena, and we'll see you on Avalon."

"As you wish, Princess."

Olive stood on her toes and pecked Athena's forehead. "We're leaving, Bastien." She walked with her Thronsden until they were out of sight.

That's three promises to keep. Don't lose myself. Come home. Make haste. Her injured hand hadn't stopped trembling since she grabbed the key. "I know," she said aloud. "I don't want to let them down again either."

Of all the emotions, she hated trepidation most. Fear of failure wasn't what she needed. It would only get in her head and interfere with her promises.

Her fists tightened around the key. "I won't fail again. I'm bound by my promises, after all."

The bike's engine roared. Athena listened to the hum, thankful it dispelled the silence. She saluted at Zenith Palace and took off into the night.

Makoto

Makoto's heart sank as Athena departed the atrium. *I had the same feeling on the beach when I was a girl. At least this time I understand why I feel such loss.* Gratitude helped assuage her melancholy, and there was solace in sharing a proper goodbye this time.

"Cousin?"

She looked up at Richter's concerned countenance. "Yes?"

"I'm to help move the emperor to his chambers. I hesitate to ask but—"

Not that I had a proper goodbye with Father. Frustration bubbled within her like the magma in the heart of Mount Kauneus. But Richter didn't deserve to be its target. Just as Athena hadn't earlier.

"You need me to give you a wide berth." Makoto stood, dusting herself off. "Thank you for your assistance, cousin."

"I could say the same to you." His eyes silently swept over the charred remains of several hounds. "I imagine the damage would've been worse without you. What was that, Makoto?"

"I..." Her fingers scratched against her mother's gem. Coarse grating filled her ears. Long, sharpened nails curled from her fingertips. *Another side-effect?* "I'm not sure. Excuse me." She stood beside Ephraim. "I need your hand."

"You shall have it." He took her hand, either not noticing the nails or not caring. "My ear and shoulder as well."

"Not yet. We'll talk, but..."

302

Richter and the servants gingerly lifted her father. They carried him slowly, communicating each step and adjustment of their grip.

Tis as if he were a delicate piece of furniture. She kept waiting for his eyes to open. For him to scoff with a deep throated "Buh." But his eyes stayed closed, his voice silent.

Makoto squeezed Ephraim's hand.

"Should we move to your chambers?" he asked.

"No," she said. "I still have business. If we're to leave for Avalon, I want a plan before we retire."

"Then we shall see Countess Reina?"

Makoto nodded. "Yes, we—" She noticed Olivia walking away from Amelia and Reina, clenching something in her hand.

"Olivia!" Makoto called. She and Ephraim caught up with her sister and Thronsden. "Where are you going?"

Bastien rounded upon Makoto. "Are you Olivia's keeper, Princess? Must you know her whereabouts at all times?

Makoto flinched, not at his words but his eyes. She understood his desire to protect his charge. But the accusations and distrust in his countenance hurt. "I only—"

Ephraim squeezed her hand. "Is it odd to be concerned for her sister's safety on such a night, Bastien?"

"No," Olivia agreed. "Bastien is tense is all. Think nothing of it. Reina wishes to speak with you regarding tomorrow's travel." She opened her hand to show a long black key. "She tasked me with delivering this. It seems our dearest elder sister neglected the key to her vehicle."

How like Athena to not think everything through. "Thank you for assisting our elder sister."

Olivia cocked an eyebrow. "You thanking me? I never thought I'd see the day. Especially one in which I owe you my life." She stowed the key in her dress pocket. "Tell me, sister, how should I repay this debt?"

"I wouldn't go that far. Bastien would have saved your life."

"Possible. I don't doubt his ability, but twas *you* who did it. What do I owe you?"

Makoto lightly shook her head. "Please. There are no debts owed between family."

"As you wish. But you will accept my gratitude."

"Of course."

They kissed each other's cheeks and embraced.

"I'll see you in the morning," Makoto whispered.

Olivia said nothing. She signaled to Bastien, and the two exited the atrium.

Ephraim frowned at them. "I apologize for my brother."

"No need, Ephraim. Tis been a long evening for us all. Hopefully speaking with the countess won't make it too much longer."

She and Ephraim joined the trio of Amelia, Kalus and Reina. Klaus clasped his brother's shoulder. They shared a curt nod and stood behind their charges.

Amelia smiled through her dour countenance, as she touched Makoto's forearm. "You're going to be alright."

Her words struck a chord. Lord Bahamut chastised her. Bastien judged her. Her own frustrations wanted to consume her. Reassurance wasn't anticipated but welcome all the same.

"Thank you." Makoto's words were barely above a whisper. She touched her sister's delicate hand. "It seems my travel schedule has been updated, Countess."

"Correct. I've read about the ihmelääke flower in the past. It blooms annually on Avalon upon the night of the Phoenix Moon."

That's eleven days away. A plague of doubt seeped into Makoto's frustration. "Do we have enough time?"

"In theory, yes. We can divide your journey into four legs." Reina held up four fingers. "I estimate it should take three to four days by horse or carriage to reach one of the ports.

"Next, you charter a ship. The time varies depending on the mood of the available captains and how susceptible those moods are to being bribed."

"What's stopping us from using one of Father's warships?" Amelia asked.

Reina raised an eyebrow. "Warships? Uncle Rudolph dismantled his seaworthy vessels after he returned from Avalon with Makoto. The remnants of his ships can be found in the mines, weapons, or occasional museum piece. The only ships available are civilian vessels in Morgana's Bounty and Gravesend Bay."

"Could we not request a ship from Regent Josephine?" Ephriam asked.

"We could, Ser Thronsden. However, my fastest raven will take several days to make the round-trip from Mount Kauneus to Avalon," Reina said. "I'm afraid Regent Josephine's help will cost too much time."

Makoto crossed her arms. "We can't estimate how long it will take to cross the water without an evaluation of the vessel."

"Correct. Uncle's old warship could cross the ocean in one night. Another vessel could take three days," Reina said. "Assuming a maximum of two days to procure the vessel, it could take a total of nine to reach the island. At worst that gives you two days to rest in Avalon to locate the flower before it blooms."

Even if we find the flower, it may take an entire week to return with it. "How long does he have?"

Reina folded her hands behind her back. "The All-Mother mentioned nukkuva kuolema. Tis a notoriously slow acting poison, but the time varies based on the victim's health and access to other medicine. He should survive at least a fortnight with proper care. Rest assured, I'll prepare a map, itinerary and provisions by morning."

"The four of us will leave at dawn," Makoto said.

"Then I propose you retire for the evening. It won't do to travel with a poor night's rest." Reina paused. "Actually, could you make it five? I want to send Anna as my eyes and ears."

"I have no objections, and I doubt Olivia will take issue." Makoto dipped her head. "Thank you, Reina. We won't forget your assistance."

"I shan't let you. It's bad form to ignore good favor. I assure you Amelia is in good hands between Klaus and I." Reina outstretched her hand. "You're free to inspect them if you wish."

Makoto shook her cousin's hand, noting the firmness of her grip. "You're stronger than you look, Reina."

"A useful card to keep up my sleeve." Reina smirked. "Though I doubt as useful as your cards, Makoto. Thank you for using them to help my sister. I don't know what I'd do without her."

I didn't realize she and Margaret were that close. "Of course. Always a pleasure helping family."

"Quite. Excuse me, cousins. I have a long night ahead of me and need to get started." Reina pecked Amelia's cheek and beckoned Margaret and Anna to follow her out the atrium.

"Makoto," Amelia said. "I'll bind you to the same promise as Sophia. Promise not to lose yourself along the way."

The sharpened glint of her new nails caught Makoto's eye. *What does it mean to lose myself? For my body to change or memories to return?* "I don't expect to return from Avalon the same person, Amelia."

"Nor should you. I only ask you not compromise your character along the way. Don't let the ambitions of others suffocate your own. Don't let your path be stained with regret. Do what feels right, sister. Father always trusted your judgment, and I trust the same."

Father offered both the crown and his endorsement of my actions with it. His trust was plain to see. And I will pay it back in kind. "Have you always been this wise?"

"When I'm not playing matchmaker." Amelia giggled. "Do you promise?"

Makoto touched the scales upon her breast. "Yes, and I shall make the same promise I forced upon Athena. I will return home to you." Her lips curled. "And I will turn your promise upon you, *Your Grace*."

Amelia pouted. "I don't much like the sound of 'Your Grace.' But I promised Sophia my best, and I will keep that promise." She tugged Makoto's hand. "One last hug before you go?"

"Of course. I cannot deny Her Grace's first request."

Makoto embraced her little sister. It felt more bittersweet than the hug the four of them shared in the White Hall.

Only two short days and so much has changed. Father poisoned. Athena already gone. Amelia left behind. My family fractured just as we were made whole.

She thought once more of Asuka, and the warmth leaving her mother's body. *Perhaps it was never quite whole to begin with.*

Makoto took Reina's advice of rest to heart, but her mind and body refused to comply.

Innocuous memories of her father haunted her throughout the night. Him serving cake from the first anniversary. Listening to a bedtime story of a race between him and Charlotte Thronsden. Going fishing by the lake house.

Memories may soon be all I have left. I know better than most how ephemeral a memory can be.

"Tossing and turning won't make dawn arrive faster, Makoto."

"No, but it makes time flow quicker than when I'm idle." Makoto bit her lip. "Which I suppose is all the more reason to relax. Time is Father's greatest enemy." She sat up, hugged her knees, and rested her chin betwixt them.

Ephraim stood from his chair and sat at his princess's side. "I hate to ask a stupid question, but how are you feeling?"

"I don't know how to answer that, Ephraim. Father told me when we first met that my mother died on Avalon—that he couldn't save her. I had no memory of her then. Not even a face. And now I remember feeling the warmth leave her body."

Makoto's nails dug into her knees. "I've lost two parents in two nights. I had the power to fight but not the power to save. Does Avalon mock me for rebuking it as home?" She cradled her mother's gem, feeling a slight warmth in her chest but a chill in her hands.

"Are you ready to talk about what happened in the atrium?"

Makoto nodded. "I heard my mother's voice call to me. She told me to trust in our Holy Mother—I think she meant Avalon itself. I did, and I felt..."

"Powerful?"

"Free." She reveled in the memory of that feeling. "And I refused to let those daemons trample upon my domain. Their existence was an insult. But without you and Lord Bahamut, it would have been for naught. Thank you, as always, for being at my side."

"Of course, my greatest duty and pleasure is to support you," Ephraim said with a sullen countenance. "I worry about you, Makoto. It's just as Amelia said. I don't want to see you lose yourself upon this journey."

"I doubt I have the capacity with you by my side. You keep me grounded, Ephraim. Give clarity when I need it. You always have." She paused for a moment. "This is a personal question. Feel free to refuse an answer."

"Always a good start to a question," he chuckled. "What is it?"

"How did you cope after losing your parents?"

Ephraim exhaled. "You're right about it being a personal question, but I don't mind answering. First, my brothers helped a lot. Klaus remained strong for us, and Bastien would stay up for hours talking with me about our parents. We hurt together, but we healed together too. Not all at the same pace. Bastien took it harder than I did."

If only I had the same luxury. I'll have Olivia, but I don't foresee us crying together. "You said 'first.' Is there a second thing?"

"You, of course," he replied with a smile.

Makoto scoffed. "How, pray tell, did I help?"

"You gave me a distraction. Getting to know you, exploring Zenith Palace together. I had so much fun that I didn't miss my parents when I was around you. There were times I almost felt guilty, but you were exactly what I needed."

He reached for her hand. "Thank you for being there when I needed you, Makoto."

She took his hand and laid her head upon his shoulder. "I'd say it's my pleasure, but honestly it's my debt. I've needed you for so much, Ephraim." She closed her eyes. "I don't know what I'd do without you."

"Would you like my advice?"

"Please."

"See him tonight. We may be too rushed in the morning or you too tired to commit the memory. Don't let the last image of your father be of him carried away."

"I think that's for the best. If I can't sleep anyway, I may as well make use of my time." She lightly squeezed her Thronsden's hand. "Come, Ephraim. My father awaits."

It took only a few minutes to reach the emperor's chambers. The guards stationed outside bid them enter without issue.

Ephraim stood in a corner by the window with his eyes trained on the door. Makoto sat in an empty chair beside her father's bed. He lay wrapped in sheets of gold and scarlet. Peaceful but lonely in such a large bed.

Hämärä hung beside the bed. Its familiar glint sent a cold shudder up her back. She turned away and admired the five portraits decorating his room.

Her father stood with his siblings in and his empress in the first. Isabella didn't smile, but her eyes seemed less distant. Makoto recognized Aunt Josephine from pictures. It was remarkable how strongly Amelia resembled her, far more than Reina or Margaret.

Josephine shared her brother's golden hair, though her blue eyes were a brighter hue. She was almost unnaturally beautiful. Like her daughter, Makoto found her difficult to read.

Emperor Rudolph stood clad in armor for the second picture along with three women: amber-eyed Charlotte Thronsden, the silver-haired woman from yesterday's vision, and Makoto's mother.

Scarlet pauldrons adorned Tamamo's shoulders, while a helmet shaped like a dragon's head encased her own. A chain-shirt painted to resemble scales covered her chest. Makoto scratched at the scales on her own chest.

Father told me she saved his life. It must have been around that time. Makoto glared at the silver-haired woman. *Kagura, how do I know you? Did you take my mother from me? Are you the treacherous High Priestess?*

Makoto found no High Priestess in the third portrait. Instead, Charlotte Thronsden sat upon the White Hall's throne with a lit cigar dangling from her grinning mouth. A young Ephraim sat on her lap with Bastien and Klaus behind them. The boys wore suits, with only Bastien seeming uncomfortable in formal attire, while Charlotte's sleeveless shirt showed off her scars.

An older man stood behind the boys. His scars appeared to be from shaving rather than combat. Sunken green eyes and slouching shoulders showed his tired soul. But his smile showed none of it. *They all have his eyes, but only Ephraim has his father's smile.*

The other painting without her father depicted Makoto and her sisters. Athena stood cross-eyed, wearing dentures with bad teeth. *I remember this. Olivia and I were furious at her for ruining the picture. It wouldn't be the last time—I still remember how slimy the slug felt. To think Father kept this awful picture all these years.*

The final picture rested upon an easel by the window. Her father walked through the rubble of a misty city. He held the hand of a black-haired girl no older than Makoto when she left Avalon. They shared neither smile nor glance, but Makoto felt the girl's comfort from holding his hand.

She grasped her sleeping father's hand. "You had the strangest habit of turning orphans into princesses. I cannot speak for Olivia, but my gratitude cannot be repaid within one lifetime."

She kissed his forehead and embraced him. "But I shall not stop trying. I will save you, Father."

Makoto sat with him for several moments before pulling away. As she did, her hand caught in his pocket, touching something cold: a silver locket with the word *Rakkaani* engraved on its face. *That's Mother's word.* She opened it without hesitation.

Rudolph and Tamamo smiled, walking hand in hand down the shoreline. A young scarlet-haired girl sat in the sand, beaming up at both of them. She held her mother's gem to her eye level. *Please, show me.*

The room around her disappeared. A gentle breeze lapped against her cheek. The bite of salt in the air caressed her tongue. Giggling filled her ears. Makoto trudged through sand and water up the shoreline.

"Mama! Papa! Come play with me."

"Papa will be right there, rakkaani."

Makoto's heart skipped a beat. It was a voice she knew well, albeit younger and stronger than she'd heard in quite some time.

Rudolph Friedrich von Kauneus dashed toward her. He embraced and hoisted her upon his shoulders.

"Be careful, my loves," a woman called from beneath a parasol. She resembled an older Makoto down to the scarlet hair and pendant around her neck. "I'm afraid she's more fragile than your eldest."

"Buh," Rudolph scoffed. "You worry for naught, Tamamo. Makoto is fragile as an oak. She will not break easy."

"See, Mama? Papa understands." She held up her arms. "I'm strong."

"Humility clearly runs in your blood, Rudolph." Tamamo shook her head but chuckled. "So long as you're careful with her, my love."

The clatter of the locket striking the ground released Makoto from her reverie. She was back in her father's room. There was no beach, no breeze. No mother.

She studied her father's face. "Papa..."

"Did you say something, Makoto?" Ephraim asked.

"Yes." She picked up the locket. "I had another memory."

"Of your mother?"

"Yes—a happy one, this time." She hesitated before adding, "My father was there."

"Emperor Rudolph or your blood father?"

"See for yourself," she said and tossed him the locket.

Ephraim caught the locket. His eyes darted between it and Makoto but didn't seem surprised.

"You knew?" she asked.

He shook his head. "Suspected. I overheard Mother jest more than once of his Avalon wife. That and the pained look in his eye when you called him father made me suspicious."

"Then why..." Makoto wasn't sure which question she wanted answer first. "Why did he look pained for so long when if I called him Father? Why such hatred for Papa... for himself?"

Ephraim frowned. "I imagine both share the same answer. He loved your mother and didn't feel he deserved to be your father after failing to save her."

"Then he hid the truth from me out of guilt?"

"Perhaps. That or fear of what Isabella may do."

Makoto thought of Suilla trapped for years in that tower. *A fate Father spared me. I cannot thank him enough.*

He tossed the locket back. "What did you see?"

"We were playing on a beach. I was younger, maybe a year or two before I came with him to Kauneus. I called him 'Papa,' Ephraim. Tamamo—my mother, she called him 'my love.' I think we were a family before she died... before she was murdered."

"Do you have any clues regarding her killer?"

She shook her head. "The killer's body and voice were shrouded in haze. I remember an axe with a blade sharp enough to cut through moonlight. Perhaps Aunt Josephine learned something during her time on Avalon."

"I'm not sure trusting her is wise, Makoto. Reina is no pillar of virtue, but even she despises Regent Josephine. I urge caution around her."

Makoto looked again at the locket. *I am, and have always been, my father's daughter. He kept me close to his heart all these years. Loved me for who I am. To think I doubted him for so long.*

She pocketed the picture and returned the empty locket to her father's pocket. "Thank you for your advice, Ephraim. I wouldn't have learned this if I hadn't visited tonight."

"Shall we return to your quarters?"

"I'd rather stay with my father tonight." *In case this is our last time.*

Ephraim studied her for a moment. "I have a personal question for you as well, Makoto. But I'll warn you it's morbid."

"Always a good way to start a sentence, Ephraim. What do you wish to know?"

"The gods forbid we fail to save your father, would you want to become emperor?"

She frowned. "You're right. Tis a morbid question."

"Forgive me," Ephraim said with a dip of his head.

Makoto remembered the crown of flames blazing upon her head. She relished the freedom it granted her, as well as the power. *Tis my birthright the same as the other's. But only I had his blessing to wear it while he drew breath.*

She felt something wet between her fingers. Makoto's right hand encircled her father's throat; elongated nails dug into the edge of his skin. She quickly pulled her hand back, noting a small cut on her father's neck. A drop of royal blood trickled down her nail onto her palm.

Why... why did I do that?

"Makoto?" Ephraim started toward her. "Are you alright?"

"Yes," she said quickly. "I... I've changed my mind. I'll sleep better in my own quarters." She covered her trembling nails. "You'll be staying with me tonight?"

"Of course. I won't let you out of my sight after what happened today." Concern darkened Ephraim's countenance. "Are you sure you're alright?"

"Yes. Thank you."

Makoto made her way to the door. Ephraim escorted her outside and toward her room.

"No," she said.

"No, you're not alright?"

"I mean no to your earlier question about being emperor. The Orichalcum Crown has adorned my head long enough for one lifetime, Ephraim."

"Then we'll be sure it stays on your father's."

She reached for his hand but he didn't take it. *Does he think I'm a monster too? No longer a beautiful fire but one that reduces its world to cinders?*

Makoto caressed her nails. *No, not Ephraim. Never Ephraim. He promised to stay by my side until the end of the world. And I'll need him to.* Her father's blood trickled down her hand. *Who knows what a dragon is capable of without restraint?*

Frustration continued to simmer. She thought of her parents' laughter upon the beach. Of the life she nearly had. A faceless assassin robbed her of her mother's love. Another dared to wrest her father's as well.

I am Makoto Clarissa vi Kauneus. I shall not be haunted by faceless phantoms. They will be brought to light—to judgment! I shall show them no mercy.

She clutched the gem tightly. A blanket of calm enveloped her, smothering her frustration. *I am also Makoto Akemi, daughter of Avalon, and I shall not lose control again.*

Makoto returned to her bed, able to relax. One particular memory of her father refused to leave her mind. His first and most important lesson.

Beauty in Strength. The creed rooted itself into every part of Makoto's life. Mercy and control. Hammer and dagger. Bastien and Ephraim. Kauneus and Avalon.

Dragon and princess.

Olivia

Olivia stared at the blank canvas. The brushes betwixt her fingers and toes twitched but were otherwise still. It wasn't that she lacked inspiration. Far from it. The issue was having too much. There were so many images in her mind at any given time. Putting them on canvas exorcised them, but there always were others to take their place.

Olivia initially pursued art as an outlet for her energy and outbursts. But she continued upon Athena's encouragement. Her sister took an interest in her hobby—even going so far as to call it talent. Drawing, painting, composing. It all helped Olivia fill the void when Athena left her behind. Just as she was doing now.

The memories of Nova City were the strongest. A shopkeeper in grey overalls delivering food to the children's center. The shopkeeper's wife complimenting Olivia's little pink dress. The chilling whistle signaling destruction, and the sweet couple's faces splattered against the pavement when the monsters attacked.

Olivia still smelled the crumbling husk of the children's shelter. Heard the panic in the adults herding the kids into a cellar. The oldest girl went back up to find survivors but never returned.

That left seven children in the cellar. There was enough water for them to live comfortably for three days. The twins died on the seventh day. Then the energetic girl with the pigtails. The boy who never washed his hair. The girl who always cried. And the boy who pulled on Olivia's hair and called her ugly.

She dared not dwell on the subsequent days, but the imprint on her senses remained. The musty smell of the cellar growing acrid with decay. The cool metallic taste of blood upon her parched lips. Gnawing hunger churning in her stomach.

Try as she might to exorcize them from her mind, they always returned. After all, Olivia remembered everything.

Instead, she focused on the memories after emerging from the cellar. Sweltering light sapped her remaining energy. She wandered in delirium until she came across a figure.

Olivia thought the woman a wraith. Silver hair and dark eyes seemed too ethereal to be human. The woman cast an ominous shadow matched only by the growing hostility in her eyes.

Olivia scratched her throat—still feeling the white-haired woman's blade cutting into her flesh. Black blood trickling onto the kama's tip. There was no sympathy, no empathy in the woman's eyes.

But Olivia was spared when a scarlet-haired woman bade the other to sheathe her blade. She was rescued when Rudolph took her hand. His rugged hand, caked with the blood of monsters, had been so comforting. It always remained comforting.

"Why?" She asked him one summer's day by the lake house. "Why did you save me?"

"Buh," he grunted, as he often did. "You wouldn't release our hand when we pulled you from the rubble. You imprinted upon us like a wounded dog."

"So I am your pet?"

"You are our daughter the same as Athena. You are the beauty to her strength. Not that you'd know, but she's matured since you joined our family. We think having a little sister to spoil and protect gives her purpose."

He clutched her hand, as he did so many years ago.

"You have a gift, Olivia. Do not succumb to sloth nor be enslaved by expectation. Be happy, child—*my* child. Tis our commandment to you. Do not forget our words."

Of course she remembered. She remembered everything.

Olivia gathered her materials and left the atelier. Bastien awaited outside. His toad-like face regarded her with surprise.

"Princess? I thought you were asleep."

"We're going to see my father."

"I'd advise against leaving your room tonight, Princess. We don't know if any of those things remain in Zenith Palace."

"Then it's a risk we shall take. I wish to commit my father's repose to memory before the morrow."

Bastien scowled. "Your father lays dying, and your greatest concern is capturing your newest masterpiece."

"Of course. Tears are temporary, Bastien. Art is eternal."

"Temporary is longer than nothing. You haven't cried at all."

Of course not. She cried enough in the cellar. Tears took nutrients her body needed that she couldn't replenish. "Nor do I intend to. Tears are a waste of salt."

"Your heart is black as your hair," he growled.

"I'm going to see him. If you're so concerned about my safety, you will accompany me."

She walked off without another word and quicky heard him shuffling behind her. Bastien scowled but said nothing further.

He was kinder when we first met. She remembered the dimples from his smile. The large boy tripping over his feet and words to impress his princess. He told stories of his mother, brother, and the adventures he hoped to spend with Olivia. His enthusiasm faded, as he wasted his years by the atelier door or within Morgana's court.

The only ill-suited pair of princess and Thronsden. I almost feel bad for him.

She entertained the idea of exchanging Thronsdens. Klaus's taciturn demeanor suited her penchant for quiet. He could be a bit strict for her liking, but she supposed discipline could do her some good.

Ephraim, meanwhile, would make for an excellent companion. They didn't often interact outside shared glances in the dining room, but he took interest in her work. *I doubt he would chastise me for wishing to see Father. No doubt he's encouraged Makoto to do the same.*

The first memory of Makoto wasn't pleasant—few of Olivia's memories were. But she felt it captured the nature of their relationship. Olivia had been painting in her lake house room when she noticed the little red-haired girl playing with Athena. She watched them for several minutes before closing the blinds.

I've always had trouble letting Makoto in. First, she was an unworthy distraction. Then I antagonized her as the rival for my family's attention. Now my attempts to mend our relationship are fruitless. She thought of the portrait she slaved over yesterday. *I thought for sure that one would work. I suppose it did in a roundabout way.*

Olivia stopped outside her father's chambers. She heard whispering inside, which didn't disturb the guards. "I wish to see my father."

"Of course, Princess. Your sister is in there already."

"Which one?"

"Princess Makoto."

I was right about Ephraim. If Bastien hadn't been needlessly stubborn I could have been here first.

Bastien tensed beside her. *Nervous? Not his usual reaction to Makoto's presence.* She considered pressing the issue by forcing him to accompany her inside. *No. Makoto will doubtless be furious if I intrude upon her mourning, even with Bastien as a goodwill present.*

"I won't disturb their time alone. Thank you for your service." Olivia dipped her head and continued walking.

"Are we not returning to the atelier?" Bastien asked.

"No, Bastien. That would be in the other direction."

"To the atrium then?"

"Correct. Tis a lovely spot when quiet."

She passed Amelia's room on her way without a sentry outside. *Klaus must be keeping vigil inside. Good. She does better when he's close by. Most people don't appreciate how fragile Amelia is. I pray she can sleep tonight after what she experienced.*

It's why Olivia strove to not make the same mistakes she had with Makoto. After all, she had to be the big sister with Athena gone. It only made sense to treat the youngest with care.

She and her Thronsden reached the atrium steps. Most of the viscera had been cleaned, but there were still bloodstains amidst shreds of flesh and lace. Olivia descended the steps until she reached the scorch marks. She replayed the memory of her sister devouring a crown of flame and spitting it at the monsters.

It would make a sublime portrait but not tonight.

"Princess, may I speak freely?"

"So long as you know I likely won't listen." Olivia flipped to a fresh page of her sketchbook. She closed her eyes and pictured the guests. Harley stuck out in her mind, as he often did. She thought of the companion he arrived with. *Yes. That should do for tonight.*

"I advise you not accompany Makoto to Avalon."

"Oh?" Olivia began sketching Harley's well-endowed escort. "You wish to see my father die, Bastien?"

"Of course not," he snapped. "I only think it wise to avoid your sister."

"Uncommon of *you* to suggest that. Weren't you gazing at her longingly while you danced?"

"That was before…" Bastien lowered his eyes toward the scorch marks. "Before *this*."

Olivia paused. This was no jest or trick. Bastien appeared genuinely worried and resentful.

"You distrust her after she saved you?"

"I distrust her after she nearly burned down the atrium. She's dangerous, Princess. She and her people always have been."

"She is my sister. *I* am her people. Your brother is one of her people."

"My brother is a good man, but his attachment blinds him."

"Does my attachment blind me?"

He studied her for a moment before shaking his head. "No. You are attached to nothing. What blinds you is the illusion of her control. You saw the outburst at dinner last night, and now you see what lurks beneath the surface."

"What lurks beneath the surface is my sister. We may not share blood, but we share a family. An insult against her and her people is an insult to me."

"You take enjoyment in insulting her."

"A privilege that does not extend to you. This conversation is over."

"I—"

Olivia's glare silenced him.

"Very well, Princess. What have you decided to draw?"

"Harley and his companion. I'm sure you noticed her."

He grunted but didn't disagree. "Speaking of Morgana's property, may I ask what was in the letter?"

"What letter?"

His brow furrowed. "The letter he delivered to you yesterday. He placed it upon your chair in the atelier."

"Bastien, I don't know what you're talking about. Harley didn't deliver a letter."

She remembered Harley's visit. He bothered her, but she enjoyed the distraction and ensuing head massage. She left him to join her sisters for tea, and he left upon her return.

But she didn't remember a letter. Thus, he couldn't have delivered one. After all, she remembered everything.